PHIL BOWIE

Author of *GUNS*

"Fast, engaging – a fine debut."

—Lee Child, NY Times bestselling author of the Jack Reacher series.

"Bowie is a skilled writer. I wouldn't have guessed this was his first novel."

—*Clayton Bye,* gottawritenetwork.com

Medallion Press, Inc.
Printed in USA

DIAMONDBACK

PHIL BOWIE

DEDICATIONS:

For Aaron Roberts.

Published 2007 by Medallion Press, Inc.

The MEDALLION PRESS LOGO
is a registered tradmark of Medallion Press, Inc.

Typeset in Adobe Caslon Pro
Printed in the United States of America
10-digit ISBN: 1-9338364-3-1
13-digit ISBN: 978-1-933836-43-0

10 9 8 7 6 5 4 3 2 1
First Edition

ACKNOWLEDGEMENTS:

Thanks to my news reporter mother, Edith, who used words so well, to my woodworker father, Erol, who used his hands to seek perfection, and to my sister, Nancy, who has never lost confidence in me. Thanks to Ken Gruebel and Dr. Richard C. Boyd, and especially to Naomi Dixon for excellent criticism and suggestions. Thanks to Helen Rosburg along with her talented staff at Medallion Press for their fine work. And thanks to so many others who have helped along my path.

I love the Great Smokies and hope the good folk who live there will forgive those certain licenses I've taken for the sake of this story.

CHAPTER 1

Snakes, he thought.

It was late on a blowing gray day. There was a fitful rain not much more than a heavy mist. Dirty cold clouds were scudding low over the brooding ridge five hundred feet above the steep-sided gully he had found that morning, following a trickle uphill from a branch of Jonathan Creek. On some dim level he realized he never would have spotted the small black opening in the gully wall if the sunlight had not struck it just right through the forest trees that were fuzzed with the early growth of spring, and if he had not been in just the right place. The opening was naturally concealed among a jumble of mossy rocks by old deadfalls and tough-as-cable thorny vines.

There was something about those rocks.

Maybe somebody had piled them up there?

He had walked through the woods to the dirt road and had ridden his bicycle back home to drop off his pan and ragged backpack and pick up a flashlight, the skinning knife his daddy had given him so long ago, and his leather work gloves, figuring the gloves and knife would help him get through the vines.

He had a strong notion about that black opening.

By the time he made his way back to it, the sky had turned leaden as it often does in the Great Smokies, populating the dank forest with unsettling shadows.

Grabbing onto saplings to maintain shaky footing on the flank of the ravine and skidding on the damp leaves, he lowered his considerable muscled bulk down through a prickly tangle. The thorny vines plucked at his jacket, caught in his holed jeans, and raked his shin bloody. He picked his way through, hacking clumsily with the dull knife, parting the vines with his gloved hands. He slipped on a mossy rock and banged a knee hard.

He had a faint, icy feeling that something did not want him here, something old and musty brushing near and pushing at him. He looked around but saw nothing lurking among the trees.

That dark opening was drawing him closer.

He shivered like a wet dog, shaking the bad feeling off.

Ducking under a rotting, fallen birch that was braced across the gully, he thumped his head, but ignored the pain because the opening was directly in front of him now.

He tugged away the looser rocks, rolling them back clicking against each other. There still wasn't enough room for him to see much inside. A large rock blocked most of the opening.

One day when they were wrestling a stump out of a field together, his daddy had told him, "Mose, maybe God ain't give you the brains of a yard dog, but He sure as hell made you bull-strong. Don't you never turn it against nobody, boy, or you'll likely kill 'em without even half tryin'."

And Moses never had. He'd got mad at things that didn't want to work right and at some people, like a few who snickered at him, but he always just went off by himself until the mad went away.

He pulled hard at the boulder, but it would not budge. He scooped away some of the dirt at the base of it, starting to sweat despite the cool air. There was just room enough for him to put his back against an angled plane of it, bend his knees, brace his boots against the gully wall, and heave, grunting, the rock digging coldly into his back, his log-sized thighs starting to burn, until he felt it give a bit. He set himself in a fresh position, took two deep whooshing breaths, and heaved again, closing his eyes and gritting his teeth, and the rock slowly moved aside a few inches. He scraped away more leaves at the base of it and dug at the wet soil with his fingers, exposing a thin root, which he grabbed with both hands and yanked until it parted.

He dug some more, thinking of the old skinny hound that had passed away on him just a week or so ago, how it used to paw at mole runs out behind his cabin, getting its gray nose dirty and making him laugh. Every day since, he'd kept looking for that old deer dog to be at the back door, wanting food scraps, and he'd had to tell himself over and over it would not be back again. How could it rise up out of the hole he'd buried it in? No more than his old daddy could rise up out of that hole in the churchyard where they'd put him a long time ago.

He heaved against the cold stone again and again, his back starting to go numb, inching it aside until at last the opening looked big enough to let him get through.

He stood back, breathing deeply and wiping the sweat out of his eyes with the backs of his gloves. He looked at the dark shadowed hole and somehow knew it went deep.

Maybe snakes in there.

He had felt little fear in his forty-three years. Once he had somehow found himself in a thickening crowd at a country fair. He could sense the jumbled thoughts of all those around him. The whole world seemed to be closing in, and he lumbered out of there as fast as he could.

Another time was the day his daddy died and he suddenly knew he was all alone in this world and that made him cry hard and long.

The worst was that warm sunny day when, as a boy, he was sitting on the tilted front porch floor of the Georgia cabin with his back to the grayed clapboards. He picked at the paint flaking off of the warped floorboards, his mind filled right up to happy with the pretty summer songs of the birds all around in the woods. It was warm and humid, and his eyelids were heavy.

He fell asleep.

He awoke to see a shadowed, lumpy mass under his daddy's empty rocker. He sat up straighter, peering at it, and it shifted shape, rising up, weaving. It opened its mouth, which was all white inside and looked soft as a pillow. But this thing was bad, he knew down deep. Something very bad that could hurt him.

His daddy came out onto the porch, saw the thing, and said, "Mose, you stand up real, real slow and you just ease on over this way. Do it right now, boy."

But he could not. He was frozen with an icy dread in his hollow gut. The thing had small, shiny bead eyes, slitted like a cat's eyes, but steely-cold and unblinking. And fixed on him. Its body was thick as his arm, but it had a rat's tail. It closed its mouth, tasted the air with its tongue, and glided closer to him. He was scared he'd pee himself if the thing got any closer.

But it did.

"Okay, Mose, boy. You just sit there real still." Time seemed to slow way on down, and he held his breath. He was shaking, but he could not stop it.

His daddy ducked into the house, reached up above the door, and came back out holding the single-shot sixteen-bore shotgun loaded with double-ought buck. His daddy aimed it down at the thing and said, "Mose, boy, I hate to shoot it with a scattergun that close to you. Just maybe it will back on away."

The thing turned its head toward his daddy and then back at him, and he stared at it. The skin looked smooth and dry, and there were darker markings under the almost-blackness of it. His daddy had talked a lot about evil in the world and how we all ought to stay away from it, and that's what he thought now.

This thing is evil.

It moved like oil toward him again. There was a sound that stunned him. The thing exploded into a shredded red mist, part of it writhing sideways and rolling up against his bare foot. When he screeched and jerked his foot back to *get away* from it there was a searing pain just above his ankle.

His daddy knelt and looked at his feet and legs, wiping away the thing's blood with his big rough thumbs. He said, "It's okay, Mose. I creased you with one of them pellets. He didn't bite you. Sorry, boy, but that was a granddaddy cottonmouth. Meanest snake God ever made. Didn't think there was none left hereabouts. It's a nasty thing. Poison eats away at your skin so you can't hardly doctor the bite. Come on in, boy, and we'll clean that out with the peroxide and bind it up."

He trembled with the vivid cottonmouth memory, but told himself to stop it. He worked the gloves off, wiped at his face, and with the flashlight in his left hand and the skinning knife in his right, he got down on his belly and used his elbows and knees to crawl into the hole. It was tight. He had to twist his shoulders to fit himself inside.

He had discovered this place because the branch flowing into Jonathan Creek had run out of what he'd been looking for right about where this trickle tumbled down through the forest. He had moved up the branch over the last months, patiently panning, engrossed in the one thing his daddy had taught him that he knew he was good at doing all day long. And there had been steady color. Not a lot of it, only very light traces, really, not enough for anybody else to care about, but steady. Then suddenly it had run out. He ranged on up the branch for miles but found no more, so for days he worked back downstream and tried to find just where he picked up color again. For some reason he could never have explained, this steep trickle down through the rough ravine caught in his mind, so that morning he followed it up away from the branch. And found the small black opening.

There was a loud dry rustling and he thought, *rattlesnake.* The flashlight flickered off, leaving him staring into blackness that seemed to come right up against his eyeballs. He keened, shook the flashlight violently, the batteries made contact, and it blinked on again, but weakly. He was holding his breath, his skin prickling and his brain screaming for him to back on out of here, but the light calmed him enough so he realized the rustling was only old dry leaves that his arm was stirring. He blew out a big breath and panned the light around. He was in a space that opened out into a cave about ten feet wide and three or four feet high. It was hard to tell how deep it went because it curved away. The floor was littered with rotting forest debris. The first thing he saw was most of a cracked clay pot a few feet off to his right. He poked at the pot with the skinning knife, and pieces fell off of it. There was some kind of design carved into it like nothing he could remember. It was pretty. He picked up a shard and managed to work it into his shirt pocket and button it there.

To the left there was an overhead rock shelf that angled down to the right and disappeared beneath the cave floor maybe twenty feet from the cave opening. The glitter of quartz ran like the Milky Way through the shelf.

And mingled in with the quartz, there was color. Much, much more color than he had ever seen. A creek of color. A river of color.

He wriggled closer, and the flashlight blinked out again. He growled and shook it. The light came back. He just stared at the thick irregular streaks and splotches of color for a long time.

It was so, so pretty.

He reached out and probed at the color with the knife. His heart beat faster when the knife tip traced a nice scratch. There was a place where the quartz was cracked. He worked the tip of the skinning knife into the crack and pried until an inch of the knife tip broke off. His daddy would be mad. No, that wasn't right. Daddy was a long time gone now.

He sighed and forced the blade, thicker now, into the crack. He rested the flashlight where it would shine on the crack, and pounded the knife in deeper with the palm of his left hand. Then with both hands he pulled on the handle. It bent, close to breaking again, but a piece of quartz the size of his palm and an inch thick snapped loose, falling onto the cave floor in front of him, stirring up a moldy smell. On the back side of the quartz piece, the color was rich and dull, and he knew for dead sure it was real. And there was a whole lot of it. Maybe enough of it right here in his hand to get the cabin fixed up better. Maybe even enough to get tools so he could make a new cabin if he could find somebody to tell him how to do that. He grinned and let out a shout. He looked at the broken pot and the funny markings on it. He picked up two more pieces of it and dropped them inside, along with the quartz, which just fit. Holding the knife and flashlight in his left hand and the pot in his right, he started backing out of the cave.

There was a bad moment when he thought he was stuck in the cave opening, but he wriggled around using the toes of his boots to inch himself backward while he stretched out one arm, and he made it back out. The light was fading fast, but he stayed to roll loose rocks back over the opening, filling in with leaves and chunks of the dead birch until it looked right to him.

He would never tell anybody about this place.

It was going to be full dark pretty soon, and he knew there would be no moon or stars to help him. It was a good way back to the dirt road. And the woods would be black as the box his daddy was in. He had forgotten to put good batteries in the cheap flashlight or to bring some spares along in his pocket.

"Moses Kyle, you're dumb as a bobwire fence post," he told himself.

He forgot things all the time. But he knew he would never forget how to get back to this place.

He stumbled down the bank of the ravine to the main branch and began following it toward Jonathan Creek, the pot under his arm, the forest growing darker rapidly all around, the flashlight flicking off and then on dimly again when he would shake it enough. It was starting to rain now, drops pattering softy down through the trees, and the footing was increasingly slippery. With the sound of the rain all around, he would not be able to hear the creek to help guide him. A twig poked his forehead just above his right eye, and he rubbed his head with his fingers.

He fixed the place in his mind, going over and over it. Up Jonathan Creek to the big creek branch that ran for a way beside the long mountain. On up that branch into the valley a mile or so beyond where the dirt road stopped, past a creaky old bridge, to a stretch of slow water and the pool with a boulder in the middle that looked like an animal. A ways beyond the boulder a pine leaned out over the creek. Beyond that pine there was the trickle coming down a gully on the right. All he had to do then was climb up through a steep part of the gully and that would lead him right to it.

He shouted again at the thought of it.

The most magical place in the whole world.

His place.

CHAPTER 2

On Sunday evening, John thumbed the pause button for the VCR as old Hank came into the room, asking, "What you watchin' there?"

"*The Legend of the Lone Ranger.* You remember the Lone Ranger?"

Hank sat in his stuffed recliner and said, "Sure. Me and Hattie used to watch it on a black-and-white TV that was mostly like watchin' a snowstorm, and it blew about two vacuum tubes a week. At the end of each episode, somebody like a scruffy kid would ask, 'Who was that masked man?' And some old codger like me would say, 'Boy, you seen them silver bullets in his gun belt, didn't ya? Rides that white stallion he calls Silver? That there's the Lone Ranger. And then up on a ridge that big white horse would rear up and paw the air and the Ranger would holler, 'Hi-yo, Silver. Awaaaaay!'"

"Right, and they'd play the *William Tell Overture* in the background. Who was his sidekick, and what was the name of his horse?"

"Tonto was the sidekick; that's way too easy. Used to call the Ranger '*Kemo Sabe*,' which I think meant somethin' like friend, but I don't remember the horse's name."

"I read somewhere it meant trusted friend. The horse was Scout. You want me to rewind this so you can see all of it?"

"Scout, that's right. Naw, just crank it up from here. Where'd you find this one?"

"Bought it in that flea market over in Cherokee for three bucks. Merle Haggard sings in it. Jason Robards is President Grant. Christopher Lloyd is the bad guy. Klinton Spilsbury is the Lone Ranger, and Michael Horse is Tonto. This gang wants to carve out a hunk of Texas and start their own state. They kidnap Grant while he's on a Western train tour so they can force Congress to cave in to their demands. Our guys have to set things right."

"There was a few different actors played the parts way back in the thirties," Hank said. "Along about the fifties I remember Jay Silverheels played Tonto, and Clayton Moore was the Lone Ranger for a long time. Never heard of the two in this here story."

"Me, neither. They do a pretty good job of it, though."

They shared an interest in the lore of the Old West and often indulged in their own kind of trivia game about it. John had a collection of old shoot-'em-up Western movies, wore jeans with scuffed goatskin ropers and occasionally a black leather Stetson, drove a white Jeep Wrangler that usually wore a coat of dust, and liked to read Elmer Kelton, Louis L'Amour, and Tony Hillerman yarns.

John pushed PLAY and they relaxed, engrossed in the movie.

John owned a small log house in a clearing on the steep flank of Eaglenest Ridge overlooking Maggie Valley in western North Carolina. He shared the place with octogenarians Hank and Hattie Gaskill. When he'd first met them, they were fugitives from a rest home, hiding out on the deserted Outer Banks island of Portsmouth, four hundred miles east at the other end of the state, enjoying some last days of freedom. John had been living on nearby Ocracoke Island at the time under the assumed name of Sam Bass, running a shoestring air-charter operation. Federal marshals had set up that identity because he was in the witness-protection program, formally known these days as Witness Security or WITSEC.

He was still in the program, though the threat to him had been nearly eliminated, but now he was going under the name John Hardin, his own choice. After John Wesley Hardin. Fastest gun in the Old West.

Hattie, however, had convinced herself he was actually her son, Roy, who had disappeared in a raging storm along with the other hands on an ocean trawler that had shouldered into cold, malevolent green seas in a storm far out over the Grand Banks. She believed he'd had to change his name to John Hardin because he had done some dangerous secret work for the government. He and Hank maintained that fiction for her sake. He had actually been in touch with the old couple's lawyer to let him know, along with their remaining few family members, that he would take full responsibility for them, including any financial responsibility for whatever expenses Social Security and Hank's modest pension did not cover. Nobody had raised any objections.

It was a good arrangement. Hattie cooked for the three of them, frugally and nutritiously. Hank did chores around the place, helped with the remodeling, and brought in some extra money playing fiddle in the valley regularly with a bluegrass combo.

Most days now he never even thought of his real name. To the world he was John Hardin, a lean, somewhat taller-than-average man with a mass of graying black hair, looking at middle age just over the next rise. He ran his small business, Hardin Charter and Sightseeing, out of the Asheville Regional Airport using his lone Cessna 182, usually clearing enough to pay the bills and gradually finance work on his log home, where he was, for all intents, Hank and Hattie's son, Roy. He did occasional small remodeling jobs around the valley to supplement his income, especially during the colder months when the aerial work declined.

They watched the movie in companionable silence, and chimed in together for the "Hi-yo, Silver.

Awaaaaay!" at the end.

Hank stretched, yawned widely, and said, "Well, guess I'll hit the sack. Got a busy day tomorrow. Got to mow the lawn, mend that porch table, tend Hattie's garden some. I swear I never worked this hard. Even in the army. Between what-all chores you and Hattie need done, a man don't get *no* rest around here."

"I'll bet you bellyached plenty in the army, too. I don't know how Hattie's put up with you all these years."

"I don't, neither, come to think on it. By the way, speakin' of Hattie. She wants to talk with you. She was up in the loft readin' a while ago. Good night, *Kemo Sabe.*"

Hank went off to their bedroom, and John climbed the stairs to the loft, where Hattie was in her rocker sleeping, head on her shoulder. A mountain cookbook, which he'd found for her in the flea market, lay open spine-up on her lap. Since coming to live with him, she had seemed to shed a few of her many years. She and Hank were as happy as he had first found them to be out on Portsmouth Island in the little ghost town there. Both of them still had wrinkles in their wrinkles—not much help for that at their ages—but they had shed the rest-home depression and had reclaimed a serenity that graced their relationships with each other and with him. He was deeply pleased to have them here.

John gently took the book, marked her place with

a knitting needle from the side table, and set it aside. She stirred awake, her faded blue eyes momentarily confused, and smiled up at him. She tucked a wisp of fine white hair behind her ear with a fragile blue-veined hand and said, "Roy, I swear, you just seem to get taller and stronger all the time. Did you get some of that huckleberry pie?"

"It must be your cooking, Flutter. I sure did, and it was great. Ate too much of it, as usual. Hank said you wanted to talk with me about something?"

"He did? Oh, yes, I surely do. You know the Benfields picked me up for church this morning like they usually do?"

"Yes. Are they doing okay?"

"Just fine, at least near as I can tell, though I know she still has those bad headaches sometimes. Makes her get cross with him, but he knows it's only the pain. It was a good service. Reverend Boyer talked about love, the different kinds of it and the bright magic of it and what a blessing it is in our lives. How it can make the whole world look fresh. How it can heal and hold a person high and sometimes just purely fill up your very soul. I've surely been blessed with an abundance of it, especially from my Hank over all these years. And from you. I put an extra dollar in the collection plate. The church ladies donated money for flowers, but I don't know why; I could have brought some of that budding rhododendron from out behind our garden. There weren't too many people in church, and not nearly enough children ever come these days. I don't know how their parents expect them to grow up with any real values if they don't know anything about faith. Did you know they can't even mention God in the schools these days?"

John smiled and waited. It sometimes took a while for Hattie to get to her point.

She seemed to collect her thoughts and said, "But I wanted to talk with you about Mose Kyle."

John remembered the name and seeing the man walking around the valley here and there. A large, slow-moving, slow-minded man who kept to himself. He attended the little stone Presbyterian church where Hattie liked to go. John had driven Hattie to church on those Sundays when her friends, the Benfields, couldn't pick her up, and had seen Moses Kyle sitting by himself in the back and ducking out as soon as the services were over. On one Sunday Hattie had introduced Moses to him at the start of a service, and John had sensed the man's immense quiet strength in his handshake.

"Mose didn't come to church today," Hattie said, "and I think something bad is happening with him."

"Flutter, you said there weren't many people there today. Some Sundays are just like that. Moses probably had something else he needed to do. Or he plain forgot. You know how he is."

"No, Roy. Not Mose. I've been going to that church now for over a year, and Mose has never missed a Sunday. Not one. He's a bit slow-witted, yes, but he's a nice man. He has a good heart. Sometimes we sit on the wrought-iron bench under that big oak in the churchyard and we talk. He makes his own way in this world. He's honest. He knows things lots of people don't. Simple things. But rock-solid truths, do you know? And he's a believer. He would never miss a Sunday unless he was really sick or something worse. I'm afraid he's in bad trouble. He doesn't have a phone, so I can't try to reach him."

"I'm sure he'll turn up next Sunday, and you two can talk again."

"No, Roy, I just *know* something bad has happened. Maybe we should call the police?"

"I don't think they'd do much. The way they'd look at it, Mose just missed church. A lot of reasons for that."

"Then will you go by his place tomorrow and see if he needs anything?"

"Flutter, I've got a pretty busy day tomorrow. A long photo flight that will use up most of the morning. I want to get it done in still, clear air if I can. The weather people say showers will move in for the afternoon. Then I have to put the plane in the maintenance hangar for its annual inspection and start on that work. It's a two- or three-day job even if we don't find anything wrong. I wanted to stop at that new builders' supply place in Asheville to get plywood for the porch ceiling and some other stuff I need around here. There's your list of things you wanted at the grocery, too."

"My list can wait, Roy. That will give you some time. I think he lives in a small place a good ways back up on Big Pines Trail."

There was such concern in her expression that he smiled and said, "Okay, Flutter. I guess I'll just have to make the time. Tomorrow I'll see what I can find out about Moses."

The relief showed in her eyes. "You're the best one Hank and I had, Roy. Thank you, son."

After Hattie had gone to join Hank in their bedroom, John poured a glass of ice-cold cider and took it and three of Hattie's ginger cookies out onto the porch. He stood at the rough-sawn cedar rail and looked down on Maggie Valley. The air was chilled but smelled freshly of all the promises of spring, with a nice whiff of fresh-cut grass floating up from some yard below. The sky was as clear and clean as black ice, and strewn with a mind-stretching profusion of incredibly distant alien suns. The outlines of the mountains forming the flanks of the valley were a shade blacker than the star-lit sky. Highway 19 curved gently along the valley floor, outlined by the lights of the village motels, restaurants, and strip-mall shops. Occasional cars moved slowly. At the far end of the valley, the road curled up across Soco Gap, heading for the town of Cherokee on the reservation.

It should be a fine morning for taking the aerial

photos. He would get that job out of the way before the winds began swirling around and over the peaks, burbling with turbulence like a mountain stream and bringing in the predicted cold front with its out-riding rain showers.

Moses Kyle.

He was pretty sure there was nothing seriously wrong.

But although Hattie was troubled with an aging and sometimes erratic mind, she did possess an uncanny prescience. He'd told himself more than once not to discount her premonitions and intuitions too readily.

He would keep his promise to check up on Moses tomorrow.

He took a long pull of the pleasantly tongue-stinging cider and looked up to see Orion boldly outlined.

Tonight, for some lurking reason, the ancient warrior's light-years-long sword seemed poised above the beautiful valley.

CHAPTER 3

When he awoke, Moses was tied to a cold metal armchair with ropes padded with rags. He looked down at himself and saw he had no clothes on.

The chair was the kind you'd find in somebody's backyard, made out of curving steel strips. It was springy, and when he moved his head, it rocked. He strained against the ropes but could hardly move his arms or legs. He pushed his bare feet against the concrete floor, and the chair yielded backward a few inches and then resisted. He relaxed the pressure on the floor, and the chair rocked slightly. His hands were numb. There was a dazzling glare in his eyes from a bank of three square caged work lights on a yellow tripod stand. The floor was cold and greasy. He squinted against the brightness. There were a few small windows high up, not letting in much light. It was early morning. Or maybe late in the day. He was in some kind of garage or maybe a barn. It smelled of old oil and wood rot. He realized there were two figures in the shadows behind the light bank. He squinted harder, trying to make out who they were, deeply ashamed that he had no clothes on.

One of the figures spoke in a rumbling voice roughened by a punch to the throat during an all-out brawl two decades before and two packs of cigarettes every day since. "Hey, Mose. Sis and me are real sorry about the ropes, buddy, but we got to hold you still while we have a talk."

"Who . . . you?" Moses mumbled.

"Now see, that ain't important, Mose. What's important is we need for you to tell us where you got that pretty piece of quartz. You tell us that, we take off those ropes, give you a cool drink of water, let you get dressed—your clothes are right over there on the bench—and you can walk away. You don't, we got to find a way to make you tell us."

Moses shook his head. It felt like his brain was loose in there. "My place. Never tell anybody. I found it. My place."

He'd been in bed only half awake. It was early on Sunday morning, the first gray light coming in the cabin window and the birds calling so prettily to each other in the forest outside. Suddenly there was movement beside his bed, and he tried to sit up, but two large tattooed arms grabbed his arms and held him down. There was somebody else beside the bed. He caught sight of a needle like the doctors used. He felt a sting in the side of his neck and faded back into sleep, thinking, *Today is church day.*

"Now I *like* a stubborn man, myself," the biggest shadow behind the lights said in the scratchy voice. "Shows backbone, you ask me. But Sis here, she don't. You don't want to go gettin' her pissed off, buddy, you really don't. There was this one time Sis had a real stubborn man. She waited till he was drunked up on corn, see, come and got me, and we tied his ass to the bed with ripped-up sheets, put a paper bowl on his chest, filled it with lighter fluid, poured like a puddle into his big 'ol beer-belly button. Woke him up, let him see and smell what kind of a fix he was in, and then she lit him up." The shadow laughed. "Flat lit that boy up, she did, and we got the hell on out of there. You might could say he died of smokin' in bed. 'Course the double-wide burnt right down to the frame, but, hell, it was only a rental." And he laughed hard again. Wound up coughing wetly.

When he got his breath again, he said, "Yep, I could tell you lots of scary stories about Sis, buddy. Anyways, here's how it is. You just now much as went and told us there *is* a place where you found that quartz. We know you been pannin' Jonathan Creek a long time. We figured you followed one of them branches off Jonathan up onto one of the hills, and maybe there was what looked like this cave and you went in there and found this old Indian mine. That was good work, Mose. Findin' what lots of folk been lookin' for a long, long time. Damned good work, buddy. See, all we want is a fair share. We'll help you go up there on that hill and get all the gold out. You know you can't do that by yourself. So where'd you find it? Setzer Mountain, maybe? Or up around Moody Top?"

"Indian mine?" Moses said with real surprise.

"You had a piece of a pot in your shirt. Buddy of mine says it's old Cherokee stuff. See, we know a lot of it already. We can probably find it ourselves, anyway, now we know it's there. But why don't we share it, Mose? Wouldn't be right for us to keep it all ourselves after you went and found it and all; we know that. We're real reasonable. You're a church-goin' man, ain't you? Bible says we ought to share, don't it? Well, that's all we're askin' here, Mose. Share. Must be more'n enough for us all up there. We help you get it and sell it for top dollar, and then you can move out of that shack and get into a real house. Get yourself a woman wants lots of pretty trinkets to warm up your bed and do things you probably only seen in pictures. Live like a real man and not some raggedy-ass bum. What do you say here, Mose? We don't want to waste all day gettin' this done, buddy."

Moses shook his head emphatically. "No. It's my place. Mouth dry. Sticky."

The big shadow reached for something, and a tattooed hand came into the light, holding a bottle of water. The bottle tilted, and water trickled onto his knee, running icily down his shin. "This what you want, buddy? You can have all you want. It's good and cold. Just tell us where you found that mine. We'll draw us up a map so we won't forget how to get there. It'll be like a treasure map. You'll have a copy. And Mose, buddy, we won't tell nobody else. That's a promise. Be just our secret. We don't wanna have to do bad things to you here, buddy. What do you say?" He took a long drink from the dewy water bottle himself.

Moses clenched his jaw and said, "No. Don't want water. Don't care what you do. It's *my* place."

Neither shadow moved. There was quiet for a moment. The smaller shadow was smoking. He saw the glow of a cigarette and smelled it. He heard a mockingbird going through all its calls outside.

The big shadow said, "I'll go in and talk with the Preacher for a bit. See what you can do with him. Just don't start havin' so much fun you forget we don't want no marks on him."

The big shadow stood up from a chair and walked away. There was enough light to see the man had wide shoulders and long hair tied back in a ponytail. A tall door opened with a hinge-screech and then closed.

After a while the other shadow dropped the cigarette onto the floor and put a foot over it.

Stood up and came closer.

A skinny woman with long red hair, in jeans and a white T-shirt, her face mostly hidden from the light, but her eyes were bright. Startlingly blue and clear. He blushed. She bent slightly and let her hand trail along his leg from the knee up over his thigh, and his leg muscles tensed. She had long, bloodred nails.

Her hands and arms were densely freckled. A fine-linked gold bracelet tickled the hairs on his leg. She scratched the inside of his thigh lightly with her nails and watched his muscles jump. Did the same to the other leg. She ran a warm soft palm across his chest and belly. Back and forth lazily. Stopping to pinch his nipples and brush them with her thumb. Caressing his belly. Going teasingly lower.

She moved the tips of her nails along his penis. As lightly as a breath. He felt himself growing hard and tried to stop it. She took him in her hand and stroked gently. Slowly. A hint of a cold smile hovered at the corners of her mouth. He stared into her eyes. Eyes like purest gemstone. Could not look away. He was really hard now, automatically trying to move his hips some.

Then, still stroking him, she cupped his scrotum lightly in her other hand, and a delicious thrill coursed through him. Her cold smile widened.

She began to squeeze with her cupped hand, increasing the pressure just slightly but steadily. He tensed and shivered. He whimpered and shook his head. He started to go limp, and she held the pressure steady.

He shook his head in jerks and whispered, "Please, Lady. Don't. Don't." Her face was still shadowed, but her eyes were bright and hard as wet stream pebbles. She increased the pressure a small fraction, starting to grind, and he could not look away from those blue, blue eyes.

She squeezed harder. Testing.

And yet harder.

He was keening now with each quick, sharp breath he took. It was like a shining, chilled blade edging deeper into his lower belly.

She studied his wide, staring eyes, saw the pupils contract with the exquisite pain, felt him spasm all over with it. She could control it perfectly now, ease off when he came too close to passing out, then bring it all back to hold him right on the very edge of the abyss. And she could do it over and over until he would flinch if she merely moved a hand toward him and until he begged her and cried like a kicked child and told them what they wanted to know.

She hoped he would not tell them too quickly. That he would resist for some time yet.

She was getting wet.

She could almost feel the pain herself now and she reveled in it.

Savoring his long high scream.

CHAPTER 4

John lined his Cessna 182 up at the end of Asheville Regional runway one-six and sighted down the 8,000-foot asphalt ribbon. Some pilot who had departed fifteen minutes earlier had spotted two deer cropping vegetation near the far end of the runway, but they weren't anywhere in sight now. In his headset, the tower voice said, "Whiskey Romeo, you're cleared for takeoff."

He thumbed the push-to-talk switch and said, "Whiskey Romeo, cleared for takeoff. Thanks, Asheville." He pushed the throttle smoothly all the way in with the palm of his hand, the strong Lycoming under the cowling cleared its throat, building up to full bellow, and the Cessna picked up speed quickly. He tested the elevator, keeping the nosewheel precisely on the flashing centerline dashes by gentling the rudder pedals. He let her lift off by herself less than a third of the way down the strip. The airspeed jumped up to eighty knots almost as soon as she broke free, and he felt the familiar shot of euphoria as he ceased to be a gravity-tethered human being and became a wilder creature of the limitless sky. Not quite as free as a falcon doing lazy, instinctual aerobatics far above a valley or an eagle effortlessly riding the standing wave above some ridge, but close.

He banked away northeastward into a clear cool morning. The ocean of air was silken smooth. There was some fog lingering like smoke in the valleys, but that would soon burn off.

Perfect conditions for aerial photos.

The stone Biltmore Estate lay majestically below in its own spreading forest preserve. It was still the largest private home in the nation, a monument to old wealth and the profligate days of the capitalist barons propped up by thousands of workers laboring in near-slave conditions. Asheville lay beyond, drivers rushing along the main arteries to another workday. He kept climbing as the Swannanoa River, jewel-like Kenilworth Lake, the I-240 Beltway, and the Blue Ridge Parkway passed below in succession. Hardly any vehicles in sight on the Parkway this early.

He had to photograph a large tract being considered for purchase by a condo developer between Beech Mountain and Banner Elk, about eighty-five miles from Asheville, then swing over into Tennessee near Gatlinburg on the other side of the Great Smoky Mountain National Park and shoot a site for a proposed new restaurant so the investors could study the surrounding traffic patterns and sight lines for the signage. He would also shoot some random scenics this clear morning, just to build up his stock, which had proved profitable for sales to chambers of commerce, ad agencies, and an occasional magazine doing a feature on the mountains.

He located the condo tract using the color GPS in the center of his panel, once again marveling at the accuracy of the instrument and the wealth of information it yielded. He set up a run over the tract and a thousand feet above it, using the remote to trigger off a series of straight-down digital images with the camera hung on a homemade bracket beneath the floorboard, shooting through a hole cut in the plane's belly. He made two more runs from different directions, then circled the tract to shoot some obliques through his open side window with a handheld Nikon, guiding the plane only with his boots on the rudders, checking around occasionally for any other traffic.

He climbed another thousand feet and did it all again. When he was satisfied he had it well covered, he swung away toward the southwest, making for Gatlinburg as the day warmed brilliantly all around and some of the oldest mountains on the planet, softly carpeted in their spring greens, brushed by below, telling himself it must be some kind of fraud to charge people for doing this.

When he landed at Asheville, he taxied to park in a slot on the wide apron across from the maintenance hangar for the scheduled annual inspection. He tied the plane down to the rings set in the pavement, retrieved the belly camera, and walked over to talk with Ben Eckles, the mechanic—a squinty graybeard with an encyclopedic knowledge of light plane anatomy but the personality of a pit bull—who said he was ready to tow the plane inside and park it in a back corner.

"You can start uncowling it right away," Ben said. "Remember I keep a neat hangar. Put my tools right back where you get them from. Wish I had the money I lost from stolen tools all these years."

"Can't do it right away," John said. "There's something I have to take care of first this afternoon. Something that just came up. A promise I made."

"A promise? I promised we'd get your job started this afternoon, right? So I made the time. I got a schedule to keep here. Besides you, there's an overhaul and two other inspections I got to get cranking on. Listen, I'm not pulling yours in until you're ready to get to work on it. You think you can find somebody else let you do most of the work yourself in their hangar, use their tools, and not charge you an arm and a leg?"

"I appreciate all that, Ben. I'll try to get back here tomorrow morning at the latest."

"Well, maybe there'll be space for you. Maybe not."

John walked to his rented T-hangar to get his Jeep.

On the forty-five-mile drive back to Maggie Valley, he stopped in the town of Clyde for a quick lunch salad, keeping another promise to Hattie that he would try to eat better. Cut down on the fast-food junk. While he munched, he thought. Since mid-morning, Hattie's words had been tugging mildly at him. Her feeling that something was wrong concerning Moses Kyle. Even if everything turned out to be okay, he didn't want Hattie fretting all day long about it before knowing. He'd have to at least try to find out something for her before he became engrossed in the annual inspection. The day was balmy, so he put the top down on the white Jeep and got back on the road.

It was early afternoon when he turned off Highway 19 onto Big Pines Trail. The narrow road through the woods was paved for the first two miles. There were only a few small houses and mobile homes. There was a neat yellow cottage with burgundy shutters set back behind a patch of thick lush grass. A shapely dark-skinned woman in tight jeans and a navy blouse tied under her breasts was pushing an old-fashioned reel-type mower through the fairly tall grass with some difficulty. Pushing and then pulling the mower back for a fresh start, and pushing again. Hardin's gaze lingered on her for three seconds, but then he had to pay attention to his driving because the road abruptly became washboarded, potholed gravel and there were some tighter turns as it followed alongside a creek. The Jeep bounced and rattled.

A quarter mile farther on, there were two shuttered cottages that were probably vacation or summer places, and another quarter mile past them, the road petered out to become what looked like an old logging track. A tin-roofed cabin sat in a clearing by the creek. MOSE was childishly hand-painted on a board nailed to a nearby tree. The cabin had been painted a startling electric blue not long ago, clapboards and trim alike.

He stopped the Jeep and got out.

There were no sounds but the low, steady chuckling of the creek and some songbirds far off in the forest. He walked around the cabin. There was a chopping block with an axe buried in it, beside a cord or so of split firewood stacked against the back outside wall. A utility shed was tacked onto the back of the cabin, padlocked. He cupped his hands around his eyes and peered through a dusty window in the door and dimly saw a wide shelf with what looked like a big pie pan and some other things on it, a wooden stool, a worn backpack stuffed with something sitting on one end of the shelf, the usual tools hanging neatly on nails driven into the wall and exposed studs.

Around in front, there was a porch with a single white plastic chair on it and a rusty bicycle propped against the wall. He called out, "Moses. Moses Kyle?" but got no reply and for some reason expected none. The cabin looked empty.

He went up onto the porch. The front door was open an inch. He pushed it farther open enough to get a good look inside, then remembered Hattie's anxious blue eyes and decided he might as well go on in. He scuffed his boot soles on the jute welcome mat. The place was sparely furnished but neater than he would have imagined. Floors clean. No dust on things. Two rooms and a cramped bathroom. The larger room was the main living area. It had a kitchen sink in one corner with a few cabinets, recently painted the same vivid blue as the outside of the cabin.

Washed dishes sat in a plastic drainer on a counter beside the sink. An ancient refrigerator. A small propane-fueled cooking stove. A bachelor-sized microwave. There was a worn couch and a stuffed armchair, a round dining table with a wilted bouquet of spring flowers stuck in a coffee jar. An oscillating fan on its stand in a corner by a window. No curtains on the windows, but the glass was clean inside and out. No TV. A big ghetto-blaster-style portable radio/tape player/CD, though, on one of the tables. He inspected a stack of old cassette tapes. Willie and Waylon, Haggard, Dolly, Kristofferson. A few bluegrass compilations. Moses certainly had excellent taste in music. Give him that.

A square woodstove made of plate steel was set away from one wall on a raised brick pad. A lingering scent near the stove of many a hickory fire. There was a metal shower stall in the bathroom. An old metal medicine cabinet above the wall-hung sink.

The bed in the other room was disheveled, a thin blanket wadded up near a pillow, sheets trailing along the floor, out of place considering the general rough neatness in the rest of the cabin. Most of the man's clothes were hung or folded and stacked in an old-fashioned hardwood wardrobe. John could not remember the last time he'd seen one of those in use. From the days all the way back before closets. There was a dresser with a mirror screwed to the wall above it. Some of the mirror backing had flaked off near the bottom edge. A worn leather-bound Bible sat on a lamp table at the head of the bed. No other books or magazines or newspapers in sight anywhere in the cabin.

He went back out. The door didn't latch the first time he closed it, and he had to pull it shut a second time with some force before he felt the latch click home. He left it unlocked in case Moses had just forgot and had no key with him.

Back down the road, he stopped the Jeep even with the yellow cottage, cut the engine, and called to the woman. "Excuse me. I'm looking for Moses Kyle?"

She stopped mowing, wiped her brow with the back of her hand, and said, "Yeah, well, I'd like to know where that big gorilla is myself. He was supposed to be doing this."

She walked over to stand beside the Jeep.

They looked each other in the eyes, and neither said anything for a moment. She had long brown hair, so dark as to be almost black. Deep, feral amber eyes and mocha skin the texture of silk.

She said softly, "What?"

"I'm sorry," he said in a whisper.

He cleared his throat and said, "Don't mean to stare. It's just you're reminding me of someone I knew."

She smiled. "Now there's a line right out of some low-end meat-market boozery. Just kidding. I'm guessing you had a major thing for this someone."

"Yes."

"Yeah, well, sorry. Don't mean to pry."

"About Moses Kyle. I wondered if you've seen him recently."

"Not for a week or so. I work a night shift at the casino, so our paths don't regularly cross. He was supposed to cut my grass and trim the bushes. It's been a good arrangement. I bought that reel mower last year, figuring it would give me some exercise, but I'm really not crazy about physical labor, and he can use a few extra dollars. Until now he's done a good job."

"Maybe he forgot."

"I suppose. You know, though, there *was* one thing I noticed. Early yesterday morning, sometime just before dawn a car came by, going slow. It was unusual, because there are only two cottages besides Mose's place farther along the Trail, and they both belong to summer people who don't show up until after Memorial Day, after school is out. Half an hour later, the car came back out, going a lot faster, slinging gravel."

"Did you see what kind of car it was? A police car? Or maybe some kind of emergency vehicle?"

"Nope. Just heard it. Not likely it was an ambulance, though, because Mose doesn't have a phone to call one. Why are you looking for him?"

"You're right. He couldn't call out for any kind of help. He didn't make church yesterday, and a friend of mine is concerned about him."

"Not like Mose to miss going to that Presby church."

"Is there anyone else who might know something?"

"Not that I can think of. Mose pretty much keeps to himself. Did you notice if his bike was gone?"

"It's on his porch. The door was open a crack, and I went in. The place is pretty neat, except his sheets were half off the bed onto the floor, like he got up and left in a hurry."

"Strange."

"I'm beginning to think so."

"Well, if you find out anything would you give me a call? Kitty Birdsong. I'm in the book."

"John Hardin. I've got a place up on Eaglenest Ridge. I'd appreciate the same."

"Hardin. Okay. Well. Guess I'll see you around."

"Don't let them give all their money away."

"Excuse me?"

"Over there at the casino."

"Oh, yeah. Not much chance of that. Fact is, the casino owners don't deal in chance at all. Not from their end. All the numbers are on their side, believe me."

"I do," he said. "Thanks for talking with me." He started the Jeep and got it moving, catching a side-mirror glimpse of her standing there in her ankle-high grass, watching him drive away.

He parked the Jeep in the side lot at the low, nicely landscaped brick municipal building in the village on Highway 19. The three-officer police department was housed in a three- or four-room side office with its own outside entrance. A pleasant secretary who looked like she had just got out of high school told him Sergeant Boudreau was the only one in. A voice in the other room said, "Send the man on in, Ruthie."

Boudreau was a short muscularly chunky man who looked stuffed into his uniform. He had biceps, vined with blood vessels, that were straining his short sleeves. His hair was cut to within an eighth inch of his shiny head. He didn't get up from his desk, where he was doing paperwork.

"I'm John Hardin. I live up on Eaglenest Ridge."

"What can we do for you, Mr. Hardin?" He looked down to scribble something on a form.

"I'm trying to find out if a man named Moses Kyle is in any sort of trouble."

Boudreau looked up from the form and said, "Moses? I doubt it. He's simple, but he stays out of trouble, far as we know. You think he did something wrong?"

"I know this sounds lame, but he missed church yesterday, and I understand that's not like him. I checked by his home, and he's not there."

"What's your interest in Moses, anyway?"

"I don't know him personally, except to recognize him around town. An elderly couple lives with me.

Hank and Hattie Gaskill. Hattie goes to the same church and is concerned about Moses. I'm just trying to find out if he's okay."

Boudreau put his ballpoint down and leaned back in his swivel chair. "Well, Mr. Hardin, you tell Miz Gaskill that Moses probably just forgot it was Sunday. Like I said, the man's a simpleton. It's a wonder he remembers his own name most of the time. I hear he sometimes stays gone off in the woods for a few days at a stretch looking for a big strike."

"A strike?"

"It's how he makes a living, if you want to call it that. He pans for gold in the creeks. Finds a few flakes here and there, just enough to pay most of his bills. Probably works twice the number of hours at it he'd work on some kind of regular job on a garbage truck or washing dishes, and probably doesn't make nearly as much on an average. The man's a local joke."

"So he's a prospector?"

"That's the joke. Hasn't been any gold to speak of in these mountains in many a decade."

"I don't know. Sounds like an honest endeavor to me. Maybe more so than what some lard-ass civil servants do I've seen hanging onto public teats."

Boudreau squinted and turned a shade darker. He stared for a few seconds while John held his own gaze.

"Tell you what, Hardin. We hear anything, we'll get in touch." He picked up his ballpoint and went back to the form.

He stopped by the secretary's desk. She was grinning up at him.

"Ruth, do you suppose I could borrow your phone book?"

She reached for the book on a shelf behind her and handed it to him. He thumbed through it, copied numbers onto his shirt-pocket pad, and thanked her.

"Thank *you*, Mr. Hardin," she said, suppressing a giggle. "You have a nice day now."

"Ruthie," Boudreau said loudly. "Get in here."

John sat outside in the Jeep and used his cell to call the Haywood Regional Medical Center in Clyde, the Swain County Hospital in Bryson City, and the Harris Regional Hospital in Sylva, which were the top three places Moses might wind up if he was seriously injured or sick. It took a while to plow through the systems at each place.

Nobody had any record of admitting or treating Moses Kyle.

Rain clouds were rolling in low over the valley. He put the top up on the Jeep, fired it up, and drove slowly through the village. Not many people around this early in the season. The shops were pretty much deserted. A few late lunchers at Mama Guava's little Cuban sandwich place and at Country Vittles. All the motels had their vacancy signs lit hopefully. Nobody on the sidewalks who resembled Moses Kyle. He turned off of Highway 19 and shifted down for the switchbacking climb up the narrow paved lane to

Eaglenest Ridge.

There was a battered pickup in the clearing in front of the house. Hank was on a stool on the porch with his fiddle. A man in a tattered straw hat who looked even older than Hank was seated on the porch steps, strumming a well-used banjo. They were working their way through "Golden Slippers," Hank double-stopping most of it and the banjo player's picking hand blurring. John stopped on the brick walkway, put his hands on his hips, tapped a boot, and nodded along with the snappy rhythm. They finished with a flourish, both grinning.

Hank said, "This here's Pete. Ain't a half-bad picker for a transplanted Yankee, is he? Pete's from Pennsylvania."

He reached down to shake Pete's gnarled hand and said, "That sure sounded pretty good to me."

"I know there's the garden chores to do," Hank said, "but we got us a gig Saturday night at the Opry. We'll be openin' it for Fairchild and his bunch. You know, warmin' up the crowd. Pete come by figurin' we ought to practice some more. Fiddle just kinda climbed outta the case by itself and crawled up here onto my shoulder. Gonna rain pretty soon, anyway, so I won't be able to work in the garden. What you doin' back so early?"

Raymond Fairchild was a widely known Cherokee five-string banjo picker and Bluegrass Hall-of-Famer. The Maggie Valley Opry House was Fairchild's musical home.

John said, "Checking up on you. Might have known you'd get sidetracked by the first good picker to come along. Guess I'll have to see if I can sneak into the Opry Saturday night somehow. You'll have to answer to Hattie about the garden chores on your own. Can you guys do 'Old Joe Clark' at all?"

Pete grinned wider, poised his pick, and nodded at Hank to start them off. Hardin sat at the other end of the wide porch steps and listened through that one and "Wabash Cannonball" and an impossibly fast "Turkey in the Straw."

He said, "I think you missed a note on that last one."

Pete said, "Well, I had this mean uncle when I was a kid. Used to tickle me in the ribs till I cried. That was my uncle's favorite note. Haven't played that note since."

John left them to it as they started in on "Tennessee Wagoneer" and went looking for Hattie. She was in the kitchen deftly assembling an apple pie. She gave him a questioning look.

"Sorry, Flutter. I couldn't find out anything about Moses. Stopped by his place, talked with the police, even called the hospitals. No sign of him."

"Oh, Roy. I've been so afraid for him. What can we do?"

"I don't know much else to do. I don't think many people really know him well at all. He's one of those people you just get used to seeing around once in a while and never think twice about, I guess."

"Yes. I don't believe he has any family left. And not many friends. But there must be somebody who knows where he goes and what he does."

"You're right, there must be somebody who sees him fairly regularly. He buys groceries somewhere, and clothes and supplies. I was told he looks for gold dust in the creeks. He must sell what he finds to somebody. I guess I could try to find out who that is, ask if they've seen him lately."

"I don't like to take you away from your work any more for this."

"Too late to make it back to the airport today and hope to get much done. I'll go get your grocery list and ask around some more."

She looked off through the kitchen window and said, "He's in a dark place, Roy. Some kind of bad, dark place."

CHAPTER 5

He was alone in blackness except for weak starlight leaking through the high-up windows.

He had been sleeping some, and his neck hurt because his head had been hanging down. Still tied tight to the metal chair. His hands and arms and butt were numb. He tried to shift in the chair. He had only a foggy idea how long they had kept him here. All day Sunday and then another day, at least. So it could be Monday night. It seemed like longer than that, though. He remembered they had let him up to stagger over to a dirty bathroom in a corner of the barn, his untied hands burning like bunches of briars sticking him when the blood started running back into them. They had let him drink some water, too, laughing at him because it was hard to hold the coffee jar the scummy water was in with his numb hands. He fumbled and finally dropped the jar to shatter on the concrete.

The skinny woman had spent a lot of time with him, doing things that sent him off into a crazy-white fireworks place of pain so bad it filled the whole inside of him and the whole world around him. Letting him slowly wander back, her clear blue eyes studying him. Smiling at him. Moving her hands lazily toward him and watching him try to flinch away from those long, red nails.

Sending him away again, screaming.

But he had not told them what they wanted to know.

He tried to move his fingers, but could not even feel his hands. His neck muscles were cramping, and he moved his head around as much as he could to loosen them up. He pressed his feet against the cold concrete floor and strained his legs, his thigh muscles standing out like tree roots, but the bonds would not give any and the springy chair just rocked back and forth. He was hungry. He wanted to drink his belly full from a mountain creek almost clear as air and lie down on a thick bed of cool dark-green moss off in the forest a long way from everybody else. Look up through the trees at the sunshine falling down all around like hazy-bright angel paths. Listen to the birds talking so pretty to each other.

He thought about the place he had found.

"Mose, boy, I told you never to fight anybody."

It was his father's voice, and he whispered, "Daddy?"

"I told you never to fight anybody 'cause you might kill 'em and not even mean to. But that don't mean for you not to stand up and be a man like any other. Some in this world will poke fun at you. Tease you. Try to fool you and take what's yours. Laugh at you and call you stupid or touched. But you ain't really stupid or touched, Mose. You're a good boy. When you know somethin' is right, you go ahead and stand up for it. Don't you let nobody tell you different. You're gonna be okay, son."

His daddy. Not here and now, but back when he was sweating in that bed and passing away. Leaving him all alone in this world.

"Be okay, Daddy. Won't tell them. Our place."

He smiled and rested his head on his shoulder, drifting off.

He awoke to see three shadows behind the hot lights. The woman, he knew right away with a stab of dread. And the big-shouldered man with the tattoos. And now another man, who moved into the light to look down on him. A mass of white hair brushed straight back. Tall and thin. A face deeply lined, with eyes that burned into him like a hawk's eyes.

"Are you a believer?" the old man asked in a deep voice.

"What?"

"Moses Kyle, do you believe in the one and only pure God?"

He licked at his dry lips with his sandpaper tongue and said thickly, "Yessir. I do."

"That mine of the heathens you found. It was God who guided you, one of the least of us, to it. And us to you. You have served as the instrument of the One Pure God, and that gold will be used to do His purifying work. If you are a true believer you will retrace for us that pathway God laid out for you with His infinite blessing. You will now tell us how to find that place where He led you."

Moses stared into the burning eyes for long seconds. He shook his head and said, "No. Sir. My place. God took me? Maybe. Maybe did. Maybe wants me. Have it."

The fiery eyes pierced him. "Very well. We will test your belief in the way of long ago. In the way that He told us to do it in the Bible. Mark sixteen, verse seventeen. 'And these signs shall follow them that believe; in my name shall they cast out devils; they shall speak with new tongues; they shall take up serpents; and if they drink any deadly thing, it shall not hurt them.' Those are the gospel words of our One Pure God."

The big-shouldered tattooed man bent and slid a dirty white cooler into the light. The cooler lid had some small holes drilled in it. The old man unhooked a bungee cord that encircled the cooler, holding the lid closed. He lifted the lid, reached carefully inside, lifted out a handful of leaves, put them on the floor. A musty smell drifted up.

There was a rasping-buzzing sound like no other coming from inside. A primal sound that razors right to the spine of any hearer. The way a sudden whisper in surrounding supposedly empty blackest night can instantly galvanize an instinctive warning.

The older man moved his hand slowly down into

the cooler again, fingers spread. Darted his hand the last few inches in fast, and began lifting the thing out. It was long and thick and marked in shades of brown. Almost-black squares all along it.

Moses went winter-cold hollow inside and stopped breathing.

The big-shouldered tattooed man said, "What the Preacher's got by the neck here is your eastern diamondback. This one's near five feet and close on a dozen pounds, not full-growed. Bought him as a baby from a man down to South Carolina. See, we got like a serpent collection. From all over. Mean-lookin', ain't he? Them ridges over his eyes make him look always pissed off and mostly he is." He laughed softly.

Moses began to quiver all over.

The tattooed man went on, "See him lickin' the air? What he's doin' is tastin' for you. Tastin' to see if you're scared. Now *I* can tell you're rabbit-scared 'cause you just wet yourself a mite, even though you ain't had much to drink lately. This rattler, I guess *he* can tell you're scared with that whippity tongue he's got. Tell you what else, Mose. Look close at his head. See them holes near his eyes? Them eyes're just like a cat's, ain't they? Anyway, them holes under his eyes is pits. Uses 'em to feel your heat. Why they call 'em pit vipers. He can hit you square-on even in the dead of night. This one's got a load a poison in him to kill a damned cow. Sorry, Preacher. Rattlers're somethin' else. Took one apart once to see how it works. Skin is tough and dry.

Lot of rib bones strung out from the backbone make it real bendy. Just one lung about half the length of it. Fangs fold up inside the top of its mouth. They're hollow, like curved needles." The man held two hooked fingers toward Moses. "I still got the head bones and them wicked fangs at home. They pump the poison into you, see."

The thing was half twined around the old man's forearm, half hanging down. Tongue flicking at the air.

The bright beady eyes not blinking. Looking right at Moses.

Moses was whispering something frantically over and over, and the tattooed man leaned in close to him. "What's that, Mose? Your daddy? No, son, don't think your daddy can help out here. Nossir. Less *he* knows where that Indian mine is." He laughed again.

The tattooed man went on, "Seen a man get bit once. Strike probably hurts like hell, least the man sure looked like it did. Probably like when you go and sudden get a big splinter. But the holes don't plug up, see, 'cause the poison goes right to work, eatin' away at your skin, makin' your blood watery. Pretty soon you start bleedin' all inside. You got to know it's a bad way to die."

Moses was breathing with sharp gasps, his eyes wide, keening with each exhaled breath, so the man spoke louder. "What the Preacher might be gonna do, he might be gonna lay it right there in your bare-assed lap. See if you're a true believer. See will it hit you like God's lightning two, three times if you're not, or if it just curls up on top of your warm privates there and goes off to sleep, if you are. I was in your fix, I'd prolly try not to shake like that. Your belly's just a-quiverin'."

With what might have passed for a trace of pity, he looked at the big naked man tied in the chair and said, "What you think it's gonna do, Mose?"

CHAPTER 6

Early on Tuesday in an Asheville Cracker Barrel, John met with an out-of-state resort developer he'd shot aerials for several weeks before, showing him the images stored on a laptop. Before turning a disc of all the images over to the developer, he loaded some of the shots they picked out together onto another disc on the spot. He would send it express with a note to the Raleigh graphics company working up the sales brochures and ads.

He spent the next two hours in the maintenance hangar at the airport, working on the Cessna, uncowling the engine, taking all the inspection plates loose, removing the seats and carpeting, jacking up the wheels so he could grease the bearings. He resolved to skip lunch because of the big breakfast he'd had.

Just after ten, he left a griping Ben Eckles to do the actual exhaustive inspection, washed the grime out of the pores in his hands and from under his nails as best he could, wrapped a piece of masking tape around a skinned knuckle, and drove the Jeep back west.

The previous afternoon he had asked around town. A girl in the general store thought she remembered seeing Moses buying a few groceries early this past Friday or maybe Thursday morning, but he could find nobody who had seen him since.

Back up Big Pines Trail, he parked by Moses Kyle's cabin, knocked loudly twice with a knuckle, and waited. The door was still unlocked, and he went inside. There was still no sign of the man, and everything was as he'd found it the first time. He took some time looking around. He found only those things you might expect under the kitchen cabinets, cleaning stuff mostly. One drawer held a cluster of flatware, another had a jumble of tools, scissors, electrical tape, and so on. In the upper cabinets, there were a few dishes, pots, a frying pan, canned goods, a box of cornflakes, a can of cashews, and some crackers. There wasn't much food in the refrigerator, just orange juice, half a gallon of whole milk, a half-eaten brick of yellow cheese that was getting hard on the corners and had teeth marks in it, two eggs left in a carton, some dill pickles, a wrinkled apple.

The dresser in the bedroom held a few folded clothes, including three pairs of extra-large jeans, red long johns, boxer undershorts, T-shirts, and a pair of overalls. There was an old pair of large-sized boots in the wardrobe. Two jackets, one of them heavy winter weight. Hung-up shirts in plaid flannel, and some that were lighter-weight denim, all worn and wrinkled but clean.

There was a straw hat on the top shelf of the wardrobe, and a larger lump of something beside the hat. He poked the lump with a finger. Something hard. It was covered with a black T-shirt and a faded red baseball cap. He took the cap and shirt away to find a broken clay pot about seven inches tall and as big in diameter.

He lifted the pot down. It looked old; the bottom of it was permanently discolored with some kind of stain, and a patch of moss was stuck to it. The pot was a rich brown at the bottom, shading to almost ebony where it flared out gracefully near the top. There were strange incised symbols all around it, and two broken pieces inside the pot. He set it on the bedside table and tried the pieces. They fit, but there was at least one more piece missing. It was most likely Cherokee pottery, of course.

He thought, *Why were you hiding this, Moses? You find this out in the woods? A treasure for you?* If Moses had found this somewhere recently, maybe in or near some old Indian burial ground, had he gone back there to see what else he could find? He might be camping out in the woods there for a few days, poking around, like the cop Boudreau had said he did sometimes, but that just didn't feel right. For one thing, when he'd looked into the shed window out back the first time he'd come here, he had seen a backpack and what was probably the gold pan Moses used. *Shouldn't you have those things with you, Moses?*

On impulse, John used the T-shirt to wrap up the pot with the shards in it and took it with him. Somebody might have an idea where it had come from, and that could be a clue where to find Moses. He left feeling like a thief.

In the village he stopped at the Smoky Mountain Rock Shop, housed in a fieldstone building with a gravel parking lot under some oaks near Jonathan Creek. Plywood tables arrayed outside held hundreds of chunks of glass in many attractive translucent shades and fanciful abstract shapes, compartmentalized trays filled with glass marbles, bits of quartz, broken chunks of geodes, and all kinds of glinting stones, most of which he could not put a name to.

Inside, there were more plywood tables displaying large half-geodes, glittering shades of violet inside and bearing price tags in the hundreds, along with decorative clusters of white and pinkish six-sided quartz crystals, polished thin geode slices hanging in the windows to catch the sunlight, cases filled neatly with gold and silver jewelry made with semiprecious stones like garnet and opal and sapphire.

The portly balding owner, Ted Shoop, was loading a rock tumbler in a back corner. He looked over his shoulder and said, "Well, it's John Hardin. I hope you're here to buy a geode for a grand or so. You're only the third customer I've had all day." He closed up the tumbler, turned it on, and covered it with a plastic storage bin to cut down on the noise. He walked over to stand behind the sales counter.

He said, "You must know, don't you, that you've got the same name as a famous Western gunslinger. John Wesley Hardin. Some said he was the fastest, bar none."

John said, "Is that so?" He picked up a three-inch flint spearhead from a box filled with them. Used his thumb to test the scalloped edge, which was sharp. "Where do you get all of this stuff, Ted?"

"All over the place. I buy that glass outside by the ton from a guy who comes around once a year in a truck. He gets it from some glass-products factory in Pennsylvania. It's leftover stuff. Knows I'm a sucker for it. Apparently nobody else is, because I don't sell much of it. I keep thinking of this or that piece of it on somebody's coffee table, or in their flower bed where it will catch the sun, you know? Or in a fountain. I think it's beautiful. That flint spearhead you're holding is from Trenton, New Jersey. Old Polish guy makes them in his apartment in just a few minutes each. You ought to see him chipping away. Kids badger their folks into buying them. Some of the stuff is actually from the mountains here. Those garnet necklaces over on that rack, for instance."

"Ted, do you know a man named Moses Kyle?"

"Kyle. No. Don't think so. Wait a minute. Isn't that the man you see walking around town sometimes? Big. Kind of slow-moving. They call him Mose.

Don't know him personally. Why?"

"He's been gone for a while and nobody seems to know where. I've been trying to locate him because a friend of mine is concerned about him. Heard he makes a living panning for gold in the creeks around here. I figure he has to sell what he finds, probably somewhere close because he doesn't drive, and I thought you might either buy from him or know who does."

"Not me, but hang on and I can give you a few names." He went to a cluttered rolltop desk in a corner, found a pad, flipped through a large address book, and scribbled on the pad. He tore off a page, came back, and handed it to Hardin. "Here you go. Six places where he might sell gold within a reasonable distance, the only places I know of. Three aren't within any kind of even a long hike, but I figure a regular buyer might come to see him. 'Course these are all established businesses. Three of them I don't know personally, but I do know they all buy gold at least occasionally. He might possibly sell to some middleman—excuse me, middleperson—in which case, good luck finding out who that could be."

"How much gold could Moses be picking up in the creeks around here?"

"Not a lot these days, I'd think. There was a time, though, when some people really got rich on it. Gold's been found in more than a dozen of these western counties, I do know that. You've heard about the old Reed Mine?"

"Never did."

"Back about eighteen hundred or so, a kid named Conrad Reed picked up a nice-looking rock in Little Meadow Creek over in Cabarrus County and lugged it home. Weighed seventeen pounds. His dad, John Reed, used it for a doorstop a couple years, then found out it was a gold nugget worth a small fortune. He waded around in that creek on his farm and turned up a lot more. They say he filled a quart jar with nuggets in half an hour. Turned into a rich full-scale gold mine. About that same time, another guy named Barrington spotted gold in a creek in Stanley County. Dug a couple feet into the creek bank and uncovered a nest of it, worth a hundred grand at eighteen dollars an ounce." He poked at a hand calculator. "That would be about three-point-seven million at today's prices. Pretty tidy.

"A few finds like that started the first gold rush in the country, well before California. There were dozens of mines all over. For the next fifty years, North Carolina was the biggest producer in the country. Partly why they set up the mint in Charlotte back in the mid-eighteen hundreds. Charlotte and Brindletown were gold boomtowns. Gold Hill was built near some rich veins, and it was like a Wild West frontier town. But all the mines gave out, and as far as I know, nobody's found anything but slight traces in these mountains in a long time now."

"Interesting. And thanks. I'll take a couple of

these Polish spearheads. What else have you got that a seven-year-old boy might like?"

"How about a phantom crystal? Over there on that table. Those clear quartz clumps. Look at a few of them up close. You'll see milky shapes inside. Sometimes they resemble faces or animals. You have to use some imagination. You can even find quartz with ancient water trapped inside."

John found a cluster around a single, much larger crystal three inches long. Inside the long crystal was a shape, if he held it just right, that could be a bird in flight. He paid and left.

At home he reported to Hattie, who was sitting with Hank on the porch swing, that he still didn't know where Moses might be, but would keep looking. She nodded sadly.

Hank said, "Roy, me and Hattie figure we'll go down to the church this evenin' with the Benfields. There's a supper meeting about the spring festival. They'll pick us up."

Hattie said, "I can make you up a good plate you can warm in the microwave whenever you want to."

It was early afternoon, and he decided he was hungry after all. "That's okay, Flutter. I'll take a walk and grab a burger in the valley. Might have a beer while I'm at it. I'll rustle up something myself if I get hungry again tonight."

He walked down into the valley and stopped at the Salty Dog. An old pickup and a black chopper motorcycle were parked in the cramped lot.

It was pine-paneled inside, with NASCAR neons on the walls, five TVs displaying various sports silently, a small stone fireplace, scraps of raunchy T-shirts tacked up here and there. He sat at the deserted bar and ordered a draft and a cheeseburger plate all the way, knowing he was probably about to take in at least a month's worth of trans fats, which Hattie had been reading about and warning him against. There was the rumble of a powerful motorcycle outside.

He was looking at his slightly seamed reflection in the back-bar mirror, wondering how he had piled up so many years so quickly.

Kitty Birdsong walked in wearing tight jeans, boots, and an open jean jacket over a nicely filled white T-shirt. She sat at a small round table. Her hair was pulled back in a ponytail with a braided leather sleeve. When she spotted him, she lifted an eyebrow, smiled, and beckoned him with a head motion. He joined her at the little table, careful to avoid touching her knees with his own.

She said, "Well, have you found out where Mose has been hiding?"

"No, and the more I ask around about him, the more uneasy I feel. I'll keep at it and hope he turns up. Did you get your lawn mowed?"

"Yes, but don't ever buy a reel-type mower for the exercise. It's like kickboxing to lose weight. Not worth the pain."

"How are things at the casino?"

"They're raking it in, as usual. The latest thing is an ID tether. You clip one end to your shirt and plug the other end into the slot machine in front of you. We tell the gamers it's so they can win extra prizes if their slots pay off. A six-pack of Cokes. An extra twenty bucks. Whatever. Actually, the tethers help us identify the rollers and track their play. If they're good spenders, we lay on more hospitality for them. It looks weird, though. They're all lined up like robots, touching the slot screens with their fingers, like they're touch-talking to them, and plugged in with the tethers. I keep thinking the next step will be brain tethers. A player will stick one end into the slot and the other end into his ear. He won't even have to pull the handle. He'll just have to imagine Donald Trump broke or something to trigger the slot. And we'll be able to tell if he plans to stay and blow all the rest of the rent money or cut his losses and leave. If he even thinks about leaving, we'll inject a shot of his favorite booze right through the tether to keep him happy."

"I don't think your bosses would like to hear you talking like this."

"You're right. And the pay is okay. Keeps me in groceries and an occasional rib eye. The place just gets to me once in a while. The other day I stopped and looked around, and I realized what had been bugging me for a long time now. People don't make the dominant background noise in the place. The machines do."

"You must be Cherokee to be working there."

"I'm one-eighth redskin, but only about thirty percent of the employees have Indian blood. Used to be sixty percent when the place opened."

She ordered a tuna-steak sandwich and a bottled water, and the waiter, who also served as the bartender, said he'd bring the order to the table.

A muscular blond man in dirty jeans, a black T-shirt, and a leather skullcap came into the bar from the back room. He walked over, put a paw on the back of Birdsong's chair, leaned down and planted a quick kiss on her forehead. He said, "Kit, babe. Your stud muffin's here now, so you can get rid of this guy." His T-shirt said, "Let's Play Carpenter. We'll get hammered. Then I'll nail you."

She rolled her eyes and said, "Mr. John Hardin, this is Brandon Doyle, who rides that loose collection of worn-out Harley parts outside. It's black, like his heart."

Doyle grinned and offered his hand, and John took it. Doyle tried to crank on some force, but John's own grip was strong. There was a flicker of irritation in his eyes. But he grinned. "John Hardin, huh? You know there was a famous desperado had that name. He was supposed to be a fast draw. You fast, John?"

Kitty said, "Brandon, go lift your leg in the men's room. We're trying to have a conversation here. I realize you don't know what that means. You might want to look it up."

"She's a tough chick, Hardin. You sure you can

handle her?"

John looked at him for three seconds. Said, "Tell you what you could do, Doyle. While you're in the men's room, pick one of the numbers on the wall. Probably still not too late for you to get a date."

Doyle went still and glared for several heartbeats, then he grinned, patted Hardin on the shoulder, said, "Later, my man," and walked over to sit at the bar.

Kitty said, "Sorry about that. At a really low point in my life, I dated him once. Just once. He's got those high handlebars on his chopper they call ape-hangers, and that's appropriate, believe me."

John decided he liked her deep shining amber eyes with the faint smile lines delicately etched by her temples. There was toughness there. Resiliency. A hint of mischief. And honesty.

He said, "I have something I picked up in Moses Kyle's house. An old clay pot. Likely Cherokee. Maybe you could tell me something about it. I thought it might be a clue to where he can be found."

"A clue, huh?"

"So call me Sherlock."

Her eyes were frankly appraising, and her smile was genuine. "Okay, Sherlock. I don't know a whole heap about things Cherokee, but if I can't help, I'll point you at somebody who probably can. Where is this pot?"

"Back at my place up on Eaglenest Ridge, but I don't have a car. I walked here."

She cocked her head and said, "Well, after we eat, why don't I take you home and you can show me this artifact? I've got a while yet before I have to go help fleece the tourists."

"Okay."

The waiter brought the food, and they chatted as they ate. She said, "You know, I don't think Mose has been gone all that long. Couldn't he just be off camping somewhere in the woods?"

He ticked off the reasons he thought something was out of focus about all this. Moses uncharacteristically missing church. The disheveled bed in the cabin. The backpack and gold pan left behind in the shed. The vehicle Kitty herself had heard going by her place. The unlocked, unlatched door. "Even if Moses meant to leave his door unlocked, I think he must have known about the faulty latch and would have closed it right just out of habit," he said. "Looks like he left in a hurry, and that presents questions. How much could Moses have had to hurry about unless something was wrong?"

She nodded.

She picked up the check before he could reach for it, said, "You get the tip," and went over to the bar to pay. He put down a tip and followed.

She was talking with the bartender. "Mike, do you still have that old black helmet with the skulls all over it?"

The bartender bent, rummaged under the bar, and came up with a scuffed half helmet painted with skulls caught in spiderwebs.

Kitty said, "Mind if I borrow it?"

"What's mine is yours, darlin'. The food okay?"

"Let's just say it goes with the décor."

"Aw, you know you won't get a better sandwich in the valley, darlin'."

"Just kidding. It was fine."

Doyle was at the end of the bar, noisily wolfing a large burger.

John followed her outside. She stopped by a powerful-looking red motorcycle with studded saddlebags hung on it. She handed him the helmet and said, "Here, put this on. I think it will fit. You and Mike are about the same size."

"Wait a minute. This is yours? You expect me to ride on the back of this thing? What is it, anyway? A Harley?"

"No, it's a Honda. VTX thirteen hundred. Nice clean driveshaft instead of a belt or a chain. Wet clutch. Liquid cooling so you don't fry a cylinder at a long stoplight in the summer. It's a great bike. Why not ride on the back? Do you have something against female bikers? It's just supposed to be a male macho thing?" She lifted her helmet off of the rearview mirror and deftly strapped it on. Pulled on some thin gloves she got out of a leather bag behind the windshield.

"Not that. It's just—"

"Oh, come on." She threw her leg over, sat in the saddle, and lifted the bike off of the kickstand. "Okay, get aboard. Put your feet on those pegs. Don't be leaning out to the side. Just sit straight and hang on. You'll be safe."

"It's a pretty steep climb up to my place."

"I ride this all over these old mountains. I can do steep. If it will make you feel better, we'll take a slow ride up to the gap first, let you get comfortable with it."

He had just climbed on and secured the helmet and was trying to figure out some way to hold on without getting personal, when Brandon Doyle came outside, a can of beer in one paw. Doyle grinned and hollered, "Hey, babe, your gunslinger looks real nice on the back end there."

She started the bike, and the sudden heavy rumble drowned out Doyle's laughter.

She turned her head and spoke back over her shoulder. "You can put your hands on my waist. It won't mean you're making a commitment."

So he put his hands on her waist. He fumbled and, not meaning to, got one hand under her jean jacket momentarily. She felt warm and firm through the soft T-shirt cotton. He tugged her jacket hem down and placed his hand on the outside. The insides of his thighs were unavoidably resting against the outsides of her hips.

She drove them smoothly along Highway 19 through the village, adding power as she began the long curling climb up through Soco Gap. He could smell the freshness of the forest and feel the temperature cool abruptly when they banked around a corner.

The sparkling pavement scrolled rapidly by beneath them. He liked the rush and buffet of the wind and the primal thunder of the exhausts. She was obviously a good rider.

He began to relax and wonder why he had never considered buying one of these things before.

After three miles, she turned them around carefully in the gravel parking lot of a closed produce stand. The pipes popped and rapped sharply as she kept it in the lower gears on the downgrade to let the engine do most of the braking. She ran back through the village at five miles an hour over the limit and took them easily up the steep lane to Eaglenest Ridge, John pointing the way to his place.

They dismounted. Hattie was rocking on the porch. She stopped rocking and looked suspicious.

Kitty took off her helmet and said, "That your mom?"

"Yes and no."

"What, you're adopted or something?"

"Yes and no. She might call me Roy."

"Roy."

"I'll try to explain sometime."

"That ought to be some story."

They walked up to the porch, and he introduced the two women.

Hattie was tentative. She said. "Roy, I think those things are dangerous."

"Kitty just gave me a ride home, Flutter. And she's careful. A good rider."

Kitty took a seat on the bench, and he went inside to get the pot, which was still wrapped in the black T-shirt. When he came back out, the two of them were chatting amiably. Hattie laughed at some comment he didn't catch and said, "Yes, he surely is," and looked at John with amusement in her eyes.

"I am what?"

"Never you mind," Hattie said.

He sat on the other end of the bench with the pot in his lap and let the two of them talk, mostly discussing mutual acquaintances in the village. They obviously liked each other. Kitty was a patient and considerate conversationalist, and naturally friendly. He began to feel good that she was here at his home, but he pushed the feeling away.

When Hattie excused herself and went back inside, Kitty sat beside Hardin. He unwrapped the pot and handed it to her.

She spent a few minutes looking it over. "These markings are in the old language. It's Sequoyah's syllabary, which was introduced almost two centuries ago. It made the whole tribe literate overnight back then, but it's not used a lot now. I don't know enough to tell you what it says, except it's about some special place I think was claimed by the Wolf Clan. And I think you're right. This is old."

"Moses had it covered up on a shelf in his wardrobe. Looked like he was hiding it."

"Do you have a pad and a pencil?"

He went inside and got them from his desk in the living area. He couldn't find the plastic sharpener so he whittled the pencil to a point with his pocketknife.

She held the pot in her lap, placed the pad on the flat bench arm, and studied the markings, copying them onto the pad with care, while he in turn studied her in profile. She held the pot shards in place to get the markings just right. Erasing several times and drawing parts of the inscription over.

She reminded him so much of Valerie, stirring in him an unsettling confusion of strong feelings. A soul-swelling memory of great love. An abiding abyssal void of great loss. And threading through all that was a strange tug, tender and faint, of something that might have been new hope. He made an effort to push it all out of his thoughts.

She finished her sketching, tore off the page, and folded it to fit into her jean jacket pocket. Buttoned the pocket over the soft swell of her left breast. "I'll show it to Zeke at the casino tonight. He cleans up, works a shift that overlaps mine. He'll be able to tell us what it means."

"Appreciate you doing that."

"You have me curious. And a bit afraid."

"What do you mean?"

"Well, either sweet ol' Mose is just going to walk out of the woods pretty soon, all sheepish and apologetic and smelly. In which case we'll give him his pot back and all laugh about it. Or he's not going to, and we might track him down. But if he's been really sick or hurt someplace since early Sunday or before, it's already getting to be long enough now that we could be too late."

CHAPTER 7

Moses could not remember if he had told them how to find his special place and that made him afraid. He did remember thinking he could tell them some *other* place where he could have found the pretty river of color in the rock wall. Maybe a deep cave he knew about on the back side of Setzer Mountain.

He could tell them about that cave. Or maybe he already had.

He was alone again in the dark. And he had lost all idea of time. His neck hurt from hanging down. His butt and back hurt from pressing against the metal chair. He hurt where he was tied and in all the places the red-haired woman had worked on him. He had screamed and cried until his throat was raw, like he had pieces of glass caught in there, and his voice didn't work right anymore. Slept some when they went away and left him alone. Dreamed nightmares about black bead-eyes and curved needles and red-painted razor blades. He had been very hungry for a long time, but he didn't care about food anymore. He was thirsty, though. Almighty thirsty. More thirsty than anybody ever had been before, he thought.

He slept again. Drifting feverishly.

Dreamed of screaming.

In his dreams the white-haired man dribbled scummy water from a glass onto his lips, and he licked at it greedily even though it was warm as blood.

He thought about the deep cave on the back side of Setzer Mountain.

In his dreams he told them something.

Suddenly they were all there behind the lights again, and there was weak daylight coming in the high windows and Mose was half dreaming their voices. The dirty cooler was close by on the floor, but closed up. The tattooed man was nodding and smiling at him, and he begged for water.

The tattooed man said to the woman, "The Preacher and me'll go see."

And Moses was alone again with the red-haired woman.

After a while she came into the light.

She had no clothes on, either. She had freckles all over. She brushed her tangled hair back and smiled her grin-smile, her blue eyes glittering as she began to work on him.

Doing something to herself this time, too.

But he smiled to himself even through the building pain. Because he had dimly figured out if she was hurting him again that must mean he had not told them what they wanted to know yet.

She would not want to hurt him anymore if they knew where his special place was, would she?

CHAPTER 8

The Wrangler sat parked on the sand beside the rutted lane in the shadows. She got in gracefully. Tried to start it. There was a silent white flash that became a horrifically beautiful blossoming fireball engulfing the Jeep—meant for him—and he slammed awake, sitting up in bed deep into the night, his fists clenched into hickory knots up close by his head.

It had been months since the nightmare had visited him.

Valerie.

She had died when a trio of hit men had come after him on the Outer Banks island of Ocracoke. They had nearly killed him. Left him for dead. He certainly would have been dead had Hank and Hattie not saved him and nursed him back to health.

Months later, with the help of Valerie's Cherokee grandfather, Wasituna, he had trained and toughened his body and his mind. Then he had gone after those who had killed her so indifferently.

He knew why the nightmare was back. This woman Kitty Birdsong had set him thinking of Valerie again with fresh poignancy and bone-deep sorrow. If there had been a woman on the planet with whom he was destined to walk, that woman had certainly been his Valerie. And she had died because she had known him. The guilt of it was lodged in his soul like a stone. That another woman should be occupying his thoughts as any more than an acquaintance seemed some kind of perversion. He stared at the shadowed ceiling for a long time before he could push the nightmarish afterimages out of his mind.

He finally looked at the clock on the nightstand. Five thirty. He got up. Showered. Shaved. Dressed, and went downstairs, determined to face the day with new resolve.

Hank had put the coffee on and was poking around in the kitchen. "Mornin', *Kemo Sabe*."

"Hank." He made himself a cup of the aromatic coffee and forced a smile. "Sometimes when I fix up my first cup in a morning, I think about cowhands around an early morning fire someplace in the wilderness, watching a scorched enameled pot, waiting on it. I know it tasted like nectar to them, too."

"That's a scene from many a Western. Saw a good one last night on TV after you hit the sack, by the way. *Broken Trail.* Robert Duvall plays a tough old bird named Ritter. Thomas Haden Church plays his nephew, Tom. Always liked both those guys. Like

Duvall 'cause he's got 'bout as many wrinkles as me and looks like he earned every one. Church just looks and acts like a natural cowboy. Anyway, Ritter and Tom are drivin' horses to a buyer in Wyoming and they get sidetracked rescuin' five Chinese girls and a bad-abused whore from a mean whorehouse owner. Based on a true story."

"I remember it. Saw it myself again a month back. They had to bury one of the girls who died of tick fever, and Duvall said, 'We're all travelers in this life. From the sweet grass to the packing house. Birth to death. We travel between the eternities.'"

"Don't know how you remember so much. Me, my brain's turned to oatmeal pretty much. Got a good stumper, though. Louis L'Amour story they made into a movie called *Hondo*. Early fifties. John Wayne's a cavalry dispatch rider with a mean dog. There's a lady settler raisin' a young son by herself. Here's the stumper. There was a army scout in it went on to get famous on TV in a Western series. Who was that?"

He thought for a few seconds and said, "Oh, yeah. James Arness. The series was *Gunsmoke*. Sidekick was Festus."

Hank shook his head. "Don't know how you remember so much."

"You do all right, Hank. Haven't stumped you lately, either."

He ate three of Hattie's oatmeal date turnovers and carried another cup of coffee to his desk in the living area. He sorted through some of his best scenic aerials stored on the hard drive, made up a disc with examples in all four seasons, and packaged it for the requesting editor of a monthly publication in Brevard along with his standard rate sheet. He did some billing and wrote out a proposal to the geology department at Appalachian State University in Boone to help them conduct an aerial video survey of three mountain creeks. Caught up on his mail and e-mails and did some filing to the three tall cabinets lined up by the desk.

After nine, he started calling the list of possible gold buyers that Ted at the rock shop had provided. The first one he chose was a jewelry store called Baxter's in nearby Waynesville.

A woman answered, "Yes, good morning. It's certainly a glorious one. How may Baxter's help you today?"

"My name is John Hardin, over here in Maggie Valley. Could you tell me if you know a man named Moses Kyle? He's something of a local prospector, and I thought you might buy his gold from him."

She took only a moment to answer, repeating the name to herself and searching her memory. "No, I'm sorry, but I don't think I've ever heard that name before, and I'm the only buyer here. We do buy gold—old family jewelry, rings from failed marriages, which I always find very sad, even gold fillings on occasion—but I can't recall anybody ever bringing in any dust or nuggets to sell. Frankly, I didn't think there was enough of it left in the creeks around here to make it pay very well."

He thanked her and hung up. He was thinking he ought to go back out to Mose's place to see if he had shown up there, when the cordless phone on the desk rang loudly. He kept the volume turned up so both Hank and Hattie could hear it from almost anywhere in the house.

Kitty Birdsong said, "Hello, Sherlock. Just called to say there's still no sign of Mose at his place. I'll keep checking. Also, old Zeke didn't come to work last night, but he's supposed to be there tonight. I figure I might find somebody in Cherokee today who can read the old language, maybe at the museum, but I could also do some asking around about Mose here in the neighborhood and that might be more useful to us. Then see Zeke tonight."

"Sounds good. I'm trying to find out who was buying gold from him."

"So. I'll check around here, then. Call you if I find out something."

"Good."

"Maybe later . . ."

It was an opening. An invitation. They were both looking for Moses now, but there was suddenly a hint of something more. A subtle offering. If he even tentatively explored that, it would be a departure from his current acquaintance-relationship with Birdsong. And it would seem to be a betrayal of Valerie. Of her memory. He could not stand that.

He said, "I'll call you if I turn up anything."

"Okay. So . . ."

He hesitated. Said, "Talk to you later," and hung up.

Thinking of those deep amber eyes.

He called two more places on the list of potential gold buyers—a jewelry store in Clyde and another in Sylva. Nobody at either business had ever heard of Moses Kyle.

He punched in the number for a dealer in coins and antiques in Lake Junaluska.

"Yes, I know Mose Kyle," a man named George Rogers said right away. "I've bought gold dust from him time to time. He's pretty good at finding it. Haven't seen him in about a month or more, though. Why?"

"He hasn't showed up at his home for a few days, and friends are concerned. Did he ever mention roughly where he goes looking for dust?"

"Anybody who pans tends to keep where they go to themselves. At least partly because they're most often on somebody else's land. Same way with the metal-detector bunch."

"Did he ever say anything about finding Indian artifacts? Especially an old Cherokee pot?"

"No, Moses never has a lot to say about anything. He just comes here now and then on an old rusty bike. Brings me dust. I weigh it up, pay him a fair price in cash, he goes on his way. I suppose he could have come across some old Indian stuff, though, much as he prowls the backwoods."

"Mr. Rogers, I'd appreciate a call if you see Moses." He gave his home and cell numbers, and the man agreed to call if he should encounter Moses anywhere.

He made a call to a Cherokee metalsmith who did a quick search of his address book and said he had no record of a Moses Kyle.

The last name on the list was a tourist attraction near Frankfort. A man with a scratchy voice answered gruffly, "You've got Cagle's Gem and Gold Mine."

"I'm John Hardin in Maggie Valley. Do you know a man named Moses Kyle?"

There was a protracted silence on the other end of the line. Rasping breathing. He waited. But the man said nothing.

Louder, John said, "Hello?"

"I'm here. Moses Kyle ain't here."

"Who am I talking to?"

"This is Orin Cagle. Why?"

"Mr. Cagle. I didn't think Moses would be there. I asked if you know him."

Another long silence. "Yeah. I know him. Haven't seen him."

"Do you buy gold from him?"

"I don't see that's any of your business."

"I guess it's not, really. Moses hasn't showed up at his house for a few days. A friend of mine is concerned."

Another long silence. "Well, I hear he goes off by himself a lot. In the woods. That's where he could be."

"Look, if you see him, I'd appreciate a call. John

Hardin."

The voice said, "I could do that."

He gave the man his numbers and hung up, a strange feeling about the call lingering.

◊ ◊ ◊

The tattooed man folded the cell phone. He said, "That was Orin. Some guy named Hardin just called him lookin' for Kyle."

The Preacher was quiet and brooding for so long the tattooed man thought he must not have heard.

Then the Preacher said, "Find out what you can about this man. He might know of the gold. And we need to ask Moses Kyle if he told this man or anyone else that he found it."

◊ ◊ ◊

John brought along a lunch that Hattie had made for him and spent the afternoon working on the airplane's annual at the airport. He left a scowling Ben Eckles to finish it up.

"Next year I don't believe I'll let *anybody* do *any* of their own work," Ben said. "Not a damn one of 'em appreciates it. You tell me another mechanic lets his customers get away with it."

"Ben. You're a friend. And the best wrencher I know. But . . ."

"What?"

"You're a grouch, Ben."

"Yeah, well, you tell me what airplane mechanic isn't, after dealing with *pilots* for a couple decades."

He was late for supper, but Hattie warmed a meat-loaf plate for him and he ate it out on the porch, watching Ma Nature use the lowering sun to paint the sky three-dimensionally, revising colors, trying various hues, outlining selected clouds, suffusing others thoroughly to make misty confections of them.

He wondered if Moses Kyle was out in the woods somewhere. Rough camping. Watching the same display.

Or lying with a broken leg. Hurting. Dehydrated. Starving. Calling for help with nobody anywhere close enough to hear.

The sunset subsided into shades of violet and gray. The mountains softly silhouetted.

Still a beautiful sight if you could look forward to tomorrow.

Probably a grim display for somebody who could not.

CHAPTER 9

Kitty Birdsong called early on Thursday morning. "Still no sign of Mose at his cabin, but I've got some good info about that Cherokee pot for you. It will cost you lunch."

"That's fair. How about Mama Guava's at twelve-thirty?"

He spent the morning doing paperwork and talking with clients on the phone.

At twelve thirty he parked the Jeep next to the glittering red-and-chrome motorcycle in front of the tiny restaurant. She was sitting on the steps, her back against the porch post, one leg stretched out, wearing tastefully sequined jeans over mirror-polished black-cherry boots. Her wide-collared shirt matched the bike. She had the shirttails knotted under her breasts to reveal a modest band of taut belly. Her long hair was tied back smoothly into a ponytail. It surprised him how much he enjoyed seeing her again. They sat at a small table on the porch and both ordered loaded

Cuban sandwiches.

"So what does Zeke think about the pot?" She took a sip of water and said, "He agrees it's old. Wood-fired. The inscription tells of a sacred yellow cave of the Wolf Clan."

"A yellow cave?"

With sparkles of excitement in her eyes, she said, "I figure that could mean gold. Do you know much about Cherokee history?"

"A little."

"I did some brush-up reading this morning. About my ancestors. You know the Cherokee, or the *Tsalagi*, had been around for hundreds of years by the time you white men showed up wearing too many clothes, with greed in your hearts and lies on your tongues. We were one of dozens of tribes populating this whole hemisphere. We probably broke away from the Iroquois to the north at some point. And we were doing very well at it, thanks. Living in harmony with nature and pretty much with each other. Taking only what we needed. Making beautiful and useful things like pots. Baskets. Moccasins. Babies. The Cherokee people lived in neat houses with woven walls. Never teepees. Men and women shared power in the seven clans. Do you know we Indians, collectively, came up with nearly half of the whole world's leading food crops—corn, beans, tomatoes, potatoes, peanuts, sunflowers, and gave them to you, no charge? You, in turn, stole our land and gave us measles, yellow fever, empty promises. Booze. Rock and roll. Gangsta rap."

"If I'm not mistaken, you gave us tobacco, too. We've given you cell phones, don't forget. And PC games. And Hollywood. And motorcycles. And I am buying you lunch."

"Lunch. Big deal, after you guys took western North Carolina from us. I can thank a guy named Soichiro Honda for my motorcycle, and when I ride it I have to dodge American motorcycle parts and leaked oil spots all over the place. And before you give us any more shiny trinkets like made-in-China cell phones, which incidentally I despise, I'm telling you I'm not signing anything."

A waitress brought the food. The sandwiches had to be compressed considerably before they could be bitten into. John and Kitty attacked them.

She took a break and dabbed her mouth with a napkin, which drew his attention to her full lips. She said, "Anyway, about a hundred and seventy years ago, you guys invited us to leave these rocky ol' good-for-nothing mountains and move to the beautiful promised land of Oklahoma. We sort of liked our mountains, so we took it to the Supreme Court and they ruled we could stay. Andrew Jackson, that creep, ignored the court. A Cherokee brave saved him from a Creek tomahawk in the War of Eighteen-Twelve, but do you think he appreciated that? Old Hickory, they called him. They must have been referring to his brain. The only president in history who ever blatantly defied the

Supreme Court. He signed a shady little piece of legislation called the Removal Act, had us rounded up into concentration camps, and told us to start walking into the sunset. Into a cold winter. Sent a gang of soldiers with bayonets to help us keep up the pace. About four thousand bodies later—people lost from exposure and white men's diseases and brutality—what was left of us were camped out in the wastelands of Oklahoma. Along with remnants of most every other tribe that had lived east of the Mississippi. It was sort of early time-sharing. A stubborn few hid out in the woods and stayed here, which is why a wonderful reservation casino gets to take your rent and grocery money and car payments from you today."

"Maybe you ought to quit working there and get a job teaching history."

"My point to all this is when you guys asked us along for that westward stroll, a few of my people took pains to conceal and keep secret some of our stuff here, like a gold mine or two, or so the legend goes. When so many died on the Trail of Tears and shortly thereafter, secrets died with them."

"A sacred yellow cave. You think Moses might have found one of those old lost mines?"

"It's possible."

"And you think maybe he went back there? He's filling up his overalls with nuggets? Or maybe he got into some kind of trouble. Hurt himself. And that's where he could be."

"Something like that."

"It's pretty thin. Just based on that pot."

She spread her hands and said, "I know, but what else do we have?"

"Right. Nothing. Maybe it's been long enough the cops will be willing to help now. I'll go see them this afternoon. Don't think I'll tell them about this mine theory, though. It seemed like Moses was trying to hide the pot. If he has found a gold mine, it's his business, and I guess we probably should respect his right to keep it a secret if that's what he wants."

"I agree. But if we could find such a mine, or at least a rough location, that might help find Mose. I'll do some more research. Talk to a few old-timers on the reservation. See if I can get some idea where to start looking."

They finished obliterating the sandwiches.

He said, "You ride that Honda everywhere?"

She took a sip of water from her straw, focusing him on her lips again. "Just about. Not in heavy rain or below freezing. I like the freedom of it. Controlling that power. There's the hint of danger, which adds spice, I guess. Mostly, though, you *see* more on a bike. Especially the sky. And you smell the flowers and feel the wind on you and sense the changes in the air. And it sips gas. It's a lot better than riding around in a steel cage of a car."

"I can understand all that."

"Think you'd like to ride?"

"I guess it's on my try list now."

"Cool. Grab for it."

"Good sandwich."

"Yup." She was smiling.

"Guess I'd better get going."

"Me, too. Thanks for lunch."

He went inside to pay the check, and through the window he watched her don her helmet, lithely mount up, crank it into a rumble, and ride away, her smile lingering with him.

When he pulled the Wrangler into the police station lot, Boudreau was standing by a cruiser with the door open, about to get in. Hardin walked over and said, "Afternoon, Sergeant Boudreau. Is the chief in?"

"Nobody but me, and I'm on my way to a meeting at the sheriff's department. If you've got something to say, make it fast."

"It's still about Moses Kyle. No sign of him anywhere since Sunday or before. I think he might be in serious trouble."

"I thought we went over that, Hardin. Kyle's only an IQ point or two above imbecile. You can't expect him to act in normal ways. I hear he stays gone out in the boonies for days at a time. This is probably just one of those times."

"Don't think so. He left his backpack and his gold pan in his shed. There are signs he had to leave in a hurry. Even left his door unlatched. It feels like trouble."

"It *feels* like trouble, huh?"

"Look, Boudreau, what harm would it do to ask around? Or at least put out a notice with a description to be on the lookout for Moses? Maybe you're right and he's just gone camping, but what if we find out he's been in trouble all this time and your people took no action when you were asked? If you've got a notice out, you're at least covered, right? I know you want to do the right thing here."

Boudreau considered. He said, "I'll bring it up with the chief at this meeting I'm supposed to be at in ten minutes. Might let the sheriff's people know while I'm at it. Somebody from the Highway Patrol will be there, too. Maybe we'll decide to put out a bulletin."

"Appreciate that."

"Keep your foot off the gas in that Jeep. I've seen you over the limit at least twice now. Hate to write you a ten-over ticket. Mess up your insurance." He squealed the tires leaving the lot.

He would have to tell Hattie he'd done what he could for now about Moses. There was nothing more he could think of to do.

CHAPTER 10

John heard nothing until Kitty Birdsong called him shortly after dawn on Saturday morning. "Hope I'm not calling too early. No news about Mose on my end. Still no sign of him. How about you?"

"Not too early. Nothing on my end, either. I'll check in with the cops today. Maybe they've found out something."

"What else are you doing today?"

"Not a lot planned, but I have a standing to-do list that's pretty long. I need to get some work done around here."

"I just took a short walk. The sky straight up is deep spring blue. Brand-new clean. I'll bet you can see forever from the Parkway. It's a gorgeous day. How about we start it off with an old-fashioned high-cholesterol breakfast at Country Vittles? I'll buy. I can summarize what I've been reading on lost Cherokee gold."

"Give me thirty minutes."

Hank was in the kitchen getting coffee. John told

him he'd be going out.

Hank said, "Me and Hattie think it's great you've got yourself a girlfriend. Hattie says she's really somethin'. I don't see a thing wrong with her bein' some years younger than you, either."

"She's not my girlfriend. We're looking for Moses Kyle together."

"Sure. Whatever you say, *Kemo Sabe.* That's what we'll tell people when they ask, then. It's just sort of a private-eye thing. Best way you two figure to go about doin' that is with you up tight to her on the back of her motorcycle. Before you go gettin' a tattoo, though, with her name on it, you and me should probably have a talk."

"I think you and Hattie ought to mind your business."

"Hattie figures you *are* her business. Anyway, I got a real stumper for ya. No way you're gonna get this one. You remember a story called *The Comancheros*?"

He nodded. "John Wayne's a lawman working undercover to catch gunrunners."

"Right. Wayne and Lee Marvin get drunk together and sing a song. What's that song?"

"Give me a minute." He snapped his fingers. "Got it. 'Red Wing.' I've heard you play it pretty well on that beat-up old fiddle."

"Dang. Don't know how you remember so much."

When John arrived at Country Vittles, Kitty Birdsong already had a table for them. They ordered eggs over easy, grits, and cornbread with honey.

He said, "So what have you found out about lost Cherokee gold?"

"It's definitely more than some murky legend. Indians used to carry dust they got from the creeks in bird quills to pay for things they bought from whites at what I'm sure were exorbitant prices. The Cherokee routinely mined gold and silver. In fact, Sequoyah himself was a silversmith. And there's apparently still a lot of gold left under these hills. I found this one article by a geologist online who says it's estimated only twenty percent of it has been mined out. That leaves a whole lot, because for a long while there, in the eighteen hundreds, millions in gold came from all around here. For a fifty-year stretch, *all* the gold officially minted in the country came from western North Carolina. People have looked for the Indian mines on and off since the Trail of Tears, with no success. Old Zeke thinks he remembers reading a vague description of a Wolf Clan mine location in somebody's handwritten family journal years ago. I've got him trying to track that down for us. I've started a file folder with Internet downloads and notes I'm collecting from library books, old newspapers, magazine articles. Maybe we can condense it into something useful. Anyway, it's pretty interesting. I'll keep at it."

When they finished breakfast and went outside, Kitty unbuckled a saddlebag cover and produced the borrowed half helmet decorated with skulls. She said, "I figure you might as well start learning to ride today.

I've got just the place for it."

"I really ought to get some things done around my house."

"There's no adventure in that. You can spare a couple hours this morning. Do your chores this afternoon. Come on."

They rode out of the village and ribboned up through Soco Gap, the bike rumbling deeply. The sky was that rarest glowing sapphire-blue, with a few tastefully patterned patches of high snowy cirrus. An impish breeze was buffeting them playfully and coaxing the trees to dance in their fresh spring finery. Two hundred feet above the saddle of the Gap a flock of songbirds danced a harmonious ballet. The air was cool in the shaded road curves, eddied with tantalizing scents of mountain wildflowers.

With his hands resting lightly on her waist, he could feel her warmth through her red cotton-canvas Western shirt, and the play of her muscles as she controlled the bike with skill. She smoothly carried them down into the forested valley and idled them through Cherokee village with its gaudy signs, tin teepees, aromatic leather stores, and gift shops piled with Indian trinkets made at slave wages in Taiwan and China.

Place is so tacky it has a certain appeal, he thought.

They pulled into the very large parking lot for the tribal bingo hall, empty this early in the day. She killed the engine, put down the kickstand, and they dismounted.

"Okay," she said. "First a lecture. This bike weighs seven hundred pounds, but the center of gravity is low, so it's fairly easy to balance upright standing still, as long as you never let it lean too far. Once you're moving, you won't notice the weight at all. The bike will go where you look, so never fix on an obstacle if you don't want to hit it. Beware of sand and gravel, especially in a turn. If the road is wet, avoid the center of a lane where cars drop oil, and stay off of the painted stripes; they're slick as ice when they're wet.

"Watch out for deer, bears, dogs, birds, potholes, rumble strips, litter, roadkill, shredded truck tires, stuff blowing back out of pickups and trailers, stones kicked up by dump trucks, and, worst of all, every other vehicle driver, every cager, that comes along, because it will be a reckless idiot with a cell phone stuck in its ear. They'll pull out right in front of you like they haven't got any brains, crowd you out of your lane, and tell the investigating officer sorry, they never even saw you.

"Try to leave at least three seconds between you and the vehicle ahead so if it straddles something nasty in the road you'll see it in time, or if it blows a bald tire and starts doing skid-donuts you can swerve out of the way, or if it stops quick so the driver can read a lotto billboard you won't smear your nose all over its rear end. Other than that, there's hardly anything to worry about. So mount up, stand it up straight with your feet, and get the kickstand up."

He did as she said. "Okay, how do you do a wheelie?"

"If you ever dare to attempt a wheelie on my bike, I'll give Brandon Doyle five dollars to come over to your place and breathe on you. Now pay attention. Let's go over the controls. The squeeze thingy on your left grip is the clutch. You shift with your left toe, one down for first, then hook your toe under the lever and click it up for neutral and on up again as you accelerate until you hit fifth gear. Use the clutch to shift each time, of course. You'll learn when to shift it. Press the rear brake with your right foot. Your right hand's got the throttle and another squeeze thingy for the front brake. Got all that?"

"Yes. Horn? Directionals? High and low beams?"

"All with your left thumb. Right thumb has the kill switch and the starter switch. Get in the habit of always shutting the bike off with the kill switch, by the way. Then if you need it quick someday, you won't be fumbling for it. Ignition key's down to your left under the seat."

"Got it."

"The first thing you have to know about is what we bikers like to call the friction zone."

"The friction zone."

"You being a somewhat virile male specimen, I know precisely what the primitive part of your brain is thinking right now, but don't say it."

"Somewhat virile?"

"Okay, some females of the species might consider you quite virile. Maybe even four or five on a scale of ten. Anyway, the friction zone is that area of this wet clutch where it's slipping, which doesn't hurt it at all. To ease the bike into motion, you put it in first gear, let out the clutch until it starts slipping, and away you go. You can hold it in a slip to creep along, in a line of traffic at a light, for example. What we'll do now is a power walk. You'll put it in first, let out the clutch until you're in the friction zone, and give it just enough gas to creep while you walk the bike along with your feet. You'll take it straight over there to the far end of the lot in a slow power walk, stop, and shift it into neutral. I'll walk along beside you. Okay, turn on the ignition, make sure you've got it in neutral by looking for the green light right there by the speedometer. Then crank it. Clutch in, shift into first, get into the friction zone, and power-walk it. Go."

For most of the morning, she brought him along, making him first ride the bike slowly in straight lines, then in broad circles. Showing him how to walk the bike backward out of a parking space, to stop fast and safely in straightaways and curves, and how to stop and start on an incline by putting just his left foot down so he could hold the bike in place with his right foot on the rear brake. Told him how to swerve around an obstacle, and counter-steer at speed through turns and serpentine curves. Showed him how to maneuver in tight quarters at slow speed by riding the rear brake and looking where he wanted the bike to go. He liked it, concentrated, and learned quickly. She made him repeat maneuvers until he began to master them, and she nodded in serious satisfaction each time he did a particular maneuver well.

He finally stopped the bike, killed it, and put it on the stand. He dismounted and looked the bike over closely. “This is quite a machine. Be nice to see what it could do when you let it out.”

“I’ve had the needle pegged and it felt solid. Smooth as silk.”

“It was a good lesson. Thanks. Why don’t you let me buy you an early lunch?”

“Today, there’s a better idea. Come on.”

They stopped in front of the rustic War Bonnet Restaurant in Cherokee village. She told him to sit on the steps and relax. In ten minutes she came out holding a large brown bag, which she stowed in a saddlebag.

They mounted up and she guided them out of town to the entrance of the Blue Ridge Parkway. They climbed into the forest along the gently curling pavement. There was only an occasional vehicle. Back over her shoulder, she shouted, “We own this road today!”

And to him it felt as though they did.

The air cooled as they climbed higher, running the ridgeline. There were far sun-washed vistas, first to one side, then to the other. They ran through a series of damp tunnels blasted out of the rock, the bike exhausts filling the arched tubes with crackling thunder. Eight miles along the twisting road, Kitty pulled into the Big Witch Overlook, and they sat on the idling bike for several minutes, enjoying the view of rank on rank of ancient hazed ridges.

They rode the parkway for another ten miles and dismounted at Waterrock Knob. It only seemed natural amid all the beauty when she took his hand, smiled, and said, "Come on." They climbed the short empty trail to the top of the breezy knob, where they could look off into four states. Still holding her hand, he felt like a high-school kid again.

He asked, "What are these flowers?"

She pointed. "There's a bed of bluets over there. They call the tall white plumes goat's beard. We've been riding past fire pink. The rhododendron is just starting to bud."

They got back on the bike, and the road climbed higher still. Coming around some curves, with sheer cliffs rising close by the road on one side and dropping off precipitously on the other, all they could see was sky. The pavement was patched here and there where rocks that had been split off from the cliff faces by ice had tumbled down and dented it. They were getting close to the tree line. Strong cold winds had bent and gnarled the few low evergreens living at these heights. They made another stop at the Richland Balsam Overlook, highest point on the 470-mile-long parkway at over 6,000 feet. They stood close, not talking, shading their eyes with their palms and pondering the distances.

She said just above a whisper, "*Shaconage.*"

"Excuse me?"

"Cherokee for blue. Those farthest mountains are a blue like hickory smoke, and they're just so ghostly beautiful."

They glided along for another ten miles and stopped at a deserted parking area. She retrieved their lunch from the saddlebag, handed it to him to carry, and they made the steep, scrabbling half-mile hike to the "Devil's Courthouse," where they could see the virgin mountains crumpled away in every direction. It took a few minutes for them to regain their normal breathing. Sitting closely side by side on a tilted granite slab, they ate tuna salad in pocket bread, munched crisp salted apples, and drank iced tea.

She said, "Food tastes better outdoors."

"I know. Maybe something about prehistoric campfires in our genes."

They munched for several minutes, finishing the food and savoring the last few sips of tea.

"That view hasn't changed much in uncounted thousands of years," she said, a fan of delicate squint lines in her satin skin giving her profile a primitive quality as her gaze traced the far ridgelines, the breeze lifting her hair.

He nodded.

Sensing his scrutiny, she turned her face toward him and looked deeply into his gray eyes. She was vulnerable. Expectant.

He focused on her parted lips, shook his head slowly, and whispered, "Ah, God. Valerie." Saw her wince and look quickly away.

He rubbed at his eyes with his fingers and said, "I'm sorry."

"Not a problem," she said, smiling distantly. Not meeting his eyes. She collected their refuse in the bag. "Guess we'd better be getting back before a bear sniffs out this little picnic and comes begging."

They rode down off of the high ridge on Route 215, switchbacking through tight descending curves, their ears plugging with the increasing pressure, over a stone bridge past a waterfall decorating a mossy cleft like liquid lace. Farther on, Lake Logan coruscated in the sunlight. They idled through Waynesville in sparse traffic, and finally returned to Maggie Valley.

She dropped him at Country Vittles so he could pick up the Wrangler.

He said, "Thanks for the lesson. And for the ride. And lunch. I owe you one."

She shook her head and gave him a sad smile. "Enjoyed it. I'll see you."

He nodded and watched her ride away.

He felt empty. As though he had just hopelessly lost something priceless.

CHAPTER 11

After services on Sunday, Orin, Frank, and Sis Cagle stayed with the Preacher in the sanctuary of the Masada Undenominational Church of the One Pure God.

Frank Cagle rolled up the right sleeve of his plaid shirt to scratch a chigger bite on his large bicep. The furiously itching little red dot happened to be on the muddy yellow beak of his buzzard tattoo, so he could see it. He squeezed it hard with his dirty fingernails, producing a drop of watery blood and maybe the tiny burrowing chigger itself. He said, "So what does he say we do now, Preacher?"

"He says he will ask the owner to sell."

Orin Cagle was a pudgy man with small nervous eyes. He said, "And what if he don't want to?"

The Preacher focused his fiery eyes on Orin and said, "Then we shall seek the way to persuade them. The others will help. What have you found out about this man Hardin?"

"He's not nobody," Orin said. "Runs some kind of airplane photo business out of the airport in Asheville. Lives in his own place up on Eaglenest Ridge in Maggie with two old people, likely kin. Got him a goddamned squaw girlfriend named Kitty Birdsong. A real hot piece, though. Two of them been askin' around a lot. I don't like that at all."

"Watch your unclean tongue, Orin Cagle. The One Pure God has a terrible retribution planned for those who would blaspheme within the four walls of His sacred place."

Frank Cagle rolled his shirtsleeve back down, buttoned the cuff, and said, "No need to be tellin' us about blasphemery, Preacher. 'Specially Sis here. Figure she's done paid. Think she was about fifteen when Daddy Cagle caught her out back in the woods that time, had his favorite deerhound tied to a tree. Rag tied around its muzzle. Sis was workin' on it with a pair of channellock pliers. Daddy Cagle stripped off his belt right then and there and laid into her. You talk about blasphemery, now, she was spittin' and swearin' at him like you never heard. Accusin' him of all grades of dirty deeds in the dark. Daddy Cagle got blotchy red in the face like he sometimes did and said it was the devil himself spoutin' out of her, and it wasn't by no means the first time either, nossir. Me and Orin wasn't more'n kids ourselves. Daddy told us hold on to her real good, and Orin was cryin' like a baby. I didn't want to do it, but Daddy laid a fist into me like to make me puke, so then I done it. He got Granddaddy's old pearl Buck knife from his front pocket. Blade was wore skinny, but Daddy kept it honed sharp as a straight razor. Cut her tongue out. I held on to her real tight while he done that so he wouldn't maybe slip an' cut her worse. I had to carry her 'cause she passed out, and when we got back in the yard he pitched it to the sow. That was a day not forgot."

But the Preacher was staring off into some far place and did not seem to have heard. He knew the story. Scowling with concentration, he said, "This Hardin and the Indian. Keep close track of them. Use some of the other disciples if you have to."

◊ ◊ ◊

John spent a week taking aerials for two developers and a graphics agency and flying members of a North Carolina State University lab who had a grant to study dying trees along the Smoky Mountain peaks. It was their theory the damage was at least partially caused by air pollution blowing east out of large coal-fired generating plants in Tennessee, and they had set out to either prove or disprove that. He lost himself in routine chores and paperwork, and worked into the nights and for twelve hours one day installing a new stand-up shower and sink in the upstairs bathroom and repainting the walls.

Moses Kyle had not shown up again in church the

past Sunday. Nor had he been back to his cabin, as far as Hardin could tell the last time he had stopped by there to check. There was no word from the police.

On Saturday morning, with darkly brooding rain clouds pushing in low from the north to brush the mountaintops, he made a phone call and drove the Wrangler east out of the valley on Highway 19. A mile from town, he noticed a rusted-out red pickup of indeterminate model a hundred feet back, but thought no more of it until it turned behind him onto 276 and stayed at least three or four cars back through downtown Waynesville. It was still there when he turned west onto 74 heading for Sylva. On an open stretch, he slowed down ten miles per hour, enticing the pickup to pass, but it did not. It looked like two men in the cab, but he couldn't see clearly through the truck's windshield glare. He thought, *Who are you guys?* He sped up, and the pickup stayed well behind but still in sight. Near Sylva he turned off the main highway onto a narrow secondary road, the red pickup went on past, neither occupant apparently looking his way, and he dismissed it.

He drove through rolling valley farmland for three miles, turned left into an upsloping gravel driveway, and stopped outside a neat white farmhouse set among some tall pines in a spreading meadow.

As he was getting out of the Wrangler the screen door banged open and a thin boy in jeans, tattered untied sneakers, and a baggy, faded green T-shirt darted across the porch and leaped down the steps. Hardin braced himself and the boy jumped at him, administering a choking hug. "Sam," he said. "Are we going fishing? Where's all your stuff?"

"Hello, Curly. It's supposed to rain a waterfall pretty soon. I thought we'd go into Asheville, do some shopping, get a cheeseburger and a smoothie, maybe catch a movie. How does that sound?"

"Sweet. I can spend some of my birthday money. Get a computer game."

The boy was seven-year-old Joshua Lightfoot, Valerie's son, who was living here with an aunt of Valerie's and the aunt's husband.

The boy called him Sam because that was the name he'd been using in Witness Protection when he'd met Valerie and Joshua out on Ocracoke Island.

The middle-aged dark-haired Cherokee woman, Lisa Crow, came out onto the porch, smiling warmly and wiping her hands on her apron. She said, "I just took a deep-dish peach pie out of the oven. Can I interest you in a wedge with some cheese before you two go off adventuring?"

"I'd walk ten miles for a slice of your pie," he said. "Has this wild Indian been behaving himself?"

"No more than a seven-year-old buck ought to. He's full of curiosity and mischief. Keeps Wahna and me on our toes."

He reached back inside the Wrangler and brought out a small bundle, a red bandanna, loosely tied. Josh opened it to find a flint spearhead and a small quartz cluster, and he lit up with a grin.

"The quartz has a ghost eagle inside it," John said. "Hold it like this. See it right in there? Look close. And that's a flint spear point. Be careful with that thing. It's sharp. It belonged to a fierce Cherokee war chief who used it to fight off Andrew Jackson's soldiers."

"Really?" the boy said.

"Well, okay. I really got it from the Rock Shop in the Valley. But it ought to work just fine for fighting off imaginary soldiers. I got one for myself, too. One day we'll make sticks to lash them onto. The bandanna is what cowboys used for all kinds of things. As a mask against breathing dust on a cattle drive, for instance. You can wet it and tie it around your neck and it will cool you down in the summer. In the winter it will keep your face warm."

"Thanks, Sam. Will you tie it on?"

He tied it loosely around the boy's neck.

After wolfing down triangles of warm pie with milk they drove off in the Wrangler, rain pattering on the canvas top.

In Asheville he parked in a mall lot and during a lull in the rain they ran hand in hand for the entrance. With some persuading, Lisa Crow had told him a list of things the boy could use. They started in a shoe store and together, after some debate, chose a pair of sneakers that did not light up or contain retractable rollers or look like something an alien might be shod in. Another shop yielded underwear and socks, a pair of jeans, and a Superman T-shirt. In an electronics shop the boy selected a used computer game that did not seem to be too bloody. They ate lunch in a Chuck E. Cheese and took a walk around the large mall, looking in windows, pitched pennies into a fountain to make secret wishes, and rode the escalators, and caught the latest Disney offering in the multiplex.

On the ride back, the boy was quiet for a long time, looking out the passenger window at the rain. At a stoplight he turned to Hardin. There were tear tracks down his cheeks.

"What is it, Curly?"

The boy said in a raw whisper, "Mom." He snuffled and wiped at his face with the back of his hand.

He pulled the Wrangler over into the vacant lot of a church and shut it off.

They sat together quietly, the rain tapping on the canvas top.

John watched the rain make halting, torturous tracks down the windshield. Like tears. He said, "I miss her, too, kid. Every single day. Badly. Look at this church. It's there because of a power people can't see but still believe in. It's something like that with your mom. She still lives." John touched his temple and then the boy's temple and said, "In here and in here. Her spirit lives. Your great-grandfather Wasituna told us that, remember? We have all the living memories of her. How good she was. How beautiful she was inside. And all those fine times we had together. Do you understand?"

The boy nodded. "It hurts."

"Yes. But you're strong. What we can do is be what she wanted us—expected us—to be. You're a good boy. She'd be proud of you. Just keep on being you, study hard in school, try your best at everything you do. I'll be here for you."

Joshua considered all that. He nodded slowly with soul-deep pain behind his brown Indian eyes, but with a centuries-old innate stoic strength as well. Her strength.

The boy looked through the windshield.

Through the tears.

He said, "Okay. I guess we can go on now."

CHAPTER 12

"Who was the killer?" Hank asked.

They were on the porch, waiting for supper on Saturday evening, talking about a 1970s movie called *The Missouri Breaks.* Hattie had shooed them out of the kitchen.

John said, "That's easy. Marlon Brando. He played a regulator named Robert E. Lee Clayton. Shot a Creedmore rifle that was accurate out to five hundred yards. Great story. What was the name of Jack Nicholson's character?"

"Tom Logan. He was a small-time rustler that a mean cattleman hired Brando to kill."

"Right, and the cattleman's daughter was sweet on Logan. Can't remember who played the cattleman, though."

"Well, hallelujah. I found somethin' you don't know. It was Frederic Forrest. I think you owe me a superburger at the Salty Dog. With Vidalia onion rings."

"Nope. Don't think so. You didn't specifically ask

me who the cattleman was. And you don't want Hattie finding out you're even thinking about eating fried onion rings, anyway. She'll make you eat oatmeal for a week."

"Okay, then, how did Nicholson kill Brando in the end?"

"You'll have to do a lot better than that. Snuck up on Brando while he was camped out in the woods and cut his throat."

"Dang," Hank said.

The three of them ate Hattie's dandelion salad and seasoned broiled rainbow trout that Hank had caught in Cataloochee Creek, with steamed broccoli and baked sweet potatoes. Hattie brought out a surprise wild blueberry cobbler, but firmly allowed the men only one generous helping each with their coffee.

After the men had done the dishes, they all got comfortable in the living area in front of the TV. Hattie took up her knitting. Hank flipped through to the local news channel.

The president promised that the threat of inflation was so negligible as to be laughable, but a Haywood County tourism official was nonetheless concerned that steadily rising prices were going to cut visitor traffic in the mountains this season. The brakes on an eighteen-wheeler hauling frozen foods had failed over in Jackson County, sending the rig off of a low bluff into the woods and littering a sizable area with thawing low-calorie pizzas and diet dinners, but the driver had escaped serious injury.

The male anchor with piano-key teeth grinned and said, "Well, Katie, I guess the bears in Jackson County will be eating well tonight."

The dazzling female anchor said, "You're right, Skip. But at least they won't be gaining too much weight." They both laughed attractively.

Her sunshiny smile faded, and she took on a serious expression. "Now this on a tragic note, Skip. The body of a Maggie Valley man was discovered this afternoon on the border of the Smoky Mountains National Park by a group of Girl Scouts who were out camping."

Hattie abruptly set her knitting aside and put a hand to her mouth. Hank turned up the volume.

"The girls of Scout Troop Sixty-Four were hiking in the forest near Little Bald Knob when they came across the body of Moses Kyle. Haywood County Sheriff Newton Fields had this to say."

A fit, crisply uniformed man with a fringe of close-clipped gray hair put on reading glasses to deliver a statement written in the stilted, impersonal language that seems to be universal with law enforcement. "Two Haywood County deputies and two EMTs in a Maggie Valley Rescue Squad vehicle responded to a cellular phone call at two thirty-six p.m. today. A male body was located approximately one hundred yards from the end of Sheepback Road. The body was positively identified as that of Moses Kyle of Maggie Valley and was transported to Haywood Regional Medical Center in Clyde for disposition. Sergeant Michael Boudreau of the Maggie Valley Police Department is credited with conducting a thorough investigation into the disappearance of Mr. Kyle.

The female anchor went on. "Sheriff Fields added that had the scout troop not made the discovery it is likely the deceased would not have been found for some time, due to the remote location and the fact that the last three miles of Sheepback Road are seldom used. The cause of death has not been officially released." She brightened like a sunrise and said, "On a happier note, Skip, the week is looking great for all kinds of activities, including the popular annual Spring Arts Festival in—"

Hank thumbed the mute button. Hattie shook her head, tears in her eyes, and said, "Oh, poor, poor Mose. He was such a good soul."

John got up and rested a hand on Hattie's shoulder for a moment. He took the cell phone out on the porch and called Kitty Birdsong. "Did you watch the news?"

"I saw it. They found Mose. At the least he died out there in the woods, where he loved to be."

"I'll find out about services and call you."

"Thanks, John. I'll come by to see Hattie tomorrow. I know she's mourning. She and Mose shared a sort of special closeness."

"That would be good of you, Kitty. Thanks."

◊ ◊ ◊

They were stopped in the driveway of the Cagle place late on Sunday afternoon, headed in opposite directions. Frank was just getting home, and Orin was going out to get groceries. In his black Hummer, which was burbling nicely with its dual glass-pack mufflers, Frank Cagle was taking up most of the driveway, so Orin Cagle had the outside wheels of his blue pickup over in the tall grass. Orin stuck his big elbow out the window, leaned to look up at Frank, and said, "I just heard a bunch of Girl Scouts found Kyle yesterday. Our luck."

Frank said, "Not a bad thing. That Hardin and the squaw'll stop lookin' now. Oughta be nothin' to tie him to us."

Orin said, "You talked to the Preacher today after church?"

"Yeah. Wants us to keep on Hardin's ass a while but so he don't notice it. We got a few of the others on it. Preacher says he and the Man will take care of the rest of it. They'll call on us if we're needed."

"Frank, I swear I wish we never got into it at all. Sometimes I think about what it's got to be like locked up and I get cold in the gut."

"Don't worry about it. What can anybody know?"

Orin wiped a paw over his face, shook his head, and said, "Well, we're in it up to our bellies, so I guess there's nothin' for it now but to hang onto a tree branch.

You goin' to church Wednesday evenin'? They'll lay on hands for Yoder."

"What's wrong with Yoder?"

"They say he's got a bad pump."

"Got that snake pickup trip over to Tennessee, but I'll meet you at the church. The Adams woman's supposed to sing. That one's sure got a set on her, don't she? Like to lay hands on those."

"Sis can ride with me."

◊ ◊ ◊

On Monday morning John rose at dawn, dressed in shorts, a T-shirt, and scuffed skin-fit moccasins, and went running along the rough four-mile ridge trail he'd made through the woods behind the house. He carried a baseball-size stone, squeezing it alternately fifty times in each hand as he ducked and dodged through the low brush and trees as fast as he could, rapidly picking his footing with care and trying to do it as quietly as possible, the way Valerie's grandfather, Wasituna, had taught him. He tried to do the trail at least three times each week. He ran the total of eight miles in just over an hour and returned to the house blowing and wheezing and promising himself he would make the workout a daily routine until he won back peak fitness. When he got his breathing under control, he dropped to the dewy grass and did a hundred push-ups. There was a particular smooth creek stone in Hattie's rock garden that weighed about twenty-five pounds, and he used it do sets of fifty curls and lifts, alternating each arm. He finished up by lying on his back, hooking his toes under the end brace of the picnic table, and doing a hundred sit-ups. He took a fast shower and ate a pancake breakfast that Hank fixed up.

He drove the Wrangler to the airport and flew a brief photo sortie, then spent some time servicing and cleaning up the Cessna. He met with Fred Quick, the hefty operator of the fixed base operation, or FBO, about an upcoming two-day air show on the field. He would be offering sightseeing flights during the lulls in the aerial displays. After they had agreed on the details, Quick asked, "By the way, are you planning on selling your bird?"

"No, why?"

"Just wondered. A guy came by a couple days ago asking about you. Wanted to know which hangar was yours. Seemed odd. The thought crossed my mind you might be selling your plane and he might be a prospect, but then again, this guy was in a beat-up old pickup that was about two decades old. Red, I think. Caught sight of it out in the lot when he was leaving. He didn't look like he could even afford that. But you never can tell, can you? I said he could take one of your fliers there on the counter and call you."

"Did you get a name?"

"I asked, but he said it wasn't important and left."

"What did he look like?"

Quick thought a bit. "Don't remember too much. Average. Short brownish beard. Middle age. Looked like he'd spent a lot of time outside. Farmer's cap. If I'd thought it was important I would have pressed him for a name or a phone number."

"It was probably nothing. Some back country farmer wanting a ride up to look over his timber."

"That's pretty much what I figured."

John said, "Anyway, don't worry about it." They shook hands and he left, thinking about the rusted red pickup that had seemed to be following him last Saturday.

On the way back to Maggie Valley, he picked up two gallons of waterproofing stain for the porch decking at a Home Depot in Clyde. The Haywood Regional Medical Center was close by, and on an impulse he stopped there.

A busy woman with frizzed hair was managing the reception desk. Between incoming phone calls, he asked, "Excuse me, do you know who I might talk to about the Maggie Valley man they found dead in the woods on Saturday? His name was Moses Kyle."

"Who? Oh, yes, the one the Girls Scouts discovered. Poor little girls. Stumbling onto a grisly thing like that. I suppose you'd have to talk with Dr. Linda Gravely, the medical examiner."

"Is she available?"

The woman said, "Excuse me," and took another incoming call, handling it briskly.

Back to him, she said, "Hold on, I'll check." She

punched in a connection and spoke briefly. "Yes, Dr. Gravely happens to be in and can give you a few minutes right now if you'll go to her office. Through those doors, down the hall to the right, last door on the left. Have a good day."

Dr. Gravely was an attractive ash-blonde in her thirties, seated erect and unsmiling at her desk. He introduced himself. She nodded and gestured toward a straight-backed metal chair. He sat.

She said, "Yes, sir, may I ask how you knew Mr. Kyle? Are you related in any way?"

"No, he was an acquaintance of mine. A friend of a friend named Hattie Gaskill. I was curious about the circumstances of his death."

"We have not been able to locate any relatives, and I was hoping you might help."

"Sorry."

"What did you want to know about Mr. Kyle?"

"Whatever you might be able to tell me, I guess. How he died."

She thumbed through a low stack of files in a wire basket, came up with one, and opened it on her desk. Perused it briefly. Looked at him with iridescent green eyes and said, "I've ruled it misadventure."

"Misadventure?"

"Mr. Kyle died of snakebite. One of the pit vipers, of course. Our only native venomous reptiles. A large timber rattlesnake probably, judging by the extent of tissue damage and internal bleeding, and by the width of the puncture wounds."

She consulted her file. "There were two strikes. One to the abdomen near the navel and the other located one inch below the left nipple in the chest. That one did the most damage because it was so close to the heart."

"That's it, then?"

"Yes, Mr. Hardin, that's it. If you hear of any living relative of his, we would appreciate that information."

"My friend doesn't think he had any relatives left. About his death. Isn't that unusual?"

"Snakebite? We average five cases in Haywood County each year. Rarely a fatality, though, because the victims usually receive antivenin treatment in time, so, yes, you could say it is somewhat unusual."

"I mean the locations of the bites. Wouldn't you expect a snake to strike somewhere on the legs?"

"Not necessarily. A victim might be climbing a steep rock pile on all fours, or clambering in a crouch up a bluff, or entering a cave prone when encountering a snake, so a bite could be almost anywhere on the body. I understand there were no such terrain features near where the body was discovered—I did inquire—but Mr. Kyle could have walked a distance after the incident before becoming incapacitated. It was simply his misfortune to be alone and too far away from help."

"Moses Kyle spent a lot of time in the woods. He was no novice. I would think he'd have been aware of the dangers. It seems strange he'd have let himself be bitten."

She stood up and glanced at her watch, signaling

an end to the discussion. He kept his seat.

She said, "I understand Mr. Kyle was mentally challenged and—"

"You know, Doctor, I'm getting tired of hearing that. We're all mentally challenged in some way. Moses was a good man from what I've heard. He was out there every day making a living on his own, which is by no means easy these days. He was skilled and successful enough at what he did. I believe he lived an honest, quiet, ordered life, deserving of our respect. I don't like to see him written off so casually."

She squinted at him and her cheeks colored. "I think that's all the time I have right now, Mr. Hardin, so if you'll please leave."

He got up, nodded to her, and made it to the door when she said, "Oh, hell, wait a minute."

He turned and looked at her.

She said, "Close that door and sit back down." He did. She sat and stared at the file folder for a moment, tapping her unpainted nails on it. She regarded him seriously. "Off the record, I agree. There *is* something slightly strange about this. The body was not in good condition. It had been there several days, as nearly as I could determine. There had been a lot of internal bleeding precipitated by the venom, and the skin was badly discolored, but I noticed several anomalies. I couldn't be certain, but there seemed to be some bruising around the forearms and biceps. There was a small, moon-shaped puncture inside the right nasal passage, on the septum. The right nipple was lacerated and swollen. And then . . ."

"What?"

"The testes were damaged, almost crushed."

"So what could all of that mean?"

"I don't know. Maybe he was climbing a steep creek bank, the snake struck him twice, rapidly, he lost his grip, and fell. None of this is enough to make me question my ruling, you understand, but, taken together, it is . . . unsettling."

"I know the feeling. There were signs he left his house in a hurry. He didn't take his backpack, and somebody heard a vehicle possibly going to and from his house early on the morning we think he might have disappeared."

"I'll tell you what I'll do. I'll have another talk with the two deputies who responded. Ask them to look around Mr. Kyle's home more closely. But I doubt it will yield much more than we already know, which isn't really a whole heck of a lot. If we turn up anything, I'll be in touch if you'll leave your number or your e-mail address. Write it on this pad."

"What will be done with the body?"

"Probably cremation at the county's expense. I understand the Presbyterian church in Maggie will hold a memorial service Thursday afternoon."

"Well, thanks, Dr. Gravely."

"Linda. And I have to tell you I resented your self-righteous attitude. What to you might seem like callousness or indifference is simply professional procedure. I do care. And I do my job well. Good day to you, Mr. Hardin."

"John."

He offered his hand and she shook it.

Once. Firmly.

◊ ◊ ◊

John had picked Kitty up. There were only twelve people at the service in the stone Presbyterian church, including the minister and the organist. The tall, narrow stained-glass windows sifted the sunlight into spectral hues. John, Kitty, Hank, and Hattie shared a pew near the front. He was in new jeans, shined ropers, a white shirt, and his only sport coat, with a tie borrowed from Hank. Nobody had been able to find a photograph, so there was only an arrangement of mountain flowers that Hattie had placed in a simple vase in the center of Moses' shallow battered gold pan on the low table below the pulpit. She had also helped choose three hymns.

They sang "The Old Rugged Cross" first, and the minister, a middle-aged man named Boyer, spoke about the fragility of life and what a precious gift every hour of every day is for each of us. About the impossibly long odds against having been granted an opportunity at life at all. About the mystery of God's plan. He said, "No one of us here on earth seemed to know Moses Kyle all that well, although he and our sister

Hattie Gaskill shared a special affection. But there is One who did know Mr. Kyle well, indeed, and in turn, Mr. Kyle believed wholeheartedly in Him."

They sang the old hymn "My God and I." There were tears in the eyes of the women as they all sang about God walking out into a light-drenched meadow hand in hand with a believer.

After "Amazing Grace" and the benediction, they lingered outside, shaking hands soberly all around. Kitty hugged Hattie and came to stand beside Hardin. She was dressed tastefully in gray slacks and a white long-sleeved blouse.

John said, "Hank and I are going to scatter his ashes. Would you like to come along?"

She nodded, dabbing at her eyes with a tissue.

They took Hattie home and then John drove them toward Asheville. Nobody spoke much on the drive east. They stopped at Cotton's Mortuary in Clyde. John went in and got the gray, eight-inch cubical pasteboard box of ashes. Hank was in the backseat. He took the box and held it on his lap.

Kitty said, "Where are we going?"

"The Asheville airport. I have a light plane that I try to make a living with."

"I assumed you just did home remodeling jobs. Saw your ad in the classifieds."

"I do some of that on the side. Helps me afford to be in the flying business."

The day was brilliant, with clean fair-weather

cumulus clouds crowding in from the east to lavishly decorate the sky starting fifteen hundred feet above the peaks.

Kitty sat in the front passenger seat of the Cessna, and they donned headsets, taxied out, and took off into the brilliance. The mountains were dappled with slow-moving shadows. They climbed up through a hole and leveled out at eight thousand feet, some of the clouds billowing up in fanciful shapes as high as ten thousand feet. One misty cloud valley had a rainbow bridging it. John gently banked around to head west, the Lycoming in the nose drumming smoothly, cool air rushing in the vents.

Kitty looked around and said over the intercom, "It's so beautiful. It's a cathedral today. And you get paid for doing this?"

"More or less. By the time I take expenses out, some months are skinny. Then I go redo somebody's bathroom or tear into a rotted porch."

"Well, I envy you."

"You think you'd like to fly?"

"I guess it's on my list of things to try."

"Might as well try it right now. Fact is, I could use your help."

He ran through the major panel instruments—airspeed, altimeter, vertical velocity, attitude indicator, directional gyro, rate of turn, and tachometer—pointing to each and explaining its function. Like every other light Cessna, this one had dual controls. "Yoke works intuitively. Push or pull to go up or down; turn it to bank. If you wanted a climbing left turn, for example, you'd simultaneously pull back and rotate the yoke to the left. You'd also add left rudder to control the yaw and make the turn smoothly coordinated, but don't worry about using the rudder pedals at all just yet. Go ahead and take the yoke. That's it. You have the airplane. Not a tight grip. Just firm. And don't let yourself tense up. Relax. Think smooth and easy. Look at the horizon, and try to keep the same distance between it and the nose; that will help you fly level. Try to stay within a hundred feet of this altitude and hold a course of two-seven-zero. I'll watch for traffic. There you go. You're doing fine."

He guided her through several gentle turns, climbs, and descents, and she took to it naturally. They flew on west through a fantasy sky of fathomless cobalt blue filled with half-mile-high cloud pillars and canyons and soft rills that mimicked the hills below.

When they were over the heart of the Great Smoky Mountains National Park, nothing but crumpled wilderness quilted with cloud shadows in all directions, he talked Kitty through a slow descent until they were five hundred feet above the ridges. He throttled back, and she held the plane steady while he opened the side window, the slipstream holding it up under the wing out of the way. Hank passed the box of ashes forward to John.

For a moment they ghosted in shadow past a magnificent cloud column hanging in the air by some celestial magic, and abruptly broke out into sunshine again.

John said, "Goodbye, Moses. We figured this is where you'd want to be." He removed the lid and tilted the box out the window, the slipstream plucked at the contents, and the ashes streamed back in a long gray wraith, quickly dispersed to invisibility by the clean wind.

Kitty nodded and said, "Go with God, Mose Kyle."

Hank said, "Amen."

CHAPTER 13

The Preacher began the services with a verse from First Timothy, "I exhort therefore, that, first of all, supplications, prayers, intercessions, and giving of thanks, be made for all men." And they immersed themselves in a long prayer session, everybody kneeling on the hard floor backward with their elbows on the pew seats, eyes tightly closed, all saying individual prayers aloud at the same time.

Finally they stood one by one, still praying and calling on the Spirit, and the Preacher shouted over all the mingled voices, again from First Timothy, "I will therefore that men pray every where, lifting up holy hands, without wrath and doubting." They raised their hands, fingers spread and reaching, and they swayed and called out to God and testified.

Two men unpacked acoustic guitars, and a teenaged girl with severe acne pulled a well-used tambourine out from under a pew, and they sang the old hymns they knew by heart. "Pull Off Your Shoes, Moses," and

"Running Up the King's Highway," and "Zacchaeus Too High in a Sycamore Tree," and "Amen, Amen, There's a Higher Power," and "Amazing Grace."

The Preacher seated the congregation. With the Bible held open on his palm to give him all the authority he needed, he spoke for a full hour and a half with increasing intensity, perspiration beading his forehead, about the myriad threatening evils of the world beyond the church doors, citing the scripture continually from memory.

He spent a half hour on the signs of the approaching final battle. "Hold your Bible in one hand, and hold a newspaper in your other hand. All the signs are there for any sinner to clearly see. Satan's soldiers all over this world are rising up to make war on God's people. Matthew twenty-four: 'Ye shall hear of wars and rumours of wars. . . . Nation shall rise against nation, and kingdom against kingdom; and there shall be famines, and pestilences, and earthquakes, in divers places.' Read your newspapers. And we see in Luke twenty-one: 'There shall be signs. . . . Upon the earth distress of nations, with perplexity; the sea and the waves roaring; men's hearts failing them for fear, and for looking after those things which are coming on the earth. . . . When these things begin to come to pass, then look up, and lift up your heads; for your redemption draweth nigh.' And Jesus told us, 'Behold the fig tree, and all the trees; when they now shoot forth, ye see and know of your own selves that summer is nigh at hand. So likewise ye, when ye see these things come to pass, know ye that the kingdom of God is nigh at hand.' Look at the fig tees, you sinners. Look in your newspapers. Time is short. Are you ready?"

Nearing the climax of the sermon, he shouted, "You unclean sinners. Do you want a last chance to set your feet on the one and only shining path that leadeth to Him? Are you ready? Do you believe?" He brushed back his shaggy white hair, his fiery eyes boring holes in those who did not seem to be giving him their utmost rapt attention. He clapped the Bible closed and rested it on the pulpit.

There were shouted *Amens* and *yes, Lords* from among the fifty-seven souls seated on the straight-backed rickety pews.

He called on eleven members to rise and move to the front of the church and stand beneath the pulpit. "Werly Fulks, you shall serve as my James. Lloyd Dobbs, you are my Matthew. Jeremiah Quaid, you shall take the place of Peter. Come now. Rufus Blinder. Levi Stengler. Wilbur Pugh. All of you come forward now to stand with me."

Levi Stengler was tall, lean, and very strong, and he never smiled. Wilbur Pugh was forty-one. He was short, bald, and wore thick glasses that enlarged his eyes. He had dropped out of school in the sixth grade with failing marks, unable to fathom much of what was going on there, and had never had a job. The Preacher had made him an honorary disciple and paid him to be the church caretaker because Pugh's father, confined to a Bryson City rest home, donated heavily to the Masada Church every year and had written the church into his will.

The Preacher named the others, including Frank and Orin Cagle, and they gathered at the front of the church until all the disciples were present. It was a ritual at every one of his services.

Presenting the disciples.

His disciples.

There was no Judas.

He said, "And now, brethren of God, if you be believers, I call down the Holy Spirit upon you, to be with you and to be in you in this most holy place, and I tell you that you will *feel* it right on down to your very toes. Close your eyes now, and you will *feel* it descending down, down through the top of your head and into your lungs and through your heart and guts until it runs all through your veins and drives out all sin and all doubt. Can you feel it? Each and every one of you. Do *you* feel it? *Tell* me now."

They called out, "Yes, I do, Preacher," and "Yea, Lord," and "I feel it now."

"Why does God send down His Spirit to dwell in each one of us today? Because He *trusts* in *you all*," the Preacher thundered, sweeping his outstretched hand to indicate the whole congregation of the Masada Undenominational Church of the One Pure God. "He trusts each and every one of you lowly earth dwellers who say you believe in Him to shun Satan—yea, *shun* Satan and all his unclean, darkest angels that try every hour of every day to reach up under your ribs and grasp your very heart and eat of it."

The Preacher gripped the pulpit where his hands had worn through the finish over the years and had stained the oak dark with his fervent sweat. The cords in his forearms stood out taut. He was thin beneath the too-small black robe he had recently decided to wear, but his muscles were strong as braided whip leather. He spoke in a low, intense rumble. "Now for the big question, brothers and sisters. The most important question of your short, sin-filled lives." He increased the volume until he was shouting the question, "Brothers and sisters, DO YOU TRUST IN HIM?"

They shouted back, "WE *TRUST* IN HIM."

He opened his Bible yet again and held it on his outstretched palm, thrusting it toward the congregation. "Now then, hear the Word. Mark sixteen, verse seventeen. 'And these signs shall follow *them that believe*; in my name shall they *cast out devils*; they shall *speak with new tongues*; they shall *take up serpents*; and if they *drink any deadly thing*, it shall *not hurt* them.' Do you *believe* those holy gospel words of our One Pure God?" And he screamed out, "WELL, DO YOU?"

Fifty-six of the souls came back at him with a chorused, "YES." that shook the church. Sis Cagle could not, but she stared at the ceiling with her jewel-blue eyes slitted, as though looking for angels to descend through the tin roof.

They were spirited now, some rocking back and forth on the pews, some gripping the pew backs in front of them, some murmuring unintelligible prayers. And a man in overalls at the back shouted out, "Test us, Preacher."

Frank and Orin Cagle went into the room behind the pulpit. They came out carrying a large plastic cooler between them. They set it down in front of the pulpit. The lid had been drilled with a dozen random half-inch holes. "In The Name Of God" had been hand-painted in blood red on the side of the cooler. The Preacher came down from the pulpit, drew back the sleeves of his robe, opened the lid, and reached inside, and the murmurings and shouts from the congregation increased.

He lifted out a pygmy rattler in his right hand, holding it by the thick body so the head and tail draped, and a dangling eighteen-inch copperhead in his left hand. He thrust them high above his head and turned around to display them slowly. "Hear the word of the One Pure God. Acts twenty-eight: 'And when Paul had gathered a bundle of sticks, and laid them on the fire, there came a viper out of the heat, and fastened on his hand. . . . And he shook off the beast into the fire, and felt no harm.' *How* could Paul show the barbarians of Melita that day his power over that viper? My brethren, Paul felt no harm that day, even though the viper affixed to him and hung from his arm, because he was a true *believer.* And so the full power of the Spirit entered his body, brothers and sisters, and the Spirit protected him from Satan's lowliest, most treacherous, most vile creature." He looked at each snake he was holding, and thundered out, "Behold the faith and trust of another *true believer.* Now who among you will do the same? Who of you sinners will *trust* in the One Pure God that ye shall come to no harm?"

Two days before, the snakes had been fed live white mice, and early that morning the Preacher and Frank Cagle had chilled the assorted serpents down on ice until they were lethargic. They had used special membrane-covered bottles to carefully milk them of their yellowish venom, which they sold to a Charlotte lab for use in manufacturing antivenin. With the Preacher's help, the Cagle brothers hunted some snakes down in the mountains. They bought and sold, bred and traded other species all over the southeast. They sold some specimens to other snake-handling churches at a nice profit. The Preacher's cut was a good, steady source of additional income for the church.

There was ice in the cooler, and the old window air conditioner near the front of the church was laboring at a high setting.

The smiling disciples passed a pair of young copperheads from hand to hand. Frank lifted out another copperhead and gave it to an obese woman who had come forward. She held it high, turned in a slow circle, and cried out a long ululating string of non-words, speaking in a tongue only God could interpret. Others followed to take up the serpents, a man in overalls holding a canebrake rattler high and prancing gleefully in circles as though to some angelic refrain only he and God could hear, lifting his knees and grinning.

When the snakes began to stir from the warmth of the hands, the Preacher closed down the ritual, and the snakes were placed one by one back in the cooler, which Frank and Orin carried out. They sang three more hymns, using the old books with the shaped notes. The Preacher announced a birthday and reminded them of the Wednesday evening service, which would include another laying on of hands for a female member troubled by demon-induced headaches, and a special collection for the roofing-and-steeple fund.

After the service, Sis Cagle went out to the Hummer to wait, and Frank and Orin stayed with the Preacher.

Frank said, "They burned Kyle. I hear Hardin scattered him all over the Smokies. That should be the end of it."

The Preacher nodded, squinted at each of them, and said, "Yes. We can hope it will be the end of it. But we want them watched for a time, anyway. I will instruct Werly and Lloyd and Jeremiah and the others. Orin, count today's collection."

◊ ◊ ◊

Late that afternoon, John was out back splitting and stacking a pile of hickory fireplace logs with a twelve-pound maul, sweating freely, giving his whole upper body a good workout, trying to perfect his aim with the heavy maul, making the logs fly apart in single powerful strokes. Hank swung the screen door open, called to him, and mimed holding a phone to his ear. He leaned the maul against the chopping stump, re-rolled his left denim shirt cuff, and went inside, hoping it might be Kitty and smiling at the thought.

She said, "I've been thinking."

"You want to trade that bike in on an airplane?"

"No. I think that's the same as with a boat. Easiest and cheapest way is to make a friend of somebody who already owns one. You have your plane, *Angel*, and we're friends, aren't we?"

"I guess we are, at that."

"'Kay, then. What I've been thinking is there might still be a lost Injun gold mine out there somewhere. Mr. Mose Kyle's mine."

"Could be, I guess."

"Then what do you think about us trying to find it?"

"You think we could?"

"I prefer to think Mose did. So why couldn't we find it, too?"

He considered for a few seconds. A feeling was beginning to take hold despite his efforts to deny it. Mine or no mine, the prospect of spending more time with Kitty Birdsong pulled at him like the promise of something glowingly, impossibly wonderful just over the next ridge. Something golden.

He said, "Okay."

◊ ◊ ◊

Werly Fulks took his position in the Masada Undenominational Church of the One Pure God seriously. In a special service two years back, the Preacher had pronounced him not only elder deacon, but also a favored disciple. He had always given generously to the church, as had his daddy before him. His daddy had also started the logging company. Werly was forty-seven and had once been well-muscled from working in the woods, but since he had hired a larger crew of younger men, he now spent most days on the phone in his home office, or riding around from logging site to logging site in the battered pickup to make sure the men were working and not sitting around talking. He had grown a middle roll of loose flesh, and muscles had begun to go slack, not that he couldn't still work the biggest chain saw all day long with the best of the men if he should ever want to. He had gone to work right out of high school in order to help his father and uncle run the logging business. When they had both passed on, he had inherited it, and, with the help of a sister, who had finished school and was good with numbers, had prospered. He only had a fringe of hair left, but took alternative pride in a close-cropped beard.

He did whatever the Preacher expected of him.

The Preacher and Frank Cagle had asked him to keep a watch on this man John Hardin, who represented a threat to the Masada Church, and on the woman Kitty Birdsong. It was not an easy job. It took time away from his business, and it was difficult to monitor their movements without being spotted. He believed he had already gotten too close in his red Dodge pickup one day when he and Lloyd Dobbs had been following Hardin, so he was trying to follow from farther away, driving his sister's tan Neon, and was using six other disciples to fill in those hours when he could not do the job himself, and to check up on one of them while he was checking on the other one.

It was not necessary to follow them constantly because their daily patterns had begun to emerge. The girl worked a late shift at the casino in Cherokee, often riding her motorcycle there. When the man headed toward Asheville in his white Jeep, he was most probably going flying to take pictures for somebody or taking somebody up to look around, just doing his job. There were routine trips for both of them for groceries or other errands. The man worked on house-repair jobs around Maggie Valley. On some Saturdays he drove the Jeep over to Sylva to spend time with a boy about seven or eight years old, on a small farm there. One of his fellow watchers had found out the boy's name was Lightfoot. Living with a couple named Wahna and Lisa Crow. Probably kin to the boy. All of that only required loose watching. If the two got together on their time off, though, Fulks wanted himself or somebody to be nearby to find out what they were doing that might in any way threaten the beloved church he had come up in. He would take in everything, make some notes, call around to the other watchers every few days, and report regularly to the Preacher after Wednesday evening services.

He was parked now in the narrow lot in front of a strip of shops. The woman was across and down the street, standing by her motorcycle outside the Salty Dog, talking on her cell phone. He used a small pair of his sister's binoculars, leaning back in the seat, making sure nobody was watching him, to see she was smiling. Maybe talking with Hardin, then? Scheming up something.

She closed the phone, put on her helmet and gloves, mounted the motorcycle, looked both ways for traffic. She pulled out onto Highway 19. After she went past, he waited for two cars to go by in the same direction before he followed.

◊ ◊ ◊

The man in Bryson City had the latest coins out on his desk, admiring them under his desk lamp with a magnifying glass. It was a rare collection of five-dollar gold pieces privately pressed by the gunsmith Christopher Bechtler himself in the 1830s, part of more than

$2.2 million in gold coins the Rutherfordton, North Carolina, man produced himself over a nine-year span before the Charlotte mint took over. The coins were precisely weighed to be intrinsically worth their face values at the time, and had been widely circulated. Utterly unaffected by time or the elements, these were still beautiful, and worth a whole lot more now. He loved the rich color of them, and their silken feel.

He took a call his secretary said seemed important, and heard, "When are you going to approach Prescott?"

"I thought I made it clear you're not to call me here."

"God is with us in this we do."

"Yes, well, you keep telling that to your congregation. Let me deal with Prescott. And call me only on my home office line I gave you."

"There are others who are . . . interested. It would be good to get the business done soon."

"What do you mean by others?"

"Friends of the man who found it. They may know about the lost . . . site. I am having them watched."

"Listen to me. You need to think about that. Something like that has to be done very, very carefully. Nothing can happen that could possibly lead back to us."

"We will take care. But you must do your business soon."

"The elder Prescott might not be amenable, I'm afraid. He has big plans. His son almost certainly would be. It's a shame we can't deal with him instead."

"I understand the son is the only heir. Is that true?"

"Yes. What are you thinking?"

"Do the business soon." And the line went dead.

He had gotten far too deeply into this far too quickly. What had seemed a simple and quite possibly an immensely lucrative deal was becoming a dangerous maze. But there were always many paths to choose from that could take you to different destinations.

He only had to select the least risky. And along that selected path perhaps find ways to arrive at this particular destination in primary control and for a majority share, if at all possible. He would call Prescott from home that evening to set up a meeting. Face-to-face he could be intensely persuasive.

CHAPTER 14

Early on Tuesday morning John took a steaming cup of Hank's good coffee and the cell phone out onto the porch and stood at the rail. The sky was decorated in pastels, miles-long ripplings of thin, high cloud like medieval banners heralding the dawn. Birds were exchanging greetings from tree to tree. A heavy dew was beading the grass and speckling the Wrangler. A soft breeze carried the fresh scent of a new day, mingled with the musty lingering night perfume drifting out of the woods. The shadowed valley below was stirring with occasional cars. He checked his watch, shrugged, and thumbed in Kitty's number. She answered with no trace of sleep in her voice. He said, "How about breakfast somewhere?"

"Joey's shouldn't be packed if we get it in gear soon. A pile of French toast would do me good. We could just skip lunch to compensate. Meet you there?"

"I'll pick you up, if that's okay. After we eat I'll be going to see an old Indian friend. You're welcome to come along."

"Just give me ten minutes to comb out the night snarls."

He got the old clay pot, still wrapped in one of Moses' T-shirts, and placed it carefully on the floor in the backseat of the Wrangler.

Through breakfast they talked about nothing important in a reserved but comfortable way. When their bellies were warmed and pleasantly full, he drove them over the gap to Cherokee.

Kitty said, "Who is this we're going to see?"

"His name is Wasituna Lightfoot. His father, a man named Goingback Lightfoot, lived to be a hundred and five and was said to be one of the last Cherokee witches. I can't pronounce the name for witch too well in your language. Starts with that combined tee-ess sound."

"It's *Tskilegwa*. You start with the tip of your tongue touching the roof of your mouth. Like *Tsalagi*, which, after about ten thousand years, you tongue-tied white-eyes came along and bastardized into 'Cherokee.' Another word is *Tsali*. He was the elderly gentleman, you'll remember, who refused the government invitation to go on that little hiking adventure to Oklahoma we wound up calling the Trail of Tears. His arrogant Injun stubbornness got him shot. Now they name gift shops and sandwiches after him."

A mile outside Cherokee, they climbed a steep switchbacking gravel road through woods to a tilted clearing where there was a cabin with a green tin roof and a mossy stone chimney built up on the end wall. He parked beside a fifteen-year-old pickup and set the emergency brake well, a habit he had acquired soon after moving to this steeply rumpled country. There was a view down on part of the town in the valley. A slightly bent old man came out onto the porch, dressed in jeans and a loose shirt colorfully beaded in angular abstract patterns. His coarse black hair was streaked with gray and tied back into a ponytail. He raised a weathered hand in greeting. John got the pot from the backseat, and he and Kitty walked up onto the porch. John introduced her. The old man took her hand and held it, looked into her eyes for a moment, smiled, and nodded.

He said, "Come. Come inside. I have fresh-brewed tea."

They sat at his rustic dining table with fragrant cups of scalding hot tea flavored with herbs, Kitty taking polite glances around at the photos on the fireplace mantle, the dream catchers on the wall, a collection of well-used river-reed blowguns standing in a rack. She studied the old man, whose leathery face was a tracery of deep permanent creases and webbings of smile lines. His smile revealed a few teeth missing. There was a comfortable aura about him—a man happy in the time granted him on the planet and at peace with his life, with a store of rare wisdom collected over many decades.

He said, "So what brings you both here to see this old man today?"

John said, "A man named Moses Kyle was a prospector. From Maggie Valley. He managed to make a living panning for traces of gold in the creeks. He died of snakebite recently. Kitty and I think he might have found an old Cherokee gold mine." He unwrapped the clay pot and set it on the table in front of Wasituna. "I found this in his house."

The old man studied it, running the tips of his wrinkled fingers over the incised symbols. He picked it up to test its weight and turned it over for detailed inspection. He said, "Wolf Clan. A sacred yellow cave. Yes, this could tell about one of the lost mines. *Daloniga*. Gold. And now you two want to find it."

Kitty nodded, and John, for some reason feeling guilty under the old man's gaze, said, "I guess that's our plan."

"Why do you want to find it?"

Kitty and John looked at each other. He thought she looked guilty, too. She met the old man's gaze and said, "It could mean a lot of money, frankly. There's that, up front. But also in part we think of it as Moses Kyle's mine, if it really is out there. We'd be rediscovering it for him, too. We might be able to do some good with at least part of the money, maybe in his name."

Wasituna studied her. He nodded and said quietly, almost to himself, "Yes, the rainbow and the pot filled with gold."

Kitty said, "You think we're chasing a fantasy?"

The old Indian shook his head slightly. "No. The

mines are there. At least two of them, from what I have heard and have read. But do you remember the last time you saw a rainbow? How you felt? A rainbow is a gift to us, among all the great abundance of beautiful gifts to us in this earth life, and so it is sacred. It has a wonderful magic that pulls at you, that speaks to you and beckons you. But a rainbow is only an illusion, as it was meant to be. It appears in the sky not to guide us, but to make us feel and think. There are no real places for a rainbow's ends. The ends of it shift away from you as you change your position." He pointed at Kitty. "You see where you think one end of it falls to earth." He pointed at his own chest. "Standing on the next mountain, I see a different place where the end falls to earth. We both believe we are right. But we both would be foolish to think a rainbow could lead to a pot heaped with gold or to anything we could touch with our hands. We can only touch a rainbow with our minds. You can take a picture of one with a camera or with your mind, but nobody can own one."

Neither Kitty nor John said anything.

"This trail you are choosing. The path to Mr. Kyle's mine. From where you are, it looks like a shining rainbow with an end just out of reach. But it could be only illusion. Only a hope that Mr. Kyle had. If it is real, there could be bad trouble along the way. Greed will be close by in the shadows. Waiting. And wherever there is greed, there is always danger as a companion."

Kitty pursed her lips in thought. She said, "Yes,

sir. I work in the casino. I see the rainbows in people's eyes. And I see greed in there, too. It has the power to change people. Make their eyes go dull and empty. Make them forget you never really get something for nothing. There's always a cost."

"There is never enough to sate greed's hunger or slake its thirst. Watch the rich ones. They always want more, bigger, better, sooner, longer. Caught in greed's snare." Wasituna nodded and smiled. "I don't mean to say you should not take this trail. Only that you should be careful along it. Don't let it change you. Let me talk to a few of the old ones. Do some reading. Maybe I can help."

Kitty said, "We appreciate that, old father."

Wasituna held up a gnarled finger. "A moment. Before you go." He got up, went into a back room, and came out holding two traditional Cherokee blowguns, perfectly crafted from river cane, one six feet long and the other four feet. Each had a lashed-on thong with a hawk feather. He had a dozen darts for each blowgun in deerskin quivers. He held them out to John. "One for you, and another for the boy the next time you see him. Tell him he must practice many hours before he can call himself any good."

"They're well made. Thank you. I'll give Josh his when I see him next Saturday. And I'll practice, too."

"Tell him to paint a rabbit on the side of a cardboard carton. Tell him to stand with his back to the carton, maybe twelve feet away at first, with the blowgun at his side as he would carry it in the forest, then whirl around, bring the gun to his lips, and fire a dart at the rabbit as quickly as he can without even thinking. He will miss and miss, until one day he will begin to hit. And another day he will begin to place the dart where he wills it to go at twenty feet. Tell him then to come and match his skill against my own." He smiled and nodded. "Walk with the wind."

In the Wrangler, winding back up over Soco Gap, John said, "If Moses did find an old mine, looks like there are three possibilities. It could easily be on national forest land. A few hundred thousand acres of that around here. Nantahala or Pisgah. I don't know how the bureaucrats would look at people who found gold on that land."

"Surely they'd settle for a sizable finder's fee, at least?"

"There was a guy named Mel Fisher, spent sixteen years looking for a Spanish treasure wreck off Florida. A seventeen-hundreds galleon called the *Atocha*. The bureaucrats kept quiet all during that hunt. He finally found it down near the Keys. Turned out to be worth four hundred and fifty million. There's a museum in Key West about it. They sell jewelry made from Atocha silver. Anyway, the state of Florida jumped in with both feet and claimed it. The lawyers had a money party. It went all the way to the federal supreme court. Fisher finally won, but only because he was able to prove the wreck lay just outside Florida waters. Fisher made all his investors—the people who hung in there and backed him all those years—well off, by the way. I think it's a good story."

"If it is on public land, we'd have some clout because we'd be the only ones who know exactly where it is. I bet we could make a nice deal up front just using that."

"Maybe."

She said, "The other two possibilities, of course, are the mine could either be on reservation land—which would be pretty ironic because it once belonged to us anyway—or it could be on private land. Best we could probably hope for in either case is a finder's fee, I guess, but that could still amount to a big hunk of money, if the mine is anything like as rich as others they found around here way back when."

They rode in silence, thinking, John guiding the Jeep through the switchbacks.

Kitty said, "Wasituna is her grandfather. Your Val?"

He felt her looking at him as he concentrated on the road. "Yes. After Valerie died, he helped me."

When Valerie had died in that searing fireball of a bomb planted in his old Jeep on the Outer Banks island of Ocracoke and he had escaped the hit team with his life, he had found his way here to these mountains. He had stayed with the old man, who had helped heal and strengthen his body and train him to stalk and to kill. And then he had gone on the hunt. Wasituna was the only person in the world who knew it all.

He said, "He's a good man. I can only hope to

gather in about half the wisdom he's got stored up."

"We Injuns respect the old ones. You white-eyes tend to just sort of toss yours away when they get used up."

"I know. That's partly why Hank and Hattie live with me. They shouldn't be tossed away. They're good friends."

"She was beautiful. Valerie. That was a nice profile shot of her looking out over the mountains. I noticed one of the other photos on the mantle back there. It showed her holding a baby."

"Her son, Joshua. Seven now, living over near Sylva with kin. His dad died in a car wreck before he was born. I see him most Saturday afternoons. Sometimes he spends the night in my loft. Got a cot set up there for him."

"The boy Wasituna made the short blowgun for. It's good he has Wasituna. And you."

"Thanks."

Neither spoke for a minute.

She said, "So. Where do we go from here?"

"Maybe you could keep on with your reading, ask around among folk on the reservation. Rumor. Hand-me-down legend."

Kitty said, "Sure. And I could try to find out something about the legalities involved with discoveries of artifacts or, you know, resources, on federal lands or on the reservations. Maybe there's a record of finds. What the finders got out of it. Precedents."

He said, "I figure Moses was restricted pretty much to the practical range of his bicycle. A reasonable distance he could go out, pan for some time, and get back in daylight. What's that, a radius of fifteen miles? Let's make it twenty to be surer. The area formula is pi times the radius squared. So square twenty miles, you get four hundred. Times pi, that's well over twelve hundred square miles. About half of it national forest. Includes a chunk of the reservation. Big area. Got to narrow that down somehow. I could go around to the people who bought his gold, talk to them in more depth. See if Moses might have hinted at some general area he'd been exploring over the last few months of his life."

"People are going to be curious why you're asking. Before, you could have said it might help find Mose. What will you say now?"

"I don't know. I heard about Moses, how he made a living panning. Like to try it myself on weekends. Been wondering just how successful Moses was. How he went about it. Where he spent his time looking. If I find any gold, would they be interested in buying from me?"

"You ever sell cars?"

"I'm no salesman. But I don't mind talking with people. There's usually a way to draw them out. Really listening to them seems to help for a start."

"It would be pretty cool to actually find this mine, wouldn't it? Could be worth millions, you realize. I'd have a whole collection of motorcycles, like Jay Leno."

"I could buy a King Air or two and fly high rollers

and their nieces to Vegas."

"I'll hire you to fly me to Paris every Tuesday so I can try on the latest fashions made from scraps of silk and baby seal. Acquire a collection of blood diamonds, get a weekly do and a pedicure from some guy called Andre."

"I could have a castle built on Eaglenest Ridge. Wine cellar. Indoor Frisbee court."

"A bedroom for every day of the week."

"Hire a chief servant."

"And a chief chef." She raised a finger. "Oh, and I know. How about getting one of those Hummer limos that looks like a strip mall on wheels? Take your valet about a week to wax it."

"Those things are pretty stupid, aren't they?"

"They're only cool in America. Except, of course, for those hot sandy countries we've drenched in money in exchange for them drenching us in their oil so we can burn ten million lights we don't need. We've made pretension a fine art. We admire a celebrity wedding that cost a million. Look what some people will pay for a Rolex, when a thirty-dollar Timex from Wal-Mart keeps perfectly good time. It's no wonder people wearing rags around the world don't like us much."

"Maybe we don't need to get rich after all."

She said, "Well, I wouldn't go far as *that*. Let's at least give it a try."

CHAPTER 15

First you got to season it, rough it up so it'll work best. Come on, I'll show you," Effie Traylor said. She was a tall, fit, sun-browned woman with handsome features and alert blue eyes, somewhere in her seventies, wearing a man's plaid shirt and clean denim overalls, her hair pulled back under a green John Deere cap.

John and Hank followed her outside behind the twelve-by-twelve-foot gem shop built at the back of the gravel parking lot near Darkwater Creek. She stopped at the long wooden flume, which was supported on a framework of two-by-eights to divert water from the creek. She immersed the shallow green plastic pan in the flow, scooped up a handful of coarse gravel from a pile beneath the swift-running flume, and used it to scrub the pan vigorously with a callused hand. "Takes the shine off this plastic, lets the water spread out, run over the surface, 'stead of bubblin' or layin' in pools."

John had decided to learn something about prospecting. A pleasant young woman in the Visitors'

Center in the town of Frankfort had suggested in a low confidential tone that he talk with Effie, owner of the Traylor Ruby Mine a few miles out of town along a narrow curled road through dense woods.

From a shelf in her shop, Effie had selected something called the Garrett Gravity Trap Gold Panning Kit, which included a fourteen-inch green plastic pan, a nesting perforated sifter pan for culling out larger pebbles from a pan-load of gravel, a small needle-nosed "Gold Guzzler" plastic suction bottle, and a pair of magnifier tweezers, both of the latter to be used for extracting flakes and grains of gold from the bottom of the pan. There were two small screw-top vials for holding the gold, and an instruction booklet. He'd paid her cash for the kit.

"'Course you ain't likely to get rich at it," Effie said, "but a lot of folk seem to like it just for the fun of it. Go out in the woods on a Saturday, get their hands dirty, forget about workin' behind some desk starin' at a computer all week."

Looking over the flume setup, Hank said, "Anybody ever find big rubies here?"

"Biggest one ever found in this valley," Effie said with pride. "One the size of a golf ball four years back. That big enough for you? Got a picture of it on the wall in the store. Check it out. And Darkwater Valley's the *only* valley in these mountains native rubies *ever* been found in. Don't you let nobody tell you otherwise. Most of these other so-called mines, what they do is they salt their buckets with gemstone chips you can buy cheap by the bagful, worth next to nothin'. They dig their bucket dirt out of a side hill someplace when nobody's lookin'. Mix in the glitter junk. Rippin' people off, you ask me. You want the real thing, you pick a place their sign says 'native stones only,' like my sign says right over there. You ain't goin' to find a handful of worthless junk in every bucket, but if you got some patience you just might turn up a real nice ruby you can get set in a necklace for your woman, or some smoky garnets make a nice pair of earrings. People over at the Chamber of Commerce don't like me talkin' this way, but I don't give a darn about that chicken-necked bunch. I go my own way, and I tell it to you true. Always have."

A lone customer, a heavyset man wearing a floppy-brim safari hat, was seated on a rough low bench facing the flume. He was dumping some gravelly dirt from a small galvanized bucket into a square, shallow, screen-bottomed wooden box, washing the dirt out of the box by immersing it in the cold, clear water rushing along in the flume, then picking through the bright wet pebbles with tweezers, hunting for the elusive glint of a garnet or a ruby. Hank walked over to watch.

Effie called to Hank, "Why don't you try it for yourself? Take a couple those buckets over there. Just filled those last evenin' myself. Come from the bottom of a pool in the creek. Ought to be good stuff. You can pay me later. Only a dollar a bucket."

Hank rolled up his shirtsleeves, took two small buckets from a line of them, sat on the long bench in front of the flume ten feet from the other miner, and went to work with a screen box.

"I knew a man named Moses Kyle from Maggie Valley," John said. "He managed to make a living panning for gold all over the mountains."

"Never heard of him," Effie said. "Anyway, this here's a ruby mine. Not much gold in Darkwater Creek, so I wouldn'ta crossed paths with your man, likely. Only carry some gold prospectin' stuff 'cause my Donald liked to do it. He passed on ten years back. Good man. We made it together forty-four years. Been a couple slick talkers come sniffin' around here since. Lookin' to partner up. Got their eyes on my acreage here, see. But this mountain girl wasn't born yesterday, nossir."

"Maybe they're not just eyeing your acreage, Effie."

She smiled, lifted an eyebrow, and nodded.

He said, "Could you give me a few tips on gold hunting?"

"You'll find veins of it runnin' through a deposit of quartz most often, and sometimes alloyed with silver, or in placer deposits. Could be tons of it left under these mountains, who knows? You're lucky enough to find a vein in a cave or wherever, then you just start diggin'. Mother Nature scraped some of it out of God's original rock that she broke up and scoured with glaciers, or she washed a lot of it out over a long time—thousands and millions of years. So you can find it mixed with gravel. But you got to know where to get your gravel. Bed of a river or a creek is a good bet. You got to dig down for it. Gold's like rubies or garnets or sapphires or emery—all those corundum stones almost hard as diamonds. All heavy, so corundum stones and gold bits find their way down deep, just above the hard pack or the bedrock, that's where I get my ore buckets here."

Hank had moved closer to the other miner, who was offering him advice good-naturedly. Hank seemed totally absorbed by the process.

John said, "The gold tends to settle out wherever the current slows down?"

"That's right. A pool bottom just after a stretch of rapids could be good. Or a pool in a creek bend. Maybe the upstream point of a sandbar. Sometimes gold *is* nearer the top of the overburden, say if it's a time after a big flood, then gold can get churned up so it's not so deep. But generally you dig deep, right to the bedrock if you can. Other places to look are cracks and crevices in creek rocks where sand has washed in. Take yourself a garden trowel or a big-bladed screwdriver; scrape out that stuff in the crack. Could have some color in it. My Donald even used a dentist's pick sometimes.

"Next problem you got is to get rid of everything in your dirt that ain't gold. Lot of ways to do that. Cheapest, but slowest, is to pan it. You got to wash out the dirt, swirl everything around in the pan with some water until the water gets muddy. You let some muddy water slop out over the side—three times is good—and keep on adding water till it's clear. You got to learn the right touch. You don't want to let too much slop out or there could be some gold go with it. Takes a bit o' patience. Then you pick out the pebbles. You're real lucky, one o' those pebbles could be a nugget. Maybe you got black sand on the bottom of the pan—heavy minerals—and maybe you can use a magnet to pull that out. What you got left in the bottom of your pan might be gold bits shinin' up at you all pretty. If it's scattered on the bottom, you tilt the pan and tap it some and the gold collects in one place. They call that walkin' the dog. Pick your gold out with tweezers or suck it up with that bottle in your kit. Then all you got to do is take your poke to somebody you trust to weigh it up right by troy ounce and pay you a fair dollar. Good luck there."

"I heard a man named Cagle around here somewhere buys gold."

Her face darkened. "There's three Cagles. They run a so-called gold mine over at the foot of Corkscrew Mountain, and I hear they do buy gold. Go all over lookin' for it, matter of fact. Pay folk bottom dollar for teeth fillins', old rings, dust from hobby panners don't know any better. But you listen to what I'll tell you. I don't like gossip or talkin' behind backs, but you need to stay clear of that lot. They're in with some bunch that babbles on and plays with fire. Two brothers and a sister who's kin to the devil himself. Their daddy might have *been* the devil himself. Bear of a man with mean eyes. Brought his family in here from Kentucky maybe thirty-five, forty years back now. Bought a whole side of Corkscrew Mountain from a widow half gone in the head. Old man Cagle ran a still up on Corkscrew, someplace up behind their farm. In a cave, I heard. Sold go-blind shine to the Cherokees. Everybody knew it, but he never got caught. One mean creature, let me tell you. Used to beat his wife, they say. She died of a bad heart. He went full crazy finally, killed a man I heard owed him fifty dollars, in a beer bar over near to Bryson City, and beat two other men bad with a hoe handle at the same time. They locked him up in Butner and somebody knifed him dead in there. Good riddance, I say."

Hank apparently had found something in the bottom of his screen box. John and Effie walked over to peer into the box.

Effie said, "Yep, that's a nice-sized garnet you got there. And you ain't even paid me for your buckets. Beginner's luck."

She helped Hank pick through the rest of his bucket-loads, but they found no more gemstones.

They walked inside her cluttered shop so Hank could pay. There was a lighted glass-topped display case by the register, filled with a colorful scatter of glinting rough gemstones. Hank leaned over to look.

Effie said, "Maybe you could use a nice stone for

your missus? Or a granddaughter?"

Hank tapped the glass with his finger, indicating a hexagonal green stone a quarter inch long. "What's that one right there?"

"That there's beryl. Found it myself. Her eyes acquired a glint as she crossed her arms, smiled, and leaned on the case. They were almost head-to-head, looking down at the gems. "Good stone for a man. Long time ago they used to think it made you unbeatable. Banished fear. Made a man smarter and cured him of laziness. You need that one for yourself? You could get it cut and polished—I know a man who could do a good job of it for a fair price—and it would make a nice ring. Or maybe a tie clip?"

"They believed all that, huh?"

"Some people still do. I ain't going to tell you they're right or wrong. They say stones have different vibrations, like. You take emeralds. They're your high-class beryl, clear deep green. Well, they say emeralds are antidote for poisons, and they can ward off demons. Then there's your malachite, which is another green stone that can turn away the evil eye. Hindu Indians think rubies are even better'n diamonds. If you wear one on your left side, it'll help you get rich, they say. You take your topaz, now, there's an interestin' stone for a man like you. Soothes wild passions. Gets more powerful as the moon swells up bigger. Or maybe the purple one there. It's amethyst, another one I found in these mountains. Symbol of truth, hope, love. Passion."

John could have sworn the old man blushed.

Hank said, "What's that one?"

"The olive green one? Chrysolite. That's another one protects against evil spirits. Egyptians said it ought to be pierced, set in gold, strung on the hair of an ass, and tied hangin' off the left arm, you wanted its full power."

Hank paid her twenty-three dollars for the ore buckets and the small rough amethyst, and she gave him a note about where to get it cut and polished.

An SUV crunched into the parking lot, a family of five piled out, and Effie walked out to greet them.

In the Wrangler, tracking the narrow road back toward Frankfort, Hank said, "That's a handsome woman back there. Got to admire her, runnin' that place all by herself. Seems to do okay at it, too."

"Didn't know you had a roving eye."

"You mean a man my age? I'm Hattie's right down to my toes, but that don't stop a man from lookin'. We're pretty simpleminded, all us men, when it comes to women. Don't take much to turn us on. But we're just doin' our job, ain't we? Main reason we been put here, seems to me, is we're supposed to run down the ladies. Way we're built, and we can't help it. It's the women complicated the whole thing with a thousand and one rules for the game. Hell of a lot simpler back in caveman days, I expect."

"Got to agree with that. Half the time we don't

even know which rules apply, and they're always subject to change."

"Speakin' of females, you and Kitty Birdsong gettin' serious lately? That's one fine young woman."

"I told you. We're just friends."

"Sure. You say so."

Changing the subject, he said, "John Wayne was Army Captain York. Henry Fonda was a real stubborn Colonel Thursday, wouldn't listen to York. Shirley Temple was in it. Indians broke out of the reservation, mostly because of abusive treatment by a corrupt government agent, and started marauding. Cochise was the bad guy."

"Lemme see. Lemme see. Oh, yeah, *Fort Apache*. Late forties, maybe early fifties. How about this one, late sixties. Two outlaws with the law hard on their heels, 'specially a lawman in a white straw hat. Story took place in Arizona and Bolivia."

"That all you're going to give me?"

"What, that ain't enough? Got you stumped?"

"Newman and Redford. *Butch Cassidy and the Sundance Kid.*"

"Dang."

Thirty minutes later, after twice consulting a map, taking a wrong turn, and having to backtrack for three miles, they pulled up in the shadow of Corkscrew Mountain and parked in front of a run-down operation with a faded sign that said "Cagle's Gem and Gold Mine."

Hank said, "This place is a mite off the common track, ain't it? What're we doin' here?"

"I don't know. A feeling. I talked over the phone with a man at this place when I was calling around to people who buy gold, back when we were trying to locate Moses. This one was a strange conversation."

Appraising the place, Hank said, "Well, I can believe that."

It had probably once been a prosperous, fair-sized farm. A two-story house in need of paint, several outbuildings strung back away from the road, overgrown fields bordered by fieldstone walls that had slumped here and there. A hopelessly rusted old Farmall tractor sat forlornly in tall grass and brambles close beside a tilted gray building behind the house. A long tin-roofed shed ran alongside the road, with a mossy, badly leaking wooden flume carrying water from a trickle of a creek—not much more than a brown-water ditch—that paralleled the road. There was a gravel lot on the other side of a culvert. There were two cars in the lot, and two couples were seated on benches in front of the flume, absorbed in working with screen boxes. A collection of about twenty two-gallon galvanized buckets sat by a crusted pile of gravelly dirt at the end of the lot. An unsmiling long-haired stocky man in his thirties, dressed in a frayed plaid shirt and dirty jeans, was picking lazily at the pile with a long-handled spade, slowly filling more buckets. When John and Hank walked over, he spat tobacco juice to one side, rearranged the wad in his cheek, and said, "Help you?"

John said, "Mr. Cagle?"

The man looked both of them over, shook his head, and said, "Not me. Just work here. You wanna do some mining?"

"Maybe. What could we find?"

"You got your rubies. Your amethysts. Your garnets. Man right here just found a nice little sapphire." One of the women seated at the flume smiled and held up a bright chip. The heavyset man walked the few steps, took it, and held it up to the light. "This here's called citrine. You're doin' just fine, lady." He gave the chip to her, came back to stand in front of Hardin and lean on the spade handle. He chewed twice and said thickly, "Or you can try your luck for gold. You don't know how, I can show you. We got pans, everythin' you'll need. Got a few buckets left we just dug from a real good spot in a cave up on the hill. Could be real rich. Only ten bucks a bucket. So what's your pleasure?"

"I'm thinking of doing some prospecting in the creeks around here, and I'm looking for somebody who'll buy whatever gold I might find."

"You'd have to talk with Orin Cagle about that."

"Where can I find him?"

The man spat sideways again. "That's him comin' up right there behind you."

He and Hank turned to see a beefy man coming across the tall grass from the house. About five-ten with a protruding belly, dressed in overalls over a T-shirt that strained to contain large arms. His face was shadowed by a dirty ball cap. Twice he glanced over at the white Wrangler. When he got closer, the tobacco-chewer said, "These two are wantin' somebody to buy their gold. Told 'em they'd have to talk to you."

Orin Cagle nodded. His eyes were piggish and suspicious in the shadow of his cap brim. He seemed to be nervous. He said, "So you got gold to sell?"

"Not right now. Hope to have some, though. We bought some gear, and we're about to start looking in the creeks around here. Heard you're a buyer. Fact, I talked with you a while ago over the phone."

Orin nodded again. "We buy sometimes."

John said, "I had a friend who did pretty well at prospecting. Man named Moses Kyle. You ever buy from him?"

"Think I told you on the phone. That would be our business."

John watched the man's eyes and said, "Moses Kyle died out in the woods. Circumstances seemed strange to me. Here's a man who's spent a lot of his life out there. He knew what he was doing. Knew the dangers. Yet he died like a novice. Didn't even have any of his prospecting gear with him. No backpack. No drinking water. Died like a dumb city man out there in the boonies hiking for the first time. Think about it. Doesn't that seem strange to you?"

"Wouldn't know nothin' about any of that. Lot of

things out there can hurt a man. Look here, you find gold, give us a call. Right now we got to get back to work."

John looked around at the leaking flume, the paint-peeled buildings with rust-streaked metal roofs. "Yes. I can see a lot of work gets done around here. Maybe we'll be back, then. Talk some more."

Orin Cagle watched Hardin and the old guy walk to the Wrangler and drive away. The tobacco-chewer said, "What the hell was that all about? Somethin' about those two didn't seem right."

Orin stood there looking at the road for several seconds after the white Wrangler had disappeared around a wooded bend. He said, "Get some more buckets filled. I'll salt 'em myself later. You put too much of the shiny stuff in 'em." He walked back to the house.

Wild hydrangeas along with delicate bluets and fire pink, flaring in the late afternoon sunlight, decorated random patches of brush along the country road. Hardin was quiet, thinking, his hands automatically guiding the Wrangler.

Hank said, "Somethin' about that Cagle back there. You made him jumpy."

"I know."

"Why, you figure?"

"Effie told us this Cagle clan aren't known for honest dealings. I think if he didn't know Moses, he would have plain said so and been done with it. This seems too far out for Moses to have come on his own to sell his gold. He had other buyers closer. So this Cagle may have either met Moses somewhere or come to his place to buy. Cagle could figure he must have been seen with Moses, so he didn't deny knowing him. Maybe he cheated Moses somehow in the gold dealing. I don't know—maybe didn't weigh up the gold fairly, or owed him but wasn't paying, something like that."

"He's sure holdin' something back. Man's got mean eyes, too."

John nodded, thinking, *Did he recognize my Jeep?*

"Well, where we goin' from here?"

John checked his watch. "We've got time to stop in at another buyer on the way home if we make it quick. Don't want to keep Hattie waiting for supper."

"That's right. Potpie and skillet cornbread tonight. She said something about carrot cake, too. I can taste that already."

◊ ◊ ◊

Orin Cagle took the cell phone into the backyard. Punched in the number with a fat finger.

Frank Cagle said, "What?"

"It's Hardin. He was just here with some old guy. Askin' questions."

"What questions?"

"Said he was gonna hunt gold, needed somebody to buy it. Talked about Kyle. Lot of crap."

"What you tell him?"

"Nothin', Frank. Told him we had work to do,

and he left. But he knows somethin'. I could feel it. What are we gonna do?"

"You sure you didn't say no more'n that?"

"I swear it, Frank. But I don't like this guy sniffin' around like this. What are we gonna do?"

"Orin, you always did worry enough for three men. Don't think Hardin's nothin' to worry over. But I'll have another talk with the Preacher. Meantime you just keep on keepin' quiet."

"You think I'm gonna *tell* anybody anything?"

"You listen to me, Orin. You get two beers into you and you like to get loose-mouthed. You know you do. So you got to have a few, do it right there in the house until we get this sorted out, you hearin' me?"

CHAPTER 16

Gideon Prescott—Gid to his many friends—wanted his own version of Grandfather Mountain. It had been a lifelong dream, and Hugh Morton had long been one of his idols. Gideon had recently taken early retirement from a successful veterinary practice in order to pursue his dream.

At 5,964 feet, Grandfather is the highest point in the Blue Ridge Mountains. Tall enough so it can at times create its own microclimate. Hugh Morton had made the Avery County peak into one of the most environmentally significant mountains in the world. It was recognized by the United Nations as an International Biosphere Reserve, one of 324 on the planet and the only one privately owned, with forty-seven rare and endangered species of animals and plants.

Shot-and-rescued bald eagles can live out their lives unmolested. Peregrine falcons can hone their aerobatics riding the invisible torrent that often wraps the mountain with swirls and eddies, and occasionally bursts over the peak with such strength as to create a smooth standing lenticular cloud like a cold halo. Lithe panthers and placid black bears are contained by a clever system of cliffs and ravines in natural settings on the mountain's flanks.

Tourists by the thousands per month show up to pay admission, hike the trails and picnic, gingerly walk out onto the windy mile-high suspension footbridge for the vertiginous views, see the creatures in the musty nature museum, spot birds through binoculars, and photograph each other against fall foliage vistas. The annual Highland Games and other doings help to pay the taxes and expenses and take in a good profit.

Gideon had bought an expensive Nikon and had attended a nature-photography workshop on Grandfather, founded years back by Morton, who'd earned a reputation as a fine photographer of the hazy mountains and their elusive creatures he had so loved.

Gideon had sufficient acreage, acquired by initial bequest and careful subsequent add-on purchases over three decades, to create an attraction similar to Grandfather, though at 3,750 feet, his mountain was somewhat less grand than Grandfather. Working with a young Asheville architect, he had developed a plan and was close to acting on it. He would call his mountain preserve Medicine Ridge, honoring the Cherokee blend of natural, spiritual, and mental traditions that make up their idea of perfectly healthy living. Medicine Ridge would have preserves for threatened species to include hardwood groves, red wolves, and rare birds attracted by special plantings of flowers and shrubs. A rustic restaurant situated just below the ridge crest, so as not to mar the natural skyline, would serve organic foods and include a store that would be an outlet for Cherokee arts and other mountain arts and crafts, with invited crafters demonstrating their skills. Horseback and hiking trails would wind over the mountain's flanks.

At fifty-six, Gid looked a decade younger, with only a slight thickening around his waist and a slight thinning of his close-cut graying brown hair. His green eyes glinted with life and were framed by smile lines that bespoke his usually affable character. Now that he had some time, he planned to work out regularly and regain the sturdy fitness he'd so taken for granted in his youth. He was still young enough, he figured, to see his dream become real, though he'd been cheated of full enjoyment of it when leukemia had patiently stalked and finally claimed his beloved Miranda five years ago.

He still had hope that his son, Coleman, would realize what Medicine Ridge could mean to generations to come, and begin to show an interest in sharing the dream.

Gid had insisted that Coleman forsake his friends long enough to join him for dinner this Saturday evening. Gid had chosen the Jarrett House in Dillsboro, which served excellent food family style, and where

Gid, Miranda, and Coleman had often enjoyed country meals together when Coleman was a mop-headed, curious boy unable to sit still longer than thirty seconds. There was a wait, as usual on any weekend. They sat side by side in white wicker rockers on the porch.

Coleman was fidgeting, and Gid wondered, not for the first time, *Are you on something, son?* Maybe something he'd gotten from one of his shiftless friends?

Coleman said, "We should have gone someplace else. How long did they say we have to wait?"

"Thirty minutes. But no matter. I want to talk with you, anyway."

Coleman rolled his eyes, sighed, and looked absently across the street at the people walking past the village shops.

"What are you going to do with your life, Cole? You're twenty-three, and you still don't have a plan. You put off college to figure things out, you told me. See some of the world. Do some thinking. You've never held a job longer than a few months. You're in with some people I don't like. They seem to demand all your time. Years are going by, Cole. You need to make some decisions."

Coleman mumbled something.

"What's that?"

"I said you do what you're good at, and I'll do what I'm good at."

"What does that mean? You saying you're only good at partying? At wasting time?"

Coleman in profile, with his thin aquiline features, reminded Gid painfully of Miranda. The boy's face became flushed now, and he wrung his long-fingered hands, his elbows braced on his knees like he was about to bolt. "Look who's wasting time. You've got this crazy idea of building some kind of backwoods Disneyland. You know what people are saying? How am I supposed to feel about that?"

There were only Miranda and himself to blame for Coleman's flawed character, Gid knew. After three miscarriages and a precarious pregnancy that was most definitely going to be her last she had finally succeeded in having this boy, and so had spoiled him badly. Gid had seen it happening, but in deference to Miranda had never intervened in any meaningful way. What Coleman wanted, Coleman always got in ample measure. However Coleman chose to behave was always excused, rationalized, forgiven.

We did him no favors, Gid thought.

"Listen, son. I don't want to get into another head-butting contest with you. That's not going to get either of us anywhere. But I will tell you this. I don't care if anybody thinks Medicine Ridge is a crazy idea. People tend to scoff at a lot of ideas. At dreams. Grandfather Mountain works, and Medicine Ridge will, too. There's a place for you in this if you'll just give it a try. All I'm asking is, will you please think about it? Come with me next week to meet the architect. You might like him. He's a real fireball. Full of enthusiasm and great ideas. When you see the whole plan—"

"I'm going to the restroom." Coleman got up, brushed his long hair back nervously, and moved off inside the restaurant.

Gid studied the hand-cut gingerbreading that decorated the porch of the old inn, evidence to him of a seemingly outdated era grounded in a simple work ethic and a simple pride in skills learned and a plain code of honor earned, and said quietly, "What should I do, Miranda?"

A woman seated nearby said, "Excuse me, sir, is something wrong?"

Gid cleared his throat, shook his head, and said, "I'm afraid it's nothing I know how to fix, but thanks for asking, ma'am."

◊ ◊ ◊

Two days later, Gideon arose shortly after dawn, as was his habit. He dressed in jeans and a favorite beaded belt, a flannel shirt, and well-worn boots, walked out to the shed behind his home, and saddled his frisky young sorrel quarter horse, Stormer, talking quietly to the animal to keep him calm.

With the help of horse-loving friends, Gid had made a trail on the flanks of his mountain, the first in what would be a network of trails for mountain visitors. He put Stormer into an easy walk along it, climbing in three switchbacks, noting a new deadfall he'd have to make time to clear away. He could cut the tree up to replenish his store of firewood, and could certainly use the exercise.

The early sun was burning soft stripes into the mist that lay like hovering smoke throughout the surrounding forest. The farther-off trees looked surreal and ghostly. The leaf-matted trail was damp from the night, and Stormer stepped along quietly, the saddle making familiar leathery creaks. The horse's warm breath blew visible in the dawn chill.

This was Gid's favorite time. A time for collecting thoughts, making plans for the day ahead, a time of serene near-meditation when he could enjoy his dream. He knew some of what he envisioned was probably too ambitious or not economically viable, at least at the outset, but that was the beauty of a dream. It could be as grandiose as you chose to make it. Practicality could always step in later with its coldly calculating logic to scale it back to something workable. Gid believed most people started out by timidly limiting their own visions and so never climbed very high in life. He liked to set his own goals right up there on the highest peaks, and this was his time of day to give his imagination free rein to embellish and reshape his dream of Medicine Ridge.

But this morning Coleman was still heavy on his mind. He had slept only fitfully the night before. Through friends, he'd done some checking on the crowd his son was associating with and had not liked what he'd learned. Worst of it were the rumors of drugs, not only of using them but also of dealing them. He had resolved to confront Coleman about it and not let up until he got some answers. *I'll do it tonight. I'll be damned if I'll lose him, too.*

The trail straightened out and dipped down into a long depression. Stormer knew the trail well and wanted to run, so Gid let him out into a gallop.

At a slight bend where the trail began to climb again and the brush was dense, a large gray shape stepped out onto the trail close ahead, big arms raised and waving, shouting, "*Heeahhhhhhh.*"

Stormer whinnied and reared violently. Gid made an awkward grab for the saddle horn, but it was damp with dew and his hand slipped away. He lost the reins, and he fell back, instinctively tucking his head close to his chest and raising his fists up by his ears. He hit the ground hard, glimpsing Stormer dancing away back along the trail, his eyes wide and fearful. The impact, mostly on his left shoulder and side, stunned him, but there was no pain.

He rolled onto his back carefully and looked up to see a massive blurry figure moving in to study him. The man was muscular, with long hair tied back into a ponytail.

Gid wanted to tell him he shouldn't have done that. But the pain was building now, and he could not get clear words out.

He groaned and managed to mumble, "Why . . .

you do that? Why?"

The man seemed preoccupied, as though studying the situation in detail. Offering no help or apology. In a rasping voice, he said, "It's pretty gravelly here, so no footprints. I'll scratch out any I made off the trail, but it's mostly just thick leaves. Got these work gloves on, so no prints on anything. What you think, Mr. Prescott? Maybe you fell harder than that. Maybe you broke your neck from that left side there. You think we can do that so it's what they'll figure happened? I used to wrestle some. It's fake bullshit, mostly, but if we use a full nelson sorta sideways and really crank it on quick-like, that ought to get her done. You think?" He coughed into his fist.

Gid tried to push him away as the man knelt with a low grunt and took up position, but the big tattooed arms were like tough wild vines. He could feel the man take a deep breath as he began exerting force. The man's breath stank of cigarettes. He gripped one forearm weakly and tried to bite it but could not move his head enough to the side.

He felt the pressure building, his neck bending awkwardly beyond anything that was normal, his air cutting off, his vision dimming, his last thoughts a despairing jumble about his only son. His son who did not share the dream that would now die with him, he knew.

And then the world went white.

◊ ◊ ◊

After he had locked the door of his home office, he sat behind his desk, called the Preacher, and picked up the newspaper to read the article again, his hand trembling. As soon as he heard the strong, imperious voice, he said, "Gideon Prescott is dead. But you knew that, didn't you? You had something to do with this?"

"You should be able to do business with the son."

"I could have worked it out with Gideon, but you didn't give me enough *time*."

"You said he refused."

"The man was no idiot. What better way to begin a negotiation? Refuse and see if the ante gets upped. I could have handled this, god*damn* it."

"Do not blaspheme."

"Are you *serious*? Listen to this in the paper: 'Respected community leader Gideon Prescott died early yesterday morning, apparently the victim of an accident on his property. The Haywood County Sheriff's Office is withholding details pending investigation.' Then it goes into a long listing of the man's credentials and achievements. Moses Kyle was bad enough, but he was a nobody. An insignificant nobody. And nobody cared. Gideon Prescott was known and liked all over these mountains. If there was anything, I mean *anything* suspicious about his death, they'll never stop picking at it, do you understand me? You have any idea what they can do with forensics these days?"

"God protects true believers."

He gripped the receiver with a swelling rage. "You're beyond belief. Spout that crap to your followers. Bunch of backwoods redneck fanatics. I know you better, remember. God, why did I ever get involved in all this?"

"Are you saying you will not proceed?"

"What if I just told you to go straight to hell? I had nothing whatever to do with either Kyle or Prescott. You're the one with the bloody hands."

There was only silence on the other end of the line. The fury ebbed out of him to leave him weak. He said, "Are you still there?"

Silence.

Except he believed he could hear steady, controlled breathing.

"I said, are you there?"

Silence.

He began to perspire, and rubbed his palm across his forehead. Said, "Look, I didn't mean anything by that last. It's just . . . it's just I wasn't expecting this and I picked up the paper and it just . . . it hit me like a brick. You can understand that, can't you?"

Silence.

A cold lump materialized in his gut and began to spread. He said, "Okay, okay, I'll approach the son in maybe two weeks. After the, you know, the funeral and things are sorted out. After they make a, you know, a cause-of-death determination. Will that satisfy you? *Say* something, will you?"

Silence.

The line was definitely still open. He was sure he could still hear the breathing. It was as though a cloaked malevolence hung in the void between them in stillness, but gathering itself.

Tensing.

His voice rose half an octave involuntarily. "Look, I've *said* I'll do it and I will. I'm sorry if I offended you, all right? I didn't mean it. I was just distraught. I'll do it. All *right*?"

Several heartbeats later, the breathing stopped, there was a click, and the dial tone buzzed in his ear.

He hung up, his hand trembling badly now. He thought. *This isn't like me. What the hell is wrong with me?*

CHAPTER 17

An early-morning rain driven by heavy gusts was pelting the front windows of Hardin's house when Kitty called to say, "I think we might have something on Mose's mine."

"You turn up a treasure map with a black X on it?"

"Not quite. But I know where there's an old journal with what could be a description of how to find it. Let's go to Country Vittles and chew on it, along with a haunch of greasy bacon and half a dozen eggs. I'll let you buy. Appease your male ego."

It surprised him how much he enjoyed hearing her voice. He said, "Might as well. Today looks like a washout, anyway. I'll deduct breakfast. File it under 'Hunting for Lost Indian Gold Mines.' The IRS will understand. Pick you up in fifteen minutes?"

As soon as he pulled up in front of her modest house, she came out in tight jeans and a loose light jacket over a black T-shirt, and walked to the Jeep through a light drizzle, not hunching over like most people do in the rain, but holding herself proudly, enjoying it, and he had another memory flash of Valerie.

He only had a few poor snapshots of Val, on the dresser in his bedroom, but he had a wealth of mental images he'd carefully archived. Valerie in her black two-piece swimsuit walking proudly with her innate grace and serenity, at his side along the Ocracoke Island beach on a brassy day, a breeze toying with her long hair and a low surf whispering secrets from before recorded time. Valerie contentedly, deftly cooking in her little kitchen, her forehead silken with perspiration. Valerie watching her son, Joshua, at absorbed imaginative play, her eyes full of unconditional love. Valerie looking boldly into his soul as they made slow love on her bed, flickering candlelight caught in her dark eyes like long-ago *Tsalagi* campfires.

Kitty slid lithely onto the passenger seat, unconsciously licked at moisture on her lips, and smiled at him. Her hair was lightly frosted with tiny rain beads. She said, "Morning, Sherlock."

He nodded, uncomfortable sitting so close beside this beautiful creature while he held such private and sacred images of his Valerie in his head.

He drove downtown and found a parking slot at Country Vittles. They took a corner booth inside and ordered hearty breakfasts.

He said, "So, how did you find out about this journal?"

"Old Zeke, the clean-up man I told you works in the casino? Told me he remembered a Wolf Clan friend of his who has a record that dates back to the Indian Removal. A Cherokee named Walker Shade kept it during the trek to Oklahoma, writing in Sequoyah's syllabary. There's a description in it that his friend says tells how to find a mine. When Shade got gravely ill not long after the Trail of Tears, he entrusted his record to his only son. Apparently that son was killed in a brawl before he could get back this way. The journal was passed down to his son in turn, and then by bequest to a daughter, Mary Shade Hill, who moved back here with her family from Oklahoma many years ago. She's in her eighties now. Probably about the same age as Zeke. He didn't say so, but I got the impression he and Mary were once lovers, or at least sweethearts. They were predicting rain for today, and I assumed you wouldn't be working, so I took the liberty of asking Zeke to set up a meeting with Mary for us this morning. Figured you'd want to tag along."

"Obvious question is why hasn't somebody used this description to find the mine long before now?"

"I don't know. Maybe it's too vague. Or it could be coded somehow. But we have information that nobody else has had, and it should help explain this description, or at least narrow down the search."

"Because we know the mine ought to be within Moses' working radius."

"Right."

"When do we meet Mary?"

"You've got time to finish your coffee. She lives

near town on the reservation."

Mary Shade Hill had thick, tied-back white hair and was bent under the cruel yoke of osteoporosis, but her dark eyes were lively. She wore a bright red shirt and a long flowing printed skirt. She sat in an oak wicker-bottomed chair at her kitchen table and gestured for John and Kitty to sit.

She took some time to study each of them. Squinting. Appraising.

She said to Kitty, "Ezekiel told me you are a young woman of good character. Says you do your job well."

"Thank you. Ezekiel and you must be good friends."

"We almost married. But we are both too strong-willed, and I don't think it would have worked out. Do you two plan to marry?" She squinted at John.

He felt himself flush. "We're friends, ma'am."

She smiled a knowing smile and said, "I see."

Kitty said, "Zeke told me you have a description of a mine that once belonged to the Wolf Clan."

The old woman folded her hands on the table and looked up at the ceiling. After a moment she said quietly, "I have four sons. Two are worthless. Two work hard, love their wives, do not waste their time gambling or their minds and bodies drinking, try to teach their children *duyuktv*."

"Yes," Kitty said, "the right way. The Cherokee way."

Mary nodded. "But all four are my sons. My husband is with the spirits. I have nothing to leave for my sons or, through them, to my grandchildren. If I give to you the directions to this mine and if you should find it, and if it should yield to you money, I ask for a seventy percent share to me or to my estate, to be shared by all my sons equally."

Kitty smiled and held up a slender finger. "But, old mother, if these directions are so good, why hasn't anyone in your family found the mine?"

"It is true. They have looked, and thought, and looked some more, and finally they all have decided the directions are an impossible riddle, or a joke, or a myth. All but me. I believe they are real. That the mine is real. And if you look with fresh eyes, you might find it. If you do, should I not share in the riches?"

Kitty said, "If the directions help, then a fair share, yes. But we also have valuable information, and it's we who will have to do the searching and the finding and the arranging for any profits. If your directions help, a fair share might be a third to you, and a third to each of us."

Mary laughed, got up, pulled a manila envelope from a kitchen drawer, and sat back at the table. She extracted a single piece of legal-sized lined yellow paper, smoothed it out, and donned a pair of reading glasses from her pocket.

She said, "I copied this from the translation of the original account. You can take it with you. If you find this mine and if you reap a profit, set aside one third for me, or for my sons. Will you do that?"

She looked at Kitty, who said, "Yes, ma'am."

John said, "Do you want some kind of written promise from us?"

Mary laughed again, her eye-lines crinkled and her cheeks trembling, until she began to tear up. "A . . . excuse me, a written promise from a white man?"

Kitty said, "You have *my* word, old mother. And I believe I can vouch for this man's word, as well."

"Oh, my. You should not make an elderly woman laugh so." She adjusted her glasses. "Yes, I think you can, too. One third for each of us. That's our bargain, then. Now let me read this to you. It says, 'Go to the Smoky Mountains. Go to the long mountain of long shadows, which lies on the sunrise side of the two brothers peaks and stands above the valley of the three sisters where the slow waters split. Begin there. Go up the creek on the right hand until you come to a big rock like a beaver head. Go one hundred and twenty strides to a cut. Go up the cut. Mine is under the rocks. Remember, it is protected by the spirits of the *Aniwaya*.'"

She removed her glasses and folded them with a spotted hand. "That's all it says. Nobody knows what the long mountain of the long shadows is, or the two brothers mountains. The long mountain could be a ridge. I do know they used to call corn, beans, and squash the three sisters because they planted them together. The beans clung to the cornstalks and the squash leaves shaded out weeds, so they must have planted in this valley the journal talks about. But these are probably places only Walker Shade and his family and a few others knew—so you could say it's a kind of code, I suppose. And there are many splits, many forks in the mountain waters. But still I hope it will help you. Take it and call me from time to time. Tell me how it goes, will you?"

In the Jeep heading back to Maggie Valley, Kitty read the neatly hand-printed paper again and shook her head. "Doesn't look like it's going to be much help, does it? We can check out the topo maps, of course, but this is pretty vague. It might come down to some plain ol' hiking. There are a lot of ridges and peaks in the area we figure Mose could have worked, and every valley has creeks with forks. It's going to be tough to cover all that terrain. It'll take a while, anyway."

"I don't know."

"Of course. Your plane. We'll do an aerial survey. Check out different perspectives. Take pictures. That ought to help a lot."

"Worth the try. What does *Aniwaya* mean?"

"The Wolf Clan."

"There are seven clans, right?"

"Yes, and that can be confusing The Wild Potato Clan people dug up potatoes in the swamps and along the streams, for instance, but they were also known as the Bear, Raccoon, or Blind Savannah Clan. People of the Long Hair Clan, the *Anigilohi*, wore elaborate dos, like some of your female country singers or your preachers' girlfriends, and were sometimes called the

Wind Clan. Usually the peace chiefs belonged to the Hair Clan. The Wolf Clan was the largest. Most of the war chiefs belonged. The Bird Clan people were great hunters. They used snares and spears. Good with blowguns, too. The Deer Clan people, the *Ani-kawi*, were protectors of the deer and known for speed on foot. The Paint Clan practiced healing. They used a lot of wild plants. The Blue Clan people were healers, too, and also known as the Panther or Wildcat Clan."

"You're a Blue, then?"

"Wise guy. No, my ancestors were in the Bird Clan. *Anitsiskwa.* A long time back they may have served as the messengers between settlements and to other peoples. Like the birds are messengers in a lot of Cherokee legends. Anyway, what's next?"

"We could go online and check out area maps and satellite photos, but it might be better to look at the large-scale topographical maps at the county offices. The Maggie area and a good chunk of the Smoky Mountains National Park are in Haywood County."

"The reservation is in Swain and Jackson Counties. I guess the Swain County office would be closest. Is that in Bryson City?"

They spent the rest of the morning studying Swain County maps spread out on a large table in a musty back room, with the help of an affable and patient older man who knew the area well, but with no luck.

They stopped for a late lunch at a rustic roadside restaurant and ate smoked turkey sandwiches on the screened porch in a pleasantly warm but damp breeze. Rain showers were still blowing randomly through the mountains. They ordered coffee and a single bowl of hot apple crisp with ice cream, and attacked it from both sides.

"We have a hundred-and-seventy-year problem with all this," John said.

"I know. The terrain in our search area has changed a lot over those seventeen decades. Road building all over the place. Whole towns cropping up and sprawling out."

"Some hillsides blasted down, other hillsides stabilized, swamps filled, creeks diverted or dried up. Chunks of mountains quarried. Whole forests logged out and regrown. But we'll keep looking."

They visited the county offices in Jackson and Haywood and went over large black-and-white aerial photos and more topographical maps intricately striped with contour lines, but had no better luck.

Later in the day, he took Kitty home so she could get ready for her shift at the casino. As tentatively as a bird, with a gesture that surprised and moved him on some deep level, she touched a hand briefly to his shoulder before getting out of the Jeep, and said, "Thanks for the ride, Sherlock. That was fun, even though we didn't learn a darned thing. When can we go flying?"

He looked into her eyes, cleared his throat, and said, "I've got a remodeling job I need to look at in the morning for estimating, but I'll be free after nine. Weather's supposed to improve. I'll call you."

"Good. I'll see you tomorrow, then."

He watched her walk to her house, turn, and wave. He returned the wave. The day had sailed by all too quickly. Her scent lingered in the Jeep. He realized he'd been taking mental images of her, and he once again felt guilty and ashamed of his tacit betrayal of Valerie's memory. He pushed the strong conflicting emotions aside and drove away.

The sky was solidly overcast, and the light was dimming. Halfway up the steep, wet road to Eaglenest Ridge, he could see red winking ominously through the trees ahead. He shifted and picked up speed.

Frantically flashing red lights and brilliant white strobes were garishly painting his house and the surrounding trees. Two white-clad EMTs were loading a stretcher into an idling ambulance when he pulled into his yard and stopped, skidding on the gravel.

CHAPTER 18

Hank was standing on the grass beside the driveway, tapping the fist of his right hand into the palm of his left, despair etching his wrinkled features. One EMT climbed into the back of the ambulance. The other quickly closed it up, nodded to Hank, got behind the wheel, and drove off down the hill, lights and siren strident. John said, too loudly, "What is it?"

"She fell bad, John. Hit the back steps all along her left side. Banged her head on the rail, and that don't look good. Bleedin'. I know a head wound does that a lot—seen that enough in the war, but this don't look good at all. What am I gonna do, John? I don't even remember a time when we wasn't together."

John placed a hand on the old man's shoulder, squeezed, and said quietly, "Hattie's strong, just like you. Grab your jacket, and we'll follow them. Where are they taking her?"

"Haywood."

"Good people there. They'll do everything possible."

In the Jeep, Hank said, "It's my fault."

"Why do you say that?"

"She slipped on the wet leaves back there. I shoulda had those cleaned up yesterday. Meant to. Got side-tracked tryin' to get a new tune on the fiddle just right. My fault."

"You don't need to be thinking that way, Hank. It was an accident. An accident can happen to any one of us, any minute, any day."

"She was scared."

"Of what?"

"Before the ambulance got here, I had her covered up with two quilts, pillow under her head, tryin' to make her comfortable as I could. She'd been out there by the garden seein' if it ought to be weeded, I guess. Or how she wanted to finish the plantin'. I didn't want to move her, you know? Didn't want to chance makin' it worse."

"You did what you could for her."

"She was in and out. Wasn't makin' a lot of sense. Said she spotted this man out there in the woods, and he ducked behind a tree. Scared her. She tried to get back to the house fast. The steps was wet, the handrail was wet, then there was all those leaves on the steps. Leaves're like ice when they're wet. She went down hard."

"She say what the man looked like?"

Hank shook his head, his expression miserable. "That don't matter. It was my fault."

At the Haywood Regional Medical Center in the

town of Clyde, Hank stood in front of the glassed-in reception desk and distractedly filled out and signed papers. They were politely asked to please take seats in the waiting area. A doctor would talk to them when more was determined about Hattie's condition.

John hated hospital waiting areas. They were thick with frustration, fear, despair. People trying to hang on to some semblance of normalcy after their worlds had suddenly taken dizzy, frightening swings out over the void.

Hank got up, went over to the windows, his hands jammed in the back pockets of his jeans. He stared out at nothing. A woman in the corner was feeding a baby with a bottle and talking to the little bundle, saying, "Don't you worry, honey, your daddy's gonna be just fine. You'll see. He's gonna be okay. Please, God. He's gonna be okay."

A man in dirty overalls came in holding a blood-drenched handkerchief tightly over his elbow. The woman at the reception desk called somebody and they took the man inside.

John looked at the ceiling and thought. It had been a rainy, dingy gray day. Wind stirring the indistinct shadows. Hattie might well have imagined a figure in the woods. Her eyes were not all that sharp anymore. There were times when she was vague. She had a calm, matter-of-fact belief in spirits and ghosts. Her aging imagination might well have deceived her. But for some time now, he'd had the uneasy feeling of being watched. Followed. Stalked. Could this be connected with his past? He had once flown for a wealthy dealer in light weaponry, a man whose tentacles reached around the world into many trouble spots. Dealing most profitably in death. John had seen a lot. Too much. It was why he had gone into the witness-protection program in the first place. So from the perspectives of several of his old employer's friends, maybe he'd seen far too much and thus posed an intolerable risk to them. Had old enemies found him? If people around him were suddenly in danger because of him, what should he do?

After an interminable hour and forty minutes, a young woman in white came out to talk to them. She looked competent. Efficient. She smiled tiredly and said, "We have her stabilized. She has a hairline fracture in her hip. Contusions. A badly bruised forearm. Our biggest concern is a concussion. She took a bad thump on the side of her head. It always sounds so trite to tell families we're doing everything that can be done, but that's the truth. She's in, let's say, very guarded condition. You can go in to see her, but she's sleeping and doesn't need to be disturbed, so only a few minutes, please. There's nothing you can do here. If you'll give me a cell number, we'll call you the minute anything changes."

She looked so frail in the hard-chromed recliner bed. So insubstantial. They had her bandaged and hooked up, instruments tirelessly and indifferently monitoring her life signs. Hank sucked in a breath and teared up when he saw her. Started to take her hand, then did not for fear of waking her.

John said quietly, "What we can do is go home and get together some things for her. Her robe. Pajamas. Clothes. Hairbrush. Things she'll need."

Hank wiped a veined, spotted hand across his eyes and said, "Yeah. Okay, John. Been thinkin' what she'd do if it was me. I know what she'd do. So maybe we could make a stop on the way home?"

They stopped at the stone church in Maggie Valley. A changeable Plexiglas-cased roadside sign said, "Spring—God's Greeting Card." Reverend Boyer and his wife lived in a stone cottage behind the church. John parked in the gravel lot. Boyer was in his home office, books and papers spread over his desk. He gestured for Hank and John to sit on the couch facing his desk.

Hank said, "It's Hattie, Reverend. Fell and got hurt pretty bad. She's over in Haywood. I figure if it was me hurt, she'd come here. Ask for a spot of help from the Big Man upstairs."

Boyer nodded. "Sorry to hear that, Hank. People here hold your Hattie in pretty high esteem. I'll put her on the prayer list for Sunday's program. And we might as well say a few words right now." He took a moment to compose his thoughts, then said a simple prayer asking for strength and healing.

Hank said, "Thanks, Reverend."

"You know, people in this town will do about

anything they can to help you or Hattie. Call on them if you need to for any reason. I'll go visit her in the hospital."

Boyer's wife, Susan, came into the office and said, "I couldn't help overhearing. Hattie's a lot stronger than we credit her for, Hank. And those people at Haywood know what they're about. Have you two had anything to eat tonight?"

Hank said, "No, ma'am, but—"

"Well, you just come on back to my kitchen. I fixed a big roast this afternoon. Won't take a few minutes to do up some vegetables to go with a piece of that roast, and an apple pie's almost done in the oven. Come on now, Hank. You can help. We'll fix up plates to take with you."

Hank got up and followed her. John started to get up, but Boyer held out a hand and said, "Hold on there, please, Mr. Hardin."

He sat on the edge of the couch, elbows on his knees.

Boyer steepled his fingers. "I've been meaning to talk with you. I've seen you in a back pew on occasion, when Hattie needed a ride to services. How do you like our little church?"

"Hattie loves it here. I appreciate your hospitality for her. She's a special lady."

"She told me you're actually her son, Roy."

"Long story there. But I'm just a friend to Hank and Hattie. I owe them."

"I know Hattie gets confused, slips a bit at times,

but I agree. She's among the special ones. Thinks the world of her Hank. And of you. Wishes you'd both join her in church more often. May I ask what your views are about faith?"

"I think it's great for a lot of people. Gives them hope."

"But not necessarily for you."

"Never thought much about it. I guess I have serious doubts."

"Such as?"

"Well, if there is a God, He's cavalier about our fates, isn't He? I don't understand why a perfect, loving God would allow a Holocaust. Or an Inquisition. Or kids being born with AIDS." And he thought, *Why would a great God allow Valerie to die in a bomb blast in my place?* "How many wars have been fought over religion? Millions have died in those wars over the past several thousand years. Why should we fear a God who's supposed to love us all? A lot of churches base their beliefs and rituals on some version of the Bible, but it's full of contradictions, it defies logic, it's vague, and it was only written by men. A lot of it was pulled together from centuries of hand-me-down storytelling. It's been hand-copied and translated over more centuries, with who knows how many changes along the way, and people interpret it to suit their own purposes, anyway."

Boyer smiled. "Those are pretty strong views for a man who's never thought much about it."

"Sorry. Didn't mean to rant. Or give offense.

This visit isn't about my views. It's about Hattie."

"Forgive me, but maybe something you could do for her is try to understand her. She's a believer. I mean not just a fair-weather believer."

"I know."

"I don't want to preach at you. That usually doesn't do much good, anyway, for somebody who's a hard-core skeptic. But why do you think the Bible has lasted so long? Why has it been a perennial best seller?"

"Because people fear death. They see the Bible as a possible way around what looks like personal oblivion. An alternative to just winking out in the end and falling away into the darkness. It promises heaven. A kind of after-death resort for the elite. The chosen. Maybe someplace on the other side of the Milky Way. Presided over by a nice old man with a long white beard and His martyred Son. If there's the slightest chance the story's true, they want in. Why not bet on such a dream? Nothing to lose by betting it's true. Trouble is, they get to believing their particular versions of the story so strongly they'll even torture and kill each other over it. The Catholics and the Protestants in Northern Ireland. Knee-cappings. Garrottings. Public bombings. The Shiites and the Sunnis. The hatred between Jews and Muslims. Between Muslims and Christians."

Boyer leaned back, his chair creaking, gazed at the ceiling, laced his fingers on top of his head, and said, "How do you read a newspaper?"

"A newspaper?"

"Let me suggest you read a newspaper in at least four distinctly different ways. You scan the front page. That's the hard news. You presume it's pretty much word-for-word facts, right? And you accept it. Now turn the page. There's an editorial. One man's humble opinion on something. You understand it's biased, right? Then you've got the advertising, and you presume a degree of exaggeration there, to say the least. Cream-puff Buick, owned by a little old lady just used it to go to the Presbyterian church in Maggie, and she only listened to gospel music on the radio. The last page is the comics, my favorite section. That's all metaphor and obvious extreme exaggeration. But there's a current of incontrovertible truth throughout that newspaper, can't you agree? There is a Buick, after all, behind that ad, if not an old lady. The comics hold up a mirror to us. The editorial discusses a real issue. You can see the underlying truth in your newspaper.

"You're right, the Bible didn't fall out of a cloud. But if you'll try to see it for what it is, you'll begin to perceive its bedrock truths. Of course, there are many who insist every word is inviolate, literal fact, and if that works for them, fine, but I've seen people get into a lot of trouble if they insist on going down that path. Is one of God's days in Genesis the same as our twenty-four-hour day today? I guess it's liberalism bordering on blasphemy to suggest looking at the Bible as a collection of very different kinds of writing, but I do. A lot of it is hard fact, no question. Pure recounting of history. But there's also saga. And myth, like the primeval history in Genesis. There's fine poetry in the Psalms. Epistles like Paul's letters. Illustrative stories. Wisdom it's hard for anybody to argue with. Many kinds of writing. Jesus taught most effectively with parables, fables with underlying lessons. Parts are simply intended to be word pictures, to my way of thinking. But what does all that matter? There's a broad and wonderful underlying truth coursing throughout. And *that's* why it's a best seller. I think something heavy is weighing on you, Mr. John Hardin. Up to you, but with some digging, you might find something in that obtuse old book to ease your burden. Be happy to help if I can."

"I'm not sure I belong in a church. I've done some things . . ." *I've killed men.*

Boyer smiled. "You're saying you're a sinner? I've got a church full of 'em. Me included. Jacob, son of Isaac, was one of the earliest biblical scoundrels. A real con man. Deceived his father and stole his brother Esau's birthright. Serious stuff back then. Enough so Esau vowed to kill him for it. Yet he came to be called Israel. Leader of a whole flock of sinners. We could squeeze one more in here with us, I think."

Hank showed up in the office doorway carrying a large brown paper bag in front of him with both hands. He looked less despairing. "Got supper for us here. Miz Boyer insists on it." Susan stood behind

Hank, smiling, wiping her hands on her apron.

John said, "Thanks, Reverend, and thank you, ma'am. We can both use some good food."

The brown bag filled the Jeep with a homey, tantalizing aroma. Hank held it on his lap. He said, "Thanks for stoppin', John. Feel some better now."

John was quiet for a time. After he'd parked the Jeep and shut it off, he said, "Maybe when Hattie's back on her feet, you and I ought to start taking her to Boyer's place on Sundays. I mean, more regularly."

Hank thought a bit. "Couldn't hurt, I guess."

After supper Hank collected a large suitcase full of Hattie's clothes and things and set it by the door. John called the hospital. With the practiced politeness of all such facilities, the voice on the phone reported no change in her condition and suggested they come by to see her during visiting hours the next day.

In the morning John called Kitty. The three of them met at the Haywood Center and talked with the young doctor, who said there was still concern about the head injury. "She's drifting in and out. She had a brief seemingly lucid period early this morning, but she was confused and somewhat irrational when I tried to talk with her just a few minutes ago. I think she's sleeping again. We're feeding her intravenously, and we want to do a scan today."

They spent twenty minutes by her bed as she slept, Kitty gently touching her on the arm and the forehead and talking low and soothingly to her in that ancient, instinctual way of women, while the men fidgeted and felt powerless.

John and Kitty left Hank sitting beside her and went out for a walk down the street.

He said, "She told Hank she spotted a man in the woods. Guy ducked behind a tree, and it scared her. She was hurrying back inside when she fell."

"Do you think there really was a man?"

"Maybe. Maybe not. But there's a possibility that's beginning to concern me."

"I know. I've been thinking somebody else might suspect Moses found a lost Injun gold mine."

"We've been asking a lot of questions here and there. That somebody might think we have an idea where it is."

Kitty said, "And that somebody might want it for themselves pretty badly."

CHAPTER 19

The strong Lycoming in the nose bellowed, giving its all and spinning the prop to invisibility. The Cessna gathered speed in a relatively short sprint down the runway, and they lifted off smartly into the cool dry air, ideal conditions for maximum lift. In the east the new sun was building a fire inside a long mile-high billow of cloud that lay low over the mountains, making the misty heart of it glow softly as an angel's promise. Probing, smoky shafts lanced high from around the cloud's irregular upper reaches.

Kitty said, "Wow." She was in the backseat behind John, so they could both look out the same window and discuss what they were seeing, and so Kitty could then take photos using his digital Nikon. He'd given her a quick course in taking aerials before leaving the Asheville airport. Keep the camera strap around your neck so you don't inadvertently bomb fellow Americans. Or, almost as important, so you don't lose a camera that cost thousands that I'm still paying out. Use a skylight filter. For maximum sharpness, keep the shutter speed high, and don't let the camera or your hands or arms touch the vibrating structure of the airplane while you're shooting. Avoid scratching the Plexiglas airplane windows while trying to shoot through them. Take plenty of frames from all angles. Good photographers, like those who consistently fill the pages of *National Geographic* with visual wonders, always shoot up a storm and cull it down later to a few—maybe only one—of the very best. Here's what all the buttons do. Got that?

They were wearing headsets so they could talk over the throaty voice of the Lycoming. Watching the sunrise building into a fine new day, he said, "Yes, it's nice up here. And it's always different. Makes you wonder what all the little people down there chained to the planet do."

"They actually *work* for their livings so they can keep their lawyers and doctors and politicians prosperous and their Wal-Mart stock up. In their spare time they gamble—excuse me, they game—and some of the more unbalanced ones hunt for lost Injun gold mines. And they all eat breakfast."

"I'll buy you a big lunch. Wanted to get up here while the sun's still low. Your clue sheet said go to the mountain of shadows. Now we can see the shadows."

She studied the rumpled, furred terrain. "Yeah, but *all* the mountains down there have shadows on their western sides right now. There are dozens and dozens of them. And there are creeks in almost every valley."

"Okay, so we look for features that make more or deeper shadows. A steeper mountain. A long, overhanging ridge. Cliffs. Erosion ravines. A mountaintop shaped something like a half bowl. Maybe we'll know it when we see it. Of course, it's a whole different situation late in the day, so we ought to come up again near sunset. Nothing we can do about the time of year. That can change the shadows, too. Like we talked about, I'm going to use a reasonable radius with Maggie as the center point—we'll call it the Moses Radius—and we'll try circling outward from town. Do that a couple times, maybe. If you're not starving by then, we'll grid the area in straight lines. That will cover most perspectives. 'Course it also looks a lot different from up here. It will take some imagination to understand what any given area looks like when you're standing on one of the peaks near it."

"Imagination, I have. I even sometimes imagine us actually finding this thing. Oh, look at that. Where's the zoom thingy?" She shot several frames, careful not to touch the Plexiglas with the lens.

"What do you see?"

"Two hawks over there sailing around that peak. They make it look like a ballet, only better. They stand out because of that thin mist still in the valley beyond. Think I might have got one just as a shaft of sunlight made its wings flash for a second. *That* should be a good shot."

"Sometimes you just get lucky."

John had folded a sectional chart earlier to show the search area he'd roughly circled in yellow highlighter. He pulled it out of the side pocket and placed it on the passenger seat so he could refer to it and mark it up with any promising spots. Kitty had her own map that showed topography and streams in some detail. He scanned around outside for traffic and banked westward for Maggie Valley.

It was four days after Hattie's fall. She was no longer hooked up to all the frightening electronics, but was still in the Haywood Center, in a semiprivate room with potted flowers she could plant one day around the house, hopefully. She had long periods of her old remarkable lucidity and cheerfulness, with only brief lapses into bewilderment and confusion now. Not so different from the way she had been before the fall. Hank was spending as much time as he could by her side. The doctors promised to let her go home within a few more days, but warned she must get plenty of rest until the hairline crack in her hip healed sufficiently. There would be a chromed walker and, of course, too many prescribed pills. Hank had said, "Gives me a chance to wait on her for a change. Don't know how long we can keep her in bed, though, with no better cookin' than you and me can manage. She's got us spoiled."

She had not seen enough of the man she insisted had been acting suspiciously in the woods to describe him as anything more than a darting phantom in a dark jacket and a billed cap. Hardin had studied the ground in the trees behind the house, ranging out for a hundred yards, but it was thickly carpeted with leaves that did not take footprints. Maybe the man had been a hunter looking for deer trails so he could plan out next season's stalk, or somebody out shooting squirrels, or simply a hiker, just as startled as Hattie had been. But in any of those cases, he should have seen her fall. *So why didn't he come out of the trees to offer help?*

Kitty pointed a slender dark finger past his shoulder and said, "There's your place. You have an aerial of it?"

"Matter of fact, I don't." He unlatched the window and let the slipstream float it up to hang just under the wing. He said, "Shoot. Then we'll swing over so you can take a few of your place, if you can see enough of it through the trees." She had contracted a beginner's excitement with photography, the excellent glass on the Nikon presenting the world from a whole new and fascinating viewpoint. He'd felt the same way himself when he'd first begun to use the camera.

Leaning forward on the backseat and keeping the long lens back just far enough so the hundred-mile-an-hour wind could not try to snatch it, she shot out of the window over his shoulder as he banked the Cessna to dip the landing gear out of her way. Some dark silken strands of her long hair reached out playfully in the breeze spilling in the window to brush his cheek.

She said, "Got it. This is fun."

From an altitude of a thousand feet above the tallest mountains, he started out directly over the village and flew outward in a lazily increasing spiral. There was full sun now, so shadows were prominent. They scrutinized the terrain serenely sliding by below, John trying to divide his time safely between looking, flying, and scanning the sky for other planes in the area.

He said, "Wait a minute. Look right here." He pointed with his right hand, flying with his left. "The bigger peak is Moody Top, I think. To the west we've got two similar mountains, maybe the brothers the journal mentions, a tad more than two miles apart I'd guess, and there's a creek in the valley between. Can't see if it divides."

She consulted her topo map. "Right. Moody Top. It's casting a pretty good shadow. The two brothers hills in the west could be Hemphill Bald to the north and Little Bald Knob to the south. That's Fie Creek in the valley. It's a solid crooked line, and it meanders a lot so it could have some slow-water stretches. There's a no-name crooked dashed line branching from it. I guess that means a branch that carries water in heavy weather or in springtime after a snowmelt. Maybe it carried more water a century and three quarters ago. The branch cuts right across the Great Smoky Park boundary. I'd say Fie Creek is a possible. There's a back road running through the valley near it. I'm marking it."

He spiraled out to the circumference of his charted

circle and back again to Maggie Valley, then he cut across the area in a series of straight lines to gain new perspectives. They found four more possible creeks, and Kitty marked them on her map.

He climbed in another lazy spiral to a mile above the mountains, where they could look far west into Tennessee and see rank after rank of mountains and ridges wrinkling away in all directions. The air was cold so he closed the window. He kept the Cessna in a gentle bank on a radius of a dozen miles with Maggie at the center. They were quiet for several minutes, enjoying the expansive view, then he felt the plane dip and skid a bit and she squeezed between the seats, brushing his shoulder with a warm taut thigh, to move into the front passenger seat and buckle up.

She said, "Maybe we need to think some more about that man Hattie saw."

He considered for half a minute. Valerie had never known she was in any danger because he had never told her. *She had no warning.* He took a deep breath and said, "Something I guess you ought to know. I'm not supposed to tell anybody, but I've been in WITSEC for a while. Witness Security, or another name for Witness Protection. It's a long story. Flew for a guy who dealt in weapons all over the world and saw too much, so I went into the program and changed my name to Sam Bass. This guy found out I was on Ocracoke Island, trying to run a one-horse air-charter business. There was trouble, and that's when Valerie died. The marshals changed my name again to John Hardin and I had some work done on my face. The guy I flew for is out of the picture now, but he had a lot of friends who might think I learned too much about what they do, so the marshals thought it best for me to keep the Hardin name, and I already had the whole identity built up, so it was the easiest thing to do, anyway. My point to all this is, that man in the woods might be out of my past. Not connected to this gold hunt at all. I don't want you or anybody to be in danger again because of me. Hattie's already been hurt pretty badly."

"And *she* thinks you're Roy Gaskill. With all these names, you must *really* get a lot of junk mail. Sorry. Thanks for letting me know. I won't tell anybody. It's none of my business, but you're not to blame for Hattie's accident. I don't think you should hold yourself responsible for Valerie's death, either. And listen, don't be worrying about me. We're doing this together because we both want to. I've always been able to pretty much take care of myself. But I'll keep an eye out for anything unusual and let you know if I spot something out of place. Okay?"

"Okay. I don't think Hattie down deep really sees me as her son in her more rational spells. She just wanted to so badly she constructed this fantasy. Because I think it must be especially hard to take to see a son go out on the ocean one day and just vanish. At times she might believe her fantasy on some level. She might just have to in order to live with the pain. Anyway, Hank and I go along with it out of habit. Sometimes I even begin to see them both as kin. You want to fly some?"

She took the dual yoke and said, "Okay, I've got the airplane. Which way is Orlando?"

"Let's get a late breakfast first. Pull off some power and fly about two-thirty on the directional gyro. There's a small country strip not far out of Sylva. We'll take their courtesy car. It's an old pickup held together with baling wire and a prayer. A smoker. Rumor is they crank it up sometimes in the summer just to kill mosquitoes. I know a place where they make ham biscuits so good they ought to be illegal."

They decided there was no real need to fly the Moses Radius near sunset, at least until they had ground-searched those likely spots they'd marked on the map.

◊ ◊ ◊

Later that afternoon, after he had dropped Kitty off, he drove to the Haywood Center to visit Hattie and pick up Hank. She seemed to be doing better, complaining at being kept in the place longer than necessary, asking if they had been eating too much junk food, giving them a list of more items she needed them to bring. They left quietly when she fell asleep.

At home John made edible spaghetti using a

canned sauce. They watched TV for an hour after the sun had gone down. Hank looked worn out and still deeply creased with worry, and distractedly said he was going to gather the few things Hattie had requested and turn in early.

John said, "There was one about a part-Indian Western man with a tough paint mustang. Runs an endurance race against long odds across the Arabian Desert. Going for a hundred-thousand-dollar prize. Competitors trying to kill him. At a low point he and the horse seem nearly finished, way to hell and gone from anywhere, the horse is wounded, no water, and the guy asks the spirits of his ancestors for help. It's based on a true story about a man named Frank Hopkins, actually won four hundred killer cross-country horse races in the eighteen-hundreds. Omar Sharif was in it. Viggo Mortensen played the lead."

Hank smiled, erasing some of the worry lines. "That's easy. *Hidalgo.* Good story. A scene at the end shows a herd of mustangs runnin' free. Hopkins fought to save wild horses in real life."

John had spotted a videocassette of that movie among books on a shelf in the couple's bedroom two weeks earlier when he'd gone in there to fix a sticking window at Hattie's request.

When Hank had turned in and the house was quiet, he pulled on a sweatshirt, went outside with binoculars, stretched out on his back in the cool, damp grass of his front lawn, crossed his ropers at the ankles, and looked up.

The fine-ground glass tugged them fractionally closer. Made the pinpricks become period-sized and much more numerous. Sprayed his retinas with whisper-thin million-years-old photons that could only hint to him how it all was out there so incredibly long ago. He let the Little Bear point out Polaris, aligned within a single degree with earth's spin axis and so holding faithfully constant in the night.

We probe with telescopes and sweep it with radio antennae, hoping to pick up a hint of what it's all about. Cudgel our brains over it. A lot of people just ignore the whole thing. Choose not to think about it. When Galileo pointed a homemade telescope into the void and found out earth isn't the center of everything, the Church made him get down on his knees and apologize. Forced him to spend the rest of his years under house arrest.

The abstract edge-on spattering of our galaxy ran like a river across the whole sky, and he panned the binoculars across the incredible expanse of it. He recalled an old Cherokee story about it.

People had a corn mill. They'd grind corn and leave it near the mill overnight, but one morning they discovered some of their corn was missing. The theft happened several nights in a row, so one night the people took long hickory sticks and lay in wait behind their hut. Sure enough, along about midnight a huge black dog stole down from above and started eating their cornmeal. They leaped out, shouting and waving their sticks, and the startled dog jumped up and loped off into the north sky. As he ran, cornmeal trailed out of his mouth. The trail became the Milky Way, and the Cherokee would afterward know it as "where the dog ran."

Is that a worse explanation than all of everything starting as an exploding speck, which is the best the geniuses can do? Maybe I like the black-dog story better.

That faint smudge in Orion. In the eye of the orbiting telescope, it's a tie-dyed veil—what's left of a busted sun.

Pick out a speck. How about that dim one? That alien sun I choose—so far away—maybe has its own collection of rocks swinging around it carrying God-knows-what creatures, who could right now be looking back at dinosaur-age light from our own sun. That alien sun could suffer some great internal seizure and detonate this second and by the time the blast light gets heres, we, and the earth itself, could be long gone.

It's all in such delicate balance. Old stars dying but seeding great hazy furrows of vastness with their dust. New stars born out of the dust and gasses. Black holes vacuuming up everything within their gravity fields. Quasars and pulsars signaling like beacons. Wheeling galaxies of stirred stars by the billions. All of it doing a slow dance across time to some song we can't hope to hear.

And something had to begin it all. We've always sensed it. Given it a lot of names. Feared it. Cut the hearts out of living virgins as gifts to it. Tried to glimpse it. We're born into all the endless evidences of its work, but some of us are always skeptical anyway. Or at least skeptical of all those who claim to be so certain of their particular versions of it. Their human descriptions.

Couldn't hurt, Hank had said. Maybe Hattie knows something I never did. So maybe there's a glimpse of it to be had in Boyer's little stone church.

We'll see.

◊ ◊ ◊

John parked the Wrangler in a rutted turnout by Fie Creek. Kitty's hair was held back with a black biker's do-rag printed with miniature lightning bolts. She was wearing jeans, low rubber-soled boots, and a denim jacket over a T-shirt. She shrugged on a backpack like she'd done it many times before, and she carried a short walking stick hand-carved to resemble a straightened snake with a mouse in its mouth at the gripping end. "It was my father's," she said.

He was wearing Western shin boots with composite soles, old jeans decorated with frayed holes and crusted paint splotches, a Windbreaker over a T-shirt with a faded image of the Wright Brothers "Flyer" on it, and a billed cap. He strapped on Moses' tattered backpack with an olive surplus trenching tool lashed on top. He carried a honed Bowie knife on his belt. With its heavy ten-inch brass-hilted blade, he'd found it to be a useful tool—still small enough to peel an apple yet big enough to cut brush or chop campfire wood like a frontier machete. And a formidable weapon if necessary.

She looked up at the early morning sky, painted with long soft strokes of pink and gray, and said, "I've always wondered, what if you came out of a cave you'd been in for days, losing all track of time, and you saw a low-sun sky and had no compass, could you tell if it was a dawning or a sunset?"

"There are clues sometimes, I guess. Dew. Fog. Frost."

"Maybe you'd recognize some differences in the songs of the birds. Or, deeper down, maybe you'd sense a special stillness in a dawning, a newness. Or a quality of rest in a sunset."

They set out along what looked like a long-disused hiking track that paralleled the creek. She was in the lead.

"Anyway, white-eyes, you're in my element now," she said back over her shoulder. "Injun territory."

Her long dark hair cascaded from beneath the do-rag, sheening when a sun ray stealing through the trees brushed it. Trying to look anywhere but at the backside of her jeans, he said, "Good thing I've got an Injun guide. Just show me where the yellow metal is and I'll give you a trinket. Maybe an iPod."

"If I find the yellow metal you'll owe me a whole Wal-Mart. So we're looking for a fork where the waters go still."

"Take a right there, go to a boulder that looks like a beaver, go a hundred and twenty strides. Go up another branch, and you can't miss it. This may be your element, but your people don't give any better directions than a cop does in New York City."

"A beaver's *head*. And the writer was trying to keep the location secret from everybody but those of his kin who would know what he was describing. I'd say that was pretty clever."

The trail gave way to trackless forest. They picked their way over mossy rocks and around brush and deadfalls. Muddy hillside swales fed their seepages to the creek, which happily obeyed its ancient duty of hunting lower ground until it discovered a stronger river to join, a restful lake to mingle with, or a restless ocean that could take it on a journey around the planet.

They stopped after maybe two miles for a drink of bottled water.

"You move pretty well out here," she said.

"Wasituna taught me a few tricks. I've been thinking. Moses probably didn't just stumble over this mine."

"You're saying something led him to it?"

"Suppose he was panning along in this creek, could have been over weeks or months. I don't know, stopping to check out gravel under still pools after stretches of fast water, the way that gemstone woman, Effie Traylor, told me to do it. Finding a flake of gold here and there. Maybe when he got to a fork, he panned both branches but could only turn up gold in one. So he followed that one upstream."

"So maybe a trail of gold finally led him to the mine. Sure. It makes sense."

He shrugged the backpack off, untied the small spade, and got out the gold-pan kit. He walked to the creek and looked it over. There was a shallow, relatively quiet pool on the other side in a gentle bend. Carrying the pan and trencher he picked his way across, stepping on stones, careful to trust only dry spots because the wet areas were exceedingly slick. He set the pan on the far bank, chose a place near a large rock, and dug down into the gravel, making a pile, trying to find hard bottom.

When the trencher struck a large, flat rock, he scraped along the top surface with care, and deposited a spade-full of the gravel into the pan. Squatting on his haunches, he allowed water to flow into the pan and shook it gently. He lifted out the screen insert to remove the larger pebbles, which he poked through with a finger before discarding. He dipped some more clear creek water into the pan and swirled it around three times, watching it become cloudy, letting some spill over the lip. He repeated the process several times, sloshing too much water out along with some of the gravel, but beginning to get a feel for it. He stirred through the fine sand and gravel remaining, looking it over intently. Flecks of rock and minerals caught the sun, and the sand moved in the remaining water in abstract swirls, but there were no rewarding dull gleams of gold among the bright bits of old rock. He tried three more pans but with no more luck.

He shook the final beads of water out of the pan,

put it away, and shouldered into the backpack, and they moved on up the creek. Over the next mile they stopped six more times and he patiently tried the panning, with no success. A crow laughed rudely from a tall tree nearby.

Kitty took a turn at it and said, "Well, it's fun, but either we don't know what we're doing or there's not much gold in Fie Creek."

He said, "I admit I don't know what I'm doing. There's a lot more to it than you'd think. I guess you develop skill at reading a creek so you know where it could be hiding its gold. Acquire an instinct for it. If Moses were here he could probably point out all the probable paydirt." He selected another spot and tried another pan-full.

Kitty scrutinized the creek bank, turned over a flat stone, and said, "Ah, there you are, little guy." She motioned to him. "Come here. Look at this."

He stepped over to her on selected stones, carrying the empty pan and trencher.

She picked up something that looked like a fat cousin to a chameleon, placed it on a mossy rock, and said, "It's a dusky salamander. They like being close to the water. There are creatures all around us. Neat, huh?"

Three miles farther on they came to a swampy area where the water was sluggish and choked with reeds. He stood, hands on his hips, looking around. Kitty walked a way ahead and called, "This could have been a fork at some time. The creek, what's left of it, bends off to the left, and there's a definite depression sort of wending off there to the right. Let's follow the depression for a bit."

But it didn't feel right, and before long the land tilted sideways and the depression disappeared.

Kitty said, "Looks like a dead end to me. But it's time for lunch anyway. Let's climb up that way, see where it goes."

The trees were thick, but there was not much underbrush so they climbed easily, breathing deeply, working up a sweat, wading through a profusion of low white flowers like a recent snowfall. "It's *phacelia*," Kitty said.

To her delight she found a cluster of white-striped jack-in-the-pulpits amid ferns in a shadowy glade, and stooped to touch them. They passed a blaze of fire pink, and she pointed out several closed buds of purple gentian. "They're waiting for worker bees to come along and trigger them open to give up their nectar."

They eventually came out into a clearing beneath an eroded, jumbled cliff riven with cracks. They picked out a route up to the cliff top and took off the backpacks. They sat side by side and hugged their knees. Letting their breathing settle down and their heart rates subside. There was a view out over the forest to several hazily distant furred humps, and it was as though they had journeyed back in time. No buildings or roads in sight. No evidences at all of human habitation.

He felt peaceful from the exertion. Better, in fact,

than he'd felt soul-deep inside for a long time. Content to be in this wild place beside this woman.

The forest smelled of sun-heated leaves and flowers and musty soil. Birds called to each other in sweet liquid trills higher up the hill.

She reached for her backpack and got out their lunch. They took their time with it, slathering peanut butter and homemade apricot jam onto squashed wheat bread. They munched on handfuls of her version of trail mix from a generous baggie, crunched hard tart apples that squirted juice, and took turns using a saltshaker. They drank from bottled water that tasted especially sweet after the hike.

He helped her clean up their trash and put everything away. He got two fresh bottles of water out of his backpack. She pulled off the do-rag, tilted her head back, shook it slowly from side to side, and with primitively feline motions combed her long hair back with her fingers, making his breathing quicken involuntarily. He had to look away at nothing in particular down through the trees. She leaned back, her hands propped behind her, her shoulders pulled in, and looked up at the sky.

She said, "Can you feel it?"

He studied her profile.

"We call her Mother Earth, and out here in the woods, where it's been like this since before we kept track of time, there's a spiritual presence. Everything moves quietly, everything grows and changes. Gets renewed. Everything *breathes*. There's peace here. Hard to put it into thinking terms, because it's much more involved with feeling. Somebody once said home is someplace we recognize when we're there, and a place we long for when we're away. Out here is home to me." She looked at him with a disarming openness and smiled. "I'd make a guess the sky is home to you. Where you can spread your wings and taste the wind."

"It's where I feel free."

She nodded and looked out over the forest. "When I'm home, I feel thankful, mostly. For all the beauty. For my strength. For life. What a gift it is. The Shawnee Tecumseh said, 'When you arise give thanks for the morning light. If you see no reason for giving thanks, the fault lies in yourself.'"

He had seen skies so full of light and ephemeral beauty he could only hope to sample it. To taste it. He said, "Yes."

"We're taught a lot about spirits. There's a prayer to the Great One my mother taught me. It's all about offering thanks. To the spirit of fire or sun in the east for warmth and light. To the earth spirit in the south for peace and rebirth. To the water spirit in the west for purity and strength. And to the wind spirit in the north for wisdom and giving. For the beauty of all things. Wherever I am, when I see something beautiful, I think of home. Of out here."

He wanted to say, *Lately, when I see or hear or touch something beautiful, I think of you.*

Instead he said, "The Great One. I like that. Seems to cut across different faiths. Different denominations, and the Great One sure knows there are a lot of those. Back at the eastern end of the state, churches are always splintering over some issue. If you leave your shed empty for more than two weeks somebody will start a new church in it."

They held to their own thoughts for a time.

He said, "I don't know much about you."

"We lived in Oklahoma outside Tahlequah. Moved back here when I was seven, but not to the reservation. My parents bought a small farm near Bryson City. Mom taught sixth grade. Dad had a trucking business. Hauling sand and gravel. We never had a surplus of money, but we were happy. I'm the youngest of three. A brother and a sister. They went back West. I see them twice a year or so. My parents are gone. I worked my way through Western Carolina U in Cullowhee. Majored in business. One day I'll start something, maybe selling Cherokee arts and crafts. Right now I don't want too many anchors. Got emotionally banged up in a long-term relationship, so I'm gun-shy. When things begin to close in around me, I get on the bike and let the wind blow my head clear again. I go up on the parkway and find some hiking trail into the woods, you know?"

He nodded. He wanted to touch her, bury his face in a fan of her hair.

She seemed to catch a glimpse of his mind.

Flicked a surprised glance at him and raised an eyebrow. In a subconscious, mildly nervous gesture, she used her slender fingers to gather her hair—tilting her head back to display a primitively sensual profile—and stroke it backward so it caught behind her ears.

He took a long drink from a water bottle. She retied the lacings on her boots.

A cool cloud shadow drifted over them.

She said, "So. Guess we'd better be getting back."

He checked the zippers on Moses Kyle's backpack and lashed the trenching tool in place. Giving his hands something to do.

They picked their way down from the cliff, the rocky shards of it rough and warm under their hands from the sun, and walked back through the forest that drank from the dappled sunlight and yielded up its breath for them.

◊ ◊ ◊

It was ten thirty the next morning before he could get some errands run, drop Hank at the hospital and look in on Hattie himself for a few minutes, and pick Kitty up. She put her backpack on the backseat and slid into the Wrangler. He handed her the map they'd marked up and said, "Pick one."

She studied the map. Poked it with her finger. "I liked the look of this one from the air."

"Chambers Mountain."

"The 'two brothers' could be Mill Mountain and Rocky Knob. The creek in the valley is Big Branch. It eventually joins Richland Creek a few miles south, which flows into Lake Junaluska."

"Okay. Let's try it."

"How's Hattie?"

"Fretting. Wants out of there. Doesn't think Hank and I can last long on our own cooking and she's probably right. Doc says maybe in a few more days, but she'll still have to take it easy except for brief exercise tours around the house using a walker. We can get takeout until she's a lot better."

"That's good news. Maybe Hank's finally getting some decent sleep. Not worrying so much."

"How was your shift?"

"About eleven thirty one of the gamers hit a slot for twenty thousand. The casino had a guy take a lot of pictures and got her to sign a release so they can use her to advertise. They made a party out of it. They'll enlarge her and hang her on the Big Winners wall just inside the entrance. To keep the myth alive. Nobody ever wants to know how many thousands of gamers had to lose their blouses so twenty grand merely represents a minor business expense."

They took Highway 19 east for ten miles. Junaluska was coming awake with random wind riffles breaking up the reflected surrounding mountain images into a pointillistic abstract. Just beyond the lake they took a left onto 209 North and went six miles to Big Branch

Road, a narrow lane laboriously cut through the valley woods paralleling its namesake creek. He drove slowly along it so they could study the creek through the trees. The downhill pitch seemed pretty constant, and the gin-clear water was flowing briskly. He chose a relatively straight stretch of road and put the right wheels of the Wrangler up tight against a hillside. About a foot of the Jeep was still in the road, but it was white and easy for any drivers to see in plenty of time to miss it. She had to slide out on his side.

He got out Moses Kyle's backpack, and they crossed the road and climbed down the bank to the creek, holding onto trees for support. He spotted a gravel-filled depression in a large flat boulder. High water would cover it, but it was dry now. He got out a canvas tote bag holding the panning kit and a garden trowel Kitty had contributed. He hopped stones over to the boulder, squatted, and dug out a pan-load of gravel, trying to get deep enough to scrape the boulder surface clean with the trowel edge. He dipped up some water and swirled it. Picked through the larger stones and discarded them. Dipped and swirled twice more. Used tweezers to part the sand.

Nothing.

He discarded the load and filled the pan halfway again with the remaining sandy gravel. Dipped and swirled five times patiently, working the gravel down to a sedimentary residue. Ran a fingertip in an S-curve through the fine bottom silt, and several tiny gleams suddenly blinked up at him. He felt a spike of elation and waved his free hand to Kitty.

He gathered up the canvas bag and held it with the pan in his right hand. Used his left arm as a counter-balance to hop back to the creek bank.

He handed the pan to her. Her eyes widened and she touched a fingertip into the pan and withdrew it with a golden fleck on its sandy tip. "Wow. It's really there, isn't it? This must have been what Mose felt like. Let me give it a try."

They panned more likely spots for a half hour but came up with no more color. They got back in the Wrangler and drove farther up the creek and deeper into the valley with Chambers Mountain rising up on their right, looking for any boulder that could conceivably resemble a beaver's head or a branch that might fit the journal description. There was a trickle that tumbled down from their right and ran through a culvert under the road to join the creek, and they stopped to look it over, but it did not feel right. She shook her head.

He said, "Something else. You notice all this land over on the right along here is posted? I don't think Moses would have ignored that."

They went on until the creek became even steeper and angled away to the left and up in a series of waterfalls.

"This is also pretty far out on the Moses Radius," she said.

"I think this one's a bust."

"Tell you what," she said. "There's a five-mile trail around Junaluska. Let's see if you can keep up with me on it. When you get tired, we'll stop for lunch."

"How many times you want to go around?"

CHAPTER 20

"They damn sure know somethin'. They're lookin'," Frank Cagle said. "Depends how much they know, but they keep on they could stumble onto it anytime."

They were in what had been intended as a living room by the builder of the Cagle place eighty years ago. Seated in straight chairs at a fold-down card table. The worn wide-planked floor was bare and dusty. There was a pile of rusty tire chains in a corner. Two cases of oil were stacked nearby. A bony hound was curled asleep on one end of an old cracked leather couch, its ears twitching. A single bare high-wattage bulb lit the room from the center of the ceiling.

The Preacher said, "Looking where?"

"Werly Fulks said up around Rocky Knob. Big Branch Creek runs under it in the valley. They were pannin' the creek."

"Take Fulks and one of the others. You must conceal the mine." He outlined how it was to be done so it would appear to be natural.

Later that night the Preacher called the man in his home office and said, "You need to move more quickly."

"I'm doing what I can. Do you want people getting suspicious? If they see this happening so soon after Prescott—"

"Do it tomorrow."

"Listen, it's not something you can do in a day."

"Yes. It is." And the line went dead.

◊ ◊ ◊

In the man's office two days later Coleman Prescott sat on the soft leather couch across from the desk, wearing dirty jeans and a black Metallica T-shirt, his legs out straight on the carpet and crossed, his shoulders sunk into the leather, his long hair a tangled mess, his eyes reddened and nervous.

The man thought, *He's on something. I've been talking for twenty minutes, and this idiot isn't even listening.*

Coleman said, "Can we hurry this up? I have friends waiting on me."

"Well, it's just as simple as I've laid it out. A group I represent called Mountain Resort Development Limited would like to purchase a hundred-acre portion of your property in order to create a world-class resort community. The offer capital is generous, and the resort will certainly boost the value of all your acreage. Confidentially, I would conservatively estimate a fifty percent increase in appraised value within two years. We're leaving the banks out of it, so all the interest on the transaction will accrue to you, and this will provide a steady monthly income for you. Over a twenty-year term you'll take in almost triple the offer price with the points added in. There are several reasons for the structured payment plan. It's one reason my principals can afford to make such a generous offer. It also spreads your capital-gains liability out over three years. I do have to advise you, though, we're looking at several other potential sites, so we'll need your answer fairly soon. If we do move on this right away, I think I can guarantee you a generous option to purchase the adjoining one hundred acres, as well."

Coleman uncrossed his legs and sat up on the edge of the couch, wringing his hands nervously. He snorted and said, "Well, that's pretty much all bullshit."

"Excuse me?"

"You and your buddies want my land because it's the best location you could find. You pay me as little as you think you can get away with, in portions yet, put up a cluster of condos built as cheap as you can get away with, and walk away with millions."

"Well, we're profit-oriented. I certainly don't deny that. But you understand we'll be taking a major risk—that, contrary to some reports, the resort market will continue to be healthy in this area, that materials costs will not spiral out of sight, as some analysts are predicting, that buyers will respond in sufficient numbers. And we will be putting up all the costs of surveying, land preparation, roadways, design, permits, environmental impact statement, construction, advertising. A long list of considerable—"

"Bullshit again. Here's what I want. I want to join your little group of investors. I want a slice of the pie. You understand? I want in as a full partner. And I want a million dollars earnest money up front. You go talk to your guys. It's take it or leave it, as far as I'm concerned. I plan to sell off that whole side of the mountain, and there's no shortage of potential buyers, so you better tell your people to jam it in gear if they want a piece before I go meet with a couple realtors. Might be a few days before I do that. Call me, okay?"

And Coleman Prescott got up and walked out.

◊ ◊ ◊

Kitty picked up the breakfast dishes, put them in the sink to soak, and refilled both of their coffee cups. He felt slightly uncomfortable in her modest, neat kitchen. When he had called her forty minutes earlier she had said, "I've got plenty of food here. Eggs, grits. Soy bacon, which tastes pretty good as long as you close your eyes, because it looks like toy bacon. Store-bought biscuits. I can do breakfast. The coffee will be perked by the time you get here."

She sat down across the table from him. It had been a week since their last scouting hike. He'd had to do a bathroom remodeling job he'd promised a woman three months before, working alongside a plumbing outfit that had finally found their way down a waiting list to this particular project. He had put in ten-hour days in order to complete his end of the job so as to minimize the inconvenience to the home owner, a retired widow who had unknowingly bought a whole litany of problems when she'd signed for the older home. He had not charged her enough to make more than a minimal profit after materials costs.

A sodden front had pushed in sluggishly from the west and it had rained long and hard, so they would not have wanted to go into the woods anyway for three days of that week.

It felt good to be near Kitty again.

She said, "Okay, now my belly's full you've got my attention."

He pulled the map from his jacket pocket, spread it on the table, and smoothed the creases. Turned it around so she could look. "Tell me what you think." He put a finger down on a spot. "It's not one of the possible sites we chose from the air, but it might be the right one. This long ridge here. It's five hundred feet lower than Setzer Mountain just to the west. We'd probably have spotted it at sunset."

"Oh, I see. Setzer Mountain blocks the sunlight from that ridge late in the day. Shadows it. And with long shadows, like it said in the journal."

"Something else. I went to the Maggie Visitors'

Center late yesterday to pick up a handful of brochures. Thought I might find some other businesses around here that bought gold from Moses. They had a nice graphically illustrated, laminated map up on the wall there. Thing is, that map is a lot older than what we've been using." He tapped his finger again on the spot in front of her. "About thirty years ago, this used to be called Dark Ridge."

"Medicine Ridge now, huh? It's pretty close in, too. What, not more than four miles from Mose's place cross-country? A rough hike, probably, but only about eight miles or so out and back for him. The valley looks pretty flat so there could be slower water in it. There's this dirt road going partway into the valley on the west side of the ridge." She put her finger on the ragged dashed line, brushing his finger lightly. "But where are the two brothers mountains?"

He moved his finger to the west a bit. "Look at the topo lines on Setzer. You could say it actually has two summits. Same elevation within fifty feet, with a shallow saddle in between. Not something you're likely to spot right away, especially among so many other mountains and ridgelines. The journal didn't say there were two separate mountains. It said the two brothers peaks. Why couldn't the two peaks be on the same mountain?"

She was tracing hair-thin erratic blue lines with her slender finger. "If you follow Campbell Creek up from Jonathan Creek and on into the valley, it branches off into East Fork and West Fork, and West Fork has another no-name branch here, and another skinny one farther along, here. So there are at least three forks to look at. Could be more branches that were there a hundred and seventy years ago but aren't on today's maps."

"Unless we can find the beaver boulder near one of them. That will nail it down."

"I looked up a picture of a beaver in the library, by the way. Made us a copy of it."

"When you want to go have a look?"

"Why not today?"

Kitty changed into her hiking gear. He already had his boots on and Moses's backpack in the Jeep. She asked him to put the top down, and they rode through the cool morning with the wind buffeting them to Johnson Bridge Road off of Highway 19. The paved road forked away to the left, and Campbell Creek Road went straight ahead and started out only mildly washboarded until they went past what turned out to be the last of three mobile homes, then it became rapidly worse as it meandered on into the valley, deeply potholed and marshy enough in places so he put the Wrangler in four-wheel drive to get through the puddles. They crossed a rickety old wooden bridge.

He said, "Moses' bike was crusted with mud. Maybe because he came up this road."

"Not many other people have lately, for sure."

"One set of pretty fresh tracks. Too wide apart for a four-wheeler. Washed out in places. Probably a hunter or two in a pickup sometime recently."

They caught occasional glitterings of Campbell Creek to their left. He pulled into a grassy area to the side of the rutted track. They shrugged on their backpacks, and he slipped the large sheathed Bowie knife onto his belt. They walked on, following the bank of the rushing creek, swollen by the recent heavy rain.

They stopped three times where they could find relatively quiet pools and tried panning, taking turns at it, but had no luck.

The creek was high and discolored because it was scouring dirt from its banks. They passed a large marshy pool and, farther beyond, an old dying pine that was leaning precariously out over the creek.

There was a large dead water oak twenty feet from the creek. It had a deep split in it that decay had hollowed out. Hidden at the back of the split, screwed to solid wood in deep shadow, there was a small five-megapixel Stealth Cam camera, a high-end model that had come from the manufacturer painted in a camouflage design. When they passed, it sensed their presence with its passive infrared detector and fired noiselessly three times on a medium-resolution setting. The unit was designed to monitor a trail for later hunting, recording the passage of deer or other game, even in low light or at night without a flash, but it worked as well on human subjects.

They came to a branching. The main creek bore away slightly to the left. The right-hand fork was carrying much less water. They took the right-hand fork, working their way slowly through thick brush and vines.

In a clearer stretch, there was a steep-sided gully feeding a rush of muddy water into the creek from the right. John climbed up a way beside the gully, but it seemed to flatten out, filled with matted leaves and forest debris. Water was draining out through the leaves, like several other hillside seeps they had passed. He came back to the creek, sliding in the mud so he had to hold on to saplings to keep his balance. They moved on up the fork.

She said, "I haven't seen any boulders that look like beavers."

"One back there looked like a turtle."

She said, "It's like looking at clouds, I guess. Turn your imagination loose and you start seeing all kinds of creatures."

"The creek is pretty high. Our beaver might be hiding underwater."

They kept on until the fork was lost in a swampy hillside depression. They retraced their route back to the main creek and followed it up to yet another fork. They took the right branch again. It went on for another two miles before disappearing into a series of hillside seeps.

He said, "We've been on the West Fork. The other side of this rise there's still the East Fork. We can go all the way back to where the fork splits, just after the old bridge, and go up that."

"First I think we need to refuel."

They found a large tilted slab of rock overlooking the creek, took off the backpacks, and swiveled their necks, working some stiffness out of their muscles. They sat and ate succulent Clementines, hard apples, cheese, and her homemade trail mix, washed down with bottled water.

She looked up at the long ridge. "I wonder why they changed the name to Medicine Ridge."

"Lady in the Visitors' Center said a man named Gideon Prescott owns most of the mountain. He had the name changed. Wants to make it into some kind of nature preserve. Something like Grandfather Mountain, with natural-barrier woods areas for animals, hiking and horseback trails, a restaurant selling health food, a shop selling Cherokee art."

"In Cherokee culture, medicine is a sort of mystical weaving of physical healing—a lot of which is based on herbal and holistic traditions—and spiritual healing. Medicine for the soul is as important as medicine for the body. Sounds like a great idea, but I heard Gideon Prescott died recently. Fell off a horse and broke his neck. Something like that."

He studied the ridge rising up above them. An ancient brooding land-wave frozen in time.

He said, "This Gideon Prescott is dead?"

◊ ◊ ◊

"They walked right past it," Frank Cagle said. He

showed the Preacher the images on the palm-sized digital-card reader. They were in the back room of the church after services, with Orin Cagle, Werly Fulks, and two of the other disciples, Lloyd Dobbs and Jerry Quaid, who now knew about the mine and what had happened to Moses Kyle. They were among the most loyal church members, would do anything the Preacher asked of them, and as long as they did, were to be trusted. Sis sat in the corner, leafing through an old worn and stained hardbound book of religious images. Fat silly cherubs. Angels that looked dizzy, she thought, or about to faint, or high on something. The Sistine Chapel; half the people with no clothes on, and God reaching out His hand to touch the fingertip of bare-assed Adam. *The Last Supper.* She thought they all looked drunk on the wine. That stone carving of Mary holding her dead Jesus. That was nice. How could anybody carve something like that out of stone?

Orin Cagle paced. "They could come back and find it. And all this . . . All this will be for nothing. You know what's gonna happen if they find all this out?"

Frank said, "Take it easy. We gone way too far into this thing to let off now. We just need to stop these two. Or damned sure slow 'em way on down. Lot of ways to get it done. That right, Preacher?"

Ten days before, in the first gray light before dawn, Frank, Orin, and Werly Fulks had made their way up Campbell Creek, wearing hip boots and walking in the water so they would leave no footprints. They set up the Stealth Cam, rolled the big stone sideways enough to mostly cover the hole, and carried more stones there to cover it up the rest of the way, then stuffed leaves collected at random from the creek bank below into black trash bags. They made two dozen trips lugging the bags over their shoulders up the ravine. They filled it almost level with the leaves and other rotting forest debris, and raked it all smooth with branches, until it looked like just another hillside seep. The days of rain had packed the debris to make it look more natural, and had probably erased any tracks they might have left. Frank had waded up the creek again just after sunset the night before to retrieve the card from the camera and replace it with a fresh one.

The Preacher took the small card reader from Frank and glared at the image like he could burn Hardin and the Indian woman up with just his eyes.

He said, "Yes. Slow them down. Or stop them."

◊ ◊ ◊

Later that Sunday evening, an hour after dark, the man, as was his habit, walked along the short curved bricked path lit softly with low solar-cell garden lights, across his backyard and into his home office, a large well-furnished room behind his detached two-car garage. He locked the door behind him. He put a pot of coffee on to brew, turned the HDTV on to Fox News but with the volume down, and settled himself behind his desk, beginning to organize his thoughts.

He opened the upper right-hand drawer where he kept his digital daily planner, heard the sound, and went hollow-cold inside. He whipped his hand back and whisper-screamed, "*Ah, God. AhGodahGodahGodah God*," and backpedaled his leather chair until it slammed into the wall. He got up on liquid legs and backed up sideways, frantic, trying to find the door, feeling behind himself, almost tripping on the edge of the Oriental rug, flailing his arms to keep his balance.

And saw the shadowy figure standing in the open French doorway that led out to the flower garden. He froze, the skin of his scalp prickling all over.

"Who . . . who is that?" He put his hand to his chest, where there was a sudden sharp pain. "It's *you. You* put that thing in my desk. Are you trying to give me a *heart attack?* Ah, God. What are you doing here? How did you get in? Somebody could have seen—"

The Preacher held a big rough hand up, palm out, warning him to stop talking, and stepped out of the darkness, his eyes fierce.

He said, "Sit," and pointed at a straight chair.

The man sat and held a trembling hand to his forehead.

The Preacher had a thick canvas sack in his left hand. He walked to the desk, reached into the drawer, and lifted out the darkly patterned pygmy rattler. He held it up to admire it for a moment, then let it down into the sack and slid the drawstring tight.

He said, "Sinners like you. Nonbelievers. Blasphemers. They live in ignorance of God and His wondrous power, which has no limit. Psalm Sixty-Six. 'How terrible art thou in thy works! Through the greatness of thy power shall thine enemies submit themselves unto thee.' But you show no fear of Him. And yet you turn to Him in your base needs. Where do you go when you wish to wed your whores? To the church of God! Where will your bones be prayed over? In the church of God! And when you are afraid, you scream out His name, beseeching Him to help you. Do you think God should help you? Or should He grind you to dust under His thumb?"

"Look, I met with the son. I made up a story about a group of investors who want the property to build a resort. A structured purchase plan starting with two hundred thousand front money. He wouldn't have any of it. Told me he wants a partnership in the project. And a million up front. A *million*. Told me he plans to sell that whole side of the mountain off any time now. You can't reason with this kid. I think . . . I think he's *on* something. His head isn't working right. How am I supposed to *reason* with somebody like that?"

"You will find a way. You will do nothing else until you find a way. You *will* find a way soon."

And he blended with the night outside the doorway, leaving it open to a chill breeze that lifted a corner of the drape and made it do a crazy little dance.

CHAPTER 21

The man in black stepped into the warm sunny street, a crescent shadow from his wide brimmed hat hiding his eyes. Two others showed themselves around the corner of a building farther along the street. The man in black motioned for them to find cover. One of them ducked into a deep shop doorway. The other, carrying a rifle, climbed an outside stairway to a balcony, crouched behind an ornate wrought-iron bench and went still.

The man in black shouted, "Come on out. You hear me?"

The street was quiet.

The front door of the gray clapboard building creaked open. A man emerged warily. He wore faded jeans stuffed into his boot tops, a plaid shirt, and no hat. He looked like just another ordinary cowboy. He moved into the street thirty feet from the man in black and stood facing him, his dusty boots planted shoulder-width apart, apparently unaware of the two concealed ambushers at his back.

In a clear voice he said, "Your call."

The man in black said, "I told you to get gone. I figure it's not my lookout what happens to you now."

The man in the rumpled plaid shirt said again, "Your call."

The man in black went for his gun like a striking sidewinder, but the man in the plaid shirt was already throwing himself sideways into a half-crouch, his gun out and hammering, the forty-four caliber rounds loud as thunderclaps—one shot fast as lightning to his front from the hip, then whirling and firing twice more, not a heartbeat between any of the shots, the last round blowing out a smoke ring.

The man in black looked down at his chest in surprise and shock, groped at his shirtfront with his free hand, discharged his gun at the street, and crumpled. The man in the doorway twisted out into the street and went down. The man on the balcony dropped his rifle, pitched over the railing, and fell heavily into the bed of a hay wagon.

A dart of sunlight fired from the star pinned to the plaid shirt, and the man holstered his six-gun.

Joshua said, "Cool. Now can we go get an ice cream?"

The bodies in the street stood up and, alongside the marshal, waved good-naturedly to the crowd. A honky-tonk piano started up inside the Silver Dollar Saloon, where the Can-Can dancers would flounce their skirts at the tourists again in fifteen minutes.

Kitty, John, Hank, and young Josh had ridden the inclined railway to the top of the mile-high ridge above Maggie Valley. It had been Hattie's idea for them to go spend this Saturday afternoon at Ghost Town in the Sky. She was scheduled to come back home from the hospital on Monday and had waved her hand in a shooing gesture that morning and said, "Go. Go have some fun, all of you. Take young Josh. Roy, hasn't he been asking you to take him to see Ghost Town? Well, do it then. It's too nice a day out there to be wasting it with this old woman."

They walked past the Two-Bit Hotel and Judge Fineum's place and the Olde Tyme Portrait Studio and stopped at the Iced Cream and Fudge Shoppe. The boy ordered a large double-chocolate cone. John suggested a small one to start with, and the boy reluctantly agreed. Hank bought a slab of penuche and started nibbling on it out of the paper bag. Kitty and John opted for thick milk shakes. They took their treats outside and walked out of town to find benches where they could enjoy the view. After Josh finished his cone and wiped his mouth with a small fistful of Ghost Town napkins, Hardin held him up to look through silver coin-operated binoculars mounted on a green metal pedestal. Josh tried to see the log home on Eaglenest Ridge across the valley, but could not find it until Hardin aimed the binoculars for him. The boy seemed preoccupied and somewhat distant.

John walked beside Kitty while the boy walked

with Hank to the garish amusement area, and all of them found seats on the circular chain swing, which lifted and rotated them out perilously close to a cliff edge that fell away dizzyingly beneath them down the mountain. They rode the big stomach-hollowing Sea Dragon pendulum swing, and the loop roller coaster loaded with young laughing shriekers, and the three adults stood watching Josh on the dervishing Tilt-a-Whirl, which he got back in line for three times.

After his last ride, the boy gave John and Kitty a serious look and hurried ahead to catch the Indian dance show in palisaded Fort Cherokee. They all found seats on the bleachers inside where Josh could see, and he paid rapt attention as the drums began a mesmerizing rhythm that thumped its way into the minds of the audience. An old man in traditional dress came out, raised his arms, and summoned the dancers in a deep chant. "*Yo-hoh-hee-yay.*"

The dancers came stepping out in moccasins and deerskins, rattles in hand, sacred eagle feathers adorning them. Schucka-schucka-schucka. They whirled and hunched and toe-stepped in ritual patterns from ancient centuries.

Outside, when the boy wasn't looking, Kitty used her eyes and a head gesture to say, "*Pay attention to the boy.*" Hardin walked with him, neither saying much. They stopped in the amusement area so Josh could go on all the rides again.

At the end of the afternoon, they stood in line

to ride the steep chairlift down the mountain, John paired up with the boy. They hurried into position, and an attendant held the slow-moving chair still long enough for them to get seated and pull down the restraining bar.

Hardin said, "Okay, what's wrong?"

They floated out straight until the chair lifted over the first tower support, setting them gently swinging, then began sinking silently toward the valley far below, the view vast and giddy, but the boy was unfazed, looking past his sneaker toes down to the valley and then swinging his feet back and forth. They could hear a truck laboring up a hill miles away.

Josh finally spoke. "Did you forget my mom?"

"What? No. No, Josh. I'll never forget your mother. Like for you, life won't ever be the same for me without her."

The boy pointed down toward the chair riding the cable thirty feet in front of them. "Then why are you with her?"

"She's a new friend, Curly. Just a friend."

Josh looked up at him with such searching intensity he felt compelled to explain.

He said, "Okay, I know you'll keep a secret. Back before the Trail of Tears, your ancestors, the Cherokee people, mined silver and gold in these mountains. When the soldiers came to make them move west to Oklahoma, your people did what they could to hide the mines, and only passed down the secrets of where the mines were to family members, or at least to members of the same clan. We think a friend of ours found one of those old mines not long ago, but he passed away, so we're looking for the mine now. If we find it one day, I'll take you to see it, okay?"

"For real?"

"It's a promise. Listen, after we drop Kitty off, we'll still have some time before I have to feed you and get you back home. You want to practice with the blowguns? You can draw a target on a box, and I'll pull it across the backyard on a line for you." The boy had left his blowgun at the log house, along with a baseball glove so the two of them could play catch whenever there was time.

"Cool. That's a good idea, the box for a target. Then can we eat at Salty Dog's? I like their cheeseburgers."

"We'll start off slow with the blowgun. After you get good at hitting, what you can do is keep your back to the target. I'll get it moving and then holler go, and you can spin around and try to stick the dart. It's your great-grandfather's advice. For how to practice hitting a moving target. Pretty smart guy, your great-grandfather." He rested his elbow on the chair back and squeezed the boy's thin shoulder, and they both smiled.

They watched a sleek falcon pivoting with perfect grace on the warm upslope breeze, as raptors had done in these mountains since before man started counting time.

Kitty stole an anxious glance up and backward, grinned, and nodded to herself.

CHAPTER 22

John seemed to be late with everything that day. *One of those days you can't get it all done*, he'd thought several times. He and Hank were late making it to the hospital to bring Hattie back home because the old man had taken extra time trying to dust and straighten up the house, and because John had only realized the Wrangler needed gas when they finally got on the road. At the Haywood Center the nurses took their time preparing Hattie and gathering her things.

Finally they had her home and comfortably propped up in her bed, with extra pillows and cold water with a bent drinking straw on her bedside table, her potted plants transferred to the top of a hope chest against the wall. By the time Hank had received her instructions for going about preparing lunch, and John had eaten a late lunch quickly, mostly to keep Hattie happy, he was hopelessly late for a scheduled flying job.

For the second time that day, he dialed the developer who was his client. He said, "I'm still running behind. Sorry. There's weather moving in later today, but I think we can still do the job in clear air with enough sunlight if we get moving. I can meet you at the airport office in an hour."

But there was a fender bender on Highway 19 that tied up traffic for thirty minutes, and he was late arriving at the airport, apologizing yet again to the developer, a portly, impatient man in his forties named Mack Lynch, who wanted three potential building sites shot from a variety of angles and also wanted to view the areas for himself.

There was another wait on the taxiway for arriving and departing heavies and to allow the wing-tip turbulence from the departing jet—which could flip the Cessna like a toy—to dissipate before they were cleared for takeoff.

He set a course west for a site eighty miles away in Graham County, a few miles this side of the Tennessee border, near Santeetlah Lake. A front was stampeding in from the northwest, kicking up atmospheric havoc in general—a long squall line of towering, thunderbolt-firing cumulonimbus cells, heavy rains, and turbulent winds. He wanted to get the westernmost site photographed first, before the fringes of the front arrived. At eight thousand feet above sea level, where he leveled the Cessna off and trimmed it up, he could already see the blackness beginning to amass on the very far horizon, but the day was still mostly sunny around them, with only a few high thin clouds.

After a few minutes, Lynch looked down and said over the headset, "What's all this area under us right now?"

"The Cherokee reservation." He banked the plane so the man could look down through the pilot's side window. "There's the town of Cherokee in the valley."

Lynch nodded. "On the way back, how about snapping a few shots of the acreage around the casino, if it won't cost me any extra? I'm talking with a couple Indians about building a restaurant."

John realized the man was seeing the land below as partitionable, buildable—preferably with a view—paveable, marketable. Bankable. Not so different from the way Andy Jackson's cronies had envisioned it seventeen decades before.

Just beyond Bryson City, John pointed out the old-fashioned locomotive and passenger cars running the tracks of the Great Smoky Mountain Railroad, hauling tourists from Dillsboro through Bryson City, and southwest all the way to Murphy and back.

Lynch said, "Wonder how much they net with that setup."

The vast Nantahala National Forest spread away over hills on their left. To the north, Clingman's Dome rose to 6600 feet, prominent above ranks of lesser peaks that were gathered around it, paying homage. Fontana Lake was strung out for thirty miles in front of them, woven in and out of branching valleys, backed up by a tall dam at the far end that slaked generators sending power all across the Tennessee Valley region.

Santeetlah was the headwaters for the Little Tennessee River that threaded off westward. It rested like a giant's bowl of clear nectar in a soft fold of the land, splintering the sunlight into dollar signs. They circled two areas Lynch was considering for development, and John shot from various angles the man pointed out. When Lynch was satisfied, they headed back east. Over Cherokee he shot more stills near the large low casino and its high-rise hotel that fed it a fresh, steady supply of heeled gamers. The sprawling parking lot glittered in the sun.

It required another hour to finish up what Lynch wanted, using his still camera and a small video cam for footage intended to fit into a presentation for the client's fellow investors. By then the sun was wholly engulfed by the darkness swelling tumorously along the whole northwestern horizon like something from a Stephen King nightmare.

Lynch asked him affably if he'd like something to eat, on him, and it was already well past the normal time he ate at home. Because he had left his cell phone on his bedroom dresser that morning, he called Hank from the general aviation office and said he'd be getting supper out.

They took Lynch's new GMC, which had a scattered collection of notes and brochures and receipts stuffed behind the visors and spread across the dash, and went to a Ruby Tuesday two miles from the airport. The developer got a bloody steak with fries, and Hardin heaped up a plate from the salad bar. They talked over dessert and coffee as darkness gathered outside.

Lynch said, "I hear you flew for Bobby McGinnis a few weeks back. Great guy. They say he's got some kind of hotel complex up his sleeve for a site that might be near Black Mountain, some real posh deal like the Grove Park Inn. Rooms probably four bills a night and up, but with lots of extra glitz, you know? Conference center. Tennis. Steam baths. Massages. Bidets in the bathrooms." He pronounced it bih-detts. "You shoot Bobby a few sites for something like that?"

John took a last sip of coffee, wiped his mouth, dropped the napkin onto his empty plate, and smiled.

He said, "Mack, I don't like to talk about what my clients might be doing."

Lynch frowned.

John said, "Think of it this way, Mack. Nobody will know from me what sites we photographed for you today. I figure it's strictly your business. And thanks for the meal. It was good. Why don't you let me get the tip?"

Lynch leaned back, grinned, and spread his hands, "Hey, I *like* a guy with principles, you know? You just don't run across a lot of them got serious money in the bank, though. Am I right or am I right?"

Lynch dropped him by his car in the lot by the modest general aviation building at the airport. He was about to start the Wrangler when he remembered he'd left the video cam in the kick-panel pocket on the plane. *One of those days.*

He had not gotten his workout in that day, so he took a flashlight out of the glove compartment, pulled on his light jacket against the night chill, and started walking. Three quarters of a mile from the general aviation parking lot, at a far end of the field, there were three rows of open-front T-hangars lined up near a taxiway. His hangar was all the way around in the back of the last row. The night was getting breezy, no moon or stars showing because of the encroaching overcast from the front, and there were soundless flashings low in the sky off to the northwest, like a distant battle.

There were seven hangars in a row on the back side of the buildings. His was the fourth from the corner. He was looking at the ground as he came around the corner, thinking about Kitty. An idling pickup was parked near his plane, only its parking lights on. It had no license-plate light. He killed the flashlight and walked faster. There was a man in his hangar, standing on the three-step stool Hardin usually kept in a back corner of the hangar, working on something up underneath the pilot-side wing.

Hardin switched on the flashlight, splashed the man with it, and said loudly, "What's going on here?"

The man was wearing gloves and a ball cap. He instantly shielded his face from the glare, jumped off the stool, and ran for the pickup, trying to stuff something into his jacket pocket.

Hardin began running, but the man didn't have far to go; he jumped into the truck and floored it, the driver's door slamming from the forward movement. The rear wheels spat gravel and a cloud of grit from the taxiway shoulder, spraying Hardin in the face as he raised a palm against it. He'd caught a glimpse of glasses and a graying beard. He stopped, wiped at his eyes, and trained the flashlight on the rear end of it. The tailgate was down, the bed black, but the back of the cab was dull red. Caught two numbers on the dirty plate. Four. Nine. Then it was gone around the corner of the hangar.

He went to the plane. An inspection plate was loose. He backed out two of the three screws with his fingers and used a fingernail to push and swivel the round plate aside. The aileron cable for that wing was behind the inspection opening. The steel cable had been cut, but not quite all the way through, just enough so it would probably break when he got airborne and the ailerons came under aerodynamic load. An engine failure in a light plane was bad, but fairly survivable because a good pilot could simply glide to a landing in a field or on a disused highway, or even in treetops if necessary, but a snapped aileron cable would probably result in an uncontrolled crash.

And those were usually fatal.

It was too far back to his car to have a hope of catching the pickup that way. There were at least four routes the truck could use, increasing its lead every second. He had no cell phone. His hangar neighbor, an acquaintance named Scotty, had a cherry vintage Cessna Skyhawk. Three-Three-Four-Hotel-Hotel. He knew spare keys were taped to an engine support tube inside the nose inspection hatch. He ran to the plane, yanked the hatch open, held the flashlight between his chin and shoulder, and used his pocketknife to slice through the electrician's tape that held the keys in place. He moved around the plane fast, undoing the tie-down ropes, pulling the nose-wheel chock. Climbed in and got it primed and started. Fuel gauges showing half full. Called ground control as he began taxiing out to the end of the active runway. He did a quick run-up, switched to the tower frequency, and said he was ready for takeoff.

The controller said, "That you, Hardin? How did you get Scotty's blessing to fly his cherished airplane? I thought he slept in that thing."

"Charm. Comes naturally to us pilots. Not something you guys know a lot about."

"You know there's a squall line from hell not thirty miles west? Moving our way fast."

"Just going up for a quick local. I'll beat it back." He turned on the GPS, checked and set the other instruments. "Now how about your blessing?"

"Cleared for takeoff. Monitor my freak, and I'll update weather for you."

"Thanks, Asheville."

He fed in full power and the Skyhawk faithfully

gave its all, gathered itself for a brief sprint into the building wind, and hopped aloft. He banked as he climbed to circle the field three miles out, jolting some in the prefrontal turbulence, scrutinizing all possible exit routes.

He spotted it, alone between two clumps of traffic, its taillights noticeably dimmer than those of the other vehicles, and no license light. Heading north on I-26, moving no faster than general traffic. He kept it in sight and circled higher.

A pilot acquaintance from the other end of the state, a sheriff's deputy who was sometimes called on to fly a Cessna to help track down a fleeing felon, had used his flattened hands to illustrate flight maneuvers the way pilots since the Wright Brothers have done. One hand for the plane and the other representing a fleeing perp. He'd said, "Every vehicle throws a distinctive headlight pattern onto the road, when you take a few seconds to study it. It's a combination of the light intensity and shade, headlight alignment and spread, parking or driving lights mixed in, how clean the lenses are. It's like a big old fingerprint. You get on up there to about four thousand feet above 'em where they can't hear you over the sound of their own ride, and you don't circle out too wide so the perp's own roof always masks his view straight up, and they never even know you're there. You can throttle back, do a few tight circles as you go so you don't get too far ahead, and track 'em to Hades, or set up a nice little roadblock to nail 'em anywhere you want."

The pickup, spraying out its unique light pattern, continued on I-26 for more than ten minutes, past the I-40 intersection and on through the brightly lit outskirts of Asheville. Off his left wing there was a horizon-wide army of billowing gigantic cumulonimbus with icy tops rising eight miles above the relatively puny mountains. Their angry hearts beat with bursts of lightning, their whole beings becoming visible in briefly beautiful glowings. And they were grinding closer every minute. The ground was occasionally fading out here and there as he passed through dark, gauzy wisps of cloud.

The pickup slowed and took an exit onto a road that angled tortuously away more to the northwest. Lightning revealed a gleam close alongside the road. Had to be the French Broad River, which flowed from all the way down in Transylvania County near South Carolina, up through Asheville, and on through the national forests into Tennessee to fill sprawling dragon-shaped Douglas Lake. The small town below, then, had to be Woodfin.

The pickup wound on, slower now, for another few miles, and he kept it in sight easily because there was almost no other traffic on this road.

But the sky began to choke up on him, more dark threads of cloud stealing in to obscure patches of the terrain, the lightning brighter and more frequent, the turbulence worsening rapidly. Another small cluster of lights marked a settlement. Alexander maybe? Or Marshall? He needed a map. He took note of the GPS coordinates. Memorized them.

The ground dimmed and suddenly vanished as he flew into denser cloud. Then it reappeared magically. Looked like there was a fork below. Couldn't tell which way the pickup had gone because the view abruptly disappeared again, and this time it was as though blinds descended outside all the Cessna's Plexiglas. Except for the dull embedded northwestward flowerings that signaled the even closer presence of the huge storm cells that would be packing drafts powerful enough to tear the little plane apart.

He was flying on the instruments. He was in it solidly now, he sensed, and had no choice but to turn back.

He had reduced the radio volume because he hadn't wanted the distraction. He turned it up to hear, ". . . you read me, Cessna Four-Hotel-Hotel? Hardin, are you there?"

He had no headset, so he was listening on the cockpit speaker. He put the handheld mike to his mouth, thumbed the yoke switch, and said, "Cessna Four-Hotel-Hotel. Read you five-by-five, Asheville."

"Hardin, don't scare me like that. We lost you on radar. Those cells are right on top of you. Suggest you turn east now for Marion or Hickory. They're both still VFR."

And have to explain to Scotty why his airplane happens to be at a strange airport?

"What's your weather, Asheville?"

"Marginal VFR. Ceiling twelve hundred. Winds variable and picking up. Peak gusts to one-niner. How far out are you, Four-Hotel-Hotel?"

"Fifteen GPS. I'm heading your way."

"Report five out."

When the GPS showed five miles, he called and was told winds were nearing gale force in the peaks and blowing a thirty-degree crosswind to the single runway.

The controller said, "We're going to IFR now." Which meant the field would be shutting down to all but those flying on approved and filed instrument flight plans.

"Four-Hotel-Hotel requesting special VFR." The special clearance was a last landing-option resort for anybody flying by visual flight rules when conditions were somewhat worse than marginal.

"Special VFR granted. Enter left downwind for Three-Four. Cleared to land."

The gusty turbulence was getting determined now, jolting the plane frequently and strongly. He let down to seven hundred feet above the ground to keep the long rows of runway lights in sight.

When he turned final, keeping the power up to avoid stalling in a lull between gusts, the runway was moving around in the windshield like the plane was possessed. He had to hold it in a hard left crab to keep the runway reasonably aligned in front of him. He kept more power on than usual all the way down to just feet above the pavement, the dashes flashing by below.

There is a brief time during landing when the plane has lost almost all its aerodynamic ability to fly, but has not yet gripped the pavement, so it is not really in the pilot's control and is on its own.

He straightened it up, but held the left wing down a few degrees, into the wind. The Cessna wobbled, then the left tire grabbed with a loud yelp. He chopped the remaining power, used the rudder pedals to keep alignment, and fed aileron into the wind to keep that wing from lifting. The rollout was short, and he taxied back to the T-hangars.

He pushed Scotty's Cessna back into its slot, left the keys on the dash, and tied it down. The wind howled around the corner of the building, and rain lashed loudly down onto the metal roof. He used the flashlight to search the area where the truck had been parked, and found a Phillips screwdriver and a tri-corner file on the gravel. Dropped from the man's pocket as he'd bolted for the truck.

The man had been wearing gloves so there would be no prints, but he left the tools where they lay and walked back in the soaking rain to the general aviation office, where he could call the cops.

And Scotty.

An hour later he met with two starched Buncombe County sheriff's deputies and Scotty near his T-hangar. The wind and rain had subsided. He had wrung out his clothes in the restroom, but he was still soggy.

Scotty was a muscular redhead with the prototypical temper. Red-faced, his fists planted on his hips, he said, "So you just decided to jump into *my* airplane and take off into a line of *thunderstorms*?"

John said, "Didn't see much other option if I wanted to track that pickup. Wasn't time to call you, and I didn't have my cell phone with me to call the cops. I'll ask the line guy to top up your fuel."

Scotty looked at the deputies. "You hear that? He'll pay for the gas. I want to know what charges I can press here. Theft? Unauthorized use of an aircraft? Joyriding in a bunch of thunderstorms? He'll pay for the gas, he says."

One of the deputies held up his palms in a placating gesture and said, "We'll certainly look into that, sir."

John said, "Sorry, Scotty. I might have scuffed your left tire on the landing. It was windy."

"You might have scuffed my tire? I just *bought* those tires at the last annual. You might have scuffed my *tire*?" He strode over to his storage locker, got out a flashlight, muttered, "He'll pay for the gas, for Pete's sake," and set about minutely inspecting his Cessna's gear.

One of the deputies, wearing rubber gloves, knelt, keeping his feet on the pavement, to study the gravel where the pickup had been parked, and to inspect the abandoned tri-corner file and Phillips screwdriver. He left the tools there. John showed them the open inspection port under the left wing. They shone their flashlights into the hole and took digital pictures. Made notes. Did not touch the plane. Asked questions. Asked the same questions again, but slightly rephrased. And, most importantly, did he have any known enemies who would want to do something like this?

He told them no.

Scotty came back and aimed his flashlight beam up into the inspection port.

One of the deputies said, somewhat too loudly, "Don't touch the airplane, sir. In fact, please move away from it."

Looking intently into the port, Scotty said, "Don't worry, I'm not touching anything. Well, look at that, will you? All but one strand's been cut." He counted to himself. Walked over to stand with them. "I know that cable. It's called seven-nineteen. Tough stuff. It's made by twisting seven bundles of steel wires together. Each bundle is nineteen twisted individual strands. Two thousand pounds breaking strength total. A full ton. But all you've got left here is a single bundle, less than one-tenth the breaking strength. If I recall correctly, less than two hundred pounds. You could go through your preflight ground checks, test-cycle the controls, and they'd work fine. But you take off, you put your ailerons under normal aerodynamic stress in an ordinary turn, especially in the bumpy air we have around these mountains, and this cable would be virtually certain to fail."

The deputies looked at him.

Scotty said, "I'm an engineer. I'll tell you something else. This cable moves the ailerons, which control the airplane's roll around its longitudinal axis. It's absolutely vital. I knew a man who was flying a Chipmunk in an air show once. He was doing an eight-point snap roll, okay? Quick, hard little jerks on the yoke. Well, it turned out to be a snap roll, all right. His aileron cable snapped when he was upside-down, heading for the ground fast." Scotty used his flattened hand to illustrate. "He told me he remembered thinking, 'This is really gonna hurt.' Then he decided he'd better try *something.* So he gave it some back elevator pressure and stood on full rudder. It was enough to skid and flip her over upright, and damn if he didn't wobble and stagger that sucker back to the airport and land it with just his tail controls. But this guy was a former Marine Corps fighter pilot and as sharp as they come, you understand. Somebody like Hardin here, who has no more sense than to steal a man's airplane and take off into the teeth of a squall line—somebody with limited skills and diminished cerebral capacity—certainly could not cope with the loss of his ailerons. You could probably hear the crash quite a way off. And see the smoke column from the fire."

John said, "Thanks."

Scotty carried on. "But my main point is, whoever pulled this knew precisely what they were doing. How to find the right inspection port and select the proper cable and carefully do this to it. And it would not have been all that easy to detect. I mean, post-crash. Not like putting something in the fuel, for example. This was somebody fairly clever."

One of the deputies said, "We'll keep that in mind."

Scotty waved his hand at the deputies in a dismissive gesture. "Let's just forget what I said about charges. He's got enough problems. Whoever wants to burn him down is probably a lot smarter than he is."

"Appreciate that," John said. "Nice bird you have there, by the way."

"Yes. And I like the hangar slot I have because my bird always looks that much better parked next to this wreck you more or less fly." He strode over to his big SUV, climbed in, and drove away.

The deputies said they would meet with airport security, which amounted to three rotating guards who spent most of their shifts in the passenger terminal with only an occasional tour of the airport property. They would also immediately contact the Asheville FBI people, who would conduct the actual investigation, since tampering with any aircraft is a federal offense.

In the confidential opinions of the deputies, however, there were no discernable tire tracks, Hardin had glimpsed the man wearing gloves so there would probably be no prints, and since he could not provide much of a description of the man, the offender could not likely be matched up with a known criminal or other person in the databases. And since the two numbers from the plate—especially when they had no model year or make to go on and could not even be sure of the sequence—would not likely be much help.

An hour later Hardin went through it all again for an FBI man named Donner, who brought along two technicians in an unmarked crime-scene investigation van. Donner was a serious black man in his thirties, dressed in a plain blue suit over a turtleneck, with his head shaved. The area around the plane was taped off, and Donner admonished the sheriff's deputies for not having immediately preserved the scene. John told the man about his abortive aerial chase. He also told him he could have been followed weeks ago by two men in an old red pickup of indeterminate make, and Donner made note of it on a flip pad. Donner said they would check on regional outlets for the brands of the tools the perpetrator had left behind, which were carefully bagged and tagged. He would interview the FBO operator, Fred Quick, who weeks earlier, Hardin said, had mentioned someone asking about his plane. Donner would be in touch. He should call if he remembered anything at all that might help. The airplane might be released to him by the afternoon of the next day. Donner would call about that.

Still damp and thoroughly chilled now, he got into the Wrangler at eleven thirty and headed west for Maggie Valley.

Fred Quick had said the curious stranger drove a rusty old pickup that might have been red, as best he could recall. Hardin had thought an old red pickup with two men in it had been following him. The truck he'd seen tonight was old and red. With a four and a nine on the plate. And likely from some place northwestward past Woodfin.

When he got back to Eaglenest Ridge, the house was quiet. He let himself in, changed into dry clothes, and took a cup of instant tea out onto the front porch.

The night was still and humid after the earlier storms. Slow-drifting rags of clouds, faintly edge-lit by a crescent moon, revealed patches of sequined indifferent infinity. The woods were soaked in blackness. He stared out over the dark valley. A client could have been with him in the plane.

Or the boy.

Or Kitty.

You're out there somewhere.

He set the heavy mug down onto the porch rail when he realized he'd been squeezing it hard enough to threaten shattering it. He went inside and found a worn much-refolded map. Spread it out on his desk, and began studying it.

◊ ◊ ◊

The next morning he got up before dawn, told Hank he would likely be gone most of the day on business, looked in on Hattie as she slept, and drove the Wrangler east, the map on the passenger seat unfolded to show the western end of the state.

He swung onto I-40 near Clyde, and on the

outskirts of Asheville took the exit for 19/23 North, crossing the French Broad River. He turned onto Route 251, which went through the sleepy village of Woodfin and then wound closely alongside the river as it hunted its way through the hills for miles. There was the even smaller village of Alexander, and just over a mile beyond, Route 197 forked off to the right. This was where he had lost the pickup. He took 197 and slowed down, looking on both sides for an old pickup parked near a house, or for a garage or a shed big enough to hide a pickup. There were not many houses. A rutted gravel track led off to the left, so he shifted down and climbed it to a ridge crest where there were two cottages but no pickups. One cottage had a muddy black pickup in front of it. A woman came to the screen door and stared at him with hostility. He waved good-naturedly as though he had made an honest mistake, turned around, and coasted back down to the road.

Farther along 197 he idled through the village of Jupiter. The road was looping to the east, and it eventually led back to 19/23, so he turned around and picked up 251 to follow it alongside the river again. Beyond a long lazy right-hand bend, he hit a snarl and consulted the map. After briefly joining up with 25/70, Route 251 merged onto 213, and he had a choice of going east on another long loop that went through the hamlet of Mars Hill and rejoined 19/23, or west through the tiny gathering places of Marshall and Hazlenut and all the way on into Tennessee.

There were more offshoots along the way.

Doggedly, he took the eastern choice first, studying the area near every house, exploring two dirt roads and another steep, graveled driveway.

He spent all day at it, stopping for gas and a snack, and later at a general store that had a tacked-on grill, for coffee and two sandwiches, quitting only when the light began to fade out of the sky and shadows started populating the woods. By then he was in Tennessee near Douglas Lake. He found his way to I-40 and took it south.

He would take up the search again.

It was late when he got back to Eaglenest Ridge.

Hank was up watching TV. He thumbed the mute button and looked concerned. "Long day, huh, *Kemo Sabe*?"

He smiled and said, "Some days there just aren't enough hours, you know?"

"Your lady called about three this afternoon."

"Not my lady. A friend. How's your lady?"

"Worried about you. She knows somethin's been wrong with you today. Don't ask me how she knows. I stopped thinkin' on how she knows some things about thirty years back."

"You ever get women figured, let me know."

"You took Hattie and me in. Give us a place we can hold our heads up. Work some for our keep. Treat us better'n our own kin. You ought to know what we think about you, son. You gonna tell me you don't trust us now? Or are you gonna tell me what's got you by the short hairs?"

So he sat down and told the old man all of it. Everything he knew and suspected.

Hank considered. "What we need's a few good guns. A semi-auto deer rifle like a thirty-ought-six, maybe. A twelve-bore shotgun with a box o' buckshot loads. Hang that one up over the back door or put it in the front closet. And maybe a model nineteen and eleven Colt forty-five pistol like I carried back in the Big One. Enough whack to stop a bull."

"No, I'm done with guns."

"Thought I was, too, but that was before some outlaw took a notion to kill you."

The next morning, after a call from the FBI office releasing the Cessna, he taxied it to the maintenance hangar, shut it down, and climbed out. Ben Eckles came out wiping his hands on a shop rag and went to the open inspection port under the wing.

He fingered the damaged cable and said, "Scotty told me about this. So some lowlife came onto my airport and started messing with one of my airplanes? Wait here." He went back in and brought out a key. "This fits the lock on the rollaway doors. What we'll do is replace this cable. Then we'll park the plane right there in the front corner until they nail this guy and hang him up by his heels from the wind-sock pole. Use the key to come and go as you please."

"I appreciate that, Ben."

"Didn't say it wasn't going to cost you, sooner or later. You'll owe me a big one for it. And make sure you don't lose that key."

CHAPTER 23

She was staring out the open window into the night. No covering sheet, but she was fully dressed. The single overhead light off. Her legs tightly crossed. Her fingers laced on her stomach. Noises from downstairs muffled. Her whole body was filled with an angry, humming tension that made her twitch. Knowing he was probably going to come for her again tonight. There was a rent in the screen, and mosquitoes were in the room. One was a tiny wavering continuous scream near her neck.

Hot. No air moving. Sweat on her forehead and her upper lip.

Two owls calling to each other hollowly in the darkness.

The Levirate Obligation.

They had arranged the marriage for her back when she was fourteen. He was totally bald. Thin like her, but with muscles hard as old ropes from working with stone, and skin like leather. His breath always stank.

He had died five years later when he drank the strychnine. He was the first one to pick up the cup that day in church, and some said it was because they'd mixed in too much poison. Others said it was because the Spirit had gone out of him but he had taken the cup anyway, so he was just a fool. A few said they never did think he really believed.

She had not wanted to get pregnant and had not.

Then there was that fool who had said he would take care of her and had asked her to move in with him. Nobody else would want her, she knew. Because she could not speak.

But he started drinking too much beer on weekends. Then on most nights. And finally on every night. She watched him slowly become bloated and foul. One night he swore and cuffed her hard with a big hand, and she cracked her head open on the refrigerator door handle.

It had bled for a long time.

So she had gone to get Frank.

Sometimes she could still hear the noises the drunk made later that night from the double-wide.

From within the hissing, cracking, howling, living, cleansing fire.

And she would smile inside.

Now the door opened, and for a moment he was a still silhouette in the dirty light. He closed the door behind him and moved into the room.

The Levirate Obligation.

She gripped the buckle of her jeans belt with both hands.

She heard him take off his pants and drape them over the straight chair, change falling out of a pocket to ring on the floor. His weight tilted the mattress. His knee drove slowly downward to part her legs. He moved to pull her hands away from her belt, but she tightened her grip so he held himself up on one hand and used the other to tear away the front of her shirt, the buttons popping off, to expose her breasts. She ground her teeth, shook her head, made a sound like a mewling kitten. She despised herself for that but could not stop it.

He breathed her name repeatedly and said "shhhhhhh," over and over.

He pulled at her wrists, and she could not resist his strength.

She stopped mewling, went limp, and turned her head aside to stare out into the darkness again. At first, way back when she was twelve, when the big figure would come into her room late in the night with his rough man-scent and whisper her name and have his way, she'd hated her body for the unbidden pleasures it stole from those black nights. For betraying her. But slowly she had learned to banish the feelings of pleasure and to make herself become like ice inside.

She summoned that now.

Made herself become ice inside, so she could only numbly feel his fingers working at her belt.

CHAPTER 24

Kitty Birdsong punched out of her shift at midnight. She was tired and slightly down. She nodded to the security guard, a stocky young Cherokee named Anderson, and walked out of the sprawling casino. A chartered bus sat by the curb under the wide neon-bright entrance portico, growling at fast idle, exhaling its diesel breath, waiting to pick up a load of gamers and haul them back to their hotel. She followed the curving landscaped sidewalk to the vast parking lot where the cars were thinned and scattered in patient wait for their owners. A few gamers were fanning out to hook up with their rides. A shiny metallic-gray convertible with its top down pulled briskly into the lot and selected a slot near the entrance walkway. The tan top rose up like a giant paw, and the car covered itself. Its lights winked out and it opened its doors to discharge a pair of fresh ones, who laughed at some shared intimacy, held hands, and started walking toward the multicolored splashes of neon. The couple looked happy at the prospect of acquiring some easy wealth.

She walked to where she had left the Honda lounging on its kickstand under a light, drew off the thin nylon cover that was slick with dew, folded it, and put it in a saddlebag. Her helmet was locked by its strap to the other saddlebag's buckle. She pulled it on, got out her gloves and her Roxie leather jacket with the built-in shoulder, elbow, and spine pads, and put them on. The jacket and helmet were white for maximum visibility, which she considered her best defense against daydreaming, road-hogging drivers in their plush steel cages, habitually chewing on cell phones.

John Hardin was on her mind as she straddled the bike, toed back the kickstand, fired it up, and let it warm.

The man was intelligent in so many ways. And dumb in a few others. She knew he felt an attraction. And so, certainly, did she. *Those mysterious, penetrating, magical eyes.*

She understood and admired his loyalty to the memory of his Valerie. A woman she could never hope to replace, most likely. But if the two of them continued to hang around together, prowling through the woods, sharing this lost-mine adventure, they were sooner or later going to touch souls. And, she thought with a little thrill-smile, *Then I think there'll be sparks you just won't be able to ignore, Mr. John Hardin.*

She pulled out onto Highway 19, already feeling better now with the bike under her. She stopped at a white-striped walkway to let a couple coming from the casino cross the highway, walking toward the motel on the other side of the street. He was looking down at his feet, lost in thought. She was hunched, gripping his arm. Her face was pale-white and anguished in the Honda's headlight. A portrait of bad luck.

As soon as she cleared the town there was, as usual, almost no other traffic at this time of night and, as usual, she had to resist the temptation to really let the powerful bike have its head through the twisty, demanding climb up to the saddle of Soco Gap. Had to resist pushing herself to that bright sharp edge where everything would come into finer focus and time would slow. She held off to just above the speed limit and floated effortlessly through the sweeping curves, the bike seemingly guiding itself, the pipes drumming out all other sound, the bright spray from her headlight trembling with the power.

The night was soft and humid. Mist hung in the trees, and the air was cool and clean in her lungs. The stars were scattered prettily above the sleeping silhouetted hills. A gibbous moon rode high. It was such a refreshing contrast to the carpeted artificial atmosphere of the casino, the gaudy ranked slots bleeping their mindless electronic noises as they digested the gamers' money with tireless efficiency.

For perhaps the hundredth time she had a vision of riding naked through an endless night like this, going for some far-off faintly glowing horizon, her hair billowing back, the wind washing her flesh, all her nerve endings tingling. And she twisted on a smidgen more power through a long, freshly paved banked turn.

She *owned* this night, and her soul swelled with the sheer *aliveness* of it.

She began humming the old Santana melody "Angels All Around Us", one of her long-time favorites.

Then, because she was missing being near Hardin, she sang the lonesome "Amigo's Guitar" and could hear the background Spanish guitars harmonizing soulfully in sympathy.

She stole a quick glance up at the stars. Picked one to wish on.

There was a tighter right turn around a big rock shoulder ahead. She slowed before entering the turn, looked ahead into it as far as she could see, pressed down on the right grip to counter-steer smoothly into the sweep of it, and halfway through, rolled on power to stabilize the bike and make it bite into the turn. She was about to ease off on the counter-steer as she came out of the turn and to then reverse it and bank into the next curve.

A car was parked, lights out, back in a scenic turn-out by the right side of the road.

It was aimed at her as its high beams flared alive and it leaped at her.

She first tried to straighten the bike up so she'd be able to hit both brakes hard, but there was no time.

She threw the bike over to the left, hunting for the next turn, the car coming down onto her fast from the right, so she kept the power on.

The left floorboard tilted up as it contacted the road, showering back a trail of sparks, but the soft rounded tires clung to the asphalt. She was half blinded by the brightness but could make out a patch of gravel strewn across the road ahead, right there in the next curve, nothing beyond but dim treetops and blackness as the mountain flank fell steeply away.

And knew she'd been neatly suckered.

She got off of the throttle and the bike began to slow but not nearly enough to take the left turn. She got on both brakes hard, telling herself, *Just don't lock up that rear wheel.*

The gravel flashed toward her and she felt the tires lose their grip. The bike started to slide out from under her, the road slamming her along her left side, her helmet scrape-cracking loudly in her ears.

She was still on the brakes and thinking, *hit the kill switch,* when the bike cleared through the gravel, found solid footing, and its brake-locked wheels bit, flinging itself and her up and over, and she thought, *God help me, it's a high-side flip.*

She lost her hold on the bike, and it went sliding away. She came glancing down onto grassy dirt and skidded and free-fell sickeningly.

Into a crackling tangle of something.

And then everything was quiet and woozy and the

after-image of the car lights was fading. She was seeing something. The fuzzy, broken moon. And it wouldn't stay still. Stars were slowly swirling into focus.

Her head hurt.

Her left side was numb.

Something was sticking painfully into the small of her back, but she didn't try to move. She just wanted everything to hold in place, please.

She heard herself moan softly in the quiet night.

Above on the road the car was parked. Idling.

A face under a long-billed baseball cap looking down on her out of the passenger window.

Instinctively, she did not call out. Tried to keep the world around her from moving giddily.

The car sat there idling. Then it crept away into the night, and she saw its lights feeling the way around curves up toward the gap.

She moved her right hand. Shoved the twig aside that was poking her back. Rolled over slowly, brambles scraping her helmet face shield, and tenderly used a boot to feel for the steeply sloping ground. Held on to the bushes with her right hand. Her left side was hurting now. She moved experimentally and did not think anything was broken. Felt around in the dark. Grabbing onto bushes and tufts of grass, she spent several minutes stumbling and slipping on the wet grass and climbing back up to the road. She stood there on the verge, breathing hard until the trembling in her hands and legs eased off.

There was enough moonlight to make out the bike, which lay inert farther along the road edge, its rear wheel out over the drop. *I must have hit the kill switch, after all.* She limped over to it on unsteady legs.

Thought about it.

She got down shakily onto her butt. Grabbed the front fork with both gloved hands, and pulled. The bike moved two inches closer. She reset herself painfully and tugged again. Another two inches. More tugs. More inches.

She stopped to rest. The night was quiet.

She tugged some more, until the rear wheel was over the asphalt. She had once seen a guy demonstrate how anybody could right a bike, even the heaviest of them. She moved around on the pavement to put her lower back to the saddle, held onto the handlebar with her right hand and onto the left rear wheel shock weakly with her left hand, took two deep breaths, and pushed back and up, her legs, especially the relatively uninjured right one, doing all the work. To her surprise, the bike tilted and began to rise. She pushed harder with her shaking legs, until the weight of the bike rested almost wholly on the tires. She pivoted to hold the handlebars and set the kickstand.

Took another rest, breathing hard.

Got out the small flashlight from the saddlebag. Started going over the Honda.

The left floorboard was broken off. The left handlebar was sprung up and the end of the grip was ground down badly, but the clutch still seemed to work, stiffly. The crash bar was bent and gouged. It had saved her left leg from serious damage. Saddlebags scarred. When it had flopped over in the violent high-side, it had landed mostly on the soft grassy carpet alongside the road. A fork reflector had been torn off. One of the exhausts was loose. The windshield had a large chunk out of it, and what was still attached was spiderwebbed with cracks. A cylinder cover on the right side was missing. She looked around on the road with the flashlight. Found the broken floorboard and put it in the saddlebag. *Don't want to be littering.*

Her left shoulder felt wet and burned. She aimed the flashlight at it. Seeping blood. Road rash. Big time. But the jacket had done its job, the leather abrading away but saving a lot of skin. Her left hip, too, was bleeding, a big patch of her blue jeans shredded. The left knee felt unstable now. The bleeding didn't seem to be life-threatening.

Moving like an old person, she got her leg over the bike. Sat for another minute. Reset the kill switch, and thumbed the starter. The bike responded with an angry roar.

◊ ◊ ◊

John swam up out of a dream about a golden Cherokee mask to hear a staccato rapping getting louder outside. He grabbed up his jeans, stuffed his feet into the moccasins, pulled on a T-shirt, and padded downstairs and out onto the porch.

She swung into the yard and slewed the Honda to a stop on the gravel. Something was wrong with the bike. The headlight beam was skewed, and one handlebar was bent. And it was very loud. She shut the bike down, set the kickstand with some difficulty, and got off. Moving slowly.

He met her in the middle of the front lawn.

She pulled off her broken helmet and dropped it on the ground. Put her gloved right fist on her hip.

She pushed out her chin and said, "Some scum-sucking, redneck, lame-brained, idiot murderous cagers intentionally ran me off the road just now the other side of Soco Gap. I mean *deliberately*. Set a sneaky trap for me, and I rode right into it like a fool newbie. Look at my *bike*."

He said, "Never mind the bike. What about you? That shoulder needs some attention, Kitty." He took her gently by her good elbow, helped her over to the porch steps, and sat her down.

She said, "*Owwwdammit*," as she brushed the rail with her injured shoulder.

He checked her over quickly as best he could and said, "Just a minute."

He ran into the house, past a groggy Hank who was coming to investigate the commotion. Grabbed the keys to the Wrangler. Ran back out to bend down by her. Said, "Listen, Kitty. I think we need to take you over to the medical center. Right now. Have you looked at, okay? We're going to go over here and get in my Jeep right now, okay?"

"Well, don't look at me like that. I'm not dying."

He took a deep breath. "No. No, I guess not. You did ride that wreck all the way here from the Gap. And you're really angry. That's healthy."

"They *suckered* me, John. Ran me off the road. It was a high-side, but I landed in bushes. That saved me, thank God."

"Yes."

Hank was standing on the porch, barefoot and in his pajamas, peering out at the bike.

She inspected her shoulder and her hip. "Those pea-brains did destroy my best jeans, though. Seventy-nine ninety-five with the butt sequins. And this is a three-hundred-dollar jacket. And that helmet was on a one-time clearance sale for a hundred bucks."

"How much were those gloves? The left one is pretty scuffed up."

"Twenty-nine ninety-five."

"Okay. I'll buy you a new pair of gloves."

"Great. That will make everything okay, then."

He smiled.

She looked at his feet. "So do you wear moccasins to bed? Are you trying to pretend you're an Indian?"

He bent, touched his forehead to hers, and closed his eyes briefly. Stood up and took another deep breath.

She gave him a tentative smile.

He said, "Come on. Let's go get you fixed up."

◊ ◊ ◊

She asked John to call the Highway Patrol and set up a meeting with a trooper at the scenic turnout near Soco Gap. She was bandaged, limping, and stiff, but had refused to spend the rest of the night in Haywood, and had refused any painkiller stronger than aspirin. They had stopped at her place so she could change into slacks and a loose-fitting sweatshirt.

It was four o'clock, and the chunk of moon was low in the sky when they made it to the turnout. A gray state cruiser was parked there with all its lights firing.

She said, "Why do these guys always like to use all their lights so much? It looks like a redneck Christmas decoration."

The trooper was sweeping the pavement with a large flashlight.

His name was Ramirez, and he was professional, efficient, and polite. He was using a small digital recorder to take verbal notes.

Kitty described what had happened. He listened patiently and requested she go through it all again while he held the recorder close for her. He paced the scene, speaking more details into the recorder, came back to them, and said, "Not to question your statements, ma'am, but I've seen this same sort of accident more than once before in these mountains. A motorcyclist goes into a curve carrying a bit too much power. There is a patch of ice, or there are wet leaves, or there is a fan of gravel that was spilled from a dump truck, the motorcycle loses purchase, and the rider goes down. It can happen easily enough, and there is no particular blame to be assigned."

She limped over to point at the patch of gravel, which had been thinned by the vehicles that had passed since the incident. "This was no accident, Trooper Ramirez. They *put* that gravel there, and then they charged at me out of that parking area at just the right time to spook me so I'd hit the gravel in this turn. Going fast. I fell for it."

Ramirez looked again at the gravel, the marks the sliding Honda had made, the gouges in the road shoulder where it had landed, looked over the lip of the steep bank where she had fallen, and studied the road shoulders. He stopped across the road and said, "It is possible somebody used a shovel right here to scrape up gravel and spread it into the road."

"Exactly," Kitty said. "They tried to kill me."

He got a clipboard from his cruiser and said, "I believe you, ma'am, but there is not much to go on here. No tracks. No footprints. And you have no description of the vehicle other than it was a dark car. There were probably two or more in the vehicle because the face you saw was at the passenger window. Unless the driver slid over into the passenger seat to look out. Are you absolutely sure you can't describe that face at all?"

"I was stunned, I guess. Half blinded by the headlights. I know he had a ball cap on. I'm pretty sure it was a man, but I can't give you any detail."

John said nothing. Still in his moccasins, he used his own flashlight in slow sweeps to look the whole area over.

Ramirez said, "It will have to be recorded as a single-vehicle accident with what is called a phantom vehicle involved. But I will do what I can. I will append a statement that backs you up, in my opinion. I can't guarantee they won't give you points for it, which, as you probably know, could affect your insurance rates. I hope you feel better soon, ma'am."

Back in the Wrangler, Kitty said, "Great. I got a speeding ticket three months ago. Two points. If they give me points for this, they'll probably add three or four zeros to my insurance statement."

He said, "Somebody tried to rig my airplane to crash."

"What? When?"

"Day before yesterday. I surprised the guy at it, but he ran. They're looking into it. I doubt they'll get very far."

"When were you planning on telling me about it?"

"Sorry. Tomorrow. Today."

"Somebody wants that mine. And they know we've been looking for it."

"Yes."

"So what do we do now?"

"You don't do anything but get some rest. Call

in sick for a week. Call your insurance people. I'll borrow a low-bed trailer and take your bike to a dealer or wherever you say. In a few days we'll figure out what to do."

"Okay."

"How are you feeling?"

"Like a sore loser. And like going hunting."

CHAPTER 25

At dawn, after he had left Kitty to rest at her place and had driven back to Eaglenest Ridge, John slipped his cell phone into his jeans and set off at a brisk jog along the trail behind his house. To help tone his arms and his grip, he carried a grapefruit-sized stone in each hand. Each stone was of a different weight, to help challenge and so to train his balance. He did curls and lifts along the way. Sets of fifty with each arm. Halfway through the run, he would switch the stones. He wore his moccasins and no shirt so he could feel the cool air on his skin and perspire freely, and he tried to move as quietly as possible, scanning the trail well ahead in detail so he would know where to place his feet to create the least disturbance, as old Wasituna had taught him. He had practiced it so much it required little conscious thought now, was almost instinctual, and he could traverse the ridge, cut across a valley following a deer trail, and climb another mountain flank along an old logging track like a ghost.

He often used such runs to think.

After five miles he stopped by a car-sized boulder, dropped his carry stones, took a running leap to the top of it, and sat down, his lungs feeling cleansed and his blood buzzing nicely. He hugged his knees and looked off across the forest, letting his breathing slow.

He separated all the events in chronological order since Hattie had asked him to check up on Moses Kyle, then selected each one in turn and looked at it objectively from all angles. Suppressing his personal emotions but not his suspicions or his hunches. Letting his thoughts roam free. Hunting for common threads and pulling at them. Sniffing for anything illogical or slightly skewed out of place. Small anomalies. Anything previously unseen or forgotten.

An hour into the process he went very still, then stretched out his right leg to dig for his cell phone. He had to call information first for the number.

It rang nine times before she picked it up and said, "Traylor Ruby Mine. You got Effie."

"Effie. John Hardin. We talked about gold panning."

"I remember. How's your sidekick? What was his name? Hank?"

"Doing fine. When you were telling me about the Cagle operation, you said something about them playing with fire and talking strangely."

"Did I? Oh, yeah. They belong to this bunch of fanatics that speak in tongues, test their faith with fire, you know?"

"What else does this bunch do? I think I know, but I'd like to be sure."

"I heard it said they drink poisons. They got them a church over somewhere a good ways west of here, somebody said, close on to the Tennessee line. Back up in the woods. They play with snakes, too."

"Yes, they're snake handlers."

"Pick 'em up in church. Dance around. Holler out 'Praise the Lord' a lot. You don't get bit, means you're in tight with God, I guess. You do get bit, means you ain't a real believer. I'm a born-again Baptist myself. We got other ways to spend time with God. Don't need no snakes. Wadin' up Darkwater Creek on a early mornin' any time o' the year does it for me. Every time."

"Thanks, Effie. I'll be back to see you. Probably bring along a young Cherokee boy I know. Maybe he'll turn up a nice ruby."

"You never do know. Bring that Hank, too. He's got a story or two in him, I can tell."

He got down from the boulder, retrieved his carry stones, and ran back to Eaglenest Ridge, squeezing and relaxing his grips on the rocks all the way. He set a pace that raised his heart rate high and had him sweating freely.

He got out a map and spread it on his desk, sweat dripping onto it. Effie had talked about a fanatical bunch somewhere up near the Tennessee line. He had lost the pickup when he flew into clouds that thundering night. While it was winding like a lighted bug crawling northward along Route 251, which ran onto Route 213, curving west and on into Tennessee. He had searched the area on the ground. He traced the road with a finger again now. It ran through Marshall and Hazlenut and Hot Springs, all just white dots on the map. Little backwoods settlements. A fanatical backwoods bunch. *Is this where you live?*

He didn't know for sure.

But he did know where the Cagles lived.

Hank put together an apple cider, instant-oatmeal, and crisp-toast breakfast for the three of them. He took a tray into the back bedroom for Hattie, then sat with John at the kitchen table.

The old man sipped his coffee and said, "How about one based on a true story an' set around the last century's turnin'. It had Paul Newman as the big star, and Ava Gardner, and the director was John Huston. The guy who played in *Psycho* was a preacher."

"*The Life and Times of Judge Roy Bean.*"

"Dang. Okay, what was the name of the town?"

"Vinegaroon. Gardner played the great vaudeville star Lilly Langtry. The preacher was Anthony Perkins. Newman was the only law west of the Pecos. Loved Langtry from afar. Said there was going to be peace and he didn't care who he had to kill to get it."

"Dang."

After showering, John looked in on the old woman, who was propped up in bed, interrogating Hank.

She said, "Did you get all the wash done? Remember, you'll have to iron your shirts if you don't want to look like a hobo when you go out to play that fiddle."

Hank looked at John, took the old woman's hand, and said, "Ain't goin' off to play until you're some better, Mother."

"Nonsense. No reason not to. And don't forget, if the back garden isn't weeded and turned, we won't get everything planted when it ought to go in. Did you bring in a good pile of wood? Still goes down cool some nights. And where's the paper? If you leave it out in the box, it'll get all wet. I want to get up and walk around the house longer today. I'm fit as I can be. And I don't want to use that infernal walker. I can make it on my own two feet."

John left them to it and drove down the hill to the municipal building. Chief Glen Vogel was lean, fit, and in his fifties. When John entered the office, he stood, offered his hand, and said, "Good to finally meet you. I enjoyed hearing Mr. Gaskill play that fiddle of his over at Fairchild's place a while ago. I understand the Gaskills live with you. Take a seat. I've got a few minutes."

"Yes. Fact, that's why I'm here." He sat and told Vogel about the attempt to disable his plane and about Kitty's incident near Soco Gap the night before.

Sergeant Boudreau appeared and stood in the doorway to listen.

John said, "Hattie Gaskill saw a man in the woods

behind my house recently. It startled her and she fell. Cracked her hip. She's getting back on her feet pretty well now, but I wanted to let you know about this. Maybe one of your men could ride past Kitty Birdsong's place and by my place once in a while."

Vogel frowned. "Do you have any idea who could be doing these things and why?"

John held the man's puzzled gaze and shook his head.

Boudreau said, "Motorcycles are always running off one of these mountain roads or another, and the riders always blame other drivers. And your Miz Gaskill could have spotted some hiker back in the trees, if she saw anybody at all."

Vogel planted his elbows on his chair arms and steepled his fingers. He squinted at the bigger man in the doorway for three seconds. He said, "Mr. Hardin, this is Sergeant Boudreau."

"We've met."

Vogel said, "Sergeant Boudreau, please go see about getting those new tires put on my vehicle. I'll talk with you later."

Boudreau smiled, cocked a pistol finger at John, and left.

Vogel said, "Sorry. The tampering with your plane. That's a federal offense, so I assume the FBI is involved."

"The Asheville office."

"I'll call them and see what I can find out, not that I expect them to share anything. I'll check in with

Sheriff Fields, too. We don't have a whole lot to go on right now, do we? But I'll have my men swing by your place and by Miss Birdsong's place, on a random basis. And we'll keep an eye out for older red pickups in bad shape, possibly with a four and a nine on the plate, although God knows there are plenty of beat-up red pickups in these hills. We might stop a few politely to check out the drivers; it couldn't hurt. That plate might have been stolen and not reported yet. I'll nose around myself."

"Appreciate that."

"Give my best to the Gaskills. I wish I could play a country fiddle like that."

John went home, took Hank out onto the porch, and showed him how to use the cell phone to call the police. He dropped it into the old man's shirt pocket. Hank had a strong distrust of computers, and a stubborn dislike of cell phones and all their electronic ilk.

Hank in turn took him inside and opened the front-hall closet. He reached to the back behind an overcoat and brought out an old exposed-hammers double-barreled shotgun and broke it open to show the brass bases of the twelve-gauge shells. In a low voice he said, "Double-ought buck. I borrowed it from old Pete. Right barrel's full choke for distance, the left is modified choke for closer up."

John thought about telling him to be careful with it. But Hank had come through a particularly nasty version of hell fighting with Merrill's outnumbered

Marauders in World War II, holding the Burma jungles against the Japanese.

He said, "Let's hope it doesn't come to something like that, Hank."

Kitty called at mid-day and said, "I was sleeping like a hickory log. But I woke up out of a bad dream an hour ago, wanting to wring somebody's red neck, and now I can't get back to sleep."

"How are you feeling?"

"About as stiff as that hickory log, and I've got some highly colorful patches on me. They'd make good tattoo backgrounds. I called in battered. My supervisor said she warned me motorcycles were dangerous. And I called the Honda dealer in Asheville. They'll fix my bike."

"I'll take care of getting it there. You had lunch?"

"There's not much to eat in the house."

"Give me a list. Then give me two hours and I'll bring eats for us."

"I need to educate you about proper eating times."

"It will taste better when you're a little starved."

"But I'm a lot starved now."

John borrowed a low expanded-steel utility trailer from a neighbor. The Wrangler had come with a hitch. He cranked the bike and power walked it onto the trailer, Hank passing ropes to him to tie it down.

He stopped in Maggie at a grocery store and bought everything on Kitty's list, then went by Mama Guava's for thick loaded subs.

He arrived at Kitty's door with clusters of plastic bags hanging from both hands. They sat on the couch and ate the subs. The meal made her yawn and stretch with a wince.

He told her to try getting more sleep. "Take it easy for a few days. I'll get the bike to Asheville right now, then I have some business to take care of. I'll call you tomorrow."

She cocked her head and raised an eyebrow. "What are you thinking?"

"I went and talked with the Maggie cops. The chief seems pretty sharp. They'll be cruising by once in a while. You'll keep the place locked up?"

"Why do I have the feeling you're not telling me something? Okay. But you call me no later than noon tomorrow. Or I'll be on your doorstep."

He trailered the Honda to the Asheville dealer. By the time he returned to Eaglenest Ridge and dropped the trailer off, the sun had gone and there was only a ruddy sky-glow as though from some secret fire behind the hills.

He waited for two hours after Hank had gone to bed, using the time to study a detailed map. He knocked lightly on their bedroom door and got no reply. Both of them were sound sleepers. He left a note on the kitchen table telling them not to worry. He was only going to check up on the airplane. It was lame, but it would keep Hank from calling in the law if the old man woke up and found him gone. He dressed in black jeans, a black T-shirt under a worn denim jacket, and his moccasins. He slid new batteries into his Mini Maglite and strapped the big Bowie knife onto his belt. Stuffed a pair of thin leather driving gloves into his back pocket. He slipped outside and locked up behind him. He had left the Wrangler aimed down the hill. He released the hand brake and let it coast for a hundred yards before starting it and flicking the lights on.

◊ ◊ ◊

Corkscrew Mountain was a brooding black presence rising up ahead to blot out the stars. There was a gibbous moon riding high, enough to help guide him once he'd got full night vision. He had parked the Wrangler on a gravel turnout in a bend of the narrow road two hundred yards beyond the Cagle place. Walking back, he had ducked into the roadside brush when a lone car went past going much too fast for this road, two wheels slapping into a pothole.

He crouched behind a stone wall that bordered a pasture and studied the house and outbuildings for ten minutes. A bug buzzed past his ear. It was after midnight. There was no movement anywhere. A single dimly lit downstairs window in the house. One yellowish yard light by the driveway, where a black Hummer was parked close to the back of the house, a blue pickup parked behind it, closer to the road. A purplish bug zapper on a tilted pole was steadily buzz-crackling. Ground-hugging mist was seeping through the trees. A lone whip-poor-will was calling fluidly somewhere up the mountain.

He pulled on the leather driving gloves. Keeping to the shadows as much as possible, he circled the pasture to come up on the outbuildings. There was a garage with a single dirty cobwebbed window in a side wall. The window was visible from the house. He stood by the window, unmoving, for two minutes, listening. Slitted the flashlight beam with two fingers, and peered inside. There was a dented rusty red pickup truck in there. He eased around to the front, now in full view of the house. The double doors were padlocked, but sprung apart at the bottom. He knelt and used the shielded flashlight again. The plate was dirty, but he could make it all out and he memorized it. The last three digits were 942. He was sure it was the truck that had followed him, and was also most likely the one he had tracked from the air.

He moved to an outbuilding behind the garage and looked into a window. An old riding mower, a cluster of yard tools stacked in a corner, food cans filled with screws and nails, paint cans, and a jumble of assorted dusty junk. No lock on the door. Farther back up the hill in the trees he approached a larger shed. Maybe twenty feet long and twelve feet wide. It was mostly masked by the garage between it and the house. Two spaced windows on each side. The windows were all very dirty, intricately spiderwebbed. Protected with a heavy wire mesh screwed to the tar-papered siding. He peered inside but could not make out much. Squarish wire-mesh containers on long wide shelving.

The front door was padlocked. But then he looked closer and saw the heavy lock had been swiveled in place but not pushed into locking position. It was a lazy trick he'd used himself to make his storage shed appear to be locked when he didn't want to be bothered with frequently using the padlock key.

He swiveled the padlock and slipped it out to release the door hasp, hooked it in his jeans pocket, and moved into the shed, leaving the door standing open for some light. He took four steps on the rough concrete floor and froze at the sound. A dry whispering buzz that cut right to his spine and sent a chill warning tingling through him. He used the shielded light cautiously. There was a pervading musty-sour smell like an exhalation from hell.

Snakes.

Dark, still, sinuous masses. Inside the wire cages along both sides of the shed on wide shelving. Two or three in each cage on sawdust bedding. A large dusky triangular head in the nearest cage was aimed at him, catlike eyes unblinking in the dim shielded light, tongue flicking at the air delicately. The thick snake was neatly coiled, its tail standing erect and blurring with the nerve-prickling sound it was making. There were more cages in rows along the rough floor under the shelves. He moved cautiously farther into the shed. There was a worktable at the back below some cabinets. Beakers. A sheet of labels. Two containers on the table covered with stretched rubber membranes. Some stainless tools. A three-foot thin metal pole with a crook on the end. He'd seen one used on wildlife TV shows.

A squeak behind him.

He clicked off the light and spun around, going into a half crouch, reaching for the Bowie knife and drawing it from the sheath.

A figure was silhouetted in the doorway.

Blocking it.

The figure moved slightly, and there was another squeak.

He squinted. Realized it was a woman.

And she was opening cages.

He held the flashlight a full arm's reach from his side, aimed it at the doorway, and flicked it on.

Flaming red hair. And jewel-blue eyes, unblinking in the light. Staring, like the snake's cold eyes. Jeans and a T-shirt and bare feet.

He said, "Who are you?"

She stared, utterly unafraid, raised her arm, and pointed a slender finger at him. Not at the light. At him.

And she smiled.

He started moving toward her.

Stopped.

Two of the cages nearest the door were empty.

She nodded at him, then whirled and vanished into the night.

He swept the floor with the Maglite, wishing it was much stronger to chase away the shadows.

A curving dark shape lay on the concrete between him and the doorway. Thick, and three feet long. Stirring. Its head rising up and weaving. Sensing. That wicked head turned his way, the dry tail buzzing steadily.

He moved very carefully toward it, the knife held across his body, shoulder-high and blade out, his grip white-knuckle tight. He held the light steady in his left hand, trained on the snake. His body slightly bent.

The snake stopped, raised its head more, tongue tasting. Buzz increasing in intensity.

He had no time. He moved steadily forward, his gut going hollow. When he was three feet from the snake it lunged. A blur. He uncocked his right arm and the Bowie cut a protective arc in front of him. He barely felt it when the tip caught the snake six inches below the head and flung it back and away. Another dark shape shifted close by his right foot.

He leaped for the door and began running. Low and loping, the light off, his night vision damaged, but aiming for the dim trees. Almost colliding with one. Fending it off with an elbow.

Lights going on at the house and a door banging. Somebody shouting.

He held the flashlight in his left palm and shielded

it with two fingers to give him just enough light to pick his footing. Ran hard across the edge of the meadow, trying to make the shelter of the trees beyond.

A booming gunshot behind him. Another.

Shotgun. Too far away to do much damage.

He crashed through brush and in among trees.

Ran like a deer through woods for seventy-five feet, then broke out onto the road. An eighth of a mile to go to the Wrangler. Only less than a minute, but a vehicle was starting back at the house, and he heard tires churning gravel.

He increased his speed to his limit, still carrying the light in his left hand and the knife in his right.

Headlights breaking over a rise behind him, but the white Wrangler was ahead now in the turnout. A hundred feet to go.

The lights behind him grew rapidly brighter, throwing out a long absurd shadow of himself in front of him. He could hear the car engine straining.

He made it to the Wrangler in a skidding stop, ripped open the door, threw the knife and light inside as he swung under the wheel.

The pickup behind him began braking.

He had left the key in the ignition. Cranked it fast, put it in first, revved the engine, hands ready on the wheel, but he held off.

He waited until the blue pickup had slid almost to a stop, wheels shuddering and tires yelping, just behind and to his left, then he let out the clutch smoothly, engine revving high, the Wrangler's tires dug in, and he shot away, switching on his lights, crouching against any gunshots.

He had studied a map of the area before leaving his house. Three miles ahead, a dirt track cut off to the left and across a low ridge, to connect with another paved highway beyond. The lights were brightening again behind him, even though he was doing sixty-five on a road where fifty was pushing it. He scrutinized the roadside ahead, spotted the track, shifted down, and braked, and bounced the Jeep off the road. It was bad. He put it in four-wheel drive. Considering he was in the Jeep and they were in a small pickup, that was just fine. The track was probably long disused. Grown up, with large soft spots, but the Wrangler bulled on through. He shot several glances at the jouncing rearview mirror. Saw the pickup stop on the road, nose into the track, and stop. He kept pushing the Wrangler until he was a good way over the ridge and out of sight. He stopped, shut it down, and listened. He could go ahead on the track and risk getting stuck, although he had the cable winch mounted on the front bumper and could get unstuck from almost any situation, given time. Or he could give it ten minutes and backtrack to the paved road, turn left, and take a paved right two miles farther on that would eventually lead him out of the area.

He chose to wait and backtrack. He sat in the quiet dark woods, the Jeep tilted into a muddy depression, the heat ticking out of its engine, letting his heart slow and listening to the night.

Felt something sharply painful at his hip. It was the snake-shed padlock. He dug it out of his pocket and dropped it out the window. If he had not absently chosen to pocket the lock, the woman could have simply swung the door closed and locked him inside.

He used the flashlight to inspect the Bowie. Its tip was smeared with blood.

Good.

They would know who he was, of course. Would know *they* could be followed now. *They* could be stalked.

And that was good, too.

CHAPTER 26

He stopped at an all-night convenience store and used their pay phone to call the FBI office in Asheville. Dialed the emergency number the phone message provided. A man answered with sleep in his voice, "Yes, what is it? This is Agent Donner."

"John Hardin. You've been investigating an attempt at the Asheville Airport to disable my plane. I have the plate number of the pickup the man was driving that night, and I know where it's hidden."

"Hold on. Let me get a pen."

He gave Donner all the information he had, and told him he was calling from the store.

"Corkscrew Mountain. What county is that in?"

"Macon."

"Alright. I'll call the sheriff's office there, and we'll put something together as quickly as we can. Listen, you go on home and you stay there, are we clear on that?"

He drove back to Eaglenest Ridge. The house was

quiet, the old couple still sleeping. He discarded the note he'd left on the table, took a cup of instant coffee out onto the porch, and sat on a bentwood rocker with his moccasined feet up on the rail. He debated telling the FBI agent about Moses Kyle's lost gold mine, or maybe the Maggie chief of police.

No, he decided he would not let the secret out. Not yet.

An hour after dawn, he dialed Kitty's number from his desk phone. "Did I wake you?"

"I've been up for an hour. Watching the light in the sky. Thinking."

"You up to going out for breakfast?"

When they were seated in a back booth at Country Vittles and had placed their orders, he looked into her unsettling amber eyes and said, "The thing with my plane and the thing with you and your bike. It could have been because we were getting close to the mine."

"It feels that way, yes. So what do we do about it?"

"I think the FBI may have a line on the man who tampered with my plane. I want to see who this guy is for sure. I haven't told them anything about Moses or our gold hunt."

"What do you mean, 'for sure'?"

"I think his name is Cagle. I think he bought gold from Moses. And he's a snake handler, involved with some church group over near Tennessee. He's got a collection of snakes himself. He has a brother and a sister. They're most likely involved, too."

"I thought church snake handling was illegal."

"I'm sure it is. But they do it in secret, and it's also probably something the cops and the courts don't like to interfere with because of religious freedom."

"This makes it much more likely what happened to Mose was no accident, then."

"The medical examiner was uncomfortable about it."

"It would follow that Mose told this Cagle where the mine is. Cagle wants it for himself. Except we show up to maybe spoil his party. It would probably be illegal to shoot the whole Cagle clan along with their squirmy little pets, even though they wrecked my Honda, but you know what I believe we ought to do?"

"I don't think you should be hiking in the woods. You're not healed yet."

"It's just some road rash. An everyday thing like that never slowed the Hell's Angels down."

"You're no Hell's Angel."

"Before this is through, the Cagles might debate you on that. So take me to the doctor so he can admire my new colors a while and run up his bill, then I'll change into woods gear and eat some aspirin. You're already wearing your moccasins, but we can go get your backpack and your war paint and eagle feather. Are you going to eat that last strip of bacon?"

It was mid-morning by the time he got back to Eaglenest Ridge. Kitty was waiting in the Wrangler. He called Donner from his desk and asked if there was any news.

"We paid a visit to the Cagle place early this morning with a warrant, along with the Macon County sheriff. The Cagle family is interesting. They could use a good interior decorator. They have quite a collection of poisonous snakes, and as a sideline they sell venom to a lab that makes antivenin. The pickup was there, with its front wheels off. An eleven-year-old Dodge. It's registered to a Werly Fulks with an address in a road bulge called Hazlenut. He owns a logging company that he operates from his home. Do you know him?"

"Never heard of him."

"The Cagles claim it's there so Orin Cagle can do a ball-joint job on it. He used to work with Fulks in the logging company, and they stayed friendly. Are you absolutely sure this is the pickup you saw?"

"Eighty percent."

"None of these characters show up in our bad-people databases, but there is one fact of some interest. Fulks has a private pilot's license, but apparently hasn't kept it current. The FAA has no record of a flight medical for the past twelve years. We'll be having a discussion with him today. We hope to come up with a photo soon. Maybe your FBO operator in Asheville will be able to place him at the airport some weeks before your incident. That would be something, at least. We'll see. Do you have anything else you'd care to share with us?"

"No."

"I've talked with your Haywood County sheriff and your Maggie Valley chief of police, to alert them to be on the lookout for this Fulks, and to keep an eye on you."

"Appreciate that."

He looked in on Hattie, who was sleeping, and told the old man not to expect him back any time soon but to keep the cell phone handy and the doors locked.

He decided to leave the moccasins on. He got the backpack, which already contained the panning outfit, and stuffed in four bottled waters, two hard apples, and some crackers. He belted on the Bowie and stood in his office, going over a mental checklist. He was headed out the door when he stopped, reached into the corner, and picked up the shorter of the two blowguns, which had three seven-inch reed darts in a deerskin quiver lashed onto it with a leather thong.

When he slid into the Wrangler, Kitty shifted stiffly on the passenger seat, winced, and said, "A blowgun? Are we going rabbit hunting, too?"

"Thought you might want lunch."

"You know, this Injun thing can be carried too far. You're thinking Campbell Creek?"

"Yes."

They took Campbell Creek Road off of Highway 19 and followed it on after it turned into gravel and then just a dirt track with grass in the middle, and parked by the rickety bridge. Moving at a slow pace for Kitty as she used her walking stick to keep her balance, and stopping to rest frequently, they followed along as close beside the creek fork as the terrain would allow.

Two miles from the bridge, Kitty sat down carefully on a large flat mossy rock that projected over the creek. She said, "Sorry. I guess I'm not quite as strong as I thought."

He pulled off the backpack and reached inside the top flap. "Your limp is getting worse. Here, take a drink. Just sit here for fifteen minutes. Eat an apple. Then we'll go back. We don't have to do this today."

"I'd rather be doing this than sitting on the couch thinking about it. Five minutes. Then we can keep on." She took a long drink of the water. Eased her right hip.

He sat down beside her and unwrapped a pack of crackers.

The creek widened and slowed past their rock, ripples dappling the pebbled bed with fleeting shadows that chased each other downstream. The tree canopy was combing a warm breeze and whispering mysterious primeval secrets to them. The forest scent was musky-sweet. She had her hair tied back in a ponytail with a lashed deerskin sleeve. Valerie had often used an heirloom silver-and-turquoise pin to do the same. A hazy shaft of wavering sunlight was making her dark hair shine.

He listened and said, "The birds. Beautiful. Like your name."

She glanced at him and gave him an enigmatic

little smile. Hugged her knees and gazed upstream. Did not speak for a minute.

She said, "This whole thing is a pretty wild gamble, isn't it?"

"We can do like your casino bosses do. Call it something else. A quest."

"They do have their euphemisms. They divide the year up into what they call retail seasons, as though they're actually selling something."

"Selling dreams. Like a lotto ticket. Dollar for a dream."

"I guess. I hope this mine thing was a fine quest for Mose. He must have been so excited when he found it."

John nodded and smiled at the thought.

She said, "Gambling runs all through our lives, when you think about it."

"The stock market."

"Yup. Poker chips used to be red, white, and blue. The blue ones were the most valuable. From that we got blue-chip stocks. How about the soldiers drawing lots under the cross? Two millennia ago."

"State lotteries. They rake in billions."

"'Raking it in' is a gambling term. Craps or poker. There are all kinds of terms we get just from poker. Penny ante. Stand pat. Jackpot, because in progressive poker you need a pair of jacks or better to start the betting. We assess how things stack up in life, like a stack of poker chips. The bottom chip is your bottom dollar, and the top chip is your top dollar. A buck was some kind of marker placed in front of the next dealer; sometimes it was an old buck knife, so we have the saying 'pass the buck.' Some poker tables have a slot—a hole—in the top so the dealer can squirrel the house cut out of sight, and when you're out of money you're 'in the hole.'"

"Wild Bill Hickock was holding aces, eights, and a jack of diamonds when he was shot. The dead man's hand."

"So he cashed in his chips while he was playing poker."

She went very still.

He whispered, "What is it?"

"I'm probably seeing things, but look at that rock ahead. Give yourself a few seconds."

"Yes. It could be a beaver's head. Just above the surface. And part of its back."

"It was underwater when we were here before. And we're sitting right by a long, slow stretch of creek. In fact, you could say it's been slow water ever since we began tracking this fork. The journal said, 'Where slow waters fork.'" She looked at him with excitement in her eyes.

He helped her up, and they moved along the bank until they were even with the odd-shaped boulder island out in the creek. The old journal had said 120 strides. He used a three-foot stride slowly so she could keep up, and they both counted and came to the narrow cut in the mountain's flank. Runoff had swollen the trickle flowing out of the ravine until it had washed away a lot of the concealing leaves. The journal had said the mine would be found under a rock pile. They moved up the cut. At the same time they both saw a portion of the piled stones, still strewn with some leaves, and they looked at each other.

He said, "Sit right there. You can put your back against that tree. Let me take a look."

He used a long stick to dig out more of the packed leaves. Went to work clearing away the dead limbs.

Pulled on the stone pile, rolling them back, clacking and scraping. There was a narrow black slanted cleft in the rock ledge. He came up to dig the flashlight out of the backpack. Slid back down into the ravine. Got on his knees and tried to see into the cleft. One large stone blocked the way. He stood up and looked around, frowning.

He said, "It goes deep and widens out, I think."

"What's wrong?"

"I don't know. Didn't you hear something?"

"I heard a crow way on up the mountain."

She thought, *The journal said the mine would be protected by the spirits of the* Aniwaya. But she said nothing, and only felt pleased to have discovered this quiet place. She smiled at him. "Can that stone be moved somehow?"

He rubbed the back of his neck and shrugged. He stood back and looked it over. "It's heavy. But there's always a way."

He came back for the short-handled trenching tool and began digging at the rocky soil just to one side of the stone, prying out small mud-caked rocks, scraping away soil and cutting at roots with chopping strokes. In twenty minutes he had a shallow hole excavated just beside the large stone.

She laughed. "You've got mud up to your elbows, and look at your jeans. You sure look like a miner."

"I don't think miners have to put up with heckling."

He found a strong sapling that was four inches thick at its base and used the Bowie to cut it down and strip its limbs. He chopped it off to make a pole eight feet long. He inserted the heavy end into the cleft and laid the body of it against the large stone, positioning the pole as a lever.

He put his back against the ravine wall, placed both his feet on the end of the pole, took a breath, and pushed, using his leg muscles, which were strong from his frequent runs along Eaglenest Ridge.

At first the stone did not budge, but he kept the pressure on, and then it leaned and suddenly toppled with a thud into the hole he had dug.

He crouched on his knees and looked into the darkness. Pushed the pole into the hole and swept it back and forth, rustling old leaves and stirring up a musty smell.

Thinking, *Could be a snake in there?*

She said, "Be careful. There could be snakes in there."

He got the flashlight and stretched out on his

belly. Crawled his way into the hole using his elbows until only his lower legs were outside. He stayed that way for several minutes.

Kitty said, "Okay, Sherlock, don't keep me in suspense. What are you seeing in there?"

He worked his way back out, leaving the flashlight aimed and shining brightly inside. He came up to her and offered his muddy hand.

He said, "Come on. You can get down there if you take it slow and hang on to me. You need to see this."

When she saw the gold running like a miniature frozen river through the glittering quartz, she let out a shriek and shouted, "*Mose*, you big old bear. You *found* it, didn't you?"

Outside the hole, her voice was muffled. He smiled to himself.

She touched and examined the vein in wonder, and shouted, "John, it's so beautiful, isn't it? Mose must have felt just like this."

He helped her squirm stiffly back out and climb up the ravine bank.

They sat side by side, looking at the cave. He offered her a bottle of water.

She gestured for him to keep it. "You need it after that workout."

He drank deeply, but saved half of it for her.

She said, "Oh, Mose. I'm so sorry."

"Yes."

She sighed. "So what do we do now?"

"I'll cover it back up. Try to erase most of the signs we were here. Have to leave the big stone like it is. We'll go back and make a plan."

He worked for an hour while she kept a watch on the surrounding woods.

He stood back and looked the leafy depression over. He said, "Sooner or later they'll know we were here, but this should keep anybody else from stumbling onto it."

Going slowly because Kitty's hip was bothering her, they made their way back to the fork and followed it downstream.

The Stealth Cam mounted in the dead tree passively sensed their heat as they passed and silently took five digital frames.

They stopped and sat on a log so she could rest.

She shook her head, frowning.

"What is it?"

"Well, I don't want to feel greedy about all this, but I sure do, anyway. I've been thinking how we could get the biggest possible share of this for ourselves. If we just tell the property owners it's here somewhere and we think we deserve a share, all they'll have to do is scour the whole property until they find it, and we'll be out of luck. We'll get a gee thanks. So maybe we could sneak in here with hammers and chisels and chip a lot of it out, take it two or three states away, and sell it. After all, we found it, didn't we? Don't we deserve at least a fair percentage of it? Compensation for our time and risk? Or maybe we could keep our mouths shut and make an offer to buy enough land here to build a house on. Thoughts like that. Thoughts I don't like at all. But it could mean not having to work in the casino. And maybe a chance to start a business. And a better place to live. And more *things.* But I don't feel right about it. Nobody would even know for sure it was here at all if Mose Kyle hadn't found it. I mean it could have gone undiscovered for another few centuries. This was *his* doing really, not ours. And what about the Cherokees who owned it in the first place? How do we know what's the right thing to do here?"

"Rainbows."

"Beautiful, but deceptive. This rainbow was sure beautiful. And it led us to the gold. Like some kind of miracle. But now everything has changed, hasn't it? Old Wasituna was right. Greed can change you if you're not careful. It's insidious."

He said, "One thing we can do is make sure the Cagles pay for Moses. Make sure anybody else involved pays, too."

"Amen to that."

Using her walking stick, she got to her feet. Limped two steps.

"Kitty. Lean on me."

It took almost an hour to cover the last mile. When they were within sight of the Wrangler, she said, "Well, who do we have here?"

A man was looking into the side window of the

Jeep. John pulled Kitty aside behind a large bushy cedar that went all the way to the ground and they stood still, peering through the thick branches. The man looked around and waved back along the track. Another man showed himself. They met and talked briefly, then melted back uphill into the woods on either side of the Jeep.

John had never seen either man before. They were dressed like farmers, both wearing billed caps, one in denim overalls. Average builds. Both maybe in their thirties. He eased Kitty down onto a mossy patch and took off his backpack. He thought for a moment. Untied the blowgun from the side of the backpack.

He gave her the keys to the Wrangler and said, "They most likely don't know for sure if you're with me. Get in under this tree and pull some leaves over yourself. Don't come out or call out no matter what you hear. If I don't come back, give it a half hour and then go to the Jeep and get out of here. Go see the Maggie chief."

"Why don't you just call in the cops with your cell?"

"Left it with Hank. And they would have too many questions, anyway."

"Who *are* these idiots? What are you going to do?"

"I'll take a closer look at them. You'll stay put?"

"Just don't tangle with them, okay?"

"Give it a half hour, then get out."

He jogged back along the creek for a hundred yards and cut uphill into the woods, holding the blowgun close beside his body so it wouldn't snag on anything, placing his feet with practiced care, using stones and moss and deadfalls to make as little noise as possible. A breeze rustling down the valley was helping mask sound and nudging the forest shadows into furtive motion all around. Cloud shadows were hiding and revealing the lowering sun. He cut around in a wide circle, slowed to a walk, and worked his way down the slope, skirting patches of heavier brush and tangles of vines, going from tree to tree and stopping frequently to listen and to scan the woods ahead.

He could see the white Wrangler parked below. One of the men was standing behind a fractured boulder, watching the muddy track. The man's back was to him. John was standing behind a large shagbark hickory, peering out past the rough bark. It was good camouflage, breaking up his body's outline. He waited, trying to use just his eyes to find the second man.

The man behind the boulder was fidgeting, shifting his weight from foot to foot, waving irritably at insects. He was wearing a loose plaid shirt. He reached to the small of his back, lifted the shirt, and drew out a small chromed snub-nosed revolver, checked it, and replaced it behind his belt at his back.

Moving very slowly, John pulled back behind the tree. He drew a dart free from the deerskin quiver that was tied with a leather thong to the blowgun.

The seven-inch yellow-locust dart was sharpened to a needle point. Wasituna had rolled and bound a precise measure of thistle down onto the back end of the dart—not so much that the dart would stick in the blowgun's barrel, or so little that it would lose power by letting air leak . It was the boy's blowgun. At four feet, it was shorter than the traditional small-game weapon, so not as accurate, but Wasituna had made it well, drying the length of river cane, heating it over a fire and bending it over his knee until it was straight, smoothing the bore with a length of flint-tipped wood.

The man was less than fifty feet away. John slipped the dart into the blowgun and raised it, stepping half out from behind the tree, feet shoulder-width apart and solidly planted. Letting it rest on the palms of his hands, held close to the near end, and gripping it firmly but not tightly with his curled fingers. Aiming was mostly a matter of experience, of honed instinct, as with the western gunfighters who could clear a heavy forty-four from its holster with uncanny speed and fire lethally from the hip.

This patch of woods was quiet, only a light and constant eddy of the main breeze that was flowing strongly down the valley. He felt the breeze on his right cheek. Let his brain assimilate its strength and direction. He took two deep, calming breaths. He fixed his gaze on the man's right rump. Took another deep breath and raised the gun to his lips.

The dart flew almost silently and invisibly from the reed gun and sprouted in the center of the man's right rear jeans pocket. He reacted instantly and violently, spread-eagling up against the boulder and throwing his head back, his hat falling off. In a rising high-pitched whine he screamed, "*Nnneeeowowowww*," and twisted around to look at his backside, then quickly all around at the woods, searching like a startled squirrel for his attacker, still screeching with each breath he took. John had melted back behind the rough hickory and was watching with only his right eye. The man fumbled for the revolver and yanked it out in front of himself, tangling it in a handful of shirt.

The other man, the one in overalls, came crashing through the trees from the left, holding what looked like a twenty-two target automatic in his right hand, stumbled over a rotten limb and almost fell. He whispered loudly, "What is it? Stop screaming. He'll hear you. We're only supposed to *watch* them."

The first man stopped screaming but started grunt-whining, standing bowed, alternating glances around into the woods with stares at his right buttock. He pointed at it and said, "Looklooklook. What *is* it? Pull it out. Pull it *out*."

The other man came up close to him, breathing hard. He reached out with his free left hand and grasped the dart between his fingers, and the man screamed again, "NO. Don't touch it. NONONO,"

But the overalled man pulled, and the dart came free with a spurt of blood and another howl. The injured man leaned against the boulder and hung his head, moaning. The overalled man raised the automatic and trained it around in an arc. Looking for a target. The wounded man stood away from the boulder on unsteady legs, squinting, red-faced. His hand with the shiny revolver was aimed out straight but wavering, swinging from tree to tree. The two men began moving up the hill toward him.

John slipped another dart into the gun. He could step out, fire at the one in overalls, aiming for a thigh, then run back up the hill using the hickory for cover for at least a short way. Lead them away from Kitty.

A long, piercing, ululating cry rose from the other side of the track, freezing all three men. A moment's silence. The cry rose and fell again, eerily.

The two men looked at each other and broke down the hill in a plunging rush, stumbling over deadfalls and vines, getting whipped by saplings. The overalled one stopped in a crouch by the Wrangler and a knife blade flashed in his hand, then they moved quickly back along the track, the wounded man limping but making good time, both of them throwing glances back over their shoulders.

When John walked out of the trees carrying the blowgun, Kitty met him, leaning on her walking stick and smiling.

He said, "Where did you come up with that?"

"Don't you think an Injun war cry must have sounded something like it?"

"If so, I don't know how the bluecoats ever beat you. You spooked these guys. Had them thinking they were surrounded."

"It sounded like you poked one of them with a dart. I figured since you probably only made them mad, you could use some help."

"Thanks."

"They cut a valve stem on your Jeep so we couldn't chase them."

"I saw it."

"John, *what* is going on here? Who *are* these people?"

CHAPTER 27

Werly Fulks woke an hour before dawn and got out of bed without disturbing his wife, who was snoring like an unmuffled tractor. He pulled on yesterday's pants and shirt and shuffled into the hall bathroom, where he washed his face and studied his scowling reflection in the mirror, seeing reddened, scared eyes and too much white in his dripping beard.

On an impulse, he scissored off as much of the beard as he could, then used his wife's dulled Lady Gillette to shave off most of the rest. It took a while. He looked in the mirror again.

Good. He hardly recognized himself. Too late, but he felt some better, anyway.

He went downstairs to the dining room/office in the old farmhouse and made a call, waking up his crew chief to tell him about a new logging site he wanted the men to start the next day. It was only two acres and mostly beetle-eaten pine, but he never turned down a job. He had not slept well.

He had been stupid to use his pickup when he'd tried to trick up the heathen's airplane. The truck had then been hidden at the Cagle place, but Hardin had showed up out of nowhere nosing around, with the FBI right behind. Frank had called, telling him what to do and say.

The FBI and the sheriff had appeared at his logging site the same day. Took him to the sheriff's office and questioned him for two hours.

Where had he been the night before last?

At an all-night stud poker game with three other ol' boys at the Cagle place. They would all swear to it.

How did he know the Cagles?

Orin had once worked for him, which was true.

Had he been to the Asheville Airport at any time recently?

He told them he was a pilot, because they would know that, anyway. He was thinking of getting back into flying, so he had been looking around at a few airports for any planes for sale. Yes, he'd been to the Asheville Airport recently, but could not remember the exact day.

Did he know John Hardin?

No. Not to talk to, which was true. Wasn't that the man who ran some kind of charter business?

Why was his pickup at the Cagle place?

His friend Orin was going to do a ball joint job on it for him.

What did he know about Cessnas?

Not much, because he had always flown Pipers himself.

Why was he so nervous?

Well, hell, anybody would be nervous with the FBI asking all kinds of crazy questions, wouldn't they?

They had kept at him from different directions, but he had only told them the same story. They had finally brought him back to the logging site and had left him with a warning not to leave the area, and had said they would probably be back.

He was hollow-gut afraid it was only a matter of time before the law would find out more and would then come down on him in force, and he had no idea what he would do then. He knew Hardin had probably not seen him or the truck clearly that night or they would have arrested him, but somebody else could have seen him at the airport that night and got the truck's plate number. They could be watching his house right now, out there, through binoculars. The FBI and the ATF and half a dozen of those other big-letter police.

The Preacher had assured him he'd be doing God's work by rigging that airplane. He'd been a private pilot, so he alone among the disciples knew how to do it. The Preacher had told him he'd be fighting the evil legion of the demon possessed. Something most of the world out there did not even begin to understand these days. And down deep he knew, of course, God would protect and preserve him. The Preacher had taken him aside and had told him personally, "Our God spoke, in Proverbs twenty-one: 'The wicked shall be a ransom for the righteous, and the transgressor for the upright.' Are you not one of us, Brother Fulks? And are we not the righteous and the upright? The wicked, the demon possessed, serve as our ransom. I say to you now, you are doing the work of the One Pure God. And in that same chapter of Proverbs we are told, '. . . but safety is of the LORD.' Go now, Brother Fulks, and know deep in your heart the Lord wraps you in His benevolent protection."

He knew, though, that he was a direct link to the Preacher and his followers. And the Preacher had to be well aware of that. If the law did find out more and if they did scream into his yard with all their lights flashing and their guns out, hollering at him through bullhorns, he would represent a threat to the Preacher, to the whole Church of the One Pure God, and Werly was uncomfortable with that. He had seen the Preacher in black moods when he was better left alone. Times when Werly knew he was not the only one in the church who felt such edgy fear.

But the Preacher was his unquestioned leader. On a Sunday morning when the man was standing tall in his plain black robe behind the pulpit with his long silver-white hair brushed back in waves, with the Holy Spirit fairly shining out of him, interpreting the Word of God, making the confusing words so clear, looking right into each of their souls with his blazing, righteous eyes, telling them what the One Pure God was calling each of them to do, well, there was just nothing like it.

He was akin to Moses himself come down from the mountain. There was nobody like him on this tired old earth so overcrowded with sinners of every evil kind. Werly would never betray him, no matter what. Surely the Preacher knew that. Didn't he?

He heated coffee in the countertop microwave and carried the cup and a frayed straw basket out to the chicken coop in the gray light. One of his chores every morning was to collect the eggs. He set the cup down on an old, empty wooden barrel beside the coop door. Inside the coop, he absently brushed several of the hens from their roosts, setting them to fluttering and squawking, and used his curled fingers to gently pick up seven small brown eggs and place them in the basket.

He backed out of the coop and closed the door, sticking a rusty railroad spike through the hasp. He took a sip of coffee and left the cup and the egg basket on the wooden barrel.

He nipped a few popcorn kernels in his fingers from a bag in the tin-covered feed bin built onto his shed and went around the back of the shed to a row of twelve individual low pens, spread out and half hidden back in the trees, each housing one of his fighting cocks. They were all out crowing throatily at the early gray of the dawning. He stood still twenty feet from the nearest rooster and admired him. It was a blue Arkansas Traveler, and it was his favorite. He had raised it from a chick, carefully trimming its comb back with a sharp knife during an old moon so it hadn't bled much, and had trained it the way his daddy had taught him. It was a good cutter. A real battler. It was built just right, too. Stocky, with a lot of protective breast. Werly knew this bird would always stand and fight for as long as it could hold its head up. He'd seen its spirit enough early on during the many practice fights with others among his best young cocks, their spurs carefully cuffed in leather. Now, at just under two years old, it had already killed nine tough chickens in the pits, the last three—two Blue Ridge Roundheads and a well-known Dominecker—in a single day's fighting over in Arkansas. He'd been offered two thousand dollars for the blue after that last fight. Lot of money for a chicken, but there was all that and a lot more to be had. He would fight the blue once again for real big money in two weeks, down in Georgia. The entry fee alone was two thousand, and there would be cock owners from Florida, the Carolinas, New York State, and even Canada, somebody said.

The pastime was illegal, something Werly had never figured out. He was only raising fighting cocks to do something they were natural-born to do, after all. You let two roosters loose in the yard, and sooner or later what are they going to do? They're going to go at each other until one is dead because they're some of the gamest doggoned creatures in this world, and it might take until sundown to get it done. As natural as rain. Anybody who whined about pitting chickens ought to spend a day in some slaughterhouse where they killed thirty thousand chickens or twenty thousand hogs every day, you want to talk about something wasn't pretty. At least his chickens had a chance in the pit. But illegal it was, so fights these days took place over long intervals in locations spread over several states and on private, well-posted lands in remote woods. He'd heard about a bunch of millionaires down to Texas with their own planes and all, and those boys wagered major money on their birds, a hundred thousand or more on some fights. Some day he sure would like a piece of that action.

Today he would begin a fourteen-day conditioning period, feeding the blue with high-protein dog food and milk and the best grains he'd been able to find, and vitamins, but carefully watching its weight. Just over five pounds would be perfect. He would take it out of its pen on a tether at twelve-hour intervals and "fly it" by repeatedly picking it up and tossing it so it would flap and half fly for a dozen feet. Then he would give it a good rubdown. The blue would get only water and maybe some honey early on the fight day.

He still remembered that last fight. He could feel the angry tension in the blue when he and the other owner held their birds tight and thrust them into each other, letting them peck some, "fluffing" them so they'd get right to it in the pit. Then the referee called out, "Toe the line," and Werly set the blue down on the raked dirt with its toes on the white-limed pitting line, facing the feisty Dominecker. Each bird was wearing handmade file-sharpened metal gaffs securely tied to the backs of their legs, positioned over the spots where their spurs had been hacksawn off. The blue had eighty-dollar two-and-a-half-inch jaggers on him, and the Dominecker sported glinting bayonets. The gaffs had been disinfected in case an owner should accidentally get stuck.

The referee waited to let the crowd quiet down because there was a lot of money riding on this one. Werly had fifteen hundred out on the blue at good odds. The referee called, "Pit your birds," and both men released the tails of their birds at the same instant. The roosters met in a blurred mid-air slashing flurry, but inside three minutes the Dominecker got a gaff hung in the blue rooster and Werly had to go into the pit when the referee called out, "Handle," to carefully free it without doing further damage. Both men cleaned the blood out of their chickens' mouths, but they let the birds rest for only ten seconds because they were both bleeding out pretty good. As the crowd laughed and hooted in approval, the blue went back at the Dominecker in a red-eyed frenzy, flapping and darting and trading slashes with no letup until the Dominecker lost its footing and the blue nailed him, wounding him bad. They toed them up again, the Dominecker just sitting there and wobbling its head, and the blue finished it in about five seconds. It took quick work, but he managed to save the blue with some first aid and a shot of vet penicillin.

He would retire the blue after this next big fight and make him a brood cock. Breed him with a leggy Claret he'd had his eye on for some months. When word got around good, he'd be able to sell the chicks, and even the eggs, for top money. The blue could be a brood earner for five years or more.

He squinted at the blue and tossed a popcorn grain five feet. The blue saw it instantly and cocked its head, clucking. Good. The bird was alert. Fit. But he'd be in even better shape in fourteen days. Werly was already counting the money he'd pull from the crowd around the pit.

He went back to get the eggs and his coffee cup. He took a lukewarm sip and looked at the sky, thinking about the blue, his face feeling naked and tender where he'd worked on it with the dull razor.

He caught movement at the corner of his eye. A shape appeared around the corner in a crouch. The two center tines of the dirty pitchfork took him just under the chin and drove all the way through his neck, piercing his larynx and grazing his spine on the way. Warm wetness filled his throat, welled up out of his mouth, and spilled down his chin. He could not breathe. The egg basket and the coffee cup fell from his nerveless fingers. The ground rose up and struck him numbly along his left side, and his head bounced onto the scuffed toe of a boot. He looked at the boot stitching, blinking rapidly, and the slick red-tipped boot was withdrawn.

He stared at the wet half-rotted wood of the barrel. Felt his chest convulsing.

Thought about toeing up the blue.

Waiting to release the blue's tail. Ready to let go with a secret push of his fingers just as soon as the referee called out, "Pit your birds." Hoping to give the blue a small advantage by being freed a fraction before the other bird could fully ready itself to fight.

He saw stacks of money piled high on a table near the pit and wondered how he was going to carry it all home after the fight.

Thought he heard the referee, a tall, hooded figure with the fiery eyes of something not human, call out to him over the babble and laughter of the crowd.

And he let go.

◊ ◊ ◊

At eleven that morning, John was on his computer taking notes from online sites about gold and about Haywood County land ownership records when he got a call from an important client, an Asheville graphics agency. They needed some rush photography of a four-hundred-acre site near Black Mountain. They were putting together a last-minute competitive presentation for a development consortium, trying to win a lucrative marketing contract. They would send one of their people along in the plane to show him what they wanted. Sorry about the short notice, but could he please meet the artist, a woman named Ivy who would be driving a yellow Volkswagen, at the Asheville Airport in one hour?

He didn't want to take the time for it, but it was one of his best clients, so he gathered up his camera gear and told Hank where he was going and that he would skip lunch. He coasted the Wrangler down the hill in second gear, letting the engine compression do most of the braking, and turned east onto Highway 19, heading for the airport.

He had done a lot of thinking, and would share some of it with Kitty when they met later. He would not tell her all of it.

He heard a siren wailing at a constant ear-splittingly high shriek behind him. A cruiser was coming down on him, weaving through traffic, its lights coruscating madly. He moved over into the right lane to let it pass, but it tracked him and rushed up to stay two feet from his back bumper, the siren whooping urgently now. He pulled the Jeep over into the empty lot of a defunct landscaping company and shut it down. He rolled down the window and sat there with his hands on the top of the wheel.

Boudreau bristled out of the cruiser, leaving the door open, the cruiser radio crackling, pulled his black nine-millimeter out, and held it trained on John with both hands. He was in an intent half crouch, veins standing out on his beefy arms. He edged up beside the Jeep window and screamed at him like a one-man

SWAT squad.

"OUT. GET OUT OF THE CAR RIGHT NOW. GET OUT NOW. KEEP YOUR HANDS IN SIGHT. GET OUT."

John held his hands up by his shoulders, palm out. "I have to reach down to open the door."

"IS THE DOOR UNLOCKED?"

"Take it easy, Boudreau. I can hear you. They can probably hear you over in Waynesville. Yes, it's unlocked."

Boudreau held the Glock in his right and opened the door with his left, flinging it aside so it almost banged closed again. Fumbled to grab it again and pull it aside.

"OKAY. GET OUT, SMARTASS."

John got out and stood facing him, his hands held low, palms out.

"TURN AROUND. HANDS ON THE HOOD. DO IT NOW."

John complied, bending over enough to place his palms on the hood. Boudreau frisked him with his shaking left hand.

"STAND UP. DON'T TURN AROUND. HANDS ON YOUR HEAD. LACE YOUR FINGERS. DON'T MOVE A HAIR."

Boudreau cuffed one wrist, yanked it down, and cuffed the other. Grabbed a fistful of his shirt and pulled him to the cruiser and shoved him into the backseat.

Boudreau got behind the wheel and squealed out of

the lot, just missing the steel pole that held up a sign.

They wailed toward Maggie, doing seventy, vehicles pulling over to let them by.

When Boudreau slid to a stop in front of the station door and shut the cruiser down, John said, "Okay, what's this all about?"

Boudreau glared at him through the rearview mirror. "They found Werly Fulks after you killed him, probably early this morning."

"I haven't been out of my house until you saw me on the road. And why would I kill this man Werly Fulks?"

"I know all about it, wiseass. You think Fulks was messing with your airplane. It's what you told the FBI. Except they weren't so sure he did anything, and they didn't arrest him. So you decided to take care of it yourself. Now he's dead."

"And you're going to make the TV news?"

Boudreau pulled him out of the cruiser and led him inside past the reception desk. The girl stood up and said, "Sergeant, do you really think—"

"Ruthie, shut up. Get that FBI man in Asheville for me. I'll take it in my office."

Boudreau led him to a plain twelve-by-twelve room at the back. There was a table with four heavy straight chairs. Five black file cabinets were aligned against one wall. A whiteboard was mounted on another wall. There was a window with wire screen embedded in the glass. Boudreau recuffed his hands in front and chained him to a recessed ring mounted in the floor. Looked for a card in his wallet, pulled it out, and recited his rights.

John said, “Where is Chief Vogel? I want to talk with him.”

“Sure, when he gets out of the hospital. I’m in charge here.”

Ruth appeared in the doorway and looked at John. “They think it might be his heart. Can I get you a bottle of water or something?”

“No. But thanks, Ruth.”

To Boudreau she said, “Agent Donner is on the line.”

Boudreau pointed out the door and the girl left. He followed her, locking the door behind him.

CHAPTER 28

Agent Donner was standing with Sergeant Boudreau in the reception area of the Maggie Valley Police Station.

Donner said, "So you took it on yourself to arrest the man?"

"I assumed he'd be the prime suspect. He claimed Fulks tried to sabotage his plane. You people chose not to do anything about it. So he decided to take care of things himself."

"Don't you think you should have called me first, or at least the sheriff who has jurisdiction in this case?"

"Look, I spotted him heading east. I decided, on my own initiative, to stop him and hold him. I think you should be asking *him* questions, not me. He's the murder suspect here."

Kitty Birdsong came through the double doors, still limping but not as much as the day before, her boots knocking on the vinyl tile. She shook her hair back and looked at Boudreau, Donner, and Ruth, who was seated at her desk. She said, "You've got John Hardin here, I understand."

Donner said, "Who are you?"

"I'm Kitty Birdsong. A friend. And I want to know why you're holding John here."

Donner introduced himself and said, "Calm down please, Ms. Birdsong. We only want to question him. It's just routine. If you'll have a seat—"

"What is John supposed to have done?"

Boudreau said, "Look, this is police business and—"

"If he was supposed to have done something illegal yesterday or last night, I'm telling you that was impossible. Either I or the Gaskills, who share his house with him, will swear he was with us. He and I spent yesterday out hiking. Then he stayed home all night and through midday today. Call Mr. Gaskill, or go see him."

Donner looked at Boudreau.

Boudreau said, "She's his girlfriend. And the Gaskills live with him. What do you think they're going to say? He could have snuck out of the house early while the old people were still asleep, and he had plenty of time to get back before they woke up."

Donner said, "Ms. Birdsong. Please take a seat. Sergeant Boudreau, where do you have him?"

Boudreau pointed and led the way to the back room. John was still shackled to the floor ring, sitting with his elbows on the table and his hands clasped, looking at the ceiling. Boudreau closed the door, and both men took seats on the opposite side of the table.

Donner said, "Mister Hardin."

"Agent Donner."

"They treating you well here?"

"No complaint."

"Do you know why you're here?"

"Sergeant Boudreau said something about the death of this man Fulks."

"Do you want to tell me where you were from midnight last night through mid-morning today?"

"Never left my house. I didn't attack Fulks."

Boudreau said, "You're lying. You found him outside his house and gigged him with a pitchfork, and—"

With some force Donner said, "I'll do the questioning here today."

Donner considered, squinting at John. "There's something you haven't been telling me all along, I do know that much. A large something that's behind all of this. I think I'm considered a patient and understanding man among my peers. You're approaching the end of my patience, Mr. Hardin. You and I are going to talk a lot more. And soon. But that's it for now. Turn him loose."

Boudreau went red in the face and said, "Turn him *loose?*"

"Uncuff him, apologize for any inconvenience, and let the man go. He has an alibi, Sergeant Boudreau, and you have no evidence at the present time to the contrary, do you?"

He met Kitty in the outer office and told her he had to make a quick call. He borrowed the receptionist's phone to dial the client he was supposed to fly for and found out that when he had not showed up at the airport they had chartered a plane with another pilot to shoot the photos themselves. John apologized, but it would take time to repair the damage.

He and Kitty walked outside together.

She waved a hand at her bike. "I got it back this morning. The dealership mechanic rode it here himself to road test it, and had one of the salesmen follow him. It's good as new, but it needs polishing. I've still got the loaner helmet for you, so let's go to my place and I'll put coffee on."

"Okay. Can we swing by and get the Jeep first? "

Seated at the table in her small kitchen with the coffeepot burbling fragrantly, he said, "Thanks. How did you know I was at the station?"

"The receptionist, Ruthie? She must have a thing for you. She called your house, and Hank called me." She hooked a long, silken strand of hair behind her ear. He got up to pour the coffee and said, "How are you feeling?"

"Still stiff. But I'm healing fine. So. Now?"

"Donner said there's more behind this. I think he's right. There's a lot we don't know."

◊ ◊ ◊

Coleman Prescott washed his hands again, this time in the upstairs bathroom. It was at least the dozenth time that day, but he could not help doing it. His hands felt unclean even as he was washing them with disinfecting soap, and his arms were itching like tiny spiders were busily constructing their sticky webs under the skin. He'd had no sleep for the past twenty hours, and his eyelids were getting heavy. He knew he should eat something, but the idea of food still gave his stomach a nauseating wrench. At least the old man wasn't around anymore to hammer away at him with his stupid Disneyland ideas.

He'd spent maybe fourteen or fifteen straight hours at Tina's place with Roach and Stephanie and Brenda. He dimly realized there was something funny in there somewhere.

Oh, yeah, Tina was another name for meth that some people used. *Let's do some Tina and then let's do Tina.* Roach liked to snort it and called it ice or snow and was always talking about getting lost in a great glorious freakin' worldwide snowstorm. Sometime in the past day or so, Roach had said, "You know, Hitler used to give out ice to his soldier boys mixed in chocolates. Made 'em fight like demons all day long, man. Like freakin' Nazis. True story, I swear."

The girls all routinely shot up. Stephanie had cocked her head, raised a finger, and said, "Hey, I know what. Let's all get bright and shiny." Like there was something else they might have planned on. So they did the last of Roach's glass, the really righteous stuff that could make you ten feet tall and abso-damn-lutely unbeatable and turn you into a sex machine. Two hundred a gram, but worth it easy. Tina turned up the boom box and they all got naked and went at each other like they'd never get enough, until they lost track of time, until he was beyond worn out. Until the neighbor in the duplex beat on the door and hollered he was going to call in the heat. But by then they were all coming down, anyway.

He was focused on the sink, filled and frothy with soap. He shut off the water and turned to look for the towel, his hands reddened and soft and dripping hot water, and saw the man standing in the doorway, holding the towel. Big tattooed arms, a bulging black T-shirt, dirty jeans, and long hair tied back. The man snapped the towel and the tail of it caught him full across the face, stinging like fire, stunning him, stabbing a shard of pain into his right eye, and he grabbed for the sink, lost his grip on it and sat down heavily on the toilet lid. He put his hand to his face and grasped the edge of the shower door with his other hand and stood up on shaking legs. "How . . . how did you get in here?"

"Now, see, that's the wrong question." He spoke in a rough gravelly rasp and smelled of cigarettes. He was winding up the towel to whip it out again. "But I'll give you a chance to ask the right one. The kind of guy I am. What's the right question?"

"I don't know. I—"

The towel cracked the back of the hand that was holding his face on. Made him cower and let out a short scream. Made his whole hand burn.

"'I don't know' ain't a question. What's the right question?"

Coleman held up his free hand in feeble protection. "Don't, man. Don't. Listen, just let me think, okay? Why are you doing this? Why are you here?"

"See, now you got the right question. Good. That's good. Might mean we're gonna get along just fine here. Reason I'm here is to make you see the light. Tomorrow afternoon you got a meet with a man tried to buy a piece of your mountain, but you wasn't nice to him last time. This time you're gonna sign on the lines right where he tells you. You're gonna kiss his ass, he tells you."

"Okay. Okay, man. Listen. Whatever."

The big man reached for Coleman's shirt pocket. Lifted out his cell phone. Slid it into his dirty jeans. "I bet there's some interestin' numbers in here. Your buds that do what you call crystal meth? Make it? Sell it to you? Pretty name. Crystal meth. How do you do it? Pump it in your arm? Suck it up your nose? Stick it up your butt?"

"I'll sign the papers, man. I will."

"But maybe you'll decide not to sign, come tomorrow. It's not near as good a deal as you got offered last time. But it's gotta *look* good, you know? Got to be notarized, all that. You should have took that last deal when you coulda. Thing with this crystal meth stuff. They say it makes you a big man. Talk big. Like you talked before. You want a share, you said. You want a million dollars up front. Big man. A real wheeler-dealer. They tell me it makes you forget things, too. When it wears off you. What we got to do is make damn sure you ain't gonna forget our talk here. You see? So in a bit I'll let you choose which place on you I break. I'll name three places. You get to choose one. Like I said, the kinda guy I am. 'Course you don't want to choose one, then I gotta break two places on you."

"Man . . . man, you don't have to be doing this. I *get* the message. I'll *sign*."

"'Cause, see, if you forget, you don't show up half an hour early, you don't sign on all the lines, what I maybe got to do then is set it up to look like you been makin' this crystal meth right out back in your barn and maybe get a bud of mine to call in the cops. That's only one thing I could do. Depends what I feel like. What else I could do is come back and let you pick another place for me to break. Another bone. And then, see, the deal will be even worse on your end." He coughed into his fist.

Coleman Prescott could feel the tears hot on his face, and his chest heaved in a sob.

"What else you don't want to forget is you never saw me in your whole life. You got broke up when you tripped and fell down these stairs out here. So let's you and me go and get it done."

The big man reached for him.

Afterward he lay at the bottom of the stairs on the Oriental carpet, moaning and crying and holding his bent left forearm. He heard the car start up outside and drive away. He sat up and leaned back against the banister. The room got fuzzy, and he almost passed out.

Somewhere he had a few small rocks left in a baggie, he knew. Tried hard to remember where. It was brown, weak crap. Just peanut-butter crank. *Can't smoke it with only one good arm.*

But he could crush it with the flat of a table knife.

Roll up a bill and snort it.

Get all bright and shiny again.

CHAPTER 29

At sixty-three, Lloyd Dobbs considered himself to be the best mechanic in eastern Tennessee. It was all he'd ever done since he first started taking things apart to look at their innards as far back into childhood as he could remember. His wife had died four years back, and they'd never had children, but he had what he did, and he did it well. He saw a vehicle engine as a wonderful thing. A thing almost alive. Every part, even the tiniest carburetor screw, had its special job, and they all had to be assembled right for the engine to do best what it had been made to do. A man would run an engine for thousands of miles low on dirty oil, never check the transmission, let a radiator get choked up, go to pulling a horse trailer up the hills with a six-cylinder pickup, and wonder why his engine would finally quit on him.

He had sympathy for a sick engine, and what people saw as an uncanny way with one. To him it was pretty simple, really. Was this engine getting enough air to breathe? When the cylinders took their turns inhaling, was the mixture burnable? Was enough fire pulsing through its veins to light each cylinder off at exactly the right instant? If so, and if nothing inside was broken, the engine would come back to life. He had personal rules. You didn't just grab any wrench that fit and go cranking down on bolts to get done with it, for instance. You took your time and torqued each critical bolt to the specs in the book, not a foot-pound too much or too little, so the male threads would grip the female threads perfectly. You treat an engine right and it would always treat you right, too.

Lloyd worked a four day ten hour shift at a busy independent shop in Johnson City, and on two of his off days he did jobs on the side in his own garage behind his home in a valley five miles outside Elizabethton. He spent Wednesday night and all day Sunday with his church. He always had a list of people waiting on him to get to their problems. This afternoon he had two cars pulled into his three-car garage.

A Ford Explorer was up on jack stands, waiting for him to replace its shocks and transmission filter and fluid. Beside it there was a burgundy '93 Buick, which belonged to Rufus Blinder, another of the disciples. He had promised to get it done for Rufus today. It was the car they had used to put the fear of God into the heathen woman on the motorcycle. Lloyd had noticed the brakes were fading on it that night and had got to looking under it later with a flashlight. Rufus had bought it from a Yankee, and there was a lot of rust all under it because they salted the roads up there in the winters. All the steel brake lines were corroded and leaking, so today Lloyd was replacing them. Because this model had the automatic braking system, there were more than fifty feet of lines, and because nobody stocked pre-made lines, each one had to be custom-made. A dealer would charge maybe two thousand. It would cost Rufus only two hundred for materials. Lloyd had all four wheels removed, the front end up on his spare jack stands and the rear axle supported by two long-handled hydraulic jacks.

He was on his back on a creeper under the car, working a new line into position around the gas tank, grunting because he was fifty pounds overweight. His hands were big and had always been a handicap when he tried to get into tight places. He didn't know how long he would be able to do some of these jobs because the demon the doctors called arthritis was stalking him, and the pills and the healings were not working to fight the demon off as well lately.

He was taking a brief rest, breathing hard and looking out at his fat calico cat, which had been sitting in the driveway, grooming itself. The cat's body was frozen in place, its back legs splayed because it had been licking its tail. Its head was tilted up and swiveling toward the car, its staring green eyes fixed on something.

A hand reached down and rotated the knurled

knob on one of the hydraulic jacks, and Lloyd had no time to even call out before the jack silently retracted, the Buick's rear end tilted, and the gas tank crushed the air out of his chest, the creeper wheels bending under the strain, one wheel scraping harshly on the concrete as it folded, startling the cat, which scampered under a bush and peered out in a crouch, watching the coveralled legs kick and tremble and twitch and then go still.

CHAPTER 30

John was as sure as he could be that nobody had followed them. At least nobody who'd not had any special training at it. Kitty was in the passenger seat. He turned the Wrangler onto the smooth paved drive that took a climbing S-curve through trees to the Prescott house, a modest but well-restored older clapboarded two-story set on a sloping lawn terraced with a low slate wall. There was a two-car garage connected to the house by a breezeway. He parked near the front entrance and shut the engine off.

That morning he had called a woman he knew who ran a local weekly newspaper and kept up on all the gossip around the valley.

As he looked the house over, he said, "I was told Gideon Prescott's son lives here alone. Coleman Prescott. The only child. Rumor is, he runs with a rough crowd."

Kitty said, "How are we going to approach this guy?"

"Well, we don't have to spring the news about the

mine being on his property right away. Let's try getting to know him a little first. See how it goes."

They got out and John pushed the button beside the door. Waited ten seconds and pushed it again. Waited. Said, "Maybe nobody's home."

"Do you hear that?"

"No . . . Yes. Music."

"Classical music. Come on." She walked, with only a slight limp now, around the corner and pointed to the breezeway. He followed, and the music got louder. "I think it's coming from behind the garage. That door. Wait a second and I'll tell you what it is." She inclined her head and closed her eyes. "It's 'Bolero' by a guy named Ravel. I don't know much classical stuff, but I've always liked that one. It's long and it builds and builds in volume."

They walked to the door for what was an extension built onto the back of the garage, and he rapped on it with a knuckle. There was no response. He tried the knob and opened the door a few inches. The music was very loud now, almost painfully so, and he tried to penetrate it with his voice. "Hello? Is Coleman Prescott here?"

He pushed the door open enough to see inside.

It was a home office. A large walnut desk against the far wall with a computer. A row of file cabinets. A potbellied woodstove. A window air conditioner. A bank of multi-paned windows on the end wall looking out into the forest. A drawing table with a circle magnifier light and a drafting machine in the near corner. What looked like architect's sketches thumbtacked to a wall corkboard. The music was blaring from a corner entertainment center that housed a stereo and a TV/DVD/VCR that was silently playing some promotional footage of a plastically perfect family—man, woman, a young girl and boy—hiking and picnicking with mountain vistas in the background, approaching a stone wall to look down on black bears in a wooded glade, and the father hoisting up the boy onto his shoulders and pointing at a bald eagle perched on a dead tree.

A man was seated on the hardwood floor Indian style, his back to them, wearing a dirty gray T-shirt decorated with an elaborately fierce red-eyed dragon exhaling fire. His long hair was a tangled mass. His elbows were on his knees, his left arm, the hand like a claw, was held up straight from the knee. The arm was splinted with two pieces of wood, strips of toweling wrapped around it. His right hand was supporting his head. He was not moving. The music was building even louder, threatening to overdrive the speakers, the same refrain, over and over, different orchestral instruments taking turns.

They went inside. John moved around to stand in front of the man, who was staring down at a large rendering spread on the floor. The music built to a final crashing climax, and there was a sudden numbing silence. The CD reset, and "Bolero" began to play again, relatively quietly at first. Kitty found the power button and pushed it off. John squatted in front of the man and said, "Are you Coleman Prescott?"

The man looked at him. His left eye was red-rimmed and his right eye was swollen almost shut. His face was gray and dirty and tear-streaked. He said, "Put the music back on. It was his favorite piece. He said it was like a man's life ought to be, building on itself and strengthening and growing and never giving up. Put it back on."

"I'm John Hardin. This is Kitty Birdsong. We'd like to talk with you."

"I don't have any time left. I have to be there pretty soon. But I want to hear the music again. I couldn't find the peanut-butter crank."

"This drawing. Is it the plan your father had for Medicine Ridge?"

"I thought it was stupid. I still do. Wannabe Disney crap. But it was *his* stupid dream, you know?"

"Somebody needs to take care of that arm. And you look sick. What's the matter, Coleman?"

"Sick, yeah. I guess. He made me pick one."

"Your father? Pick what?"

"Which place to break. Which bone. He laid my arm out across a stair step and used his foot. I tried to get it straight after but I kept passing out. I wrapped it up anyway. So I have to sign."

"Who are you talking about, Coleman?"

"The man with all the tattoos. But the thing is, I

don't want to sell his stupid dream, can you understand that? Because I sure don't understand it."

"Somebody wants you to sell Medicine Ridge?" John and Kitty looked at each other.

"Only a piece of it. On the other side of the mountain. Just a piece of his stupid dream. But I don't want to."

"Then don't, Coleman."

"He said he'd come back. Tell the cops I've got a meth lab out there in the horse barn. Make me pick another bone."

"When and where are you supposed to sign?"

He closed his eyes and rested his forehead on his palm. Mumbled, "Bryson City. Two o'clock. Some development company. Mountain Resorts, something. Gonna put up condos."

John stood and walked to the windows to look out. His watch showed twelve forty. After a minute he said, "Let's get him out of here. Someplace safe."

John asked him where the house keys were and asked Kitty to stay with him. He found Coleman's bedroom upstairs. There were four hundred-dollar bills in a top dresser drawer, and he took them. Threw an assortment of clothes and other items from the room and the hall bathroom into a suitcase that was in the closet. Locked up and went back to the office. They walked him to the Jeep and drove away. Within a mile, Coleman was slumped asleep on the backseat, his splinted arm in his lap. John was keeping a watch on the rearview mirror. He made three random turns through a steep residential area, picked his way back to the main road, stopped at a gas station, and watched the traffic going by. Topped off the tank and drove on.

Kitty said, "Where do we take him?"

"First thought was a motel, but he needs looking at. Let's do this. I'll drop you at your place. Why don't you get enough stuff together for a week or two, put it into your car, and drive over to my place? Ask Hank to set you up in the loft. I'll get Coleman here taken care of and then bring him to Wasituna. You and I can talk tonight."

"I don't think so."

"Kitty—"

"The first thing wrong with that idea is my old car isn't running. It's in the shop. I think it's the alternator. Secondly, you don't have to worry about protecting me. You can drop me off, though, because I want to go online and see what I can find out about this bunch. And I'm hungry. You go do what you have to for this dopehead. I'll have my cell phone handy. I'll give you the number and I'll keep my doors locked. I told you I can take care of myself. You just call me later, and we'll get together, okay?"

"I thought you hated cell phones."

"I do. The casino provides one so they can call anytime they need me, but I hardly ever carry it. My time off is mine."

◊ ◊ ◊

The Preacher stared at Frank with unblinking, depthless eyes and whispered harshly, "They arrested this Hardin, but they let him go?"

The two of them were alone in the church.

Frank avoided those eyes, coughed wetly into his fist, and said, "It's what they're sayin'. There's somethin' else. They found Lloyd under a Buick over to his place with his guts mashed to mush. A jack coulda let go. Or somebody made it let go. I'm thinkin' it coulda been this guy Hardin. Another thing. The Prescott kid never showed today. We ain't gonna get all that gold without him."

The Preacher focused on the stained plywood cross nailed to the wall behind the pulpit, but he did not see it. He was seeing the latest Stealth Cam images of the man Hardin and the Indian woman taken when they had found the heathen mine.

This Hardin and the heathen woman were demons. Sent from Satan to bring him down. How many other demons were with them? Was a congregation of demons circling around his church even now?

But in the holy power of the Spirit, he could crush demons. Indeed, he was commanded by the One Pure God to do so.

He went up behind his pulpit and picked up his much-used Bible. Leafed to Numbers 14 and read aloud, "'I the Lord have said, I will surely do it unto all this evil congregation, that are gathered together against me: in this wilderness they shall be consumed, and there they shall die.'"

He raised his right arm and pointed to the double doors. "Go. Gather the others of my disciples and all the elders. Call them. We must meet. Tell them to arm themselves. And tell them to bring food. As much as they can. Then go and bring this man and this heathen woman here. To this Church of the One Pure God. To this mountain. To this wilderness."

◊ ◊ ◊

After leaving Kitty's house, John had driven to the clinic in Cherokee. He had half carried Coleman inside. The man weighed probably less than a hundred and thirty pounds. John deposited him carefully in a stuffed chair, propping his head on a cushion from the adjacent chair, the splinted arm in his lap. He drifted back into sleep. John filled out the paperwork, using a false name, said he was a friend and would pay cash. He had the four hundreds he'd taken from Coleman's room, and enough of his own to cover what more the bill might total.

He had to wait over two hours before a young hefty male Cherokee doctor with a brush cut showed up apologizing. One of his brother's children had been injured, but not seriously, it had turned out.

They wheeled Coleman on a stretcher, still sleeping, into an X-ray room and then into an examining room.

The doctor stuck the negatives in a wall fluorescent viewer and studied them. He said, "Both bones in the forearm are broken cleanly. Easy enough to set." He turned his attention to Coleman. Took his blood pressure and temperature and gave him a general going-over. He looked at John and said, "He's sleeping like the dead. If I had to guess, I'd say he's recently come down from a speed binge. Crystal meth, most likely. He's underweight and in bad shape every otherwise. We're seeing way too much of this kind of thing around these days. Do you want to tell me what this is really all about?"

"Simple. He slipped on stairs and fell. I'm just trying to help out here. Is it going to be a problem fixing him up?"

The doctor sighed. "I don't like to sedate him in his condition. But he's sleeping pretty deeply. So we'll try it without. How about you holding him down in case he wakes up from the pain?"

John held him, and the doctor set the arm deftly. Coleman's body spasmed with the pain. He grunted, and his eyes came open, staring blankly for a moment. Then he frowned and moaned, and his eyes sagged closed again in sleep.

A nurse helped fashion a cast for the arm. The doctor said, "I'm not going to write a prescription. Give him aspirin or Tylenol, but not too many. Read the bottle. If you really are a friend, you might want to talk to him about his addiction before he fries what's left of his brain."

The bill consumed everything he had except seven singles and change. The doctor helped John carry him out to the Jeep.

He drove to Wasituna's house and left Coleman in the Jeep while he went in to talk with the old man. He brought in the suitcase and then pulled Coleman out of the Jeep and heaved him over his shoulder in a fireman's carry to bring him inside. The old man held the door open for him and led the way to the spare room. John laid him out on the bed and pulled a thin blanket over him.

In his living room, Wasituna said, "You need food."

"It's already getting dark. I should be going. Thanks for doing this."

"First, food. It will not take ten minutes. The coffee is hot, and I only have to microwave yesterday's chili. Wash your hands and sit at my table."

CHAPTER 31

When he walked into the house Hank was slouched on the couch in his pajamas and robe, watching TV and looking sleepy. He yawned and said, "*Kemo Sabe.*"

"Hattie doing okay?"

"Doin' fine. Asleep now. Your Kitty called about an hour ago."

He walked to the desk and punched her cell number into the cordless handset. It rang twice.

Was picked up.

No voice.

He said, "Kitty? You there?"

He heard sounds. Fabric ripping? A scuffling. A shouted, "*John.*" And the line went dead.

He stepped to the couch and dropped the handset into Hank's lap, saying, "Call the county sheriff. Send them to her place," and ran for the door. Grabbed the front door edge to stop himself. Tore open the closet door and fumbled for the double-barreled shotgun from the back corner and the box of double-ought loads from the shelf. He ran for the Wrangler.

Got it going and raced down the hill, squeezing past a car coming up. He hit the flashers and took the turn onto Highway 19 on two wheels, cutting in front of a panic-stopping, horn-blowing white car with its rear wheels chattering, the brakes taking hold. The Wrangler's engine was screaming as he jammed it into top gear and floored the pedal, weaving around two more cars.

It took him only minutes to get to Big Pines Trail. He shifted down and made the turn in a fishtailing, rocking, squealing skid.

◊ ◊ ◊

Hank was standing bent over by the desk, his finger marking the sheriff's number. He'd got it wrong the first time, some man angrily hanging up on him. He peered at the number and dialed again, thinking, *Why didn't I just dial 911 and ask for the dang sheriff?*

It rang twice, but a hand reached in from the side and tore the phone away from him. There were three men standing in the living room, all with their faces covered, one with a black ski mask, the other two with kerchiefs, like the bad guys in a B Western. They all had gloves on. One was wearing yellow gardening gloves.

The man holding the phone was big and well muscled, a head taller than the other two. He wore a plaid shirt, a John Deere cap, thin black leather gloves, and a red kerchief. He had a chrome-plated snub-nosed revolver in his other hand. Hank squinted at it. Probably a thirty-two or a thirty-eight. He said, "You know how to use that thing?"

Ski Mask said, "Where was he going just now? The woman's house?" He seemed to be the one in charge.

Hank retied his robe and said, "You got the wrong place, boys. Ghost Town is across the valley on the ridge over there. Don't think they'll take you on, though, 'cause you ain't near good enough."

The big one with the gun said, "Sit on the couch and be still, old man."

Ski Mask paced. He looked at the big one with the gun and said, "You stay here in case he comes back. You should be able to handle him. We'll call you."

Ski Mask left with the man in the yellow gardening gloves.

◊ ◊ ◊

Frank and disciple Levi Stengler were holding her arms, carrying her along between them. They had a dishrag stuffed in her mouth, tied in place with a strip of another towel around her head, and she had quieted down. But when they got her outside where somebody might see, she started struggling and screaming in her throat behind the dishrag and tried to kick them until Frank punched the side of her head hard one time and she went down onto the grass. Even though she wasn't moving, they held her down and duct-taped her wrists. Orin turned off the house lights and closed the door. They were not masked because Frank had said only the woman lived here, and if anybody else was here it would probably be the man, anyway. No need to cover up for either of them.

Orin hurried to catch up and said, "Frank. This is all comin' apart. You can *see* that? What can we do with her? I think you hit her too hard. They'll get us, Frank. You want to *rot* in jail? Listen, Frank."

Frank was breathing sharply. Rasping. But his eyes were set, cold. "Orin. Shut your piehole. The Preacher wants this. We'll do it. You *hearin'* me? We're gonna *do* it."

They put her in the backseat of the Hummer. Orin and Levi got in to keep her between them. Her head was laid on her shoulder loosely, like Frank had scrambled her brains already, and Orin was sweating, his whole gut stuck through with icicles and his heart racing.

Frank backed out of her driveway. Car lights flared at them on high beam, coming on fast with yellow flashes, and Orin thought, *It's all done now.*

John slewed the Wrangler to a stop, angled across the narrow road, blocking it, emergency blinkers pulsing. He grabbed the shotgun, broke it partially open to check the loads, clicked it shut, thumbed back both hammers, and got out. He stood behind the Wrangler with his feet planted and aimed at the driver's side of the hulking Hummer's windshield as it approached.

The Hummer stopped six feet from the Wrangler. Sat there with its engine running, the glass-packed exhausts rumbling.

Keeping the shotgun trained on the windshield, he moved around the Wrangler and off to the side. The driver's window slid down, and the man rested a big tattooed arm on the sill. John settled the bead sight on the center of the man's head, his index finger brushing the rear trigger. The rear window slid down, and he darted his eyes there and saw the shape slumped motionless between two men in the backseat. The big, near-side man in the back was holding a long-barreled stainless revolver on him, making sure he saw it. He focused on the driver. Long hair, tied back. The scarred face of a fistfighter.

John said, "You're going to let her go now."

The man shook his head. "Nossir. Can't do that. See, you can't shoot in the back there with that thing or you'll shut her off, too. Shoot me, and Levi'll do her right here. Or good ol' Orin back there will. I got a three-five-seven in my hand, too. It'll blow right on through this tin door and make a hole in your chest I can fit my fist in. Maybe even take a piece out one o' them trees behind you. Might pull my trigger any old time now. Say we shut each other off, then Levi or Orin only does her anyway and takes off. You ain't on top here. Best thing you could do is put that cannon down, let us tape you up, and you come along. See she don't get hurt."

John felt the serrations in the trigger. Did not blink. "You're the one who made the Prescott boy choose a place for you to stomp him."

"Made a good choice, too, for a drugger. Forearm. It's two bones, but they mend up pretty good. You're why he didn't show today?"

"So that's Orin in back. Who are you? Big Brother Cagle?"

"Gettin' tired of talkin' here."

"What do you want?"

"There you go. Smart. So how about we do this? You go on home and wait. We'll call. You ain't there when we call, I might let her choose a place to break her. You pull in the law, I'll flat shut her off. You hear? I even feel any kind o' law comin' down on us, I'll maybe use my Buck knife on her. Or a barn pitch-fork. Just as slow as I got time for."

Frank gripped the wheel with his left hand. The brake lights went out.

John tightened up on the trigger, felt it start to move. Wanting to see the face whip back dissolving under the multiple impacts of the buckshot.

Frank Cagle stared him in the eyes and held it for three seconds. Recognized something behind those eyes. He looked ahead and stomped the Hummer, and it caught the Wrangler on the right front, flicking it aside and off the road. The Hummer dug in and sped away, John swinging the shotgun off-aim and up.

Had, in fact, pulled the rear trigger, but had stopped the blast at the last strand of a second with his thumb on the hammer.

He darted to the Jeep, but the fender was crushed into the front tire. He had told Hank to call the law, and expected to hear madly shrieking sirens and see gibbering blue-and-white lights any second. He had no doubt the tattooed man had meant what he'd said. John had sensed the coiled, barely restrained tension in the man and knew he was a killer. He shut off the lights and the ignition. He put the shotgun on the hood and cupped his hands behind his ears, closed his eyes, and stood unbreathing, concentrating on the receding sound of that engine, listening for which way the Hummer would turn onto Highway 19. The fastest way to the Cagle place at Corkscrew Mountain would be right.

Faint tire squealing.

Left.

◊ ◊ ◊

The man behind the kerchief was nervous. Pacing. He had closed and locked the front door. He said, "Where is the old woman? Is the old woman here?"

Hank had been watching him. Appraising. "She won't be no trouble. Sleeps most of the time. She took a fall a time ago and she's still healin'."

"Get up. Show me where she is."

"You want to be real careful how you handle that shiny gun, now, son. I got to tell you it scares me. You got no cause to worry over us. None at all. We're just two tired old folk don't want no trouble. Sometimes I got a bother even standin' up off this couch. I'll do whatever you say. Why don't we go in the kitchen and I'll put coffee on? Looks like you'll be here a while, don't it? I mean, you got no way out of here 'less they come back, right? Yup, I'd say we're here for a good while. Sure hope ol' Pete don't come by wantin' to practice, or somebody else, maybe one of John's friends. He's got a couple real good friends who're cops. Fact, I think one's the sheriff himself. You'd best hope *he* don't show up along about now. Be tough to figure out what to do then, I guess. Glad I ain't in your shoes, son. I'd sure be frettin' how this's all gonna turn out."

"Shut up."

"What's that, son? Don't hear so good sometimes these days, and 'course I can't see your mouth."

"I said SHUT UP. Get up right now and show me where the woman is."

◊ ◊ ◊

He broke the window with the shotgun butt and reached inside to unlock it. Climbed inside and flicked on the nearest light. Picked up her cell phone from the carpet and dropped it into his shirt pocket and ran for the garage. Yanked the rolling door up. The

Honda stood on its kickstand, the key in the ignition. Searched a shelf and found two bungee cords. Rushing. Slapped the shotgun crossway on the passenger seat and snapped on the bungees to hold it there.

No good. Other drivers would see it.

He looked around, saw her white jacket on a hanger, tore it down, and used it to cover the shotgun, sticking the barrel down a sleeve and wrapping the rest. Snapped the bungee cords back on. Straddled the bike. Spotted a Mini Maglite on the shelf and got off to grab it and jam it into his back pocket, where he had also crammed a handful of shells for the gun.

Swung his leg over the bike again. Ignition on. Green neutral light on, headlight flaring out across the driveway. Clutch in. Hit the starter button.

The bike would not start.

Checked that the kickstand was all the way up. Hit the starter button.

It would not start.

Pressed the starter button three more times.

Nothing.

Think.

The kill switch. He thumbed it. Pressed the starter button again.

The bike roared to life.

He backed off some on the throttle, toed it into gear, and let out the clutch.

The Honda bucked two feet ahead and leaned heavily to the left and he almost lost it as the cold engine coughed and stalled out. Caught the lean with his left leg and hauled the bike back upright in slow motion. Grunting.

Calm down. Think.

The friction zone.

He started it again and this time let the clutch out gradually as he fed in power. The Honda responded smoothly. Out on the narrow lane, he went up through two more gears. He used both brakes, remembering to pull in the clutch just as the engine started to lug and stumble, the rear wheel letting out a yelp and the rear end drifting six inches sideways. Toed back down to first gear, slipped the clutch, and took a wobbling left out onto Highway 19.

How much time had he lost? Five, six minutes? Call it six minutes. The Hummer would most likely be sticking to the speed limit, averaging what, forty-five miles an hour through all the curves ahead? Six times forty-five is two-seventy and divide that by sixty. *Say they've got a four-and-a-half-mile lead, then.* To catch them in any reasonable distance he would have to average sixty or seventy. Practicing in the bingo-hall parking lot that one time with Kitty instructing, he had never got it over thirty. He twisted on the power in fifth gear, climbing up toward Soco Gap.

His eyes started tearing up in the increasing torrent rushing at him over the top of the windshield, blurring the road. He squinted and ducked down two inches and that helped.

Tried to draw a mental map of what was ahead. Only one turnoff between here and Cherokee. The Blue Ridge Parkway, but he discounted that. It would likely be too slow for them. Once into Cherokee they'd have several ways to go. *So I've got sixteen miles to catch up to them.*

A series of sweeping banked turns lay ahead along a newly widened stretch. He kept the power cranked on, the bike bellowing. He fumbled for the headlight switch with his left thumb. Blew the horn. Found the switch and flicked to high beams.

And knew he was coming into a broad right turn way too fast.

Backed off on the power and pressed down heavily on the right grip, counter-steering the way she had described it and the bike leaned impossibly far. There was a loud screeching that startled him. Sparks streaming from the right footboard. He kept it leaning, but it was drifting across the solid double centerlines and car lights were sweeping around the curve right at him. Couldn't make the turn any tighter, so he let up, drifted rapidly left, crossing in front of the oncoming car, running on the far shoulder only inches from the grassy verge. He brushed past the braking car, feeling the disturbed airflow on his right hand and shoulder, the car horn moaning behind him now as he cranked on the power some like she had said. The bike bit in and stabilized, darting back over into his own lane. There was a reverse curve coming up, and he had to keep the speed down for it.

Never catch them like this. Got to learn how to take these curves.

He tried to recall everything she had said about turns and counter-steering. You slow before the turn. You look all the way through it because the bike will follow your nose. Halfway through the turn, you feed in power. He tried it that way on the next turn. Not at all smooth, but it worked. So he went into the next turn carrying more power, pressing down harder on the grip to bank more steeply, cranking on the power as he drifted out. Better. He twisted on still more for the next turn. Feeling for the edge of control. There was a long fairly straight downhill reach where he could make up some time. Then the road ahead took a series of much tighter turns descending down into Cherokee. He'd have to slow for it, but so would the Hummer.

Less than ten miles now before the Hummer could take any of several directions.

◊ ◊ ◊

He had come to the casino tonight to see Kitty, but the manager had said she was out on sick leave. So he had fed sixty dollars into the slots without a single lineup. *Not my night all around.* He was down to a lousy ten-spot. Enough for a burger and a pitcher at the Salty Dog, though.

He had the iPod buds plugged into his ears with

the volume up so the decibels were colliding somewhere near the center of his brain. All his favorites were recorded on it from Sirius Outlaw Country. The Notorious Cherry Bombs were playing the last of "It's Hard to Kiss the Lips at Night That Chew Your Ass out All Day Long." The song reminded him of his second ex-wife. Like Fourth of July fireworks in the sack, but like the whole of Halloween on a broomstick when she got pissed at you for some little thing. He walked out of the casino and strode over to the glinting black Harley, which he had left just in the edge of a striped no-parking zone. Adjusted and tightened the skull buckle on his chaps to ease his equipment, shrugged into his studded black leather jacket, which he had left draped over the sissy bar. He pulled on his black half helmet. Got on and cranked it up and just closed his eyes and listened, feeling the power in the vibrating grips. He had pulled the baffles out of his Bub Jug Huggers, turning them into straight exhausts, and the guttural idling detonations were mixing in nicely with the music, which now was "If the Trailer's Rockin'" by Billy Joe Shaver. A couple walked past. With aloof distaste they eyed the big smiling biker who had his eyes closed, off in his own weird world. They both thought, *Probably high on something.*

The song ended, and Steve Earle began singing "Hillbilly Highway." He settled his gloved hands on the ape hangers and idled out of the lot. Stopped to look both ways on Route 19.

Another biker going west came by fast, stopping hard for the light a hundred feet along. It had just turned red for a line of walkers coming from the motel across the street. No helmet. No jacket. Something long and white on the passenger seat. He knew this guy. And he thought he knew this bike. He pulled out and stopped alongside the red bike. Reached into his inside jacket pocket and turned down the iPod.

Hardin looked at him, not really seeing him.

"Well, if it ain't the gunfighter. How they hangin', John Wesley? You remember me? Brandon Doyle."

John was thinking. Weighing. "I remember you."

"What the hell are you doin' on Kit's bike? And where's your helmet? You need more'n hair spray in this state or you pay a big fine. And why are you takin' that shotgun for a ride? You goin' to a shoot-out? The OK Corral?"

"Doyle, do you have a cell phone?" He reached behind to pull the jacket over the exposed shotgun barrels and tuck it in.

"Who *don't* have a cell these days? You been drinkin'? 'Cause if you have, I'll take a nip on it, too."

"Listen to me. Some men have Kitty. Three men. In a black Hummer. I'm trying to catch up and follow it."

"You serious?" Doyle looked him in the eyes. And believed him.

The light turned green and the driver behind them got right on the horn. They ignored it.

John said, "What's your cell number?"

Doyle told him and he memorized it.

The driver behind them got on the horn again with a long irate blast.

Doyle swiveled to peer into the lights and shouted, "Where the *hell* are you from? New Jersey? Go around." The white car backed up and swerved around them, accelerating with a squeal. The stunning blonde driver shot them a fierce look.

John said, "Don't call the cops. They said they'll kill her. Set your cell to vibrate and put it in your shirt. If you find them, stay well back. They've got guns. Just follow them to wherever they're going and you stop short. I'll catch up."

"Look, gunfighter, I don't find 'em and you do, you tell me where you're at and *I'll* come to *you*, hear?"

CHAPTER 32

Hattie had gotten up out of bed and moved into the living room in her robe and slippers, limping, wanting to know what was going on, why this big man was wearing a kerchief. The man with the kerchief had told her to shut up and sit down. She had told him she had to sit up in a straight chair. In the kitchen.

The three of them were seated at the kitchen table, drinking coffee. The man was having trouble holding the cup with gloves on, and had to lift the kerchief with the revolver's barrel every time he took a sip, revealing a growth of black stubble.

When the man wasn't looking, Hank winked at Hattie.

Hank said, "I was tellin' this boy how John's got lots o' police friends and how I'm glad I ain't in his place. How the three of us might be here for a long time. How we ain't no threat to him at all."

"Good Lordy, no. What could we do, anyway?"

"Just what I said, Mother. He's the one got the

gun and all."

Hattie got up shakily and said, "Well, I'm about to starve. Don't we want a piece of that apple crumb cake? I think there's enough left for us all."

The man in the kerchief said, "No, sit back down."

She smiled at him and limped toward the refrigerator.

Hank said, "She don't hear you, son. Got to speak up for the both of us. Now, you sure don't want to miss Hattie's crumb cake. Won a blue ribbon over to the Waynesville Fair. Won't take her but a minute. She'll heat it up nice in the microwave, put a scoop of her homemade ice cream on it. I can taste it right now."

The crumb cake proved even harder for the man to get into his mouth around the kerchief, but he ate all of it.

Hank said, "You need more coffee there, son. I'll get it."

"*No*, you sit right where you're at. No more coffee."

Hank held up his wrinkled palms and said, "Okay, son. Okay."

Hattie got up.

The large man said, "Sit back down."

Hattie smiled at him and took the dishes to the sink, limping, and the man pushed his chair back so he could watch both of the old people. He had a strip of ice-creamed crumb cake on his plaid shirt.

Hattie turned on the water to rinse the dishes and said, "Don't you forget to take your medicine, Hank.

Where did you leave it this time? Is it somewhere here in the kitchen?"

"No, Mother, I think it's in the downstairs bathroom."

The man said, "You can do without it tonight."

"Now, son, I got to have my medicine. You don't want to see what happens if I don't take them pills."

"That's right," Hattie said. "He could take a fit. Fall right down on the floor and go into one of his fits. He kicks and bites and yells and his eyes go all white." She opened her eyes wide.

The man said, "How come she heard you just now?"

"She's used to me talkin'. And her hearin' comes and goes, like. Depends a lot which way she's pointed. Old age is just pure hell, son. Be dang glad you're still young."

The man considered. "All right, we'll all go get your medicine. I want both of you in front of me."

When they got to the bathroom, Hattie's limp became worse and she hung back, a pained expression on her face. Hank went into the bathroom and looked in the medicine cabinet, muttered, "No, it ain't there. Wait a minute, I know where it's at." He opened the cabinet on the wall and looked inside, moving things aside and peering.

Hattie let out a shriek, and the man turned to see her gripping the back of a chair as though she was about to fall. Turned back to watch the old man. Glimpsed something blue rapidly coming at his head. Then the blue turned to black.

Hank stood over the sprawled man, one foot clamped down on his gun hand. He gripped the blue booze bottle tightly by the neck, ready to hit him again with it, but the man was out. The tall, thick blue bottle had been drilled so it could be stuffed with a string of Christmas lights. Hattie liked it on the mahogany quarter-round corner table in this bathroom with a spray of evergreen, in season.

Hattie straightened up and said, "I'll go get some of that good strong cord to tie him up, then you can call the police."

◊ ◊ ◊

John pushed the bike hard, passing all of the sparse traffic, searching for the black Hummer as far ahead as he could on the straight stretches where he was hitting seventy and eighty. He was also watching for anything that looked like a cruiser or an unmarked car. It felt as though he should have caught up to them by now. He blew through some little place he thought might be called Birdtown and found a graveled turnout, where he stopped and thumbed Doyle's number into the cell phone. It rang six times before Doyle answered, "Hardin?"

"Yes."

"I got 'em. Stayed on twenty-three about five miles, but it didn't make no sense they'd head any more south that way. South woulda been quicker for 'em to go by Waynesville. So I turned west onto seventy-four and caught 'em in about two miles. I'm stopped but they ain't half a mile ahead and no place to turn off for a while. Where are you?"

"Just came through Birdtown, I think."

"Hook a left in about five miles. At a dot called Ela. It'll take you to seventy-four and you'll only be a couple miles behind me. I'll plug in your number now. If they turn off anywhere here I'll call. Lash that damn Honda, man."

John found the turnoff. It was fairly straight and there was no traffic on it. He rode hard, coming to Route 74 in under a mile. He turned west and twisted on the power, passing a lone eighteen-wheeler growling up a long incline, and several cars. Far ahead at the top of a rise he spotted a single taillight, and within another two miles he slowed and rode up behind Doyle, who turned his head and waved his left hand.

They rode single file until Doyle slid over to the right of the lane and gestured with his left hand. John drifted the Honda slightly left until the bikes were staggered and Doyle signaled with his thumb and forefinger, making an O. The stagger made sense. Both riders could watch the road, and if the front rider stopped or swerved quickly, the rear rider had time to maneuver. John tucked in tighter on Doyle's left. When they crested the next rise, John spotted the taillights of the Hummer and nodded to Doyle. Using hand signals to communicate, they took up position a quarter mile back.

The Hummer made a right onto 143, and they slowed to let a car pass them so the Hummer's rear-view-mirror image would change. They fell back just far enough to keep the Hummer mostly in sight through the road bends. The upper reaches of Fontana Lake were spread out now off to the right.

They rode on for another ten miles. A half mile ahead, the Hummer's brake lights flared, and it turned right onto Route 28. John knew the road wound on through dense woods alongside the lake for maybe twenty more miles before crossing into the backwoods of Tennessee. The screening car kept going on 143, so they had no choice but to follow the Hummer. John knew Cagle would be checking his rear, and two motorcycles following for such a distance had to be arousing his attention. Doyle must have been thinking the same thing, because they both slowed together to put more distance, at least, between them and the Hummer. John stared at the big black vehicle on a straight stretch, knowing Kitty was inside. Maybe seriously hurt. He tried to project to her. *Hang on.*

◊ ◊ ◊

Kitty stirred in the backseat. Felt the bonds on her wrists and tasted the soap in the dishrag stuffed in her mouth. Her throat constricted and she almost gagged.

She jolted up to look around and the whole side of her head felt thick and hurt like an amplified migraine. Her left shoulder burned, and her left hip felt wet. The crusted road rash had probably split open again and was bleeding. She was between two men, the one on her left tall and sullen, holding a long stainless pistol in his lap. The one on her right was portly and nervous, holding a fat-fingered hand to his forehead and staring out the side window. The man she'd dimly heard the other two call Frank was driving.

And he was checking every few seconds in his rearview mirror, showing interest. Was somebody following them? Could it be John? Back in her house she had managed to shout out his name over the cell phone before it was batted out of her hand and then Frank had clubbed her senseless. While she'd been passed out, if John had got to Big Pines Trail soon enough to see them leaving, he might be following them right now in his Wrangler.

She sat up as straight as she could on the seat, to cover as much of Frank's rearward view as possible, and began moaning and weaving her head, fighting the gag. The tall man next to her said, "Be still."

She let out as much of a scream as she could manage behind the gag and shook her head angrily, making the headache a magnitude worse, her hair flailing.

Looking her in the eyes through the mirror—and not concentrating on the rear window—Frank said, "Ira, shut that bitch up."

The tall man transferred the pistol to his left hand, turned sideways, and grabbed her by the upper arm, right where she had suffered the road rash. It burned brightly in her head and it felt as though the muscles were being crushed into the bone. She leaned away from the man, almost passing out. He said, "Be still or I'll hit you again right there where he hit you. You understand me? Now be still." He shook her once roughly and let her go. Her left arm was numb.

She looked ahead into the night beyond the headlights, breathing hard through her nose, thinking of John.

Frank Cagle took another glance at the mirror, saw no lights, and concentrated on the road ahead.

◊ ◊ ◊

John and Doyle came around a turn in time to see the Hummer turning off to the right onto a steep rutted gravel track. Doyle looked at him, and John used his left hand to point ahead. They rode past the track, not looking at it, John catching a glimpse of a square white sign beside the track, and a mile farther on, John signaled to pull over into the lot of a defunct country store where weeds were pushing up through the pavement cracks. He rode the Honda around to the back of the rotting building, and Doyle followed. They shut down and dismounted. John unwrapped the shotgun and checked his back pocket. He had the

Mini Maglite, which he turned on, and four double-ought shells. Six shots, then, with the two in the gun. He said, "There's no need for you to go any farther. There's only the one gun."

Doyle was keeping his helmet and gloves on. He pulled up the jeans cuff on his right leg and pinched a gravity knife out of his boot top. A six-inch blade. He said, "Okay, you told me. I got this and a flashlight in my tool bag. Now let's get serious and go find Kit."

John considered. With his black jacket and helmet, he would be hard to spot, and the man looked as though he had been in a fight or two in his time.

John said, "All right, but we do this like I see it. Any problem?"

"Do it. I got your back."

◊ ◊ ◊

Frank stopped the Hummer four hundred feet up the track and shut off the ignition and the lights. He swiveled to look out the rear window. He'd seen and heard the two bikes going west and had put his window down, the sound of the bikes loud up the next hill and over it and up and over the next, and then diminishing to nothing. He was wondering if they had gone on or had just stopped up the road.

Couldn't tell.

Orin said, "What, Frank? You think somebody followed us? The cops? Frank?"

Frank said, "Orin, shut your hole." He listened for long minutes, watching the road through the trees. A car flashed by going east. He waited for three more minutes, but there were no other cars.

He reached into the glove compartment and got out a flashlight. Gave it to the tall man in the back. Said, "Levi, you get out here. Get behind these bushes and keep a lookout on the road. You see anybody ain't a member comin', you fire a shot with that pistol you got and then you get back up the hill fast."

He started the Hummer and went on up the gravel track for a half mile. There was a long low tin-roofed shed with a rough full-sized cross made of logs planted in the ground in front of it. Yellow light was spilling from the windows. There were two dozen vehicles in the lot belonging to the remaining disciples and to the most trusted, faithful elders.

It was an old farm that had been converted to a campground a hundred years ago and had once been used by a number of different churches for retreats and revivals, and as a summer camp for boys. The fields had long since grown up into brushy woods. Most of the camp buildings spread around the property were falling into decay. The two-story main house and the large barn and two outbuildings remained, farther back up on the ridge. Beyond that there was a long bluff that overlooked Fontana Lake with its drowned and dead villages embraced in its depths, abandoned sixty years ago when the dam had backed up water for thirty miles.

This property had belonged to a childless elderly couple who were members of the church, and the Preacher had persuaded them to leave all the acreage to the church in their wills.

Frank turned the Hummer in the lot so it was facing out, ready to go.

He said, "Orin, you and me are gonna take this bitch on back to the barn. Put her into a chair. I think there's a roll o' silver tape in there on the tool bench. Then I'll send Sis out to watch her and you come to meet with the Preacher and the rest. He'll know what to do."

Orin said, "Frank, you and me and Sis could just get on out of here. It ain't that far over to Tennessee. We could make it into Kentucky and stay with Uncle Ned until it gets quiet here. Can't you see this is all gonna fall apart? Frank?"

"Orin, you remember how Daddy Cagle usedta beat on us?"

"Frank, we can't go on no more. We—"

"*Orin*, you don't shut your damn hole and do like I say, do like the Preacher says, I just might see can I do a better job on you'n Daddy Cagle ever did. I don't want to hear no more out of you. You've got to the end of my rope. Now watch out how you handle her. She can still kick."

◊ ◊ ◊

The robed Preacher was on his knees on the rough boards facing his pulpit and the back wall of the church sanctuary, where there was a large painting on black velvet of lightning-laced storm clouds being ripped apart by the purifying light shafting down from heaven. He had discovered it in the attic of the farmhouse. There was an ugly water stain all along one side of the painting, but he had taken it as yet another sign from God that he was firmly on the one and only shining path.

He had prayed alone fervently right here on his knees for uncounted hours over months and years that God would help him cause this holy ground to be transformed into a world-renowned retreat for the truly faithful. He himself would go up onto the bluff overlooking the lake one morning and undergo his transfiguration, revealing his pure self to his disciples. Then they would come by twos and dozens and hundreds from all over to learn what wonders God was revealing through him alone. His disciples would tend those flocks that would come and those who would take down his words and write them into a new book of the Bible that would make believers know the One Pure God. One glorious day they *all* would gather here in these mountains, flooding into the valleys for miles around. Like all the lost of Israel. And he would reveal himself in truth to them. Those chosen would rise up out of this earthly hell into the heavens on that final judgment day. Behind him. From this holy place.

The divine reply, finally revealed to him in a dream, had been to use the gold from the heathen mine.

It could not be too late. It need not be the time for the final communion.

He rose from the floor, mounted the platform, and stood behind his pulpit, with his fierce burning eyes surveying those gathered before him. His elders and disciples. Several had brought their women. Three of them still were not here yet, but he knew one of the disciples had been left at Hardin's house.

He could sense the disquiet in them. They knew about the losses of disciples Fulks and Dobbs. They were afraid, as those first disciples had been before the evil demon-possessed ones had come to take Jesus to His earthly judgment.

He spread his arms and began in a low, sonorous voice that had the power to settle and calm them. "Hear me now. You are the faithful. Yes, you are the best of the truly faithful. Sinners all. As were the children of Israel. Yet you are the chosen of God, with whom you have a holy covenant, as I have explained it to you. Together with me you have proved your faith over and over, but we are yet again to be tested. I tell you there are demons out there all around us in this night. They seek to *destroy* your church. They want *you*. They want to *eat* of your purified hearts. But we are the faithful, my brothers and sisters. We are the true believers. Mark one: 'As it is written in the prophets, Behold, I send my messenger before thy face, which shall prepare ye thy way before thee.' Have I not served as His messenger to you? Have I not summoned down the Holy Spirit to protect us all, my brethren? You have *felt* the Holy Spirit moving in your very souls. Who here has not?"

There were murmurings of approval. One disciple shouted out, "Yes, Preacher. You have led us." Another cried out, "I have felt the Spirit." There were shouted *Amens* and *yes, Lords*.

The Preacher nodded. "And you shall yet again *feel* it so. This very night. And if the demons should descend upon us and should shake the very foundations of this, His most holy church, we the faithful will hold them at bay to the glory of God, and we will beat them back into the night. Remember those shining faithful of Masada, who held fifteen thousand demon Romans at bay for *two long years*. Are *we* any less faithful than they of old? I may call on all of you this night—which I swear to you may verily be the most important night of your lives on this earth—to stand up for the ultimate test of your faith. Faith in your God. Faith in the Holy Spirit. Faith in *me*, your messenger. Mark three, verse twenty-three: 'How can Satan cast out Satan?' And verse twenty-five: 'And if a house be divided against itself, that house cannot stand.' And verse twenty-six: 'If Satan rise up against himself, and be divided, he cannot stand, but hath an end.' And verse twenty-seven: 'No man can enter into a strong man's house, and spoil his goods, except he will first bind the strong man.' Do you *hear* the Word? The Bible tells us Satan *can* be divided and will thus fall. Yet we must not allow *ourselves* to be divided against ourselves lest *we ourselves* will fall. We must stand tall together and be strong. We must let no man—no lowly demon-possessed man—dare enter our house. Listen to me now, my brethren, as I shall reveal to you how the devil and his demons will be divided against themselves, whereupon they shall fall."

CHAPTER 33

Seated at his desk, Haywood County Sheriff Newton Fields greeted Agent Donner when the man walked briskly into the office looking like Denzel Washington on a mission.

Donner said, "What have you got here?"

"I don't know yet. Like I told you on the phone, an elderly man at Hardin's place, a man named Hank Gaskill, called it in. We found a good-sized man there tied up. A real angry man. No ID on him, and he's not talking at all. Gaskill put a lump the size of an egg on his head with a bottle and took a thirty-eight revolver away from him. We went to Birdsong's house. Somebody had broken the front window in, and the garage was open and empty. There was a Jeep Wrangler pushed to the side of the road almost out front, with a mashed right front fender. Most of a box of double-ought twelve-gauge shells on the passenger seat. It's registered to John Hardin."

"Birdsong has a motorcycle."

"Yes, a red Honda VTX. We've put out a bulletin to be on the lookout for it."

"Is that all you have?"

"That's about it, unless we can get the perp from Hardin's place to open up."

"What do you say we both work on that? Where have you got him?"

◊ ◊ ◊

John and Doyle were in the woods across the road from where the gravel drive angled up the hill into the forest. They had threaded their way here along the last stretch of road through the trees using their flashlights held low, shielded to slits with their fingers. As they had approached the drive, a gray van about ten years old had turned off onto it.

The small leaning sign close by the drive read "The Masada Undenominational Church of the One Pure God."

They were about to cross the road one at a time and work their way up the drive on each side of it when a dark green late-model GMC pickup slowed, turned in, and bounced up the hill, slinging gravel from the lip of a pothole. Two heads and two racked rifles, one carrying a scope, showed through the pickup's rear window.

Doyle said, "What the hell have we got here?"

"They're using her as a hostage, from what one of them said. So they shouldn't hurt her. Soon, at least.

We'll give it a few more minutes to see who else shows up. I don't want anybody coming up on our backs. We're not likely to get more than one try at this."

◊ ◊ ◊

There was only a single bare low-wattage bulb hanging on its cord above a workbench fifteen feet away from this back corner of the barn. The fat one with the piggish eyes had left her alone after looking her over nervously. In the struggle at her house they had ripped her denim shirt, exposing her left breast. She was wearing black jeans and her biker boots. Her hair was all over the place, making it hard to see, so she tossed her head to get it out of her eyes, and the migraine-like pain came flooding back.

Weak gray light filtered through a row of small dirty windows high up near the eaves. The barn held a dusty jumbled collection of old machinery, vehicle parts, worn-out gas mowers, tires, stacked paint cans, and various tools scattered on tilted wall benches and hung on nails in the cobwebbed studded walls. The floor was rough cracked concrete. The place smelled of old motor oil and wood rot.

Kitty's forearms were duct-taped to the arms of a rusted metal chair, the kind she had seen years ago on lawns and porches. Her ankles were taped to the tubing near the chair bottom. By pushing down on the balls of her feet, she could make the springy chair rock a few inches, but repeated rockings did nothing to loosen the tape at her ankles.

She concentrated on her right arm. There was a slight amount of play in the tape there. About an inch. The big one with the tattoos, Frank, had shoved her into the chair, telling her to be still, and the fat one had held her there from behind as Frank cut the tape from her wrists with an old pearl-handled pocketknife, then had laid her left forearm out on the metal chair arm and stripped a long piece off of the tape roll with a ripping sound. Orin had struggled to hold her around the throat from behind and also to reach around and grip her forearm. She had fought, trying to lift her forearms away from the chair arms as much as possible while Frank was trying to tape them. So she had gained that inch of slack on her right arm.

She struggled with it, repeatedly lifting her forearm against the tension of the tape, then pushing her arm forward and pulling it back, trying to increase the play. Straining. Breathing hard through her nose. The dishrag gag was wet, and saliva was trickling down her throat. Some of the rag had worked partway back into her throat, making her feel like she was going to choke, but she fought the urge and swallowed as best she could. If she started choking, she was afraid she would not stop.

She thought the tape was giving a bit. She strained harder. Laying her right forearm flat on the chair arm and jerking it up against the sticky tape again and again.

She became aware of somebody else in the barn and peered into the shadows.

◊ ◊ ◊

A cool night breeze was making the trees rustle high above them. The sounds would help mask their movements. There was a slice of moon showing occasionally through scudding black rags of cloud.

John said, "I'll go first, on the left. Give me a few seconds' lead to see if I stir anybody up, then you cross and go right. We'll take it slow. Can you whistle?"

"Sure."

"Try this." He whistled softly, one rising clipped-off tone. Like some night bird.

Doyle tried it, quietly.

"Good enough. We'll follow along the driveway until we see whatever building is up there. Any other cars come along, close your eyes so the lights won't kill your night vision. I'll find a place there we can meet and give you a whistle. Answer it and come to me. We'll decide how to do it from there. Something goes wrong for either one of us, it will be two quick whistles. Then we'll have to do whatever looks best."

John waited, listening for any other vehicles coming along the road from either direction. The breeze picked up, clattering dead leaves in the roadside ditch.

Keeping low, holding the slitted flashlight in the fingers of his left hand and the shotgun tight along his body with his right hand so it would not snag anything, he ran across the road and entered the woods.

◊ ◊ ◊

It was a thin red-headed woman. In jeans and a white blouse buttoned to her neck.

She pulled and tugged at something yellow, sliding it along the floor—a set of square work lights on a stand—until they were pointing at Kitty from the side. Turned them on, making Kitty squint, partially blinding her. The woman moved into the light and looked down at her.

The woman's face came into focus as Kitty regained some of her vision. A lot of freckles. She had rivetingly luminous clear blue eyes.

And she was smiling.

She did not look sane.

Kitty struggled harder against the tape.

The woman reached for Kitty's exposed breast. She had long nails with flecks of red polish on them. Kitty tried to pull away.

The woman trailed the nails over the flesh of her breast in a spiraling, feather-light obscene caress, watching Kitty's eyes. Studying.

Kitty went still. Glaring.

The woman took the nipple between her thumb and forefinger and began to squeeze, gently at first, making it stand out erect, then increasing the pressure, leaning in to look deeply into Kitty's eyes.

Kitty tilted her head back, the pain showing in her face, but she did not struggle. The woman grinned and bent closer, and Kitty tilted her head back an inch more, grimacing, her eyes squinted with the pain, but still watching the woman through her lashes.

The woman squeezed yet harder.

Kitty took final aim and lunged her forehead at the woman's nose with all she had, feeling the satisfying crunch of delicate bone, watching those blue eyes flare wide, hearing a gargled scream from her as she staggered back flinging both red-nailed hands to her face in shock, blood redder than her nails splashing down onto her white blouse. She tripped on a length of rusty angle iron and fell backward, her arms flailing and her nose spraying, and sat down on the concrete. She stayed there, shaking her head, looking in astonishment at the wet redness on her hands.

The woman let out a feral growl that grew into a scream of rage. She levered herself up and flew at Kitty, her hands fisted. Still screaming, she took a wide looping swing and caught Kitty on the side of her head where Frank had clubbed her with his fist and the barn lurched under her, shrank, and dimmed out to shades of gray.

The blow had partially dislodged the gag. Kitty shook her head weakly, streaks of garish pain filling her eyes. She coughed and pushed with her tongue. Spat the gag away so it hung around her neck.

The woman stood in front of her like hell's witch, legs spread and hands held high, bunched and trembling, her nose running with blood.

Kitty focused on her, glaring through the pain, and said, "What in *hell* is *wrong* with you? You fall out of the crib onto your head? Nobody asked you to the prom? Somebody broke your broom? What *is* it, you evil bitch? Your daddy spank you a lot and then maybe cuddle you up in your bed all the way through puberty? What?"

The woman froze, her blue eyes radiating hatred. She leaned almost within Kitty's range again. Opened her mouth wide, and hissed.

Kitty blinked, not understanding.

Then she did understand what she was seeing, and she swallowed with a dry throat and whispered, "Lord, who did that to you?"

The woman let out a raging howl, looked around wildly, went over to the cluttered shelf, throwing things aside in a frenzy. Junk and bolts and nuts scattering across the concrete. She found what she wanted.

She spun around to face Kitty, gripping a rusted pair of channel-lock pliers.

◊ ◊ ◊

Doyle waited for a count of five seconds after Hardin had darted into the woods. Still no cars approaching. He took a fresh grip on the gravity knife in his left hand, wrapped his right-hand fingers around the lens so it would only shine through a slit, and pushed the button on with his chin.

He ran for the right side of the track, jumped the ditch, and picked his way through a tangle of brush, heading up the hill for several hundred feet. A long way ahead, up the hill and to the left, there was weak orange light filtering through the trees. He nearly tripped on a deadfall, catching himself with an elbow thrown up against a tree trunk.

He stopped, pressed up tight to the trunk, to look around, letting his night vision get better. Was he seeing something ahead across the driveway? He stared. Shifted his focus to the side. Yes. There was an out-of-place shape maybe eighty feet ahead behind some bushes. A big rock? A dead stump? He was in a slight depression. The line of bushes was on a slight rise, and the shape was only barely outlined by the weak light ahead. The shape of a man?

Yes, because it just shifted, got lower to the ground. From Hardin's perspective, off to the left, he likely would not spot the man because that backlight would not be right. *Now what?*

He could use the double whistle.

No. *Get to the guy before Hardin does. Get around behind. Come downhill onto him. Pick up a stick or a rock and clock him. Then whistle so Hardin don't blow your ass off.*

The breeze was louder in the treetops now. *Good.*

He crouched low and began moving much faster up the hill, concentrating on the place where he'd seen the man-shape but scanning ahead for any others.

◊ ◊ ◊

The barn door creaked open and closed, and a man came in. He moved toward the light and said, "Sis? Frank sent me. Supposed to help you watch the woman. Keep her quiet back up here. Somebody heard her yellin', Frank said. Sis?"

It was Wilbur Pugh. He was the clean-up man for the church and lived in a room of the old house. He was short and bald, with white flesh and coke-bottle glasses. The Preacher had made him an honorary disciple only because Pugh's father donated heavily to the Masada Church. He was incapable of following more than simple directions.

Pugh saw Sis and walked over to her. "Geez, Sis. Did you fall? You're all bloody. Frank said to keep her quiet. The woman." He turned to see Kitty in the chair and came over to look down on her. He said, "You really need to be quiet, ma'am."

He saw her exposed breast and stared at it.

Licked his lips.

He moved closer and said, "I want to touch it."

Kitty saw the woman—Sis, he'd called her—doing something. Bending down. Putting the pliers on the floor. Picking up a three-foot length of angle iron.

Swinging it like a bat.

There was a sound like a melon dropped onto concrete, and Pugh's glasses flew off. He grunted and his eyes went wider and rolled white. He collapsed, his head thumping onto the concrete and bouncing up to press heavily against Kitty's left boot. Twitching.

The woman was breathing hard, her eyes wild. She came closer and focused those insane eyes on Kitty's head and drew back the angle iron.

Kitty tossed her head to the side to swing the hair out of her right eye. Licked at her lips with a dry tongue.

She straightened up in the chair proudly.

Gazed steadily into those blue animal eyes.

Did not blink.

Sis drew the iron farther back. Began to see this woman in the chair. Ready to die. Not afraid. She thought, *Like I used to be?*

Kitty watched as lines of anguish formed on the woman's forehead. Her mouth sagged open in a grimace, and the blue, blue eyes softened and welled, and tears spilled down to make tracks in the blood on her cheeks. Her shoulders shook and the iron bar wavered. Mewling, she tried to steady the bar and draw it back for the swing but could not. Trembling, she brought the bar out in front of her and looked at it, bewildered.

Saw Pugh's blood on it.

Gave out a despairing cry and pushed the bar away from her. It landed on Kitty's right knee, making her cringe and moan with the sudden white pain, and it clattered ringing onto the floor.

Sis looked at Kitty with soul-deep horror in her eyes. She wiped at her tears with the back of her bloody hand and ran from the barn, leaving the door half open.

Kitty leaned her head against the back of the chair. The cool metal felt good.

Closed her eyes and took a deep, sweet breath.

When her heart slowed, she looked down at her arms. Without the gag, maybe she could reach the tape on her left forearm with her teeth. She strained, groaning with the pain, blood dripping from the split in her forehead onto the silver tape, making it slick.

No, there was not quite enough play in the tape on her right arm to allow it. Couldn't reach her right arm with her teeth, either. If she could just get an inch more play on the right arm. She went back to working the right forearm. Pulling and pushing and lifting against the tension of the tape.

◊ ◊ ◊

John made out a dark line of thick brush ahead. It looked thinner toward the driveway so he angled over until he could see the drive more clearly both ways through the trees. Uphill he saw a large shadow dart across the drive. A glint of moonlight caught the helmet. Doyle, then. *Why? Somebody ahead on my side?*

John turned the Mini Maglite off and clamped it in his mouth so he could get to it quickly. He stayed inside the trees twenty feet from the drive and moved faster, tree to tree, choosing his footing by feel and the meager moonlight, the shotgun held straight up in front of him with both hands, at the ready, pushing past branches. As he approached the dark bushes, a shape rose up and a light hit him full in the face. He whipped the shotgun down to aim at the light and squinted to preserve as much of his night vision as possible. Spat the flashlight straight down at his feet. He did not want to fire because it would alert whoever was back up the driveway.

A voice behind the light said, "You stop right there. I got a gun on you. Who are you?"

"I'm here to see Frank Cagle."

"Go away or I'll shoot."

"You fire and you're dead. This is buckshot and both barrels will have a good spread. Why don't you go and tell Frank Cagle I want to talk? I'll meet him right out here on the driveway and we can talk about what he wants for the woman."

Levi had never been in anything close to this. If he fired a warning shot like Frank had said, this man with the shotgun would cut him in half. He could try to shoot the man first, but he might still fire that shotgun. He'd seen what a close load of double-ought could do to a deer.

Levi doused the light and spun around, ducking

away from that shotgun. Began thrashing through the brush back up the hill, angling for the driveway, trying to get to the church, branches whipping his arms and face. He was about to break out of the trees when a shadow came at him, swinging something. He managed to get the gun partway up and fire low before the rock caught him full in the face and he crumpled.

Doyle dropped the rock and leaned against a tree. He whistled twice. Pulled the flashlight out of his back pocket and took a look at his right leg. Holed and leaking in the calf above his boot. Hole on the other side. Through-and-through, and not a hollow-point slug. That much was good. The pain was building. He bent and felt over the man's body. He still had a pulse in his neck. Found the gun and picked it up. He sat down, put the gun in his lap, and rested his back against a tree.

John came up, the flashlight shining low, straight down, and crouched beside him. Scanned the night all around and saw nobody else. Saw Doyle's bloody leg. Said, "We'll have to get you back to the road."

"No. I just need something to make a bandage. It ain't bleedin' too bad. Be okay right here. I'll clock this guy again if he wakes up. You go."

On his knees, John slid the flashlight into his back jeans pocket, stripped off his shirt, popping off the buttons, and handed it to him. Picked up the shotgun and stood. Doyle used his knife to start cutting up the shirt.

John moved quickly up along the edge of the drive in a crouch, close by the trees, scanning for anybody in the way.

The assembled were down on their knees, praying loudly in a confusion of voices when Frank heard the shot. He sent two men with deer rifles out the front door to meet Levi and find out what was going on. The men were crouched behind a pickup together, watching the driveway and the woods for anything moving.

From behind a large tree, John used one eye to study all he could see. The windows of the building were spraying orange light out into a clearing. Maybe twenty vehicles parked haphazardly. The black Hummer was nosed out. A big rough cross was stuck in the ground out front.

Something behind a muddy pickup. The barrel of a rifle. He faded back into the trees and moved to get a better angle on the pickup.

Saw the two men. Decided. He stood out from the tree and fired one barrel, taking out the pickup's windshield. One of the men hunkered lower and tried to aim the rifle in the general direction of the blast, fired fast three times, the rounds going wild. John took aim at the front of the pickup and fired the other barrel, hearing the pellets denting into the sheet metal. He stepped behind the tree to reload, raised his chin to the sky, and let out a long loud banshee scream. Moved back around the tree, aiming, but the two men were scrambling into the pickup. The driver started it and spun it around on the gravel, slewed toward the drive, the rear wheels flinging gravel, the passenger door flapping open. They were away and going down the hill, bouncing in the potholes.

Inside the church, Frank said, "Rufus, you go out the back. This has gotta be Hardin with that shotgun. You go try to get a shot at him from the side."

Disciple Rufus Blinder held up his palms and said, "No, Frank. Not me. You go."

John ran across the clearing and up the front steps, the shotgun ready in his right hand. Used his left hand to yank open the door but stood to the side so only the barrel and part of his face showed in the doorway. A woman inside shrieked, but the man with her said, "Quiet, Emma."

The people inside were standing, everybody staring at the door, unmoving. A black-robed man was standing behind the pulpit. John centered the brass bead mounted between the barrels on the man behind the pulpit and moved inside to put his back against the wall by the door. Several of the men had rifles. Three that he saw were aimed at him. Another man held a pistol down at his side, obviously ready to bring it up and fire and trying to decide if he should.

John held his aim on the black-robed man with the fierce eyes and said, "Listen to me. I won't shoot first. It's loaded with buckshot. I've got both triggers pulled and I'm holding the hammers back. Some of you are going to die if anybody fires. Even if you kill me. I don't want to hurt anybody. All I want is the woman. Where is she?"

The Preacher pointed a long finger at him and shouted, "*Behold the demon.* He is no ordinary man. He is here to destroy us. You just heard his evil cry. But the Spirit is in you and with you, my brethren, and we must crush this demon. You are the true believers. You are my disciples, my elders, my righteous army. Together we will beat back the Romans. Together we will ascend to Him who waits for us in paradise. I tell you that you can crush any demon if you do not lose your faith. Together, now, my brethren. CONFRONT THE DEMON AND CAST HIM OUT FROM AMONG US." He stood with his robed arms wide and his head thrown back, his eyes closed.

At first nobody moved. Then a man with a scoped rifle held at his hip edged out of a pew and moved toward him. Another man raised his hands high, wiggling his fingers, his eyes closed, speaking with unintelligible mumblings, rising in intensity. Another man joined in. Some began to pray. A large woman glared and advanced on him with her hands outstretched. They crowded in closer to him all around. He sensed movement at his side and Frank Cagle loomed up out of a crouch and swatted the shotgun up. Both barrels went off, spattering the bead-board ceiling with black holes, the recoil shoving him back. A man ripped the shotgun away, dropped it, and clamped his right arm, and another man grabbed his left arm and they pinned him tightly, spread-eagled, against the wall. A cheer rose from the people. Frank shoved his chin up, slamming his head against the wall, and drove a fist into his stomach with such force the sheetrock wall gave behind his back. Pain radiated out to fill him utterly, and the church skidded sideways. He was unable to breathe, his belly and chest burning, and he took short, convulsive gasps until he could fill his lungs. Frank Cagle's face was only inches away, his breath stinking of cigarettes, his big hand gripping John's throat. The muscles in his forearm moving under the tattooed skin. John tried to work up enough saliva to spit into his face but could not.

Frank grinned, and in that grin John saw his death.

There was movement to the left. Frank looked that way and froze. The people quieted to murmurings and backed away. Frank let go of his throat. The two men kept John firmly pressed against the wall.

Sis, her tangled red hair wild, blood spattered on her face and hands and staining her blouse and jeans, moved into the church, staring directly at the Preacher. She stopped, her legs spread. Held one hand at her crotch and pointed an accusing finger at the Preacher. Some who could see what was in her eyes looked away.

Frank said, "Sis?"

The Preacher glared back at her and thundered, "*The demons are out all around us in this black night. Behold what they have done to Sister Cagle.*"

The wind had picked up and was moaning through

cracks in the window frames.

A long primal hackle-raising sound came from Sis. A low growl rising into a guttural screeching insane scream. She moved another step, still holding her crotch, her red-nailed finger pointing. Trembling now.

The Preacher shouted, "THE DEMONS. CAN YOU HEAR THEM, BRETHREN?"

Frank Cagle bellowed out, "NO. HOLD IT. SHUT UP." He coughed wetly.

The Preacher gripped his pulpit, his knuckles turning white, but he said nothing.

Frank coughed again and said, "Sis, you sayin' the Preacher took you? Like Daddy?"

Sis did not look away from the Preacher's eyes, but nodded.

The Preacher said, "She *lies*. It is the work of the demons. She is *possessed*."

Frank pointed at the Preacher and said, "NO. You shut your hole. Sis don't lie. You did her, Uncle. You don't say one more damned word 'til I tell you."

Frank looked at his sister and said in a low voice, almost to himself, "To get at Daddy, you went for what was his. You couldn't go after him. 'Cause he was our daddy. But you could sure tear up that deerhound. His favorite. Ain't that right, Sis? So *you* killed Werly, then. And Dobbs. To get back at Uncle here, you figured to tear up his church. Kill off his disciples. What'd you do? Take Orin's pickup?"

She turned her head to look at him and her blue,

blue eyes held no trace of sanity.

Orin Cagle sat down on a pew in the front and said, "Ah, God." And buried his face in his hands.

Sis was still pointing. Frank moved to her side and used two fingers to bring her arm down to her side.

He glared at the Preacher and moved up the aisle.

The people parted for him.

He shoved on the pulpit and it toppled aside.

Frank said, "You come and take her when me and Orin was both gone off?"

The Preacher said, "It was the Levirate Obligation. It is written in the Bible. When a man should lose his brother, that man must take his brother's women into his bed and—"

Frank's big hand jammed around the Preacher's throat, choking his voice down to a croak. "Now see, there's one even *I* know, Preacher. It says a man should take on his brother's *wife*, if she be willin'. Don't say nothin' about the man's daughter when she don't want to. Orin, get yourself up."

Orin stood, crying. "Frank, it's all done."

"Orin, you stop your cryin' and you go into the back room and you drag out that big cooler. Do it now, Orin."

Orin obeyed, glassy-eyed and resigned. Letting out an occasional sob. He came back, pulling a large, battered cooler that had once been red.

Frank coughed and said, "What we're gonna do now, Uncle, is see if you're a real, pure believer. How you want to do this? I'll give you a choice. The kinda guy I am. You can take your chances with the snake. Or you can drink somethin' me and Sis can mix up. We got that stuff in the back there, too, don't we? What's it gonna be, Uncle?"

The Preacher shook his head, his long white hair falling down over his eyes.

"What I thought. We'll do the diamondback test o' faith, then."

Frank ripped the robe from him and then his white shirt. Shoved him into the ornate chair on the platform, punched him once in the face to keep him still, and tied his hands behind the chair back with a strip of the robe. He kicked at the cooler three times and pulled the cover up. Ripped it away from its hinges and dropped it. The church was quiet except for the wind eagerly crying its small howlings at the windows, so they could all hear the rasping, buzzing sound. Frank kicked the cooler twice more. "We'll do it like we done old Mose Kyle, then."

The Preacher's throat was half crushed, but he croaked out, "No . . . no . . ." and shook his head.

Frank lifted the open cooler and brought it close to the Preacher, tilting it down and resting it on the Preacher's knees, slapping on the sides of it. The Preacher looked through the strands of his hair and saw the agitated diamondback rearing and tasting the air. Tensing. Striking in a patterned blur. He felt an incredibly sharp pain in his chest. And then another.

Tried to scream but could only croak. Looked down at the four seeping holes, and fainted.

The poison began its exotic work right away. It would not take long because the punctures were close to the thudding heart.

The diamondback slid to the floor and essed like flowing oil toward the darkness of the back room.

The people were dazed. No one seemed to know what to do.

Frank said, "Come on, Orin." He walked to Sis. Picked her up. She put her arms around his neck. Rested her head on his big shoulder and closed her eyes. He walked out of the church, and Orin followed.

John stared at the man who was holding his right arm pinned to the wall and said, "Let go right now."

The man looked at him and let go. John shoved the other man away hard enough to sit him down on the floor and knock his head against a pew. He bent painfully and picked up the shotgun. Broke it open so the empties kicked out, and got the two remaining shells from his back pocket. Slid them into the chambers and closed it. He said, "Somebody is going to tell me where the woman is. The woman Frank Cagle brought here."

He saw no real comprehension in any eyes. He ran out the door. Frank was putting Sis into the backseat with Orin. John saw nobody else in the Hummer. Frank glanced at John, got in, and pulled away, the wheels spurting gravel. John snapped the shotgun to his shoulder and fired at the back of it, taking out the rear window. It kept going, bouncing in the potholes. He ran.

As the Hummer blasted past him, Doyle took aim at the front wheel, leading it some, and fired the revolver three times. Was rewarded with an answering bang. The Hummer skidded and plunged off the road a hundred feet farther on, hammering into a tree.

John saw the Hummer slam to a stop and darted into the trees at his left, slowing from a run but still moving quickly. There was enough light from the Hummer's headlights to help him choose his footing, and there was not much brush along this stretch.

Frank pushed the deflated air bag out of the way, grabbed up his .357 from the floor mat where it had skidded out from under the seat, and fell out the door onto his knee, ignoring the pain. He shook his head to clear it and moved in a crouch to the rear of the Hummer, scanning for the spot where the shots had come from. He figured he'd fire once or twice to stir the shooter up, and extended his arm to sight down the long barrel.

John said, "Shotgun. On your head."

Frank stayed in position, just turning his head to the side. Hardin was beside a tree. In the shadows. But it was still a possible shot.

John said, "No. You can't make it. Not and still have a head. Put it down on the ground. Tell Orin and Sis to stay put."

John saw Frank's gun arm start swinging toward him and fired exactly where he had been aiming. At the threat. The blast took Frank's hand off with the gun in it, slapping his arm against the car. Frank screamed and grabbed at the spurting arm with his other hand, clamping it and letting out another high scream. He slumped against the rear wheel, hugging the stump to his belly and groaning.

John broke the shotgun open, pretended to load it, clicked it shut. Thumbed back both hammers on the empty gun and moved across the low ditch, aiming at the Hummer's rear window. He said, "Orin. Open the door."

Orin opened the rear door. He was crying and had his arm around Sis, who looked dazed.

John said, "Get out. Bring her with you."

He walked them back up the drive, sat them down in the middle of it, and called out, "Doyle. You see them okay?"

Doyle switched on the flashlight. "I got 'em."

John touched Orin's chest with the barrels and said, "Where is Kitty Birdsong?"

"Back up there. Up the hill. In the barn."

He came back to stand over Frank. Saw the shredded hand with the gun in it and kicked it into the ditch. Put the shotgun on the ground. Stripped off his belt and bent to knot it around the forearm just back of Frank's clamping hand. Pulled on both ends of the belt and drew it tight, and the bleeding slowed to a seep. Frank groaned and glared at him.

John looked him in the eyes and said, "Keep that tight. Or loosen it and you'll bleed out. They can dump you in a landfill somewhere. Your choice."

He picked up the shotgun and ran back up the hill. People were standing outside the church watching him run past.

He saw the old two-story house as he came around the last curve in the drive. There was a weak orange light behind the house, a piece of the barn showing. He cleared the corner of the house with the empty shotgun up to his shoulder. A back porch light was on. No lights on in the house and nobody showing anywhere near it.

She was standing in the barn doorway, her hand out against the jamb to support herself. Blood on her face, a scrap of silver tape on her arm. Her dark hair wild.

He stopped in front of her. Touched her on the shoulder and moved aside so the weak light was on her face. Looked into her eyes.

She said, "There's a dead one in there. Sis did it."

He lifted a strand of her hair away from where the blood had pasted it to her cheek. Let out a breath, the tension flowing out of him.

She said, "You don't have a shirt on. And I heard the war cry. Still trying to pretend you're an Indian?"

CHAPTER 34

Sheriff Fields said, "We've put most of it together, I think."

They were in the sheriff's office. Fields behind his desk and Agent Donner in a chair beside the desk, his legs stretched out and crossed at the ankles, tapping a ballpoint on a yellow notepad on the corner of the desk. John was in a straight chair tilted back against the wall, facing them.

Donner said, "Moses Kyle found the mine. One of the Cagles apparently bought a piece of quartz from Kyle that had a big chunk of gold in it. That Cagle must have told his uncle, Walter Cagle, the preacher, about it. Not an ordained minister, by the way. He just took over the church from the previous pastor ten years ago. They tortured Kyle until he told them where he found the gold, then killed him. They set out to buy part of the Prescott land to get the mine. They used a prominent Bryson City lawyer named Edward Kunkel, who was going to front the initial purchase money, to make the pitch to Gideon Prescott. Kunkel's late wife was a cousin to Walter Cagle. Tried to keep it in the family. Apparently only a few selected people from the church knew the whole story."

Fields said, "Various charges are lodged and pending. The Cagle woman is clearly certifiable. Orin Cagle had a lot to tell us, along with a few people from the church. Frank Cagle is up for the murder of Moses Kyle and the Preacher and for Gideon Prescott, but Frank is barely making it. We just heard they've got him reasonably stable. The doctors found something in his lungs, though. They say he might not last through a trial. Orin will do a lot of time."

Donner said, "How are your people? The Gaskills and Kitty Birdsong?"

"Okay. What will happen to this Kunkel?"

Donner said, "They'll try to nail him. But he's a lawyer, after all. He's got a lot of wiggle room. And he's well known. Connected. We'll have to see."

Fields said, "I don't know how they expected to carry it off."

John looked at the ceiling and said, "The wrong kind of rainbows."

Fields said, "What?"

"Greed. It does blind."

◊ ◊ ◊

He had called to ask John and Kitty to his house. They were in the office built onto the garage, standing around the drafting table.

Coleman Prescott eased the cast in its sling and said, "I've been talking with the architect. It won't be exactly like he planned it, but I think it will work okay. I've got a long ways to go first, and I know that. I'm in a twelve-step program. A day at a time. A higher power. Try to make amends where I can. All that."

Kitty said, "Well, you should have enough money to do this mountain up right, with the mine."

Coleman shook his head. "It's not my gold. All Dad cared about was the land. He bought that acreage from a man in Asheville who retained all the mineral rights, which I'm told includes the gold. Fine-print stuff. Any proceeds from the mine belong to him. He's a doctor."

Kitty said, "It just figures, doesn't it? Why didn't this Kunkel pick up that tidbit?"

Coleman said, "He's a criminal-defense attorney, not a real-estate man. There might be some kind of finder's fee my lawyer can negotiate with the doc, although I hear he's pretty tight. That's why I asked you here. To thank you and let you know you're both in for a good piece. If it happens."

Kitty said, "There's somebody else. Her name is Mary Shade Hill. She helped us. We made a deal with her. Thirds. If there's any money, she'll be in for it, too."

John said, "Even if there's no money, I'd think it could help you out with this Medicine Ridge thing. Take a guided horseback ride to see the lost mine of the ancient Cherokees. The famous Moses Mine."

Coleman said, "Try your luck at panning the creek. Buy some jewelry made from the Moses Mine gold. Yeah. I thought of that."

John said, "You need any aerials shot, I'm your man."

Kitty said, "You mentioned a gift shop. With Injun arts and crafts. Do you have somebody in mind to run that?"

◊ ◊ ◊

It was early on Saturday morning. John was at his desk, trying to catch up on paperwork. Hattie was in the kitchen, assembling a carrot cake. Hank was in the bedroom with the door closed. Going through his well-thumbed copy of *All the Great Western Movies*. Trying to find a real stumper for John.

The phone on the desk rang loudly and he answered it.

The boy said, "Can you please come to pick me up early? I need to talk to you."

"I can leave right now."

"Okay. I'll wait for you around in back. On my swing."

◊ ◊ ◊

Brandon Doyle was at a Bippie pump on the edge of Maggie Valley, standing with most of his weight on his good leg, feeding two gallons to the black Hog. Wearing his worn leather jacket over a T-shirt that said, "Sex Instructor. First lesson free." He had the iPod plugged in and turned up. Billy Joe Shaver had just belted out "Live Forever," and Reckless Kelly was getting into "Wicked Twisted Road." He looked up to see Hardin swinging in to stop with his arm on the door, the Wrangler idling. Doyle nodded and reached into his inside jacket pocket to turn down the music.

Hardin said, "You know anybody who's got one of those things for sale?"

"A Harley?"

"Maybe. If I don't have to take out a second mortgage for it."

"You better not tell Kit you're thinkin' on a Hog. And first you ought to learn how to ride so you don't shame the rest of us. But I'll ask around."

"Thought I might stop by the Salty Dog tonight. Shouldn't drink a whole pitcher myself."

"Now I *know* I can help you out there."

◊ ◊ ◊

He parked the Wrangler in the tilted yard of the white farmhouse that was surrounded by several tall pines and a spreading meadow. Went around to the back and fitted himself into the swing next to the boy. The day was perfectly warm, a breeze flavored with wildflowers stirring the pines to sigh in chorus and the meadow grass to ripple and sheen in the sunlight.

He let the boy speak first.

Joshua Lightfoot looked at his smudged sneakers, his expression serious, and pushed at the dirt so he swung a few feet, his thin arms bent around the chains at his elbows, the fingers of both hands curled into each other, palm to palm, in the strong grip Hardin had showed him. The cliff-climbing grip. One sneaker was untied.

He said, "I had a talk with Great-Grandfather Wasituna. I think it's okay for Kitty to be your girlfriend. If you want her to be. I don't think that will mean you'll forget my mom."

Hardin looked up through the pines and studied the sky.

A fleet of glowing cumulus clouds sailing in from the east. Like galleons come to plunder beneath the cobalt infinity. Valerie had done well mothering this boy. This miracle born of her spirit. Even for so short a time.

We live in a continuous miracle. Why do we forget that?

When he felt he could talk, he said, "Tell you what. Why don't we put the top down on the Jeep and take a ride?"

◊ ◊ ◊

Kitty was in her garage with the door open, in shorts and a halter top, her hair tied back in a ponytail. Polishing the red Honda.

The white Wrangler pulled into her driveway, its new right front fender gray primered because John had not got around to painting it. The top was down and their hair was tousled.

They got out and she met them with her hands on her hips.

He looked her in the eyes, and she held it.

A smile beginning inside her.

He said, "We thought you might like to go get an ice cream."

From the 2007 Willa Award Winner for *Hallowed Ground*

LORI G. ARMSTRONG

SHALLOW GRAVE

Surveillance on an insurance fraud case in Bear Butte County unfolds tragically for PI Julie Collins and her partner, Kevin Wells. The reappearance of a mysterious hole—cause of the fatal accident—brings about the landowner's unsettling confession; bones were recently uncovered on that remote ridge. Fearing repercussions from their illegal off-season hunting, the hunters reburied the remains and kept quiet.

Now the hole is back, but the bones have vanished.

Were the bones part of an ancient Indian burial ground? Connected to the unsolved disappearance of a Native American woman? The overworked, understaffed sheriff asks for Julie's help.

But the case opens old wounds, and she finds herself at odds with the Standing Elk family, discovering they withheld information from her in the months before Ben's death. And Julie's relationship with Tony Martinez hits a rough spot when she agrees to go undercover in his strip club.

On the wrong side of tribal politics, family disputes, and employee rivalries, Julie continues to dig for answers . . . while the personal stakes climb. In a brutal fight for her life, Julie finally comes face to face with her brother's killer . . . and realizes not all deceptions run deep.

ISBN#9781933836188
Mass Market Paperback / Mystery
US $7.95 / CDN $9.95
www.loriarmstrong.com

The Saucy Lucy Murders

Cindy Keen Reynders

Dan Lightfoot's wandering eye has finally gotten the best of his wife, Lexie. Bereft, she moves with her teenage daughter Eva back to her hometown, Moose Creek Junction, Wyoming, to be near her sister Lucy, and they open a small business, The Saucy Lucy Café. It sounded like a good idea. Hometown. Family. A career and an income . . .

But Lucy is a staunch churchgoing woman who believes her sister must remarry in order to enter the kingdom of heaven, and the reluctant Lexie finds herself dating again. Trouble is, all her dates wind up dying and visiting Stiffwell's Funeral Parlor. Gossiping townspeople begin to mistrust the sisters and café customers dwindle . . . along with the town's menfolk.

Although Detective Gabe Stevenson, with whom Lexie has a love/hate relationship, and Lucy's husband, the inept town sheriff Otis Parnell, warn the sisters not to get involved, Lexie just can't let things be. Business is down the toilet and, according to Lexie, the police simply aren't getting the job done. It's time to intervene.

And so begins the hilarious and half-baked investigation of The Saucy Lucy Murders.

ISBN#9781933836249
Mass Market Paperback / Mystery
US $7.95 / CDN $9.95
December, 2007
www.cindykeenreynders.com

For more information about other great titles from Medallion Press, visit

www.medallionpress.com